George Brown has spent [...] Asia, initially fighting terro[...] before retiring to run a pla[...] has kept close links with counter-terrorist colleagues throughout the world, and his contacts and experience have enriched his superb thrillers, including *Ringman, Pin Point, The Double Tenth, Sacrifice* and *The Envoy*.

The Contractor

George Brown

PIATKUS

First published in Great Britain in 1998 by
Judy Piatkus (Publishers) Ltd of
5 Windmill Street, London W1

This edition published 1998

Reprinted 1998

A catalogue record for this book is available from the British Library.

ISBN 0 7499 3077 2

Set in Times by Intype London Ltd

Printed and bound in Great Britain by
Mackays of Chatham PLC, Chatham, Kent

Dedicated, with affection, to the memory of
Charles Norman Buswell, OBE. MC.
An English gentleman.

And to Margaret, who joined him in 1997.

requiescat in pace

Form/Gvt27b

TOP SECRET

DISTRIBUTION: RESTRICTED/DirCIA ONLY

ORIG: SAIGON. VIA S21/CENTRAL INTELLIGENCE RADIO
    RELAY CENTER
TOD 03/22/57 19:35Z/TOR 07:38.
STATUS: encoded/SIGSALY/AXP . . . decode: Kreuznach. L.

Indication: No copies: No carbon. Original encodement attached.

DATE 03/22/57 MESSAGE BEGINS XXXXX
IMPERATIVE I HAVE FACE-ON CONTACT WITH
A SENIOR COMPANYMAN XXXXX CANDIDATE
MUST HAVE MANDATE FOR TOP LEVEL
DECISION MAKING XXXXX THIS MEETING
COULD RESULT IN THE ENHANCEMENT OF
OUR INFORMATION AND INTELLIGENCE
GATHERING CAPABILITY AND TOTALLY
RESHAPE THE COMPANY'S INFLUENCE IN
THIS REGION XXXXX CONTRACTOR XXXXX
ENDIT

Prologue

Kuala Lumpur, Malaya, March 1957

Bob Graver sat on the edge of the bed. He was draped in a large white, fluffy towelling bathrobe and sipped from a large glass of Scotch. The ice cubes that he'd liberally dosed the whisky with had almost melted, but their remains were still sufficiently active to set up a little musical jingle when he tilted the glass; a pleasant sop to Graver's tired and jet-lagged brain.

Bob Graver was one of the new type of CIA executives – Yale, non-operational, specially selected for a rapid upward trip in the Langley hierarchy. Nothing special to look at, almost the opposite; a short man, his near-sightedness corrected by thick, almost impenetrable lenses in plain wire frames, and untidily dressed, he looked more like a mature theological student than a senior member of one of the world's largest government intelligence-gathering agencies. But behind the drab, clerical exterior, Graver had not only a sharp analytical brain but the sort of gritty determination and personal courage that had first attracted him to the head of the burgeoning Central Intelligence Agency.

He peered at the sheet of paper he'd found at the KL airport dead-letter drop indicated by Contractor. Instructions, instructions, instructions. Go there, come here, stay where you like, book in there, contact me at X. Contractor didn't trust him. And why should he? He'd made a sheltered life for himself for God knew how many years; he wasn't going to give it all away at the drop of a hat to a Langley desk jockey. Graver raised the paper closer to his face. The only thing that made any sense was the name of the hotel he'd been instructed to book in to. The rest was the clever stuff – Dashiell Hammett in Chinatown, two steps forward, two sideways, and a soft-shoe shuffle down a dark alley. Graver blinked several times behind his bottle-thick lenses, then placed his glass heavily on the table beside the bed, raised the spectacles to his head and furiously rubbed his itching eyes. It wasn't just the jet-lag. Kuala Lumpur was an unknown quantity; the street names might just as well have been written in Serbo-Croat. They'd look better tomorrow. He gave a little forward jerk of his head and dislodged the glasses which dropped back neatly onto the bridge of his nose. He carefully folded the note, pressed it flat and slipped it into the back cover of the blue imitation-leather-bound Gideon which he then replaced in the slot under the telephone. He shrugged out of the bathrobe, slipped on a pair of bright scarlet cotton pyjama bottoms and, removing his spectacles, emptied the glass of whisky and switched the light off. He was fast asleep before the light bulb had cooled down.

It was the swish, swish, swish of the overhead fan that brought him back to life. That and the gentle gurgle of the phone by his ear.

'Your taxi's arrived, sir.'

What taxi? A brief pause. 'OK, tell him to wait. Give me ten minutes.' He dropped the phone back in its cradle and rolled out of the bed, showered, dressed and made his way down to the foyer. Breakfast could wait.

Graver was beyond caring. He was already soaked with perspiration when he clambered into the back of the yellow-and-black Ford; eight o'clock and the sun was already high and dragging the humidity out of where it had passed the night. The leather seat stuck to the back of his wet shirt, there was no air-conditioning and the taxi stank. He could smell the fried onions and garlic and chilli from the Chinese driver's last meal, and it didn't improve when, as the taxi jogged out of the hotel's forecourt, the driver took both hands off the wheel, lit a match and held it under a foul-smelling crumpled cigarette. Graver wound the window down as far as it would go and sucked in the exhaust fumes of a thousand overstretched motors laced generously with the spicy smells from another thousand open fires building up steam for lunch-time curries.

He caught his breath, unstuck his back from the hot seat, leaned forward and tapped the driver on the shoulder. The Chinaman didn't slow down. He turned his head and studied his passenger's face, then exhaled a cloud of smoke out of the other side of his mouth. '*Jalan Weld*,' he said, and let the taxi find its own way into Weld Road. Graver met his eyes without concern. Unlike Graver he seemed to know exactly where he was going.

A few cars behind them a white Mercedes flashed its headlights briefly twice.

Instruction No. 3: – in Weld Road a white Mercedes will flash its lights twice – get in it, say nothing . . .

Graver paid off the taxi, clambered out in the middle of the traffic and walked back to the white Mercedes. His eyes tried to pierce the smoked windscreen but all he could make out was the outline of a man's head. He pulled open the passenger-side door and scrambled in just as the jammed traffic started to move. He slammed the door shut and turned sideways to face the driver.

He was European. Hard to tell, as he relaxed behind the wheel, whether he was tall or short, but, even after a session in a KL traffic jam, he still looked cool and fresh. He wore a light blue Airtex shirt, navy blue serge shorts that rose just above the knee, thick woollen fawn-coloured knee-length stockings and highly polished solid brown leather shoes.

'You're Contractor?' said Graver. He tried not to look or sound surprised. He had no idea why but he was expecting a true-blue American, or possibly a miniature Chinaman – a sort of oriental Peter Lorre. This imitation Englishman didn't fit in with his expectations. And his question got the response he was expecting – nothing.

It was a short drive through, what looked to Graver like the better back streets of Kuala Lumpur before the white Mercedes glided into the leafy, tree-shaded carpark of the

3

Griffin Inn. Still without words, Graver allowed himself to be led to the outside covered area and a table well away from the two couples who'd decided on a late breakfast.

Contractor broke his silence.

'Drink?'

'Coffee,' said Graver, and pulled a chair out and sat down. He didn't wait for his coffee. 'OK, you talk, I'll listen.'

Contractor moved his chair closer to the table and rested his elbows on it. 'There's no need to fart around the subject. If you've done your homework properly you'll have gathered that I'm inside most governments and the military and intelligence establishments of quite a few countries in this area. At the moment the only reliable information you're getting from Hanoi or Saigon is mine and it's coming from the hearts and minds of the administrations of both capitals. OK so far?'

Graver raised his eyebrows but said nothing.

Contractor understood. 'OK. So let's scratch the surface of my problem. You've seen the depth of my penetration of the governing administrations of both ends of Vietnam. I'm in at the same level in Rangoon, Bangkok and any other country you'd care to name in this part of the world. It's up to you whether it continues.'

Graver didn't hurry with it. He said casually, 'OK, I've got the picture. But, before we go any further—' His thick glasses studied the other man's face. His eyes were unblinking behind them. 'You doing a turn for anyone else?'

'Like who?'

'Anyone.'

'There's no one can afford me. I can only play for one team at a time otherwise I get confused.' Contractor managed a smile but it didn't last. 'How long d'you want this state of affairs to last?'

'Your exclusivity?' Graver's expression didn't change. If anything he'd begun to look slightly bored. It was the same old story. The guy was putting on the squeeze for more money while the product still had a way to go. He reckoned he knew what Contractor meant. He played dumb.

Contractor wasn't put off. 'I'm talking about the extent of the circuit and its strength; the fact that we've got senior

4

administrators in all these hot spots working for the CIA. How long d'you want that to go on?'

'For ever.'

Contractor's lips tightened and the dying ice cubes in his gin and tonic played a brisk melody as he tilted the contents of the glass down his throat. 'Don't play the smart asshole with me, Graver! You're sitting on a fucking gold mine of information that's more highly classified than any other agency in the world could offer. Give a thought to what Hanoi would do to have it the other way round . . . To know exactly what cards the Pentagon and the White House have face down in front of them. The stakes don't bear thinking about.'

'And is that what you're thinking about – the stakes?'

'Money doesn't come into it. I've been given the opportunity to expand my intelligence-gathering capability tenfold – interested?'

'What's the catch?' This was what it always came down to – the catch, the tiny, almost invisible words at the bottom of the contract.

Contractor merely stared at Graver as if wondering whether his heart would stand the shock.

'Arms, ammunition, equipment?' Graver went through the mental shopping list, the usual stuff. And, of course, money; it always ended up with money, regardless of what the seller began his spiel with.

'No. Nothing like that,' said Contractor, without taking his eyes off Graver. 'Have you given any thoughts as to how I got this thing going?'

'Several, but I didn't like to ask.'

'You interested?'

'You're going to tell me anyway.'

'Sure I am. What d'you know about Chinese Tongs?'

'Tell me about them – if it's relevant.'

'It is. They're just about the biggest club in the world; every other Chinaman you've ever set eyes on is someway beholden to a Tong. The stick-wielders of the Tongs inspire more fear in a Chinaman than Himmler's Gestapo did for the Jews. And these Tong Chinese, or their eyes, are everywhere. They've got their fingers in every type of crim-

inal activity known to man – and that means everything!
And the home base for the most powerful three Tongs
is Bangkok. Mark that, Graver, not China, not Hong
Kong, but just up the road there in neutral, uncommitted,
hands-over-the-eyes-about-what's-going-on-anywhere-else-
around-here Bangkok. That's where it all happens, that's
where the Touming Guanxi rule the . . .'

'The who?'

'The Touming Guanxi. It's what the world's number-one
Tong calls itself. Touming Guanxi means invisible
relations . . .' Contractor picked up his drink and tasted it
and, under the pretence of studying the surroundings,
watched out of the corner of his eye to see how Graver was
taking it. But Graver was as much a master of the underhand
as Contractor. He showed nothing. But he waited for the
punch line, and he had a nasty feeling the punch line was
going to be hard one. A punch line that was going to cost.
But by the time that came Graver reckoned he'd worked
out most of the tangibles.

But this was the one that got away.

Even if he'd had advance warning of Contractor's
thinking and calmed himself down to logical thought, it was
still enough to send the blood rushing into his brain.

'It's all to do with Tongs, Graver, and how long you and
your people are prepared to accept their help.'

'I didn't know we were, but tell me about it.'

Contractor went over, briefly, the extent of his, and
through him the CIA's, involvement with the Touming
Guanxi and the benefits they had derived from this association. But Graver didn't need to be told this. He had seen
the volume and the quality of information that had filtered
into Langley from this area. Graver kept his head. He was
in no doubt about who owed whom thanks. But he was still
waiting for the punch line.

'What does this cost us?'

'You thinking dollars?'

Graver shrugged. 'I asked what it was costing. I can't
imagine this bunch of Chinese gangsters offering a complete
intelligence network at no cost.'

'The Tongs' help is not costing Washington any dollars,'

responded Contractor. 'Up until now it's cost a little bit of discretion on my part. A bit of glancing this way and that, but not directly at, when a few things have been going down – a few little things not exactly within the mandate of the good guys—'

'Can you go a bit deeper than that?' Graver was getting the vibes. They weren't good ones.

'There are a lot of peripheral activities in the Tongs' world, things that have no connection with American national security – as we know it. These people deal. They deal in almost every commodity and every activity under the sun—' Contractor studied Graver's tightening features. 'Are you following me?'

'Try getting a bit closer to the point. Mention something specific.'

'Narcotics.'

'That's specific enough. Go on.'

'In return for the most comprehensive spy ring in the world, I have turned my sight away from the narcotics industry run by the Touming Guanxi. The Chinese operating from Bangkok and Burma have got a stranglehold on the production and distribution of opium through this region. There's been some minor excursion into the American market but it's not yet fully established.'

Graver blinked his eyes behind the thick lenses of his spectacles. He had a good idea now where things were heading. But he was a long way out. There's an enormous divide between tacit ignorance and tacit approval. He was about to see how big a divide.

'Stop me if I'm hitting the wrong button, Contractor, but it sounds as if you're telling me that drugs are being smuggled into the States; that you know this has been, and probably is being done even as we sit here drowning our sorrows and you haven't rung the bell. Is this what you're telling me?'

'That's part of it, and if you take time to think about what you've received for turning a blind eye to something that's unstoppable anyway, I think you, and your master at Langley, will agree that the deal's a good one for us. And when the fuse does run out in Vietnam, what have you got

7

in position to maintain any form of positive intelligence – other than the Chinese grouping I mentioned earlier? And don't forget, if you get it wrong you'll be the boys who have to explain to whoever's running the show in the White House why you're being out-guessed by a bunch of jungle monkeys. Body-bags loaded with bits of young American boys piling up at Andrews is a great mind concentrator when it comes to decisions on what is ethical in the dirty game and what isn't.'

Graver didn't need pictures drawn for him. He was a political CIA man; the dirt and the muck that got splashed around at ground level were for the workers. But he was trying. 'If it's no more than the movement of a few sacks of poppy heads I think we could probably learn to live with that.'

Contractor looked hard at Graver, then got ready to ram the nail up his ass. 'It'll be more than a few sacks of poppy heads, Graver. But so far we've only touched the tip of the idea. My contacts have taken up a slightly more involved position . . .'

Graver put his coffee cup down with a thump and sat forward in his chair. 'Involved? Does that mean complicated or involvement?'

'Possibly both.'

'I'm not sure I could live with any involvement deeper than you've already outlined. These Tongs of yours are criminals. It doesn't matter how you wrap them up – silks or rags – the way you put 'em across they're no better in bed than the Chicago mobs of the twenties and thirties or today's Mafiosi – they're all fuckin' criminals and don't attract us to too intimate a relationship, no matter whether we derive a small percentage of gain. I think you've gone far enough with them. Thus far and no further is my edict to you and will be my recommendation to my principal. Is that enough? Is that what you wanted head-to-head for?'

Contractor studied him for a moment, then slowly shook his head. 'Not quite. I chose the word involvement with care. After many years of holding hands with us, of building up the most comprehensive intelligence-gathering network we've ever had out here, of giving us more than a head start in a future war, they want a reassessment of our gratitude—'

'You mean they want money?'

'No – a reassessment of our gratitude. Turning a blind eye on a minor import-export enterprise is not a helluva lot of gratitude. They want CIA involvement with them in a major takeover of the US narcotic trade . . .'

'They want what? Say that again!'

'I think you got it, Graver. You don't want it repeated. What you want is its elaboration . . .'

'No way! Absolutely no way!'

'D'you want to hear the rest of it?'

'I don't want to hear fuck-all about any form of partnership with a bunch of fuckin' Chinese criminals. Forget it. Nothing doing!'

Contractor remained calm and for a moment carefully sipped his gin and tonic. Graver took off his glasses and polished the lenses by way of therapy, his head shaking this way and that as he thought about what he'd heard. When his nerves were sufficiently quietened, he slipped them back on his nose and refocused on Contractor. 'No way,' he repeated.

'OK. Let's skip the details and I'll read you the end of the script. Sit quiet, Graver, and listen.'

Graver sought solace in his coffee and did as he was told.

'Right. Not only narcotics but drugs of every description are going to be flooding the world before the end of the century. America's going to be the hub of the industry; everything will take place there, it'll be the world exchange; prices'll be set, quantities established and shipments will leave and arrive the way any other commodity does at the moment. The only difference is that drugs will be entirely underground. Establish that in your mind, Graver. Somebody's going to run this business. It can be the Mafia, reborn Chicago mobs, fun and games with the Italians, the Irish, even Central Americans, jumping into the ring – or you can have the Chinese. With all these except the Chinese you get nothing but strife. Every agency in the country is going to be fully stretched just to try and keep the thing from turning into the biggest brain-bender of all time. There's your alternative, Graver. You can't beat this thing, but you can profit from it, and you can, to a certain degree, keep tabs on it. Make it a monopoly, make the entire drug scene a Tong-operated cartel, and you'll be able to plot its progress. They'll keep some discipline in the drug world; they'll police it; they won't let it become a free-for-all. Instead of dozens of distributors cutting each other's throats, turning the streets into abattoirs and undermining every civilised institution in every major country in the world, the Touming Guanxi will regulate it from a position of strength and will negotiate with one voice . . .'

'Nothing doing!'

'I said sit and listen. You get to air your views when you've had a look at the entire picture. Have you got that bit? That's the end line. A disaster scenario, but one with room on the tiller for your hand so that some of its direction can be manipulated. The alternative—'

'You've shown it—'

Contractor ignored the interruption. 'The alternative – a loaded runaway express, out of control with a dozen different drivers tearing each other's throats out while the thing roars off the tracks and into oblivion. And however you see it, Graver, the Touming Guanxi will in the end be top dog. It'll take them a lot longer and cost them a lot more, but you can't stop them so you might as well profit from the inevitable and keep them on our side.'

Graver lifted his cup again. Totally in control, he decided he was drinking with a madman. 'I don't buy it – the hypothesis or the scenario. And I repeat, no way will the CIA encourage anyone to take a monopoly in a criminal activity for the sake of an easy handle. No way.'

'Then try this one,' said Contractor reasonably. 'Turn it down without consideration and as from tomorrow morning all intelligence from this region going into Langley's inner sanctum dries up and the whole shebang has to start from scratch. But this time we go it totally alone; all our high-ranking informers in serious positions go up the monkey's ass. Nothing, Graver. Fuck all. From the most highly organised intelligence-gathering apparatus in the world to zilch – in twenty-four hours. D'you like that one better?'

Graver met Contractor's eyes and held them for several moments as his mind offered him a different scenario; a scenario where he was standing in the DCI's office, hands in his trouser pockets as he nonchalantly reported that they had no more Contractor, no more intelligence units in South-East Asia; no more spies, no more agents, no more informers in high places, not even in low places, and owing to his, Graver's, insistence on the purity of action of the United States of America's Central Intelligence Agency, they'd not only lost everything in the world's next cauldron but they'd got the fuckin' Chinese secret societies, who'd been falling over themselves during the last eight years or so to help, actively working against them. Well done, Robert Graver, ten out of ten for fucking incompetence. Pick your hat up on the way out.

'What's the minimum they'd accept?'

'I've just given it you. D'you want to talk to number-one son?'

'Is that possible? I don't want to have to fly all over South-East Asia to drink green tea with some Dr Fu Manchu.'

'Fifteen minutes.'

'What?'

'Finish your coffee and settle the bill while I use the phone. You can tell Dr Fu Manchu all about it in a quarter of an hour. He's waiting to see you the minute I give the word. D'you want me to do that?'

'Let's get it over and done with. No promises. I'm agreeing to nothing. Just talk. OK?'

The white Mercedes picked its way carefully along Batu Road, turned into the bigger, but less crowded Pahang Road before edging its way out of the crowd and into the scruffy Sentul Road. A short distance and it joined the main trunk route and continued north until most of built-up Kuala Lumpur was left behind.

On either side of the road tin villages had sprung up and developed, in typical Chinese manner, into shantytowns with every conceivable type of junk-shop, usually spare parts from crashed, burnt-out or unroadworthy vehicles. The roads running through these shantytowns were nothing more

11

than laterite tracks, and the deep ruts and potholes, usually filled with muddy water and dead and decomposing dogs and cats, had to be negotiated at snail's pace otherwise the car would end up as bits and pieces suspended from the nearest tin shack's beams and shelves. The sidewalks, upon which the shops, made of second-hand timber with rusting corrugated tin roofs, had been constructed, were raised wooden platforms reinforced with discarded railway sleepers. The overall atmosphere was one of desolation and resigned acceptance.

One hundred per cent Chinese, the air was at all times filled with the overpowering smell of Chinese cooking and cigarette smoke. Everybody smoked; everybody hawked and spat and everybody, until the arrival of two white-faced strangers in a German car, shouted conversation at each other at the tops of their voices. When the two Americans stepped out into the road, two thickset, identically dressed, flat-faced Chinese Tongmen closed in on them. The silence that descended could be spooned up with a wooden ladle. But nobody made eye contact. Every single man had something else that occupied his eyes until the Americans, picking their way through the puddles preceded by the two Chinese, had disappeared into one of the shanties. It was only then that the noise began again.

Graver allowed his eyes to roam as he walked behind Contractor who, in turn, moved casually behind one of the Chinese. The other Chinaman brought up the rear. The place was deeper than he had at first realised. It seemed to go on for ever: a dimly lit tunnel through every known car part – radiator grilles, old exhaust systems, thousands of retreaded tyres, batteries, bumpers, doors from every car that ever was dating back to 1930. He peered around him. Who the hell would want to come to Sentul to buy a rusting 1935 Chevvy fender?

Graver breathed deeply of the dust and oil and rubber residue from old retreads as the file came to a halt, passed sideways through a dirt-laden shaggy curtain, another storeroom, then a pine plank door. The two young Chinese joined up and stood to one side of the door. They allowed Contractor to enter but when Graver took a step forward an arm shot out, turned him sideways and, with one of them behind and one in front, they ran their hands expertly over his body before stepping to one side and allowing him to pass through the doorway.

Liu Zhoushiu sat alone in the room. It was a room that was for everything. But more than that it was a safe room in a safe house, a meeting place, soundproof and defendable with more escape routes than a rabbit-warren. A worn and badly battered desk and the chair that Liu was sitting in made up the permanent furniture; another two chairs had been imported for the honoured guests, wooden fold-up chairs cast out from some council office at about Japanese occupation time. Liu was sipping milky tea from a tumbler. He didn't stop sipping but acknowledged Contractor with a raise of the eyebrows and an exchange of expressions. He pointedly ignored Graver and listened with studied concentration to a lengthy report in Cantonese from Contractor. When Contractor finished talking he shifted his eyes to Graver and gestured towards him with his hand by way of introduction. 'Mr Jones,' he said.

Liu gave the faintest of smiles and reached a slim, delicate hand across the desk for Graver to grasp. There was no response to his smile; Graver wasn't in a smiling mood. But he did take the hand, and wished he hadn't. It was like shaking hands with an empty kid glove. No feeling, no warmth, just a gesture of Western civility that had no meaning in this section of Chinese society. 'Sit down, Mr Jones.' His English was good, without affectation. 'And tell me what the CIA thinks about the proposition Contractor has placed before you.'

Graver didn't mince his words. 'The CIA's not aware that they've been offered a proposition. The way I read it we've been offered a heavy blackmail job.' He jerked his head at Contractor. 'And if he's told you any different let me disillusion you here and now – the CIA doesn't go in for blackmail jobs of any description.' He studied Liu's expression. It was like studying a sheet of plain paper. He pushed a little harder. 'He tells me' – he raised his chin slightly in the other American's direction again – 'that without Washington's co-operation in your plans to run the

13

narcotics market in the United States you will withdraw all assistance to our security cadres in this area . . .?'

Liu allowed the silence that followed Graver's words to develop, then, after raising his glass of tea, he slurped noisily, swallowed and said in a thin voice, 'A little bit overstated, Mr Jones, but basically, yes . . .' He took another slurp. 'Except, you haven't got any security cadres in this area. Your security cadres and your intelligence and information-gathering capability are entirely in the hands of people who owe their allegiance to me.' He coughed lightly, modestly. 'They supply the CIA with what is necessary but they do not belong to the CIA. Neither can they. Without their help all your sources will dry up; and in doing so there will be no cracks left for penetration by your own people.' He shrugged deprecatingly. 'But this has already been told you by Contractor?'

Graver matched the Chinaman's expression. 'What guarantee do we have that these people will not turn sides and abandon you, as you, for example, might well abandon us once you have established your business in the States?'

'You have my word on it. I am a businessman, not a gambler.'

Graver had been neatly manoeuvred into a corner with a minimum option. He'd been boxed in. If he didn't agree there was no intelligence game worth thinking about; Liu would close them down as easily as sweeping his hand across the board and sending every piece flying. That was a non-starter. If he said he wanted time to think about it he was showing indecision. Liu wanted decision; he wanted yes or no; he wanted it now – that's what face-to-face meant. And if he said he wanted more guarantee than a middle-age Chinese Tong leader's word he'd close the meeting with an insult. Loss of face wouldn't come into it; the blank-faced sonofabitch would close 'em down out of insult and go ahead with his America plans regardless of whether he received CIA patronage or not. Graver looked at the wall. There was nowhere else for him to go. He backed away.

'What are your plans for this venture?'

Liu's face showed no triumph, no satisfaction. He was going into the United States of America to take over and run the world's narcotics market and he was going to do it with the blessing of the Central Intelligence Agency. But nothing showed in his flat, featureless expression as he calmly and systematically slurped the thick sweet tea from the glass. The noise of the gurgling liquid was the only sound in the room as the three men considered their positions. Liu kept his eyes glued to Graver's face, and Graver, fully aware of the Chinaman's scrutiny, glanced sideways at Contractor. Contractor was the only non-player. He had nothing to lose or gain; the status quo was sufficient reward for him; he wasn't going to get his balls kicked in by Langley for taking to the dance-floor with Thailand's drugs emporium. But his position, and protection by the Touming Guanxi, was enhanced – after all, he was the one who brought the Invisible Relations and the visible CIA to the same table.

But would it last?

Graver wouldn't have bet money on it. But then Graver never had been a betting man. He was a man of practicalities; betting was OK if there were no odds, everything face upwards and you bet on what you'd got, not what you thought the other guy hadn't got. But Graver's missing gambler's instinct wouldn't have allowed the investment of a broken zip-fastener on the possibility of this one lasting a year.

He was way out.

Chapter 1

San Francisco, November 1974

The two men had been sitting in a booth in the Café Flore spitting and scratching at each other across the table all evening. Nobody took any notice. Nobody ever did. What lovers did in a South of Market gay bar was nobody's business but their own.

They were an oddly matched couple. A schoolboy-size Caucasian with a spotty, adolescent complexion, sulking full lips, pale blue eyes and yellowy bleached, stubbled hair cut in the gay urchin style. He was about eighteen coming on twenty-four. His companion couldn't have been more different: short, powerfully built, squat and muscular with flat oriental features and narrow, cruel eyes that almost disappeared into the heavy mounds of his cheekbones.

The blond boy lifted his eyes for a moment and studied the two young Chinese who strolled in hand in hand and stood just inside the entrance. It was a brief glance and matched that of the elderly, sad-looking white man, in a shirt open at the neck, jacket and tie, who sat at the piano with one elbow on the keyboard supporting his chin whilst the other hand tinkled a slow, moody accompaniment to a big black youth with his eyes closed practising blues variations on a battered saxophone. The piano player took longer than Blondie over his inspection of the newcomers; saw something that the others didn't and turned his eyes away quickly, bowed his head and concentrated on where he was putting his fingers.

16

The two Chinese at the door adjusted their eyes to the gloom then, as if on command, moved to the bar and ordered two glasses of root beer. Whilst one paid, the other, dressed in skin-tight Levi's and a dark brown bomber jacket, his black hair slicked flat on his head with a white parting down the exact centre, glanced over his shoulder and casually quartered the dark room. There wasn't much to see. Most of the heads were back close together again; most were interested in nothing beyond their partner's face. No one was listening to the disillusioned old man and his tinkling, out-of-tune honky-tonk piano.

The Chinese in the bomber jacket allowed his eyes to rest for a moment on the two squabbling men then, with a slight touch on his companion's elbow, he minced across the floor to the lavatory. The barman lost interest and moved back to his friend at the other end of the bar.

In the lavatory the young Chinese removed the short-barrelled .38 from the loop on his belt and from his bulky jacket pocket drew out a six-inch metal cylinder. This he screwed tightly onto the threads cut into the outer rim of the barrel. He eased back the hammer and, with the revolver in his hand hanging at his side, walked normally through the swing door of the toilet.

His passage back to the bar took him past the table with the two arguing lovers. The man waiting at the bar, leaving the two beers untouched, moved away and walked towards the entrance. The man from the lavatory, without breaking his stride, brought the .38 up from his side, fired two bullets into the head of the thickset Chinese sitting with his back to him, another two into the face of the blond boy, then carried on walking to the door where, joining his friend from the bar, he took his hand and strolled out into busy Market Street.

It had happened quickly and without noise or commotion.

In the dark corner the two friends still sat unnoticed, one with his head in his arms on the table, the other sitting back in his chair with his head resting on the wall behind him. They weren't arguing any more. And the piano player played on.

When the bar woke up to what had happened it was

discovered that the stocky man with the Mongolian features had his face blown away. He was stone dead. Blondie had survived by a whisker and was rushed to the Pacific Medical Center in Fillmore. Ten days later he was ready to tell Lieutenant Ranny Lim of the San Francisco Police Department why he thought a couple of Chinese hit-men would want to kill him.

And he had no idea. That was until Ranny Lim went to work on him.

'You're a very lucky boy, Blondie,' was Lim's opener. 'By all accounts you should be dead. Somebody up there must like you.'

Pain and truculence guided the wounded boy's response. 'Piss off!'

The words came out indistinctly through the gaps where his teeth had been blown out, and muffled by the wads of lint and bandage that held his face together. When it was all over he was going to have difficulty finding a friend, let alone new love, with a face like his. But he didn't know that yet.

'You're known as Blondie around Castro and the Tenderloin. And that's another thing, while we're getting to know each other – do you normally wander around Castro and Sunny without a set of dog tags round your neck?'

'Whaddya mean?'

'For a boy like you it's a battlefield. Some of those hard shits out there'll empty your pockets, screw your ass off and throw it over the wall. You're a new guy on the block. None of the regulars know you; you've only been seen around for the last couple of months and then only with your Chinky boyfriend. You're not on the game, are you?'

'Why, you going to arrest me for it?'

Ranny Lim smiled lazily. Small, even for a Chinese, with a smooth face and clean features, he looked more like a high-school student than a detective lieutenant. 'Let's start at the beginning again, then. What's your name?'

'Like you said – Blondie.'

'You sure you're not called Smartass?' Ranny Lim's face remained open and his expression unaggressive. But under the words was a sharp edge which Blondie, with all his

18

animal instincts in running with the gutter mob, didn't make the mistake of ignoring. 'Because if you are,' continued Ranny Lim, 'and you want to play games, we can do it down at the station. We've got a little room for assholes there – even for those who've had a face full of thirty-eights . . .'

'I can't be moved. The doctor said so.'

'You can be. I said so. Now what's your name?'

'Philip.'

'Philip what?'

'You won't believe it.'

'Try me.'

'Morris.'

'You're right, I don't believe it. But we'll go along with it for the time being. OK, Philip Morris. We've got over that little hurdle. Now the same thing applies to the next ten questions. Try not to test my patience, Philip. OK? Let's start with: what was your late friend's name? Where was he from? What did he do? And how long had you known him?'

'Are you arresting me for anything?'

'That wasn't one of the questions.'

'You know what I mean. Incriminating myself; pleading the Fifth and all that sort of thing?'

Ranny Lim raised his eyebrows and lit a cigarette.

'You can't smoke in here.'

Lim ignored him. 'You a lawyer or something?'

'No. Why?'

'What's all this malarkey about incrimination and the Fifth? That's legal talk. Are you into something deeper than nearly having your head blown off, Philip? Was it you they were after?'

Blondie turned onto his side and, as best he could, looked Ranny Lim in the face. He squealed like a little pig with the effort of turning his head. Lim sympathised with him. He knew how bullet wounds hurt, even ten days after they'd done, or failed to do, their stuff. 'That guy I was with . . .?'

'Dead.'

'Thank you for breaking it to me so gently!'

'Tell me about him.'

'It was him they were after. He was running money . . .'

'Who're they?'

'It's your job to find out, not mine.' Blondie relented for a second. Perhaps it was pain, perhaps he wanted to get it over and done with so that he could crawl back into the woodwork. 'It was nothing to do with me,' he emphasised. 'They wanted Leong ...'

'Leong being the name of your dead boyfriend?' Ranny Lim walked over to the washbasin in the corner of the room and pinched out the end of his cigarette. He turned the tap on the ash, watched it sizzle down the drain, then came back and sat down again. He lit another cigarette. This time Blondie didn't complain. 'What was the rest of Leong's name?' he asked.

'I only knew him as Leong. He was Chinese, he was from Thailand.'

'You said he was running money – who was he running money for?'

Blondie tried to shrug but it reached the nerve ends in his damaged face. He gave a genuine groan, then rested his bandaged head on the headboard while he recovered his earlier cockiness. But it was a much subdued Blondie who finally opened up. 'I think he was part of a Chinese drug syndicate. He never mentioned it, he was very clammy on things like that. Personally, I didn't want to know, I don't do drugs. Neither did he, not the hard stuff. He used to take a pipe fairly regularly but that's not drugging, is it? I've had a pipe once or twice myself. It doesn't do anything, not for me anyway. All I wanted to do was go to sleep ...' Ranny let him prattle on. In a minute he'd probably say something. ' ... but lately, over the last few weeks, he'd been very much on edge—' Without Lim's prompting Blondie stopped to ponder this and came up with his own solution. 'I think he was dipping his fingers in the till. He had more to spend than your average money-runner. That's what I reckon – he was siphoning and they blew his head off for it. I think he knew—'

Ranny Lim broke his silence. 'What made you think someone was gunning for him?'

'He broke the rules, didn't he? He was supposed to be running between New York and London, England. He went via here to throw off the New York markers. Coming here

20

people could cover his back and make sure he had no followers. It was big money he was carrying – very big money.
But he had help.'

'What sort of help?'

'I'm not sure. But I think official.'

'Why official?'

'I went with him on a couple of occasions, just for the
trip, mind you. He used SFO on the two trips I went with
him. It seemed to me a very roundabout way to go to
Europe. After all, New York's . . .'

'Talk about the help.'

'A suit and tie at the airport walked alongside us and
winked Leong through the formalities. He wasn't stopped
or checked, not while I was with him.'

Ranny Lim's face showed nothing of what was going
through his mind. But the little bells were already ringing,
if muted. He didn't dwell on the men in suits and ties. 'You
said when you went with him he went to Europe – England,
you said?'

'Yeah. London. In the city where the business and banks
are – sort of Wall Street . . .'

'OK, so you went to London's Wall Street. Anywhere
particular?'

'The Chusan and Kowloon Bank. Always the Chusan and
Kowloon. Everyone in there was a Chink – sorry, a Chinese.
He would go to the counter and then someone would come
round and take him into an office. The manager's, I suppose.'

'Is that the only reason you supposed he was running
money – that he always went to a particular bank in London,
England? Tell me more.'

Blondie sulked for a few seconds. Lim reckoned he'd
earned it, but then decided life couldn't stand still while a
white-haired faggot with his pretty looks shot to ribbons
sulked over his memories of an ugly, squat little Chinese
with only half a head lying stiff as a plank in the police
mortuary. He gave him a gentle kick-start.

'Where'd he pick up all this money?'

'No idea – well, I do actually, or I think I do. We had a
little row – nothing important, just one of those things, and
I didn't see him for a couple of days. I thought he might be

21

seeing some old tart so, curiosity, you know, I waited outside his place and followed him. Funny thing was, these other two guys went after him too, and over the couple of days I watched Leong these two little Chinks were stuck to him like shit. It was strange, though, for a guy carrying a lot of money about he didn't seem concerned about watching his back – he didn't see them, they didn't see me ...'

Lim brought him gently back on course. 'Where did you follow Leong to?'

'Stockton Street. Twice. Same place. It's a store called Cathay Emporium, sells spices and bits of bone and rhinoceros horn for giving poor old jerkers a bit of a push when they're trying for the jackpot ...'

'You'd know all about that, Philip?'

'D'you want to hear this story or not?'

'Go on, then – you followed Leong to an aphrodisiac store in Stockton Street. What then?'

'That's where he picked the money up.'

'And these two guys who followed him?'

'Dunno. Could they be the ones who did this to me?' Blondie made a languorous gesture with a long slim hand curling towards his bandaged face. His voice cracked. 'But why me? Why would they want to do this to me?'

'It'll remain one of those big mysteries, Philip. It's going on all the time. Maybe they thought you were part of Leong's crew – or maybe his minder!' Lim didn't laugh, although the thought of a white-haired, limp-wristed pansy minding anything but his boyfriend's pussy-cat would take one hell of a stretch of the imagination. But funnier things had been known to happen.

'What's going to happen to me?' asked Blondie, plaintively.

Ranny Lim got to his feet. 'Nothing as far as I'm concerned,' he said. 'You haven't done anything wrong, have you?'

'What d'you mean – have I? I've just had my fucking face shot to ribbons. What about the people who did it? Aren't you going to find them?'

'Oh, we'll have a look here and there, Philip. But you know how these things are. Chinese – funny little mothers, they all look alike, and there are millions of 'em in SF. We'll be lucky if we ever run across these two again. But if we do I promise we'll stick your problem onto their charge sheet on top of anything else they might be done for. You're not thinking of going anywhere abroad for the time being, are you?'

'Why?'

'I might need you to come to the airport with me one day and see if you recognise anybody there. OK?'

'Not OK. I want nothing more to do with you or them. Thank you very much!'

'See you around, Philip. Get better soon.'

'Captain,' said Ranny Lim, 'it's not a question of a couple of Chinese hit-men taking out a drug syndicate's bagman. There could be all sorts of reasons for that . . .'

'Maybe it's because he was gay.'

'I wouldn't dispute that either. No, they can kill each other every day of the week as far as I'm concerned, but what does interest me is the little snippet the blond boy dropped about this money-carrier being helped through SFO customs and security formalities. A little something there that stinks.'

'Bit of corruption, you think?'

'A big bit by the sound of it. What I'd like to do is put this Flore killing on ice for the time being. We can pick it up again at any time with the stuff we have. I'd like a couple of Chinese boys for a watching job that may take a bit of time . . .'

'Stockton Street?'

'Yeah. I think I know where it'll lead – straight to a drug-runner; nothing big, just a drop for money *en route* from New York to Europe for laundering. It won't be worth closing it down and, with luck, we might trawl in one shipment before they catch on and close the place down themselves.'

'Ranny, what makes you think we'd only do one load?'

'It's that funny feeling, Captain. People in suits and ties at the airport.'

'You going to put a name to anyone – or anything?'

Ranny Lim sucked in his breath with an exaggerated whistle and shook his head at the same time. 'I wouldn't even mention my suspicions to myself. But I think I'll go and pay a visit to the airport, just for a little look round. Nothing serious, nothing official. I'll go out there for a quiet drink with an old pal of mine.'

'This guy got a name?'

'Dick Mayne, deputy head of airport security.'

'OK. Keep it cool. Don't disturb any of these people in suits – not yet; not until we know what we're getting into.'

'Nothing more than a social call, Captain. Can I have that watching team?'

'Yeah, sure – it's no big deal. Let's give it a run. Keep me in touch – OK?'

Dick Mayne had only one leg. He'd left the other one, full of 50mm bullet holes, in Vietnam, but it didn't show – he could keep up with the best of them.

His office was in direct proportion to the difference in importance between himself and the head of airport security; it was slightly larger than the average broom closet. He stood up when Lim came into the room and, without a word, twisted on his articulated heel, opened a drawer in the tin cabinet and brought out a bottle of Jack Daniels No. 7 and two small glasses. These he filled almost to the brim, then he sat down, broke his leg at the join just below the knee, and picked up one of the glasses. Not a drop spilled.

'Cheers!' He swallowed half the contents of the glass. 'Help yourself, Ranny.' He rummaged in the desk drawer and brought out a coarse paper packet of cigarettes and tossed them beside Ranny Lim's untouched glass. 'Recognise 'em?'

Ranny Lim smiled crookedly. 'It makes my lungs ache just being in the same room.' But he reached for one all the same and lit it. They were addictive – Vietnamese-grown and -made, jet-black tobacco, *thouc lao*; for those who got the hang of them and survived, it was like dragging the blast of a flame-thrower into your lungs. But it made for relaxed conversation.

Lim picked his way into the subject.

'International flights, Dick; what sort of characters would you have hanging around watchee-watchee?'

'Bit of everything nowadays. You never know what the hell's going down at any given moment. Airport people are always on the lookout and always standing by for a call from ground staff. As you know, there's a police detachment here at all times. Why d'you want to know?'

Ranny stuck his nose in the glass of whiskey and sniffed. 'People in suits?'

'Those too.'

'What would they represent?'

Mayne reached out and helped himself from the packet of *thouc lao*. He studied one of the sticks for a moment, stuck the open end in his mouth and rolled it between his lips until it was wet; the other end he dipped in the whiskey before lighting it. He coughed chestily and raised his eyes to Ranny Lim. He thought he'd got the message. 'You thinking Feds?'

Lim's expression didn't change. Neither did he nod. He kept everything very still.

Mayne dragged again on the cigarette and grimaced. 'OK, Feds. They come on the scene only if the situation calls for one or more. Usually that's done by them from the City office. They don't have a permanent stand here.'

'How about the other people?'

'Spooks? Company men? Drugs?'

'That sort of thing.'

'Tell me about it first.'

Ranny hesitated long enough for Dick Mayne to raise his eyebrows then drop them fiercely over his eyes, creating a sharp black ridge over the bridge of his nose. He had very bushy eyebrows; they looked menacing and, as Lim well knew, in this position meant he wasn't too happy with the cards he'd been dealt. He was a bad poker player but very adept at putting his feelings across without having to say a word.

Lim told him about the killing in the Café Flore and Blondie's remark about the Chinaman being helped through the international barrier with what Blondie reckoned was a bagful of used notes. Dick Mayne sat, po-faced, until Lim finished talking. He waited for him to empty his glass, then dragged it across to his side of the table, lined it up beside his and, with infinite care, poured an inch and a half in each. He studied them to make sure neither had received an advantage, then slid Lim's back to him, picked his own up and waited for the Chinaman to do the same.

'Cheers again.'

'Same to you.'

'You trying to make a problem for yourself, Ranny?'

Ranny just stared at him.

'OK. You are. CIA have a permanent presence but it's not generally known and it's never talked about. It's a sort of—' He stopped and studied Ranny Lim's features. 'I'm not sure I should be discussing this with you. Nothing personal, Ranny – I shouldn't be discussing this with anyone . . .'

'Thanks!'

'I didn't mean it like that. Oh, shit! OK – this is not for distribution around your locker room; it's for your ears only – OK?'

'OK.'

'It's a sort of highly secret international watching station. There are selected airports where this watch is in place – SFO is a four-star which means high profile, or one of the prime areas for surveillance . . .'

'Of what?'

'Imported terrorism, mainly, but a bit of everything comes in and goes out of a four-star. Another four-star is that place your gay friend mentioned.'

'Which one's that?'

'London.'

'CIA watch that as well?'

'Same as here, pal. Hang around a bit and you might hear a limey accent. It's all darks and shadows. I only hope they know what they're watching for, but, getting back to your fag and the Chinese bagman, what exactly is it that's being implied here?'

'That, Dick, is the seven-hundred-and-fifty-million-dollar question. I just don't know. Something. But what the hell it is God only knows. Where do these CIA guys hang out?'

'They're spooks, Ranny, they don't sign any registers.

26

They could be living in the parking lot for all I know. They just appear. They just happen – like spooks!'

'Is it a permanent crew?'

'I've seen the same three guys on and off. In fact the one I saw earlier today has been around for about six weeks. Maybe they do a two-month stint. Who knows? They're a law unto themselves. It's not for me to ask what the hell they're up to. Personally, I'd forget all about it if I were you.'

Lim smiled mirthlessly. 'I'm going to think about it.'

He did, for a couple of minutes, while he gently savoured his drink. Dick Mayne studied the little Chinaman while he did so. There was a soft expression in his eye. He had a lot of time for the gutsy little sonofabitch. It didn't surprise him when Lim lit another cigarette, scorched his lungs with an unguarded pull on the thick black tobacco, coughed and rapped his chest with a fist, then whooshed out the mouthful of smoke and said, 'For my own satisfaction, Dick. I think I'll take it a little further down the path. I'm going to bring my gay wounded warrior for a day out at the airport and see if he recognises anybody. As I said, just to settle my curiosity.'

'It's your funeral, pal. What if the guy who helped the money-bag through turns out to be from Langley?'

'I'll cross that bridge when I come to it.'

'You'll be advised to have a good scout around before you do that. Those boys have been known to play very rough when they're on the game. Me? Personally, I'd stick to running in whores and queers down the Tenderloin if I were you.'

'Much the same thing, this, isn't it, Dick?'

The watching team Ranny Lim had placed on the Cathay Emporium struck gold five days after their surveillance had started. A strange face arrived at four o'clock in the afternoon with a large, moulded quality suitcase. He left a few minutes later without the case and, after a half-hearted, over-confident evasion course, made his way downtown to Ellis Street bus terminal and boarded the Airporter shuttle to San Jose. The watchers split and one of the team joined him on the bus. When they reached the airport he made sure his target was safely ensconced over a plate of steak and eggs before contacting Lim.

'Let him run,' instructed Lim, when told that the courier, Chinese, had booked in for the New York flight on the return half of a ticket from the same place. 'Got a picture?'

'Several.'

'OK. See him onto the plane and then get back to Stockton. I'll meet you there. He's just a straightforward bagman, a little fish, we'd gain nothing by netting him. His masters would just close down the depot and open another. Forget him. Er – his face didn't do anything to you, did it?'

'Nope. But I was just behind him when he was asking about New York flights. He wasn't local – spoke with an accent, not Hong Kong or Singapore . . .'

'How d'you make that out?'

'They tend to talk British when they break into American. This guy had something different. Very foreign.'

'Chinese perhaps?' asked Lim, straight-faced.

'Not that either.'

'How about Thailand – Bangkok?'

'That one's out of my circle. You sure you want to let him go?'

'I'm sure. See you later.'

Ranny Lim would have bet money the new face was a Bangkok one. Blondie had been certain his boyfriend was from there. If there was something big going down between San Francisco and the outside world it would have to be Tong. Tong with a Thai accent. Thailand Tong. And Thailand Tong meant Touming Guanxi. Trouble. Opium, heroin, cocaine money, big money, if Blondie'd got his facts straight. And one of ours helping it through the gate at SFO?

When Lim, in the quiet of his office, studied the photographs of the New York man and the uglier, but dead, Leong there seemed to be a remarkable similarity. Nothing he could put his finger on, just something inside him that seemed to click – perhaps it was the flat, broad nose, or the measurements typed on a sticker on the back. He shoved the two pictures in an envelope and sent them under special cover to FBI Los Angeles for possible identification, the results of which, if any, to be communicated direct from LA FBI to Lieutenant Ranny Lim at Turk Street station, San Francisco. If the FBI were surprised that the pictures weren't handed to Lim via FBI San Francisco, they didn't show it. They weren't silly or pedantic. If a police lieutenant in one hot spot wanted to bypass his local Federals then that was his business and he'd either have a good reason or he'd fallen out with the locals – it wasn't unusual, and it wasn't their problem.

The identification came back by special courier. Positive. Both Leong and the new face were on the list. It appeared that both men were Thai nationals of Chinese origin. Ten out of ten for the agent who said they weren't Hong Kong or Singapore Chinese. Additional information on the two men indicated that they were logged by FBI as being street-level New York members of one of the primary Tongs active in the US, the Touming Guanxi, whose centre of operations was normally the Eastern seaboard. The Tong, watched but not infiltrated by the Organised Crime (Asian) Unit of the FBI, had no previous record of association or activity in either California generally or San Francisco particularly. Observation and investigation through CIA sources at Langley indicated no activity in the US within the narcotics trade.

Very interesting, thought Ranny Lim, and he telephoned his friend at the newly formed Drug Enforcement Administration's Intelligence Center at El Paso. The following day a special delivery envelope, postmarked El Paso, was dumped on his desk.

Ranny Lim's friend was quite free with his knowledge. It was limited, but pointed. The Touming Guanxi, he wrote, was the major policy-making faction of the big three Tongs in Bangkok, Thailand. It controlled almost the entire production and distribution of the huge narcotics industry in what is now loosely termed the Burma Triangle (Burma, Cambodia, Thailand), but strangely – Lim's friend had encased the word 'strangely' in quote marks and underlined it, but had given no explanation – it had never been reported as being involved in narcotics in the US.

He went on to explain that up until two years ago, when

29

the Drug Enforcement Administration had been formed, all narcotics intelligence had been handled by the CIA and it was only in these two years that the DEA had had an undercover team in position in Thailand. The CIA had never been very helpful, although it would probably be treasonable to suggest that they had deliberately impeded the activities of the new agency. This inter-departmental jealousy had kept them and the CIA at arm's length and to date the effectiveness of the DEA had been limited to tracing the source of narcotic shipments from Thailand. The DEA knew of the existence of the Touming Guanxi but their attempts at infiltration in Bangkok had so far resulted in the deaths of four special agents, two of them this month, and the disappearance of two more. DEA did, however, make a tenuous but unsubstantiated connection between an American businessman resident in Bangkok and two of the senior figures in Touming Guanxi, but this was downgraded by the CIA as a 'kite-flyer' and overlapping a CIA area of interest. But nevertheless, the report continued, this information was passed by DEA Washington to the FBI who identified the businessman as a Mr James Logan, known to have had OSS connections during World War II. The FBI asked the CIA whether they had any knowledge of this man; the CIA reported back, with a copy to the DEA for NFA – no further action – that he had no connection with Langley or any other official United States intelligence agency.

There were several more pages detailing, mainly, the DEA's attempts at breaking the ever-increasing volume of drugs into the United States from a variety of foreign organisations, but little more about the Touming Guanxi. Lim glanced briefly at the other sheets, replaced them in their envelope and put them in his pocket for when he got home and could put his feet up and study them at length. In the meantime . . . The anticipation of a quiet evening was disturbed by a call from one of his watching team in Stockton Street.

'We've got a customer for that suitcase. He dragged it out of the store and humped it down to the taxi rank. Boonie's gone with him in another taxi.'

'OK – meet me out at the airport.'

'San Jose?'

'No, you muff, SFO. And it's going out international. Meet me there. Just a minute! Have you got a camera?'

'Yeah – inst, long-range. But Boonie's got it.'

'Great. Bump into him at the airport and tell him to get pictures of everybody this guy talks to. Then you split from Boone and let him run solo. Keep your eyes open for me, Billy, but be discreet . . . See ya there.'

Ranny Lim stuck his unmarked car in the public parking lot and walked unhurriedly into the main concourse in the central terminal of San Francisco Airport. He rode up to the departure hall on the upper level, bought himself a late newspaper and lowered himself into one of the fixed composite moulded chairs that proliferated in the barn-like area in cinema-like banks and rows. He opened his newspaper and crossed one leg over the other. Billy watched him from his vantage point near the Pan Am check-in counter and, when he looked settled and comfortable, walked across the hall and sat down in the same row but a couple of seats further down. There were a lot of people about. Two Chinese men, one wearing a jacket and tie, dark brown pants and polished leather shoes, the other a maroon-and-white anorak, track-suit bottoms and sneakers, melted into the scenery. They weren't the only two Chinese there.

'No sign of Boonie or his mark,' said Billy without moving his head towards Ranny Lim. 'What the hell are we doing here?'

Lim continued reading. He didn't look up from his newspaper. 'Just sit there quietly and keep your eyes open – and try not to talk too much.'

'He could have been going for the ferry to Marin.'

'They'll be here. Trust me, Billy.'

'I might've done if you hadn't said that.'

'The suitcase is not going to be such a dumb bastard as to come straight here. He'll take Boone for a sightseeing tour of the city before he heads out this way. He'll change taxis a couple of times too.' Ranny looked up and turned his head in Billy's direction. 'What's this bagman look like?'

'Caucasian,' intoned Billy, as if he were entering the

31

details on a station charge sheet, 'age, about thirty-five, five seven to five eight, light brown hair, well dressed, good jacket, grey pants, tie, proper shoes . . .'

'Very interesting,' muttered Lim. 'They kill off their regular bagman, one who knows the form and the contacts, but who broke the law—'

'What law? He got himself killed, that's not breaking the law.'

'Tong law, Billy. Tong law – he decided he ought to have a percentage and got greedy. Not allowed – it's all in the rules. Once you've dripped your bleeding thumb onto the contract you've sold your soul; you have a brand-new lot of laws and obligations to hold up. Helping yourself out of the bag is very bad news all round; not doing it is law and obligation number one. This guy was lucky to just get his head blown off – quick and clean. They've got a lot of other little treats for team members who break laws and obligations. They must have been in a hurry. But you've gotta see their point, Billy. This one's a big 'un, it's international and they won't take less than one hundred per cent confidence in the loyalty of a money-runner. So for this deal they've changed from Chinese – I don't know what the reasoning for that is, but this new face'll be a heavily insured contract carrier. Keep your eyes peeled for a smartly dressed Chinese businessman. He'll be the insurance—' Lim's voice didn't change. 'There's Boone. Can you see the bagman?'

Billy sucked his teeth noisily. Then, 'Got 'im! He's making his way to the TWA check-in. We pick him up before he loses the bag?'

'No,' hissed Lim. 'We're giving them a free one here. Go and check with Boone whether he's made the bagman's shadow and whether everybody else interested in this game has been made and certified clean or otherwise. Check?'

'Check.'

'Right. When you've made it with Boone tell him to wander round with his camera like he's rubberneckin' and picture anyone the target talks to, even the check-in girl, but for Chrissake tell him don't point the frigging thing directly at him. Get on with it . . .'

Ranny Lim marked the target and his suitcase then got

on with his own brand of surveillance. He called up Dick Mayne on the internal phone system and persuaded him to go down into the cargo loading bay. They just had time for a quick cigarette when the TWA London via Shannon flight baggage started arriving. The bagman's suitcase was one of the earlier pieces to tumble out of the hole in the wall, and this was surreptitiously impounded and carried into the security office. There it took Ranny Lim no more than a couple of minutes to bypass the combination and trip the two solid key locks. He wasn't surprised when he opened the lid, carefully lifted out all the shirts, pyjamas and underwear, and found several layers of high-denomination used US currency bills. Dick Mayne was.

'Jee-sus! I don't believe it!'

'You'd better, Dick.' Lim emptied the bundles of notes onto the table and ran a quick, experienced eye over the haul. He reckoned about two and half million dollars; nothing smaller than a hundred-dollar bill, they were electronically wrapped in packets of $2,000. 'And if you reckon, give or take a buck here and there, that this could be happening three times a day in ten different places, we're saying *bon voyage* to one helluva load of money.'

'You might be, Ranny,' snorted Mayne. 'I'm not altogether sure I go along with this. There's something very wrong in allowing this stuff and its carrier to move on as though it's the most normal thing in the world to wander round with a suitcase with a couple of million bucks in it. I don't like it.'

'You don't know anything about it, Dick,' said Lim. 'You're just showing me the sights of this great airport of ours. This is my show. It's got absolutely fuck all to do with airport security unless I make it so.' Lim repacked the shirts fastidiously and removed all evidence that the case had been interfered with. He straightened up and met Mayne's eyes. They weren't happy ones.

'So, having helped you break the law,' said Mayne, 'you can tell me now when this bastard's going to be dragged in and put through the ringer. When he comes back, I suppose?'

Lim shook his head. 'No, pal – they can have this lot on me. I'm not interested in the money, I'm interested in the

33

chain. I've got a good idea where it came from now, and where it's going to end up. But that's not the business. How long's it been going on? How long's SFO been the gate to Europe? That's the question I want answered, Dick. Why hasn't someone been here before to watch all this going on? And what I don't like about it is that it took luck for us to see this. Luck! For Jesus Christ's sake, Dick! It takes luck for us to find there's a perfect, untouched pipeline going out of the US with millions and millions of dollars, probably all from the movement of narcotics, and if it hadn't been for a couple of bullets finding a gay, light-fingered Chinaman's soft spot and a couple going an inch too low in his boyfriend's face, this could have gone on for ever.'

Dick Mayne remained silent. He'd got his own thoughts on the subject, and they weren't very far removed from those of Ranny Lim. And Ranny Lim wasn't finished yet. He lit a cigarette and dragged the smoke from it deep into his lungs. 'And where the hell, Dick, when they're wanted, are the high and fucking mighty CIA? Where's the DEA – and where in Christ's name is the Narcotics Bureau?'

'Good questions, boy,' said the philosophical Mayne, 'but keep talking and maybe something'll ring a bell. You haven't said anything to incriminate yourself yet, but you're getting there.'

Ranny stared hard at his friend. 'If you've got something to say, Dick, say it—'

'Political,' said Mayne.

'Whaddya mean?'

Dick Mayne stared at the loaded suitcase resting on the floor between them. 'You reckon that's about two million bucks? Drug money. What's that – one month's take? Two months? A week? A day? Jesus, Ranny, no one can turn over that sort of cash money without having help—'

'I was coming to that. But I didn't reckon any political play came into it. I agree, somebody's helping the stuff out of the States – not them, not the drug sellers; first of all, with a turnover like that, the stuff's got to come into the country – think of the quantity, Dick, to generate this sort of deal – and, as you say, how many times a month? Look, if none of the people who're supposed to be looking at the drugs story are interested in San Francisco as a major player in the game, then that itself is goddamn fishy.'

'Access could be a form of payment for services rendered,' grunted Mayne, who didn't realise how close to the answer that remark put him. 'If there's anything in what you've told me so far this airport is being run primarily to exit dirty money, and to do that there must be people with airport movement credentials doing favours.'

'And that's what we're going to find out, Dick. Let's have this case put back into the loading system and let it run through. Don't even try hidden marks on it; these people know this business inside out. They've got to play the game the way they've been doing it. Anything different this time and they'll shy away like schoolgirls from a Paris *pissoir*. Like I told you, they're living on needle points; anything out of the ordinary and they'll disappear into the ground. Play it my way, Dick, no sudden moves, no dirty looks – OK? My boys have got the carrier in their sights and they've isolated his watcher. All we can do for the time being is stand back and observe—'

Dick Mayne stretched himself to his full six feet three inches and lashed out at the suitcase with his artificial leg. 'Fuck it, Ranny! I'm not sure about this. Something's itching. I'm not happy – and Ranny . . .' He put his arm on the Chinaman's shoulder. 'If anything breaks or if some stupid bastard pulls out a piece and starts blasting away, just don't forget that this is airport territory, that means airport jurisdiction and that means that I then take control. Don't you forget that, pal – any shooting and I take over.'

Ranny Lim gave a brief grin. 'Don't be a party-pooper, Dick. Whatever happens it'll all be down to you. It's going to grow and grow, this one, mark my words, and then they'll give you another medal when you blow the whole thing wide open – a medal or a hole in the head, depending who you're going to upset when their bolthole is closed down by the intrepid Richard Mayne!'

'Fuck you, Lim!'

'I knew you'd see it my way! Can we have an innocent stroll round the passenger departure area?'

'You sure he's going to London?'

Ranny flicked the label on the suitcase's handle with his finger. 'Booked through to London. But I wouldn't count on him not doing a soft-shoe shuffle before he gets there. They must have it worked out by now, unless they've all gone fucking complacent, and I've never heard of Tong couriers doing that and living.'

'What about the guy with the faggot?'

'Is he still living?'

Dick Mayne shook his head again. 'OK, Charlie Chan, let's go see what's happening up top. I'll go first. Better for the time being we're not seen together.'

As the two men came up separately from the loading-bay area into the departure lounge, Billy slid alongside Lim and murmured out of the side of his mouth, 'Our man made a phone call . . .'

Lim stopped him. 'Carry on walking. I'll meet you by the coffee bar . . .'

'That's where he is.'

'Go on, then, I'll see you there. Dick—' He didn't stop walking, didn't turn to the large man by his side. 'Give me a few minutes and meet me by the bookshop. Something might be happening . . .' Without waiting for an acknowledgement he sidestepped a woman with a trolley case and another with a prettily dressed little girl and glided towards the coffee lounge. He took one of the stools at the bar and, with his back to the room, leant his elbows on the counter. On the next stool, Billy, with a cup of coffee in one hand and a cigarette in the other, leaned his back against the counter and tried to look interested in a couple of chattering women sitting at one of the tables behind Lim's shoulder.

'He made a phone call. Boonie tried to get in close to see or hear who he was ringing but made a hash of it. It had to be an internal call.' Billy's lips hadn't moved.

'How d'ya make that out?' asked Lim.

'Because it only took a couple of minutes before he was joined by this young guy in a smart grey suit. Couldn't be coincidence. You don't come to SFO on your own, make a phone call, and within minutes meet a sharp-looking buddy. All arranged, Ranny, and just to prove it the two of 'em are sitting behind your right shoulder gassing away like a couple of old chums.'

'Who's doing most of the talking?'

'Does it matter?'

'Just answer the goddamn question, Billy.'

'Smartass seems to be in charge. Our bag-carrier is doing the listening and nodding his head. His eyes are all over the place. The suit appears to be quite comfortable.'

'Tell me when I can look.'

'Not yet! The bagman's wound up to a needle point – one of his eyes is admiring your jacket ... OK, Ranny, still not yet, but when I give the word make it casual – I'm twelve o'clock, go seven as far as the window; two men facing outward, cups of coffee, one in a dark grey suit smoking a cigarette ... still not yet—'

Lim reached sideways for the sugar dispenser and tipped it up a couple of times over his cup of coffee. 'Got 'em,' he murmured to Billy. 'Can you see a toilet sign in their direction?'

'Forget the can, Ranny! Have a look now – quick!'

Ranny turned his head casually and without looking directly at the table imprinted the faces of the two men on his memory. He didn't dwell. A couple of seconds was enough. He turned back to his coffee, drank it with a gulp, wiped his lips with a paper napkin, then stood up. He left a bill on the counter and, without another glance in the direction of the two men, walked out of the coffee lounge. The man in the suit studied his back for a second as he walked away, but it was a reflex action, it meant nothing.

Lim joined up again with Dick Mayne in the departure lounge bookshop and followed him through the back doors and tunnel to the main international departure hall.

With Ranny Lim in tow, Mayne mingled with the airport administration staff, customs, security and all the odds and sods who somehow make themselves look busy just before the departure of an international flight. It was all right for Mayne, he carried weight and authority. Nobody took any notice – he was part of the system and anybody with him was his problem, not theirs.

37

'You remember all this mention of men in dark suits?' Lim murmured to Mayne.

'And I told you you were fishing in deep and dangerous waters,' responded Mayne in the same voice, 'and I tell you again . . .'

Lim continued studying the controlled disorganisation around the departure gates. He didn't glance in Mayne's direction. 'Our bagman's picked up a friend, one in a dark suit, somebody who has business in the airport.'

'I won't ask you how you came to that conclusion, Ranny.' Mayne glanced around instinctively. 'Where are they now?'

'They were having coffee in the departure lounge. The man in the suit had a lot to say; the other one did the listening. London leaves in fifteen minutes according to the screen up there; I'd like to see the bagman through and whether anybody helps him. Personally I think it could be rewarding – are we all right here for anyone boarding?'

'If he's going to be helped he won't come through here,' growled Mayne. 'Come with me.' He led Lim through a short narrow passage to a door marked 'No unauthorised entry'. 'Anybody doing an oil job'll bring him through here. You see that door?' He jerked his head at the opposite end of the room. 'That's a direct passage to the boarding ramp. It bypasses all the hassle out there. The crew usually come this way. Here.' He pulled out a chair by a plain wooden table. 'Sit down. I'll interview you.'

He sat on the other side of the table, brought a packet of cigarettes from a pocket and placed it between them. He helped himself to one and lit it. He didn't offer one to Lim, which was just the way things should be. He leaned forward and rested his elbows on the table and allowed the first intake of smoke to trickle slowly down his nostrils. It looked like a serious interrogation was about to take place, but his eyes were in all directions.

He concentrated for some time on the one-way window that looked out on the security barriers where, quite clearly, the loading passengers could be seen displaying their passports and opening briefcases for anybody in a uniform's inspection.

'London's boarding now,' he said between his teeth, and

38

expelled another trickle of smoke. 'Watch it!' He raised his voice to its normal pitch and said, 'You must have been aware that your visa expired five days ago. I think you were deliberately—' He looked up briefly, but without recognition or acknowledgement as the man in the grey suit and his friend the money-runner, his briefcase gripped firmly in his right hand, walked past.

The runner's eyes locked onto Lim's as the two men stopped at the exit while the man in the suit pretended to examine the other man's documents.

Lim had time to study their profiles and backs, before the grey suit glanced suspiciously down the room but relaxed when Lim, in high-pitched, Chinese-inflected English, explained why his visa was out of date. But his performance was wasted. Grey-suit had picked his moment and ushered his man through the door and onto the aircraft. Seconds later, having disposed of the money-runner, he re-entered the interview room, and this time his scrutiny covered Lim from top to toe.

Whatever he was, he was a professional at it. Lim felt himself being logged in the man's face memory-bank. No question of Chinese all looking alike, not to this one; he'd know him for ever after this.

After the door closed behind him, Lim said, barely above a whisper, 'You know him?'

Dick Mayne continued to stare at the closed door over Ranny's shoulder. His face wore a perplexed, perhaps worried, look. 'You sure the little guy with the attaché case who went through with him was your target, Ranny?'

'Is that a serious question, Dick?'

'Sorry! I just don't get this – it's all wrong. There's gotta be an explanation.'

'Go on, then, ask me.'

'OK, the boy who just walked past us' – he was still staring at the door behind Ranny Lim's head in disbelief – 'is CIA—'

'What sort?' queried Lim before Mayne could finish.

'Whaddya mean, what sort? There's only one fucking sort of CIA – smart, tough, ruthless, political, too bloody clever by half, and best left well alone. What were you expecting?'

Lim locked onto Mayne's eyes. 'What you just said! I wondered whether you knew if he's drugs or illicit export of US treasury bills. They all specialise in something or other.'

'I wouldn't know. But now that *you* do, what're you going to do about it?'

'Not involve you to start with, Dick. I'm hoping my boy out there got a few instants of him and then I'll have to think about where I'm going after I've had them seen and identified.'

'You putting this in an official report?'

Ranny laughed. Not a real laugh, more a snort of scepticism. 'I've nothing to report, Dick – yet. I'll wait until I've had a night tossing and turning in bed thinking about it. I might wire Scotland Yard a description of the runner and let them pick him up – that won't bounce back at us and keeps our little ball in place. I'll have to think seriously about that one because we can't have repercussions. The way I'm thinking at the moment is that I'd like to see another run go through but this time with an official team of big heads from Langley, or wherever, to watch how their people are guarding our exits and working against the government.'

But Dick Mayne wasn't happy about it. 'Like I said, Ranny, go at it like you're tiptoeing through a bamboo minefield.'

Chapter 2

'You're attracting attention . . .'

The man in the grey suit heard the muffled squeak and adjusted his earplug. He lowered his head. 'Say again . . .'

'You're attracting attention, Hagen. A guy's been shooting films around you – he's got a couple of frames that'll have you in 'em. Deliberate.'

'Describe.'

'Heavily built, six, six one, Caucasian. Age – difficult to tell but looks hard and fit. Metal-grey long hair. Full beard, same colour. Blue and white windcheater, tartan open-neck shirt. Black trousers . . .'

'Alone?'

'No. Looks like a pair. Number two's Asian – Chinese, about five three. Features . . . Oh, fuck! Chinese features, red-and-white anorak, dark track-suit pants, sneakers—'

'Definite contact? Is that the lot?'

'So far, yes and yes.'

'Stay with 'em.'

'You aborting?'

'No.'

'Check and close.'

The soda jerk in the soft drinks booth adjusted his apron, straightened his stiff white paper forage cap and began the rounds of wiping the Formica tops of his tables. When he'd finished he looked around for a moment at the scene about him. His expression was one of acceptance. Life was boring.

41

The scene was never changing; people, people, people; people either going somewhere or watching people go somewhere. He turned away and went back to his booth and poured himself a large cardboard cup of fizzy orange squash. Then he lowered his head and spoke softly.

'See you. Come and get a drink.'

There was no response in his earpiece but it didn't worry him. He straightened up and served a man and his two grandchildren; the kids were obviously on their way out at the end of their holiday and Granddad looked fairly pleased with the idea. He wanted to talk about it but the soda jerk cut him off with two Cokes, a coffee milkshake and 'Thank you, sir – excuse me, sir . . .' When he turned back to the counter from the till the man in the grey suit was standing waiting.

'Coke,' he said.

'One of your watchers is in the coffee lounge,' the man in the paper hat murmured. 'The other one's over by the bookshop pretending not to be watching you. Hairy-face's joined up with another Chink. This one's wearing a jacket and tie. Looks smart, bright and senior – thirtyish. They're all SFPD.'

'How d'you know?'

'I fed their descriptions into the system. Our friend at PDHQ says they work out of Turk Street station. They're on an out-of-town watching brief, no details but something running on from a Chinese killing in a dive in Market Street a couple of weeks ago – that'll be a quarter, sir,' he said openly, before resuming his shallow whisper. 'Gimme a big note—' The man in the suit handed him a fifty and sucked at the straw sticking out of his Coke while he waited for the change. The soda jerk took his time sorting it out, all the time murmuring his low-level commentary. 'Greybeard and the Chinky scruff, lounging about over there, have made you, so it doesn't matter. The new one I've only just spotted. I reckon you could walk through the coffee place and give him an eyeball then we'll both know what we're talking about. Finish your Coke and go and have a look . . .' He raised his voice. 'Here's your change, sir, have a nice

42

evening . . .' And lowered it again. 'I'm closing down. See you in the parking lot in about fifteen—'

Mark Hagen walked through the coffee lounge and, for appearance's sake, stopped at the counter and ordered a cup of coffee. He didn't need it, he didn't want it, but he stirred in a cachet of sugar and left it untouched. He'd seen Ranny Lim again, and didn't like it. The man with him was of no concern; his partner with the paper hat had him marked along with the other Chinese. This one was different. This one had access to the security system of the airport and that was a threat. He was playing footsie with the one-legged deputy airport security boss, and that wasn't good news either. He didn't look round as he paid for his coffee and walked through the far exit and out into the main hall.

Ranny Lim shovelled more sugar into his coffee, then poured in two little tubs of thick milk.

He and David Boone were sitting at one of the bench tables in the main coffee lounge. He sat facing the door.

'Don't look at the counter, Dave,' he murmured as he stirred his coffee with a miniature plastic paddle. He looked Dave Boone in the eye; the warning was there. It was enough.

Boone picked up his own coffee and drank from it.

'OK,' said Lim, 'we've just had an inspection from the Central Intelligence Agency. Looks like he's on to me. Dickie Mayne reckons there's a two- or three-man team floating around on these delivery nights so, somewhere in the vicinity, there's another pair lurking in the background. I'm gonna split 'em up . . .'

'Bully for you, pal!' David Boone was an easy-going, laconical, hard man. He should have been a lieutenant like his friend Ranny Lim, or at least a sergeant, but he was content with his first grade. That was as far as he wanted to go – no responsibility except to himself, that was the way he'd been brought up; that was the way he'd lived. But he was tough, and he knew his way around. 'How're you goin' to do that?'

'I think the smartass who's just bowled through is the boss. I wanna talk to him, but not with his friends around.

I'm reckoning he's squatting outside with his car warmed up waiting for me to move. Let him stew for a bit, then I'll go off with Billy and lead him back to Turk Street. Then I'll arrest him for loitering . . .'

'I thought you said he was CIA?'

'He is. But I'm still going to arrest him for loitering. I want to find out what he's all about.'

'What's he been doing?'

'I'll tell you when he's told me. The only thing I know about him so far is that he's just helped a few million greenbacks exit the country. I'll save that one for him when he's finished lying.'

'What about me?'

'He's just stuck you in his memory bank. He's going off now to tell his back-up all about you. When I drive off with Billy I reckon our smart suit over there's going to detail a little watch on you. You can spot a watcher half a mile away, Davey. When you've spotted this one you can break his arms and bring him home to the party.'

'Why split 'em?'

'They're the best at the job. One CIA man's big trouble; two of 'em in tandem makes for one helluva situation. Split 'em, Dave. Billy and I can handle the one, and I know you can do the other.'

'You said three.'

Ranny Lim pulled a face. 'Maybe I'm wrong. I hope so. Keep your eyes open. Happy now?'

'What's happy got to do with it? It's what I get paid for. Happiness plays fuck-all part in it.'

'OK, our man's left – gone back to the parking lot, is my guess. I'm going to the washroom and then I'll pick up Billy and lead the spook to the station. Let's hope he's interested in seeing how the other ninety-nine per cent live. When we've got our guy home Billy can bring the car back here and pick you and yours up. You can feed him coffee until Billy arrives. OK?'

'Sure.'

Hagen collected his topcoat from the cloakroom, shrugged into it and waited in the shadow of the airport entrance until the dipped headlights flashed twice on the far side of the lot. He took the roundabout – the long way – to the car and made sure he had no little Chinamen or bearded photographers dogging his footsteps. He slid into the passenger seat of the car, pulled the collar up round his neck, hunched his shoulders and stuck both hands in the coat's deep pockets. 'Move it, Jack,' he grunted to the driver. The engine purred into life and the car slowly edged out of the parking slot.

They drove slowly once round the perimeter of the parking lot and found a new place close to, and overlooking, the airport entrance hall. The engine was switched off again and the two men sat and waited. Nothing more was said until they were joined by the soda jerk, minus uniform.

'Leo,' Hagen murmured into the darkness of the car. 'That little Chinaman's bought himself a whole load of trouble.' He didn't care whether Leo Penfold heard or not. He was speaking his mind. Trying to make the decision.

'Which one?'

'The smart one. I made him earlier on. He was fratting with the one-legged hero in the immigration office. If he's come into the game on his own initiative he'll have to be spoken to. Could be a colour job; could be Red.'

'Have we got clearance for Red, Mark?' said the driver. Taciturn (unusually for someone of French background), Jack Knecht opened his mouth for the first time. He was Ranny Lim's mistake he was the third man of the CIA team, menacing and dangerous.

But it seemed to be the question Hagen wanted. He grunted non-committally, then said brusquely, 'If they come out before I get back, you go with them, Jack. Leo'll point 'em out to you. And, Jack—' He turned sideways in his seat. 'Until you're told different I want 'em safe and tucked away – not dead and buried.'

Knecht didn't bother to answer. He switched the engine on and, without revving the motor, gave the inside a burst of warm air. Hagen studied his granite-cut profile for a few seconds then took his hands out of his pockets and opened the car door.

'I'll join you by phone.'

'You going to ring home?' asked Penfold.

'No choice. Hang around.'

The car door closed quietly behind him and he melted into the dark shadows caused by the shortfall of the security lighting. The two men in the car neither saw nor heard Hagen make his way back into the main building and head towards the bank of phone recesses. It was a question of knowing how to move. Some did, some didn't. Mark Hagen did everything including moving as though his life depended on it. He was as professional as they came; one of the newer breed of US intelligence operatives who would have done the job without pay – and still enjoyed it.

There was nothing about Hagen that betrayed his profession. Half an inch short of six feet in his highly polished brogues, thin-waisted but stocky and muscular, he tipped the scales at a solid 180 pounds. With good, regular features, neither pretty nor ugly, Mark Hagen had an honest, open face – it helped in the business to have an honest, open face – steady hazel eyes and a thick but short-cut mop of mousey-coloured hair. He never combed it. First thing in the morning he dowsed it with water, ran a couple of stiff brushes across it, and that did it for the rest of the day. He was in good shape. Everything was firm and hard, and health and fitness bubbled out of him, as it should for an active sporting man in his early thirties. But he'd have to watch the calories when he reached fifty otherwise he'd find stocky and muscular turning into fat and flabby – if he ever reached fifty. He had no hang-ups and no problem with women. He took them, used them and discarded them. They weren't important to him. He treated men in the same manner – he had no friends. He trusted no one. But, for all this, Hagen was one of those men who caused, among those who knew about such things, a cool, hard appraisal, a tightening of the scrotum and an unvoiced verdict – a circuit player, a Professional.

He was currently having a torrid affair. All Mark Hagen's affairs were torrid – and usually short-lived. But this one was going well. Not particularly beautiful, she was shy, had long slim legs, was a bit light around the breast but had a superb, healthy figure with gentle refined features. Mark

46

Hagen was always surprised by shy women with gentle refined features, particular the married sort. This one, who looked as though she'd be just as much at home sipping martinis in the Navy Officers Club while her husband played with his tin tub between here and Pearl, was no exception. Passion wasn't the word for it. And she looked like a virgin in the front row of the church choir with butter unable to melt between those soft, sensitive lips. The weather in this little corner of California was very hot and very humid and the fluttering evening breeze that drifted casually across the cloudless summer sky carried with it a heady, aromatic mixture that played havoc with the best of intentions. Mark Hagen put all these female extramarital sexual desires down to this evening breeze. But it wasn't for Hagen to complain. It wasn't going to last. In fact it wasn't going to last as long as even he expected.

Hagen had discovered his vocation in Special Operations in Vietnam. He had relished the fear and the sweat of the unknown working behind the enemy. He discovered very early, in his creepy-crawly world, that killing one's fellow creature was not the gut-wrenching, mind-blowing event it was made out to be. It came very naturally to Mark Hagen, and it didn't take long for the Operation Phoenix organisers to fall in love with him. Phoenix was right up his street; the identification and neutralising of communists in Saigon's area of administration. The CIA got its knuckles rapped when somebody lost his nerve and mentioned a head count of around 25,000 while he was being sick in a Saigon dope shop. It got home and the CIA washed its hands of Phoenix very quickly, but not before marking some of the more subtle and discreet operators for future employment. Mark Hagen was one of those, and so was Jack Knecht – and there were more like them. When the call came Hagen slipped out of the army and settled into his new job like a duck settling onto a ripple-less pond.

703 482 1100. He dialled the number and waited. It was the most efficient exchange in the country. 'CIA—' said the crisp voice. 'Two nine zero,' responded Hagen. It wasn't an extension, not a room, not a department. The operator knew what it was and asked nothing further. He touched the

47

disconnect button at the same time as he passed Hagen to his destination. Two nine zero was the code for the Operation Contractor mission that had been set up in the late 1950s. Two nine zero meant a direct line to the senior staff officer heading the project, and he was answerable only to the Director of Central Intelligence, CIA.

Even at the end of 1974, Contractor was still the best-kept secret of the CIA. Even the code-name CONTRACTOR was mentioned only in whispers; it had been reduced to a digital reference – 290. Hagen, like the other hand-picked field officers on the Contractor project, knew nothing of its scope, or its intentions. He knew that his mandate in maintaining the security of his part of the operation allowed him almost unlimited power. That was enough for Hagen. He didn't want to know any more. He didn't even want to know why he was shuffling couriers, usually Chinese but occasionally and exceptionally Caucasian, through the exit formalities at different airports throughout the US. It didn't concern him. That they were protected by CIA identification was enough for Hagen. But Condition Red was something else. Now, by his reckoning, but not of his doing, that security was jeopardised. It meant Operation Contractor was compromised. It hadn't happened since its inception.

Hagen kept it brief, terse and to the point. He didn't offer his assessment or his suggestions. He told it the way he saw it.

The silence coming down the phone was deafening. Hagen kept the earpiece glued to the side of his head; he daren't look away. Eventually the silence got to him and after a few seconds he thought he could hear the sophisticated humming of the tape machine. And there was sure to be one of those. One? Probably he'd switched on the whole friggin' building's listening system.

And then the silence was broken.

'Are you near your car?'

'Two minutes away.'

'Your car phone's logged?'

'Yes, sir.'

'I'll come back to you on it.'

Jesus Christ! Hagen dropped the phone on its hook and

walked briskly back to the car. Even the fucker who sits warming up the big man's toilet seat for him has to ask. And who does the big man ask? The President? Like fuck he does. He bangs his head on the table for ten seconds and then says, 'Tell Hagen and the other insignificant bastards working with him to kill the fuckin' Chinks who've dared to watch us at work, and do the same to the bearded fucker who's hooked on taking pictures . . .'

When the phone rang he was sitting forward in the passenger seat of the Oldsmobile waiting for it. He had a good idea what the message would be. It would be short.

It was.

'Hagen?'

'Yeah?'

'Condition Red, Action Purple – all principals.'

No goodbye, or goodnight, sleep well, no 'thanks for a good job well done'. Nothing like that. Just a dead car phone and no twinges of conscience. Looks like four principals walked out of their league and are heading for the blender. Hagen's brain slowed down to its cold, calculating normal while he considered the accidental deaths of Lieutenant Ranny Lim, Detective (first grade) David Boone and Detective Billy Yong. And when that was done they'd have to have a close look at Mr Richard Mayne, deputy security officer, San Francisco Airport, and holder of the Congressional Medal of Honor, to see how far he'd dug into the mess.

'It's Red,' he said to the man behind the wheel.

'Oh, shit!' said Leo Penfold from the back of the car.

Chapter 3

Leo Penfold leaned forward and said, 'Here come the two Chinks, Mark.'

'Where's the beard? Where's the fucking beard?' No panic. Hagen's voice was cold and clear; he could have been looking for the fried onions in his hot dog. He watched Lim and Billy Yong make for the dark blue Chevy Biscayne and then made up his mind. 'Damn the goddamn beard! Why couldn't he stay with the other two? Un-fuckin'-reliable, these small-town cops – why don't they stay on the streets looking after the fucking traffic! Jack,' he snapped to Knecht. 'Get out! Take your car and follow those two. Find out where they hole up and we'll sort 'em later. Play it loose, Jack!'

Knecht didn't need a second bidding. For him the operative word was 'Get out' all rolled into one. Before Hagen had finished talking he was out of the car and trotting briskly into the night. This wasn't what Hagen wanted. He'd been split three ways – intentional or accidental? He didn't dwell on it; it had happened. 'Leo, go and find the beard. He doesn't know you. I'll co-ordinate. Bring him back here. If he makes an issue out of it you know what to do. No fuss. Don't frighten the natives with bad language or noise. When you've finished with him find out where the hero hangs his pants. I'll want to talk, privately, with him. Don't frighten him . . .'

'Ha, ha, ha—' Leo Penfold gave a nervous imitation

50

laugh. Cold-blooded death talk was an unwanted thriller; not for him a career start in the bloodletting around the south of Saigon. Well brought up, good family, good school, legal university background, he thought the CIA was the perfect springboard for a lifelong career in crime prevention. It sounded patriotic too. But he hadn't got Hagen's indifference, or was it addiction, to the gritted teeth, the twitching limbs and the staring, accusing eyes of the dying man. But this wasn't the time or place. Hagen made it sound all so simple and matter-of-fact. 'Go and find the beard', and then trace the home of a one-legged war hero. It was Red and Purple – kill and dispose. Killing a beard sounded very secondary – very down-market.

'Any problems, you join me.' Hagen glanced quickly at the dashboard clock. 'By phone after eleven – OK?'

'See ya.' Leo Penfold slipped out of the Oldsmobile and into the shadows where he waited and watched Knecht draw out and filter into line behind the two Chinese in the unmarked police car. He waited another few seconds until the glowing rear lights of Knecht's car had disappeared into the stream of traffic heading north on the Bayshore Freeway, then tripped up the steps and back into the airport main hall.

Ranny Lim drove carefully out of the airport so that his follower had no trouble keeping up and then, when he joined the 101 freeway, hit the gas, and from the scattering of traffic left behind him identified Knecht's car as it joined him in the outside lane. Within minutes he hit the first of the tailbacks and stuck, without attempting any clever manoeuvres, with the mass. It soon cleared and they were on their way again. Knecht, relaxed and sure of himself, stayed with them until the traffic thinned out and Lim, fearing this would discourage his follower, turned off the freeway at the South Vann Ess flyover and took him for a short trip down Howard Street: a left at 10th Street, a quick glance to make sure he hadn't lost him, then a right into Market Street, circumnavigate the Civic Auditorium, then Grove Street and Fulton Street.

As he turned the car into Steiner Street, Lim slowed,

flicked his indicator, ignored one vacant gap and pulled into another several cars ahead. He watched impassively through the rear mirror as Knecht pulled into the first gap and, keeping the engine running, turned to Billy Yong and said, 'I think it's time to arrest our friend from DC, Billy.'

Billy jerked himself awake. 'Arrest him? For what?'

'For parking in a restricted area without a permit.'

'He's all right this time of the night.' Billy gazed about him. 'And this is not a restricted area.'

'It is if I say it is. Show him your badge and pick him up. We'll take him the rest of the way in ours. Oh, Billy—' He wound the car window down and placed the unlighted flasher on the hood. 'Be polite to him – he's one of our law enforcement brothers!'

But Billy had gone. Lim watched him approach the car and hold up an open left hand to show friendliness while his badge folder flapped open in the other to show he meant business. Knecht wound the window down and offered Billy a half-smile and a look of surprise.

'I'm a police officer—' said Billy.

'So I see,' responded Knecht. 'What have I done?'

'Would you mind getting out of the car, please, sir?'

'I'm working. D'you want to see some identification?'

'No, I want you to get out of the car.'

'OK. Er – I'm CIA,' said Knecht.

'Nobody's perfect,' replied Billy. 'Lock your car up and come with me. My chief wants to talk to you – he's along there.' Billy jerked his head at Ranny Lim's car. 'Wants to know why you've been following us from the airport. After you, sir.'

Knecht lowered his head and smiled at Ranny Lim through the open window of the car. 'Hi! Front or back?'

'Get in here,' said Lim, without returning the smile. 'In the back, Billy.' He hadn't taken his eyes off Knecht's face. 'D'you want to give me a name?'

'Sure.' Knecht looked over his shoulder at Billy, lounging on the back seat, his eyes half closed, and then shifted his gaze back to Ranny Lim. He touched his chest with his open hand and gave a little cough. 'D'you mind if I smoke?'

'Go ahead. What's your name?'

Knecht pulled his raincoat out of the way and put his hand in his pocket. 'Fred—' he replied, struggling to get his cigarettes out. But it wasn't cigarettes. Once he'd got his coat sorted out the Browning slid effortlessly out of the leather thong on his belt. Cocked, safety off, its four-inch barrel extended by a six-inch suppressor – Ranny Lim didn't even have time to look surprised.

The heavy thud of the suppressed discharge and the slam of the first 180gm SXT bullet into the side of Lim's head brought Billy's eyes open with a flash; wide awake, but he was much too late. Another thud, another liquid impact, and Billy rolled onto his side on the back seat of the car. Knecht followed Billy's head with the Browning and when it stopped moving squeezed again. The second bullet exploded inside Billy's skull and shattered it like an egg. But it was unnecessary. Billy had been dead from the instant the first hollow-nose bullet had blown the inside of his head apart. But Knecht was a pro. Condition Red, Action Purple, Hagen had said. So that was OK. That Hagen had said follow and locate was something else. Not his fault. It was the Chink's fault for stopping suddenly. Red and Purple. It all came down to the same thing in the end. Knecht had no problem with its reasoning. He swung back to the front, placed the suppressor muzzle two inches under the dead lieutenant's chin and squeezed the trigger again. Ranny Lim's head almost hit the roof of the car then bounced with a heavy thump onto the steering wheel.

Knecht gave the inside of the car a quick professional look then eased himself out through the door, gently pulling Lim's still-shivering body so that it lay stretched out across the front seat. He locked the doors, stared around him for a few seconds, then walked round to the driver's side. He lifted the flasher off the roof, tossed it inside the car and locked the driver's door.

The Browning dragged his raincoat pocket down as he walked, knees bent, head lowered, back to his own car. Not clever, but effective. Anybody watching would be hard pushed to put an accurate description to the figure bouncing along the sidewalk. He started the car, pulled away and drove to the end of Steiner Street and into Turk Street, where he pulled into another space. Leaving the engine running, he walked back to the corner and peered round at the police car. There was no one there; nobody inspecting the suspicious goings-on. Nobody had been watching from the shadows. But it didn't matter. There'd be hell to pay when Turk Street station found a couple of their Chinks chilled and stiff a few hundred yards from home.

On his way back to his car he dropped Ranny Lim's keys down a street drain. As he drove downtown, past the station, he lit a cigarette. His hand was as steady as an iron bar, and the only thought on his mind was whether Mark Hagen had had as interesting a night as he'd had. But you never knew. He drove around for about ten minutes then flicked the cigarette out of the side window and pulled into an all-night gas station slumbering just off the main road. He shook his head as he approached the office and held his hand up with the little finger and thumb extended. The Hispanic face that peered out of the guarded window studied him through narrowed eyes. He looked respectable. A finger went up, a buzzer sounded and the heavy door clicked on its lock.

'Thanks. Use your phone?'

'Sure.'

'Might as well fill 'er up while I'm waiting.' He laid the keys on the counter in front of the heavy metal grille and walked across the shop floor to the phone. He dialled and lowered his voice.

'Mark – a small problem . . .'

'Ain't there always?'

'The Chinks pulled a fast one and made me. I had to break the news to them.'

The pause was significant.

'You still there, Mark?'

'Yeah. Shit!'

'Gimme a constructive, Mark.'

'Shit again! Are they out in the open?'

'I had no choice. I've left them where they are. The gusher'll blow the minute someone walks along that sidewalk. Whaddya reckon?'

'Close the shop before it blows. I'll do that. You come out here and collect Junior and his package and meet me at point four on the 101.' Hagen glanced down at his watch. 'It's a quarter after ten; Leo'll call in at eleven, my call sign, you take him . . .' He was at his best. An emergency, a cock-up, the house was falling down, but not for Mark Hagen. The instructions and orders came crisp and fast. 'I'll clear up at Richmond and meet you and Leo at, say . . .' He glanced down again – give it anything up to an hour for the shit to hit the fan and another hour for them to stop running around chasing their arses. Two hours free for running. ' . . . half past midnight – point four . . .'

'You already said that.'

'Go!'

Knecht hung up the phone, paid the attendant and drove out of the forecourt. He pulled up again outside a lighted phone booth and left the engine running while he made his call. This time he dialled the Turk Street police station.

'Can you put a call out for Sergeant Long and have him ring me back – it's urgent. My number's—'

'No need,' responded the voice. 'He's sitting right here. I'll pass you across.'

'Long,' said a cautious voice.

'Henry, it's your father.'

'You got a problem?'

'Can I talk?'

'Sure.'

'You used to have a Lieutenant Lim and a sidekick named Billy something or other—'

'Used to?'

'Yeah, used to. There were three of them running a watch on the airport this evening. It was drop-out time. They saw more than they were entitled to. I've left my sweetheart taking care of the third but I'm not over-confident. If anything goes wrong you'll hear about it. Any mention of Lim or the airport in the next half-hour or so won't make my day. You getting my drift?'

'Yeah. Make a suggestion?'

'Go on.'

'Got a phone in your car?'

'Not for general use.'

'What's the number?'

55

Knecht gave it.

'Go to the airport and if anything comes through I'll contact you. If it doesn't you can collect your friend and take him home yourself. How d'you see that?'

'Better than nothing. I'll pass on my thanks for your help.'

'Don't bother!'

David Boone was still sitting at the same table, still drinking indifferent coffee, when, half an hour later, Penfold finally ran him down. He found himself a bench seat where he could watch the bearded man's movements and sat down with a bunch of Hawaii golfers with the fidgets.

It suited Leo Penfold's purpose as they milled about, sat down, stood up, wandered to and fro and set up a continuous barrage of drink-inspired golf chatter. He'd already worked out how he was going to attend to the beard. It was going to be neat and uncomplicated. All he needed was a little co-operation from the victim.

But Boone had spotted him. Leo Penfold was not a quiet sitter and watcher; he rather liked to think of himself as a go-getter, a man of action. It showed to a man who was everything Penfold wasn't. Boone sat where he was, drinking more and more coffee until he reckoned he'd got his watcher balanced on a fairly fine edge. Then he made his move.

He got up slowly and walked towards Penfold. No eye contact – he kept his gaze on the direction he was going and then moved across the hall to the right and along the corridor that led to the departure lounge and the duty-free shopping area. There were a fair number of late shoppers about but he made no sudden moves that might put his follower off.

If you weren't flying out and you weren't going to pick up duty-frees the corridor became a no-go zone.

Boone stopped, then turned. Penfold had nowhere to go and, looking hastily behind him at the empty corridor and pretending to search for his landing card and entry to the duty-free area, he stopped and riffled through his pockets. Another quick glance behind, and Boone was still walking innocently towards him. Penfold's hand was resting lightly on the butt of the automatic under his raincoat. Without sliding it from its leather pouch he eased back the hammer from its half-cock and began walking indecisively towards the man approaching him. *Wait until he goes past, snap weapon out of holster, turn quickly, gun up; if he gets cute it's two in the back of the head, two in the small of the back, two under the left shoulder blade – suppressor off, weapon back in its hidey-hole and continue walking back into the reception lounge, out of the airport and into the waiting car for central San Francisco.* A textbook legal take-out. That's how it should have been.

But it wasn't quite like that.

Boone, without altering pace, looking dead ahead, making no eye contact, came level with Penfold and without breaking step pivoted on his left foot, grabbed Penfold's wrist and yanked it up his back. Although taken by surprise, Penfold kept his wits about him and rolled into the pressure, allowing his arm to be pulled and going with it as he went down on one knee. His right hand, still grasping the cocked Beretta, remained jammed under his raincoat but, kicking him sharply in the back of the other knee and pulling hard upwards on the arm, Boone forced him flat on the floor. Then a hard metal object was jammed behind his right ear and a soft, untroubled voice said, 'Bring your other hand out from wherever it is and push it out ahead of you.'

'What the—?'

'Shut up. Do as I say.' The same unaffected tone, no sound of exertion. 'Bring it round your back and join it up with the other one.'

Penfold did as he was told and felt the warm metal of the handcuffs as they were tightened round his wrists. Unceremoniously, he was rolled over onto his back and the bearded man ran his hand down his right side and lifted from its leather holster the 9mm 92F Beretta Penfold should have had in his hand when he approached the man along the corridor.

But it wasn't as serious as it could have been.

Penfold kept his eyes on Boone as he calmly clipped his badge to the front of his windcheater and put away his short-barrel revolver. Boone seemed to have all the time in the world. In spite of the air-conditioning, Penfold began to sweat slightly. He reckoned at that moment he'd missed something. The man was too confident. He wasn't surprised; he looked as though he was expecting everything that was happening. So he's got back-up – where the goddamn hell is it? How the fuck did I miss it?

He locked eyes with David Boone, resting comfortably and relaxed with his back against the wall, and reorganised his voice so that there was a semblance of calm reason in it. 'You'd better have a good reason for this, pal.'

Boone leaned forward and, with his finger under the shiny badge on his windcheater, flipped it up and down over Penfold's nose.

'Is that reason enough – *pal*?' He placed both hands under Penfold's armpits and heaved him to his feet. 'You've been watching me for half an hour and then you follow me down here. You didn't lose your way, you came deliberately. You've got something on your mind – spill it.'

'Look, Officer – we can sort this out. You've made a mistake and I'm prepared to let it pass. I'm official. I'm on duty, and at the moment you are obstructing a national security matter . . .'

'Save it, brother! Don't waste your time on me. I'm just a small-town hick cop, the simple member of the team. That's why they gave me the simple job.' He slipped his arm out of Penfold's as they neared the bank of telephone canopies and squeezed him in between two empty ones. 'Don't move.' He picked up a phone and dialled, staring into Penfold's face as he did so.

'SFPD,' said a singsong voice.

'Gimme Lieutenant Lim,' he growled.

'Who wants him?'

'Detective Boone.'

'He had to go out. What d'ya want, Boone?'

'Billy Yong's supposed to be meeting me out at the airport with a car. I've got a prisoner. Lim knows all about it.'

'OK. Lim told me to field any queries for him. I'll get Billy out to you. Where d'ya want to be picked up?'

'Main entrance.'

'I'll tell him.'

Knecht's phone buzzed just as he joined the freeway at 9th Street. He veered into the slow lane, picked the handset up and held it to his ear as he cruised southwards. 'Knecht,' he said.

'You were right to be worried.'

'Tell me about it.'

'Your sweetheart has been arrested at the airport by a detective named Boone. He's waiting for a car at the main entrance to bring him into town. Is that what you wanted to know?'

'Not quite,' said Knecht laconically. 'But thanks.' He dropped the phone back into its bed and stopped the car. He eased the Browning out of his belt and checked the magazine. Four rounds light. He replaced them from the candy tin in the glove box and eased one into the breech. He left the gun on the passenger seat, cocked, safety off, with that day's *San Francisco Chronicle* resting lightly over it. He pulled into the fast lane, hit the gas pedal and cut across the freeway into the airport approach lane.

He made it look very normal. Nothing tricky, just a gentle cruise past the picking-up area. There they were. The silly bastard Penfold standing there with his hands in front of him covered by his raincoat, looking like a dirty old flasher caught on the job. Stupid asshole! Knecht could almost see the handcuffs. And the big, ugly-looking guy with the beard who'd been in the coffee lounge with the Chink detective. Penfold's target! Send a fucking boy on a man's job and this is what you get. Right. Goodbye, beard, and the board'll be clean again. Now, sonny, watch how it's done!

He made a full circuit and came round once again. He wound the window down, picked up the cocked automatic and laid it in his lap, then cruised along the collection slip road like an innocent picker-upper of a long-lost cousin who'd been told to wait outside the airport on the sidewalk. He slowed to a crawl and drew up alongside the two men. Penfold played the game and ignored him. 'Good boy, Penny!' Knecht picked up the Browning, poked his head out of the open window and shouted, 'Penfold! Get down!'

59

He squeezed the trigger three times as the bearded man swung round.

'Holy fuckin' shit!' Knecht slammed his foot hard on the accelerator. The noise of squealing tyres, the heavy smell of burning rubber and the repeated crack of a pistol followed him as he controlled the sliding, skidding car out of the entrance area. The pistol was still in his lap where he'd dropped it, and with a quick flip of his hand it was back in its original position and covered once again by the newspaper. Knecht brought the car under control and slowed down to a normal but careful speed. Instead of heading for the city centre, he took the underpass and came out on the south turn-off and, joining a small batch of cars going in the same direction, tucked himself in and began to curse himself softly and fluently.

It didn't last too long.

'Oh, Jesus! Oh, Jesus! Oh, Jesus! How the fuck did that happen?' He'd seen Penfold's head swing round. A startled look in his bulging eyes and his mouth wide open as if trying to tell him something. Then he'd seen him fall. He hadn't hung around to see what had happened or whether Penfold got up again. It was the bearded cop who should have been face down on the sidewalk.

But Boone had been there before. He knew all the unmarked police cars from Turk Street, and this wasn't one of them. He was already on the balls of his feet and highly watchful when the slow-moving dark-coloured Oldsmobile Cutlass inched its way alongside where he and Penfold were standing. Penfold gave him the warning. The quick intake of breath and the deliberate turning of his head in the opposite direction sent his hand flashing to the inside of his windcheater. The smoked windscreen, the open front window in the cold night air, the driver's raincoated arm resting on the window ledge – and then the shout and the slim, black tube snuggling in the crook of the arm.

Boone was ready for it.

He jabbed Penfold in the side and shoved him forward. At the same time, staring into the extended barrel of the weapon pointing at him, he threw himself backwards behind

Penfold's off-balance stumble and crashed onto his side, his hand trapped under his body.

He heard three dull thuds, a hiss as one bullet sliced between the arm and waist of his baggy windcheater, and two heavy, meaty thwacks as two bullets thumped into the top half of Penfold's swaying body.

Even as the car accelerated away from the sidewalk and zigzagged out of sight, Boone was on his knees, the stubby .38 with both hands wrapped round it kicking as he emptied the cylinder at the speeding Oldsmobile. Then, quickly reloading, he pointed the .38 at where the Oldsmobile had disappeared and slowly lowered the hammer. He spat a mouthful of dust and dirt onto the sidewalk and, still on his knees, revolver still in one hand, scrabbled across the rough paving towards his prisoner.

Penfold was lying on his face, hands grasping his chest and his knees pulled up as if he were fast asleep in a cold bed. Boone lay beside him and with his free hand lifted his chin and turned his head round. Penfold's eyes were open; the eyeballs, still protruding in shock, registered pain and fear.

'You knew him . . .' hissed Boone accusingly.

Penfold's eyes tried to focus but there was nothing for him to see. His eyes were operating from memory. There was a screen of red mist, and from a distance, as if coming from the far end of a long culvert pipe, a hollow, echoing voice. But it didn't make sense. Everything hurt. He couldn't say where it hurt but he felt his eyes moisten and then the mist cleared and he had a crisp, clear view of Boone's concerned, hairy face. He opened his mouth to say something, he didn't know what, anything to convince himself that he wasn't going anywhere just yet, but all that came out were the contents of his burst lungs – thick, oily blood – and then his stomach rushed along to join it. But with it went the pain. Not the fear. That was still there, but only for another second until the red mist came down again and he felt himself floating along the culvert pipe with the urgent voice getting weaker and weaker until it faded to nothing. Penfold was dead.

Jack Knecht stayed with the knot of traffic until he was able to join the 280 interstate. As soon as the first exit loomed up out of the night mist he swung off the freeway, pulled into a slip road and waited. At midnight he started the engine again, did a short tour of the district and rejoined the freeway. At San Mateo he turned onto the 92, stayed on it and obeyed all the rules as far as Half Moon Bay, then turned south on the S1. Just over five miles, between Tunitas and Martin's Beach and set back off the highway, was the El Paso Diner & Eatery in all its neon glory – Hagen's 'point four'.

Knecht pulled in slowly, switched off the engine, lit a cigarette, and waited.

Hagen was late but it didn't matter. The news was bad whether he was late or early. He slid into the car beside Knecht and told him to switch the heater on. Still wrapped in his heavy overcoat, he blew on his hands before lighting a cigarette.

'Another problem, Mark,' said Knecht.

'Tell me something new.'

'This is. I think I've killed Penfold.'

Hagen exhaled the lungful of smoke with a whoosh. 'Tell me about it.' He turned sideways so that he could look Knecht in the face.

Knecht didn't look troubled. He told it as it had happened. Hagen listened in silence. When Knecht had finished the two men sat silently smoking, staring at the blackness through the misted-up windscreen. It went on for about half a cigarette, then Hagen broke the silence.

'I'll say something for you, Jack. When you fuck up you make a helluva fucking job of it. No half-measures for you. Jesus Christ!'

Knecht remained silent. He wound the window down and flicked the remains of his cigarette out. Then he lit another.

'What now, then?'

No remorse. No regret. What's the next job?

Hagen whooshed out another stream of smoke.

'Make yourself invisible. Get as far away from here as you can in twenty-four hours, hole up for a while, and then slip back to DC as normal. Let me do the talking on this one. You say nothing, do nothing. OK?'

'Whatever you say, pal. I'll see ya on the job line, then!'

'Sure – and Jack . . .' Hagen stopped halfway out of his seat and held out his hand. 'Let's have that gun of yours before it burns a hole in your armpit.'

Knecht hesitated, then saw the reason. 'Sure, Mark.' He brought the Browning out of his pocket and held it in his hand for a moment, looking at it. 'I'm not happy running light, Mark. It's a long way to DC.'

Hagen understood. 'Take mine, but for Christ's sake don't use the fucking thing as if it were a watering can. I've got enough trouble to explain already.'

'Trust me, Mark. Thanks.'

'Fuck off!' He stuck Knecht's automatic in his pocket and stopped again. 'Spare mag, loose shells?'

Knecht leaned forward, opened the glove compartment and dropped the sweet tin in Hagen's outstretched hand. 'See ya!'

Hagen didn't hang around. He waited until the rear lights of Knecht's car had disappeared down the road towards San Gregorio, then took off in his wake. There was no sign of Knecht when he pulled off the highway at Pescadaro and broke one of the cardinal rules. He switched off the engine, lifted the phone out of its bed and dialled 703 482 1100.

'Two nine zero,' he said when the Langley operator answered, and then, after a wait while the Contractor Project senior executive was wakened from a deep sleep, or dragged off his girlfriend's complaining body, launched into his pre-pared speech. 'Our position here in SF has been compromised,' he began.

'Keep it to its bare details,' said the voice, thick with broken sleep.

'My earlier report'll be on file. I was given a Purple on four items. I had a positive result on two. Number three proved too much for Penfold and put him down. He was a San Francisco cop. There'll be some shit flying around SF.' He glanced down at his watch. 'About now, I reckon.'

'What's your own status?'

'Clean.'

'Are you clear of the area?'

'More or less.'

'OK. Get out altogether. Come back here. Say nothing to

63

anyone. Get rid of anything that might have been involved...' The instructions were coming from a now-wide-awake brain; they were shooting into Hagen's earpiece like bullets. It was good to know that somebody somewhere had a well and truly oiled finger in the evasion business. '... and I'll handle the fallout. What's the name and designation of the guy who put Penfold down?'

'Boone. A detective working out of Turk Street. He was part of a three-man detail on surveillance at SFO.'

'OK. I'll handle it from here on. You go to ground and poke your nose out of the hole only when you get to Langley. Deal only with me.'

'Name, sir?'

'Reilly.'

Hagen put the phone back to sleep and said, 'Shit!' Anyone but Reilly. Tough! Reilly'd have the skin off his back – balls-ups were his speciality; the great survivor, usually the only one left upright when at the end of the day the body-bags were laid out for a casualty count. And Reilly had made a habit of surviving when the shit was slapping around the fan. Tough on the messenger – particularly the one who brought the bad news.

Hagen pulled out of the slipway and continued bearing west until he ran into the bay road. No traffic about at half past two in the morning. He kept going until the road hit the sea and followed the mountain contour. He found a deserted stretch overlooking an area of rough, sea-scoured rocky outcrops and, keeping the engine running, stepped out and hurled Knecht's Browning as far as he could into the boiling white water below. He stepped back, reached into the car's glove box and removed the tin of sweets. It rattled like castanets as it followed the automatic into the sea. He lit a cigarette, studied his surroundings for a moment and, when he was satisfied that he was alone, got back into the Oldsmobile and continued driving south.

Chapter 4

Washington, DC, November 1974

Robert Graver, director of the CIA's East Asia Research Co-ordinate Committee, and his deputy, General Sam Reilly, faced each other across the room in Graver's personal apartments. They could talk freely. It was one of the most secure places in Washington, DC; unbuggable and unapproachable, its total security guaranteed by its situation in the heart of the CIA complex at Langley. It was a necessary setting for what Reilly had to tell his director.

Graver removed his thick-lens spectacles, peered blindly in the direction of his deputy to show that he was ready to be talked at, and began to clean them with a napkin-sized handkerchief. He lowered his eyes and breathed heavily on the right-hand lens and wiped off the condensation in an unhurried, smooth motion.

'The breaking down of the operation at San Francisco,' continued Reilly, after detailing what he'd interrogated out of Mark Hagen, 'leaves a huge question mark against the integrity of Contractor. Particularly as two men evaded the Purple directive directed against them and my officers can't say what they knew or what they didn't know about the Contractor business. Under the circumstances we have to consider that it's been compromised and that the CIA has been recognised. We've no waterproof compartments on this one; when the water starts coming in there'll be no way of stopping it. We sink.'

'The Purple can still be used,' said Graver after a moment.

'Wouldn't help. Both men who evaded the net would have made a connection between the CIA and incoming and outgoing narcotics. Hagen was sure of that. The fight at SFO was no Saturday afternoon picnic with a couple of street drug gangs knocking each other off. This was police and smart-looking guys in big black cars knocking each other off. It was seen, and one of the people who got out of the way gunned down our man who'd been briefed to bring him in. The Bureau'll be excited and so will the DEA if these two guys come out into the open. Hagen has marked both of 'em. It's my intention that he spends the rest of his life looking for them and wiring their lips together.'

Graver wasn't smiling today. He let Reilly's picturesque speech go without expression. 'Trouble is, we haven't got time for posse chases, Sam. I think we're going to have to see it as the worst possible scenario and accept that Contractor's going to come under pressure. If that happens and he's compromised or brought into the open, as you've just described, we go down the chute with him. But let me think about it. Give me a bit of breathing space.'

'Like you said, Bob, we haven't got a lot of time.'

'Then let's make full use of what we've got. We'll get together in the basement tomorrow afternoon. Before that I'll make a few calls and see if anything's floating. OK? Tomorrow, half four.'

But it was much earlier than that.

Graver poked his head round the door of Reilly's office and said, 'Cup of coffee – upstairs.'

They sat in one of the discreet corners of the upstairs canteen. It suited both men, but particularly Reilly, who needed the scope for manoeuvre, for sidestepping indiscretion. It was essential. He could feel balls-ups in his bladder.

Graver kept his voice low. 'The FBI are not interested in a couple of cop killings in San Francisco. Nobody's mentioned narcotics or dirty money to them. It's just a couple of killings well within the scope of SFPD . . .'

'You mean not yet,' grunted Reilly. If there was darkness on the horizon he'd see it, and make sure everyone else did.

'And what about this Detective Boone?' Reilly played along with the conversation; some things it was better to keep from the head of the cattle shed. He knew what had happened to Boone. He'd started a process but the cunning bastard hadn't just sat around and waited to picked off; he'd vanished into the blue. SFPD were anxious to trace him, but they wanted to do it themselves. Boone had got the message. He'd seen a CIA undercover operation. He wasn't stupid; he'd vanished. They'd had better luck with the airport security executive; he'd actually brought his report on the activities in his airport with him when the two 'officials' of the Airport Control Authority persuaded him, 'for his own safety in view of the seriousness of the situation . . .', to place himself in protective custody.

'Vanished,' said Graver.

The two men exchanged glances. Graver raised his eyebrows. Reilly said, 'I don't see a problem there.'

Graver hoped he'd read it correctly. 'The other guy's vanished too – the airport security exec.'

'Same comment.'

Graver, without moving his head, said, 'A serious damage limitation exercise is indicated. This guy Hagen?'

Reilly had already done it – he'd had Hagen's file on his desk three minutes after putting the phone down on him. 'A good one. Thorough, intelligent, cold, and bloody hard. At his grade they don't come any better.'

'Trustworthy?'

'That too. Goes without saying. He's been on the Contractor detail long enough to have proved he knows where his loyalty lies – to the Company first, last and always. We took him out of the army, Special Forces, Vietnam. He did a turn for Phoenix. I'm happy with him.'

'We use him, then. Bring him into the circle, an unknown face. Convene a meeting for this afternoon and have Hagen sit in; we'll get him involved fairly deeply, then send him out to tidy up the mess. You agree with that?'

Reilly lowered his empty cup. 'In principle. Let's keep this to ourselves for the time being and see what this afternoon throws up at us. We'll treat it as a meeting, no disaster scenarios, and watch it run. OK?'

'I agree.'

On a cold, gloomy, snow-laden afternoon the committee of the ultra-secret Contractor project sat down in a small, overheated, soundproof box in the bowels of a Langley annexe to assess the size of the bomb they'd been presented with. A bomb, General Reilly explained, that was already ticking.

The committee comprised three of the most senior intelligence executives of the CIA's innocuous-sounding East Asia Research Co-ordinate Committee; a body that had been carefully put together in the very early days of the Vietnam adventure. Its meetings were rare and this hastily convened gathering exemplified the juddering urgency that a ticking bomb had brought to bear on complacency.

There was an added dimension to the meeting.

For the first time since its inauguration a protocol was broken; an outsider had been admitted to the sanctum. Mark Hagen had been specifically ordered to attend by the DCI himself and, although he took no place at the table, he was there for all to see and later to question. He sat a sanitary distance from the table, like a pariah at a Hindu feast, alone and ignored except for the odd curious glance from the two grey faces on either side of General Reilly. He felt like a sacrificial goat.

A scraping of chairs as everyone stood up sent the dull hoods over Hagen's eyes clicking out of sight. Wide awake, he muttered like the others, 'Good afternoon, Director.'

But the director wasn't in the mood for civilities. He caught Reilly's eye, but nothing, other than tacit understanding of how this was going to be played, passed between them. 'Has Hagen been put in the picture?' he said, tersely, as he sat down at the table opposite the three wise men.

'Hagen made the picture what it is, Director,' said Reilly. 'He's the reason we've got a problem.'

'Neither here nor there now, Sam,' said the DCI, grimly. 'Does he know the basics of Contractor?'

'No,' said Reilly emphatically. 'Which is why this meeting is taking place and why Hagen is here. We are the only four people in our side of the business who know what

Contractor's all about. Those who were around when it started in '57, with the exception of yourself, are no longer active. Whatever you want to tell this man, sir, is well within your mandate. You don't need our permission.' He spoke for his two co-members. They took it for granted. Reilly was a power within the CIA, a non-political street fighter up from the ranks. No one was going to argue with him; he was going to be the next non-political Director of Central Intelligence.

The DCI shifted his glance from Reilly's heavy features to the sacrifice tethered to the wall. 'Come and sit over here, Hagen.' Hagen approached and followed the direction of Graver's finger pointing at the head of the table. It separated him from the group in the middle. It showed he wasn't a member of the club.

'Thank you, sir,' he said. He pulled the chair out so that he could stretch his legs under the table, crossed his arms and tried to look comfortable as he gazed frankly and openly at the heads turned towards him. He didn't lower his eyes; he wasn't frightened of these people.

But there was nothing aggressive about Robert Graver's manner. He left all that sort of thing to Sam Reilly, who had enough aggression for them all. He turned to Hagen, rested his elbow on the table and told him all he reckoned he needed to know about the Contractor affair. Hagen didn't interrupt, although during Graver's reading of the lesson he had ample time to speculate on why he was being told something that screamed of illegality and conspiracy. And he didn't like being brought into this select band; he felt like a prime turkey in mid-November – he'd rather not know about it. But he now realized what he'd been doing in San Francisco. He'd been escorting, on behalf of the Central Intelligence Agency, millions – probably billions – of narco-dollars out of the country and into the European laundry system. That must be worth at least a thousand years in Leavenworth.

'The point of your presence here...' The DCI had finished with the explanation, or at least all the explanation he was going to get. '... is that by your actions at SFO you have, in all probability, compromised the position of our intelligence-gathering apparatus in Asia—'

'Excuse *me*, sir—'

'Shut up,' growled Reilly. 'You're here to listen, not to make comment, or interrupt the DCI. Your position's been established – live with it . . .'

Graver continued talking as if he hadn't noticed the interruption. ' . . . an apparatus that has been running on oiled wheels, without a hiccup, for over eighteen years. An operation that has been jeopardised by a simple act of incompetence.' He kept his eyes glued to Hagen's; so did the other three men. 'If this apparatus folds somebody's going to have to pay for it with his head.' He paused and switched his gaze briefly round the table. Nobody met him. They were waiting to hear whose head. Hagen knew.

Without moving, Hagen shifted his eyes to Reilly. Reilly's eyes weren't receiving glances; he switched his eyes back to a spot somewhere in the middle of the table and said nothing. There was nothing he could say to these relieved-looking senior executives of the most powerful intelligence service in the world. They were only the policy-makers. It wasn't their fault. They'd got the bastard who they reckoned had blown their dream operation. Forget anyone else. They'd got Mark Hagen, and that's who they were hanging on to to carry the can into the Oval Office and explain to God how all this shit managed to hit the fan. But Hagen shouldered his cross philosophically. What did it matter? They'd got their fall-guy; they were, in terms of their kaleidoscope vision, off the hook.

One of them broke. He tapped the table with his throwaway ballpoint and, looking at no one in particular, said, 'So where do we go from here?'

It wasn't taken up.

He tried again. This time he managed to lock on the sacrificial goat's eyes. 'What about you, Hagen? If you've got any comments to make you can make them now.'

Hagen glanced quickly at Reilly and got a curt nod of permission.

'What's Contractor's name?' he asked.

Simple question.

You wouldn't have thought so.
Nobody met his eyes.
They looked to Graver.
'It's classified.'
Hagen kept his face straight. Twenty-five years in the company of men who closed their eyes when they shaved for fear of meeting themselves had played havoc with the DCI's fine education. Hagen had never left the gutter; a spade was still a spade, unless it was a Spade, and shit was still shit whether it was wet or dry. That was Hagen's world and he wasn't impressed with people like the God of the CIA who, like his peers, had lost the ability to use the language he'd been born with. Why couldn't he just say 'We don't know', because that's what it usually meant. 'Classified' meant fuck-all in this context; it was the same as saying 'Purple', as if 'kill' was too short a word. Hagen glanced quickly at Reilly again. Reilly held on to his eyes for the brief moment and allowed a faint, but not visual, understanding to pass between them. It was an acknowledgement of recognition between two bare-knuckle fighters in the company of a bunch of ladies' dress designers.
'Where's his centre of operation; where's he working from?'
'Same answer,' said Graver, after only a barely discernible hesitation.
Hagen didn't take his eyes off him. *In other words they'd got a heavy sleeper who'd dug himself in and they didn't know who, how or where! What a way to run a fucking spy ring.* A silence fell over the room. The men around the table stared fixedly at the blank sheets of paper in front of them; they looked like a group of mourners holding a silent prayer for a departed comrade. Hagen sat quite comfortably at the head of the table. He was dying for a cigarette but saw no ashtrays and spotted no other sufferer. He hung on to the craving; he'd enjoy it the minute he was allowed to walk outside this mausoleum. He stared at the blank faces and wondered whether it was up to him to introduce a new topic, or was this, perhaps, the set procedure for a free-for-all? He decided to wait for them to finish whatever they were thinking about and then still say nothing.

It was Reilly who reopened the agenda.

He turned sideways in his chair so that he was facing Hagen. 'This Pandora's box that your incompetence has opened has raised the spectre of a possible player in Bangkok . . .' Hagen's eyebrows rose slightly. Jesus! Now it's down to guesswork, and so much for the plain English – but he remained attentive. 'This possible player, I understand, is an American businessman operating out of Bangkok. He has something to do with supplying boats' engines and other sailing stuff . . .' Reilly wasn't a sailing man – it showed. 'His name is James Logan, but that's neither here nor there either.' He glanced sideways out of the corner of his eye at the DCI to see if he minded him pinching his phrases. It didn't matter. Graver's face, like the rest of the table, was turned to Hagen's. Hagen was beginning to feel a bit like Billy Graham. He kept his eyes locked on Reilly's face. 'But what is, is there's a possibility that our Contractor could be working out of Bangkok too. Nothing more than a possibility. Are you following me?' It didn't matter whether he was or wasn't. Reilly continued, still staring into Hagen's face, and Hagen gave him a slight nod. That was enough. 'So you will understand when I say I wouldn't like to think that the two imponderables, James Logan, US businessman operating in Bangkok, and Contractor, covert US intelligence specialist, could in any way turn into one ponderable.' He finished ominously. 'You know what I mean by that?'

Hagen kept his face straight.

But nobody nodded in agreement with Reilly. Perhaps they didn't understand what he meant. Reilly, at a nod from Graver, stood up, and the two men met each other at the far end of the room. The others sat and looked at each other, ignoring Hagen.

Reilly, six foot three, had to bend at the waist to speak with any sort of intimacy to his superior. Graver, who most of his life had perfected a way of standing on his toes without actually showing it, no longer bothered. It was, to him, one of the jewels of high office; he no longer had to pretend he was taller than he was.

'I think we can get Hagen out of here now, Bob,' he said, lowering his voice to a rumble. 'I'll fill in the words he didn't understand in private later. I think it's time for some serious discussion about Contractor. I've got a nasty feeling that this San Francisco business and these two material witnesses being able to talk about it could have the makings of repercussions that will close Contractor down. If that happens you and I go with him. I can't help thinking this thing might well have run its course and the Contractor project could blow up in our faces – I reckon we should, even at this early stage, consider demotion of the principal before the thing starts creaking.' He paused, but it was only for breath. 'You realise, of course, that if the thing does go up and comes to a Congressional investigation, it'll be your head on the tallest pole and mine on the slightly shorter one next to it.'

Graver's thick lenses didn't steam up. After twenty years in the CIA's equivalent of the electric chair it had become second nature to see the size and shape of the escape tunnel well before being taken prisoner. 'Why don't we just wait and see, Sam? Let's get Hagen back into his padded cell and sit down and talk about it. I've got a few more ideas of my own that need a bit of an airing.'

The two men went back to their places at the table. There'd been no conversation whilst they'd been at the other end of the room. No one had dared open up; they were all too intent on straining their ears towards Graver and Reilly and trying out their long-forgotten lip-reading techniques. Only Mark Hagen looked relaxed and uninterested. He was busy counting his fingers and studying the cuticles on his left hand. That was until he looked up and saw Reilly and Graver studying him. Here it comes – Leavenworth and broken arms or total exoneration and the important job of raising and lowering the barrier at the tradesmen's entrance round the back of the Langley complex. They'd told him at the beginning: 'You don't get two chances with the CIA – screw up a big one and you're out.'

Reilly gave him his orders.

'Go back to Ashford Farm and wait there until I send for you.'

Hagen stood up, face blank, arms relaxed by his side. 'Yes, sir.' He didn't meet any of the other eyes. They'd lost interest in him already. He turned for the door. No good-byes. No thank you very much. Nothing. Fuck-all.

They didn't start talking again until several minutes after the door had closed behind Hagen, and then Graver went straight into it, no preamble. 'OK, gentlemen. I've decided that Contractor's become a liability.'

It took them all by surprise. It struck them dumb. But not Reilly.

'A liability to whom?'

'Us – you, you, you' — he pointed his forehead at each of the men in turn – 'Me. And the CIA – and that means the security of the nation.'

'You mean the Contractor file goes outside these walls—'

Both Reilly's and Graver's heads shot out of their shoulders like those of startled chickens. Graver snapped, 'Like fuck it will . . .'

Reilly came in too. ' . . . unless you all want to join the Director at the bench of a Senate investigation hearing on the CIA's extra-curricular activities.'

Graver shot him a glance. Extra-curricular activities! He could almost hear the knitting needles clacking and the guillotine blade being hoisted skywards. He checked the years off on his fingers, 1957 to 1974 – eighteen years. Jesus Christ – a fucking lifetime! And even then, it could have gone on for ever, or at least until someone got too greedy. But there was no cause for greed; everyone was satisfied with what he was getting out of the arrangement, and all it took was a fucking fat little Chinaman's sexual peccadillos in San Francisco to bring the whole fucking thing down. You wouldn't believe it if you read the fucking thing in a comic paper. Graver came back from his trip down memory lane with a jolt and refocused his eyes on Reilly's granite face. Reilly was saying something. He didn't tell him where his brain had been for the last few minutes. 'Sorry – I was distracted for a moment, Sam. What was that you said?'

Reilly hadn't missed him. 'The fallout from this San Francisco fracas is beginning to spread.' He reached across the table, and poured himself a glass of water from the crystal carafe. 'I have it reliably that the DEA are trying to involve the FBI in the money-running affair; they also want to involve Scotland Yard and MI5 in unravelling the money route. They've got Bangkok in their sights as an opening gambit – sacks of money equals fields of poppy; poppy equals heroin and heroin equals Thailand, being the narcotics distribution centre for the Far East. OK?'

He left no gap for intervention. He was telling them nothing they didn't already know. 'If the DEA and its friends arrive in Bangkok in strength looking for an American operator in the marketplace they'll either frighten Contractor out of the game or expose him. They expose him – they expose us. We lose on all accounts. Either way the whole structure of CIA intelligence operations in Vietnam, Cambodia and the other gunpowder republics'll go up the Swannee. We have to cover for that eventuality.'

'How?'

'A total reassessment of Contractor's position and security,' said Reilly. 'Everyone agree?'

They all agreed.

'Meet again tomorrow.' Graver stood up. 'Same place, same time. Stick around, Sam, there's something I'd like to see you about.'

When the others had gone, Sam Reilly moved round the table and sat in the chair earlier vacated by Mark Hagen. The two heads went close together. Even though they were in the most secure room in one of the most secure buildings in the world, these men were old hands at the look-and-listen game. They took no chances. Not when the conversation was about treason.

Graver opened the betting.

'Sam, I think we've washed around the subject enough now. It's decision time.'

'It's been that since the fuck-up at SFO, as far as I'm concerned.'

'OK. Here it is, then. Contractor's got to be found and put on hold with an embargo on talking about anything he's been doing over the past eighteen years or so. But he's nobody's fool, this guy. The minute he feels time is catching up with him he'll take precautions against finding his name writ large on a sanction order.'

'Then what do you suggest?'

'Exactly that – termination of contract—' Graver's mouth twisted in the semblance of a grin. 'Demotion to non-player, or better still, termination with extreme prejudice.'

'In English, please, Bob.'

'We remove him completely from the game. And there's only one sure way of doing that. Contractor dies and with him goes the story. No one wants to talk to a dead man. The only problem with that, though—'

'Christ, Bob, can't we clear up one before we get to the next! What do we do about the Chinese?'

Graver had thought of nothing else since the San Francisco business had turned into a gusher. 'Haven't we just decided? It's all coming to an end, Sam. We play the Chinese card until the last possible minute. When the war finishes so does our arrangement with Bangkok. I stuck my neck on the line over allowing the Chinese the freedom of the United States and the reaction at the time from Dulles was, to say the least, considerably less than enthusiastic. He didn't report it to Eisenhower and no President since has been in the know. I didn't imagine, and I know he certainly didn't, that this thing would roll on and on for eighteen years. I'm not sure I would have gone with it if I had. But that's all water under the bridge. You can imagine if it came out now! Jesus, Sam, the CIA actively aiding the importation and building up of a Chinese narcotics empire in the US? Compared with this Watergate would amount to something like a piss in the Mississippi.'

'You don't have to sell it to me, Bob. I'd already decided. When we've taken Contractor out of the game there'll be no one to point fingers. Congressional hearings on mismanagement of national security are not convened on the basis of rumour. It takes evidence and without Contractor to present himself with sacks of the stuff there'd be nothing to go on . . .'

Graver smiled a sickly smile. It didn't suit his thick glasses and chubby cheeks. 'There's always you and me.'

'D'you ever hear of a guy about to be hanged shoving the hangman to one side and saying here, let me do it? I could lie to St Peter if it meant another couple of weeks before they dropped the trapdoor. A congressional? Christ! Not a hope!'

'The Chinese?'

'A pragmatic bunch of grasping bastards. They've made their pitch; there's not a lot we could do to unstitch 'em. I think they've been expecting a bit of hatchet work for some time now. They'll have covered their tracks; I don't think they're going to complain if we say that's the end of the deal.'

Graver stared at Reilly without really seeing him. Reilly, as usual, made a lot of sense; Reilly wasn't worried. But then Reilly wasn't the guy who had that little gem from Harry S. Truman stuck on his desk for all to see – the one proclaiming exactly where the buck stopped. Reilly being unworried was not a lot of consolation for Robert Graver.

Reilly was still talking. 'Is that anywhere near your thinking, Bob?'

'What?'

'You're throwing the Chinese out of the tub?'

'You read my mind. Let's play the cards as they turn up. OK?'

'OK. You agree with shunting this Hagen guy out to Bangkok with an open mandate on Contractor?'

'That's your call, Sam – if you think he's man enough for the job.'

Reilly didn't blink. 'He'll do to start with. He's dispensable. We've got plenty more Hagens if this one fucks up.'

Chapter 5

Hagen's brief was of the worst possible kind. One to one, him and Sam Reilly, no witness, nothing in writing, a verbal commitment. 'And if anything goes wrong it goes wrong with you, Hagen, not us, not the Company. Got it?'

Reilly accepted Hagen's shrug as an affirmative answer. 'Contractor – you know what I'm talking about when I say Contractor?'

'I was there yesterday, sir.'

'He's your target – Contractor. First you find him, then you ask him if he's got any material tucked away that he's saving for his memoirs; if he has you trace it and destroy it – without reading it. Then you put him quietly out of his misery. You start poking around in Thailand – Bangkok. There is a point of contact – a Chinese secret society bighead by the name of Liu Zhoushiu. I'm not sure what you're going to do with the name because he's about as easy to get at as Fidel Castro. But he definitely knows Contractor. That's all I give you.'

'What about this Logan that was mentioned in your huddle the other day? The one who interests the DEA?'

'Their descriptions don't match.'

'How old's Logan?'

'Mid-fifties.'

'So there'll be army records.'

'Nice try. It's already been done. Came up a blank sheet. He was taken straight into the OSS by Donovan, which

78

means no records exist. The latest eyeball description of Logan is of a thin, grey-haired, round-shouldered guy who looks older than his years. Pale complexion. Wears mirror shades all the time – night and day!'

'Contractor?'

'We've done all that. He was last seen in '57 so he's probably changed out of all recognition—'

'Tell me anyway – sir.'

'Over six. Mid-sandy hair. Solidly built. Light brown eyes. Good skin colour indicating an outdoor man and, like I said, they don't match.'

'Who supplied that description?'

'It doesn't matter to you.' Reilly gave Hagen what could almost be described as a sympathetic look, but it was an illusion. Hagen knew, like everyone else who'd ever come in contact with Samuel Reilly for any length of time, that if he had any sympathy, anywhere, it could be easily spread, with room to spare, on the pointed end of a needle. 'You got anything relevant you'd like to ask me?'

'Finance?'

'All resources will come through Special Projects. They'll open an account in a Singapore bank. Draw what you want – within reason.' Again, Reilly almost smiled. 'I don't want to hear of some filthy-rich bastard named Hagen taking up luxury residence in Hawaii. Anything else?' He stood up. He'd had enough. All he wanted now was to see the back of Mark Hagen and one day, in the not too distant future, hear that the Contractor file had been quietly 'exanimated'.

But Hagen had one more thing.

'Who's our base asset in the Thailand area?'

Reilly pulled a face and gave the question considerable thought. All the respectable intelligence organisations had a permanent, or semi-permanent, sleeper agent working, or lying undercover, in most of the world's interesting spots. Thailand was one of those, and the CIA was no exception. Most of these people knew each other – nothing in the open, nothing discussed, just an unspoken, unwritten understanding that half a dozen undercover agents of different nationalities could cohabitate in the same half-mile yet not admit to each other's dirty habits. Reilly stopped running the disadvantages of disclosure through his mind and offered Hagen one of his biscuit crumbs. 'Jack Krislov. Has a boat yard of sorts and does a bit of sailing around the local waters there. You can use him if you find it necessary but don't try to run him. He's not yours, he's his own man. He'll help but only if it suits his situation. He's not going to be running around carrying a gun for you. OK? If you want a bit of a hand tell him Drogheda – that's his contact code.'

'Company man?' asked Hagen, unnecessarily.

'A name in the book. He's like you. He screwed up and he's working his way back into favour. That's all you're getting. You've first of all got to get rid of a damn great black mark for incompetence before you're let loose again in this country on anything more demanding than watching the GS18's shit house in case it runs out of paper. Now get lost.'

Hagen stood and for a moment studied the top of Reilly's balding head. He knew the form. It was called the umbrella game – every fucker had one, except M. Hagen. Even before the thing went wrong they'd got a patsy; if it went right it would be smiles all round, but if the President asked what the fuck went wrong the patsy'd go to sleep in the garage with the car engine on and the exhaust pipe sticking up his arse. You can't win, Hagen – you've been given a set of dice that only throws crap.

'Thank you, sir.'

80

Chapter 6

Washington, DC, December 1974

David Boone really hadn't had a great deal of good old-fashioned fact to offer the FBI when, voluntarily, he submitted to interrogation. He arrived on the FBI's doorstep and, without preliminaries, accused the CIA of murdering two of his colleagues in San Francisco. The FBI knew all about the SF murders and took his statements with a large lump of salt. San Francisco had as big a crime problem as Chicago had in the thirties. It was the gateway into the States, the main entrance for the heroin trade. It also had the largest collection of queers and gays in the world, and where you have homosexuals snuggling up like sardines and drugs sloshing around by the bucketful, you have crime. And when you have crime you have gangs. The FBI saw it in black and white, there was no emotion, no axes to grind. This was no different, except instead of a couple of queers doing the trip it was a couple of cops. Tough – but so what? They weren't the first cops to go down in the streets of San Francisco.

But even with Boone's passionate insistence the FBI could come to no other conclusion than that this one carried nothing other than the hallmarks of a local gang settling their argument with a couple of cops on the take who'd got greedy. They considered it was none of their business unless the San Francisco Police Department made it so. And the SFPD weren't going to do that; they considered they had the matter well and competently in hand. But the FBI listened to Boone. They would listen to anybody who had a bad word to say against the people out at Langley. That the CIA had deliberately killed one of their own in front of the informant was a little harder to digest. But they listened in hope – hope without expectation. That was until Boone mentioned that the CIA was involved in the illegal export of large amounts of US currency. The trouble with this little trinket was that while his theory was reasoned and sound, the back-up to the story was pure fantasy and without a solid item of fact.

It appeared from the FBI's report that Boone, while under suspension from the SFPD pending investigation of his activities at SFO when the CIA special agent Leo Penfold had been killed, had decided to carry out his own investigation into the killing of his two police colleagues. This had led him to a man named Philip. Philip Morris, Boone told the FBI without a shade of embarrassment, and Philip Morris had been the man who put Lieutenant Ranny Lim on to the money-running activities at San Francisco Airport.

'And you have his sworn statement and his agreement to come out into the open and tell his story?'

'He died just before I got to him.'

'And this was your star witness? How did he die – not that it matters?'

'He was killed by the CIA.'

'Ask a silly question!'

'The deputy head of security at SFO testified that with Lieutenant Lim he had seen the contents of a suitcase loaded onto an international flight by a money-runner. He estimated it contained somewhere in the region of two million dollars in hundred-dollar notes. He was also carrying a briefcase.'

'More money?'

'I contacted a source in London's Scotland Yard. He said that they'd had a tip-off and had got a man into Shannon Airport, Ireland to meet the flight. That briefcase had eight kilos of high-grade refined heroin in it.'

'There's been no publicity from London. You sure you didn't dream all this?'

'Of course I'm fucking sure – I'm here, ain't I! London's

business is London's business. I'm telling you what happened here. And I did what you mothers should have done and checked the route.'

'Why Ireland? Why not direct to London if they've got the system wired.'

'This *is* the system. SFO to Shannon.' Boone was beginning to shout. He wasn't happy with the way it was going; he wasn't even happy about the way it was sounding to him. 'Shannon! For fuck's sake go and look at the place. If you're coming off an American flight you could walk through customs and immigration with a ground-to-air missile launcher hanging out of your backpack.'

The FBI shrugged. The man was talking rubbish, but they'd better go along with him. 'So we've arrived at Shannon with all our money and a briefcase full of aitch. Where do we go then?'

Boone continued seriously, 'Dublin, then train to Belfast. City Airport to Bristol – that's a place in the west of England, no customs formalities for Northern Ireland passengers, walk straight through – and that's where Scotland Yard were waiting. You want my opinion?'

'Go on.'

'This has been happening for years. It's CIA-covered all the way; every month, millions and millions and millions of dollars have been passed through this place and Christ knows how many tons of heroin. I think the British got lucky just this once because Lieutenant Lim and Detective Yong blew the thing wide open and told them about it. That's why Ranny Lim got killed; that's why the gay boy was killed . . .' He thumped the table viciously. 'The fucking CIA are up to their necks in this; they've probably got the British tied up in it too, whatever it is. You can't move this quantity of stuff around for any length of time without getting rolled by one side or the other. Ranny Lim said that Mayne, the security guy at SFO, reckoned it was a regular thing these money-runners being escorted through the formalities by the CIA. He said, in his opinion, that to warrant CIA assistance through immigration and customs, the amount of money involved would be as big as the national debt. I believe him. It's been going on under your fucking noses and you've done nothing about it.' He stopped talking and stared around him suspiciously. 'How deep are you bastards in with the CIA?'

'Don't even think about it, pal. This guy, Mayne – will he testify?'

'I read he was killed in a car pile-up on the interstate highway at Santa Clara.'

'CIA again?'

'He had no business at Santa Clara.'

'So, what it boils down to is a lot of dead people, all killed by the CIA; sackfuls of treasury notes being humped out of the country and briefcases full of millions of dollars' worth of uncut heroin being shipped across the water to London with the help of the CIA? Why is the CIA doing this?'

'It's something to do with an arrangement they have with Chinese Tongs operating in the States from Thailand.'

They didn't believe him. Of course they didn't believe him, but prudence dictated that it be mentioned to the FBI's good friend, the newly up-and-running Drug Enforcement Administration's intelligence centre in El Paso. New and keen, the DEA realized that with all the fumbling and stumbling that had gone on around San Francisco and its airport there would be no more interesting activity for some time to come. They asked for David Boone to be flown to El Paso for a little more socialisation. The FBI were glad to see him off their hands. That the SFPD were anxiously awaiting Boone's return as their star turn on the murders of two of their officers influenced neither agency's actions.

Boone was eased into a six-seater Cessna with a pilot and an FBI despatch officer for a night flight to Texas. Contact was lost just under an hour from Washington Airport, and a young couple sitting outside their camper home parked near the national park in the Blue Ridge Mountains reported to the police station at Waynesboro the following afternoon that they had heard a dull thud in the sky south-west of Crozet at approximately 2240 hours. This, they elaborated, was followed by a fiery glow like a shooting star but much slower, and then nothing. When the search-and-rescue team arrived at the spot they found bits of wreckage scattered over an area of nearly four square miles. The largest piece of the aircraft picked up was the engine; everything else had been turned into metal confetti. Three bodies were recovered. Identification was only possible by fragments of bloody, mashed jawbone containing teeth; nothing else was recognisable as human. The FBI agent conducting Boone's interrogation wondered to his wife in bed that night whether perhaps the bearded man's paranoia about the CIA might not have had some credibility. But his wife comforted him with the logic that airplanes crash all the time and they surely can't all be caused by CIA bombs. But he wasn't happy about it.

He was even more unhappy when a couple of days later a senior executive at the El Paso Center brought him to the phone with what he called 'a little addendum to the tragedy . . .' He told the investigator that one of his researchers had a short time earlier had a request from San Francisco – the same police department as the man who'd perished in the air crash. The officer had requested information on drug trafficking and the involvement of Chinese secret societies. The SFPD officer who had requested the information had, he understood, been one of the two officers murdered in their car in San Francisco. Coincidence?

When a copy of the information that had been sent to Ranny Lim was received by the FBI it turned the paranoia of a San Francisco cop into something extremely tangible. They wrapped themselves round the name James Logan and the organisation Touming Guanxi and came up with a highly ominous package. It was decided at high level in FBI head-quarters that this particular package would remain, for the time being, a little private business between the FBI and the DEA, and a middle-ranking DEA agent was despatched with a US Treasury official to London for consultation with Scotland Yard's anti-drugs unit and HM Customs and Excise Intelligence Centre.

Following these discussions a list of 'names' of suspected couriers was drawn up. Although the San Francisco route had ceased to function, other departure areas remained unaffected. All courier routes ended at the same destination, the Hong Kong & Chusan (London) Banking Corporation, Ltd, Moorgate, in the City of London. Based on Detective

Boone's assessment of the one known shipment of narco-dollars, a short period of intense surveillance on the bank revealed the huge quantities of American money changing shape and destination around the London illegal money market. It was the report of this combined British/US operation that raised the stakes, and the status of the representatives of the organisations at war with the narcotics distributors in the US. The group of officials sitting at the table in a narrow building in London was the result of a rapidly convened meeting of senior figures in the DEA, Scotland Yard's SO6, MI5, MI6 and the CIA's London head of station.

'So who's running the opium intelligence circuit in the Triangle now, Jack?' asked Henry Bradshaw, director of MI6's Far East section, of Jack Hargreaves, CIA head of station, London. 'You, or the DEA?'

'We're in it together. The CIA concentrates solely on military intelligence in that area. The DEA's interest is all areas outside that mandate. The name of the game in this instance is stopping the influx of dirty money from the United States into the UK and back into the coffers of the mandarins in whichever part of the Far East they unfold their prayer mats.' Jack Hargreaves had to handle this one with all the skill of a medicine man. His brief from DCI Langley was to get the British excited about joining them in Thailand with their Far Eastern intelligence resources as part of an Anglo-American venture in curtailing the growth of the opium industry. That was the theory. What Langley really wanted was a sideways glance by the British at a guy named Logan who sold motor-boat parts in Bangkok as a day job and the rest of the time appeared to be heavily involved in the narcotics business.

Why British? And why sideways? Why not a full frontal? Hargreaves knew when to pursue a topic and when not. This was one of those when nots. 'Why' hadn't gone very well with General Reilly at his private briefing. 'Just do as I fucking say, Hargreaves,' was the diplomatic response to his wanting to know why CIA Bangkok couldn't go knocking on Mr Logan's door and asking what the fuckin' hell he meant by, as an American citizen, floating up to his neck in Chinese shit. 'This Logan sounds like one of those sharp bastards who can smell the CIA even when covered in shit. He'd pack his bags and be off like a dose of salts if he as much as caught a whiff of the CIA. He wouldn't suspect the British of being in collusion with the CIA; he might even welcome one of their people with open arms. Solve the whole fuckin' problem if he opened his heart up to some smartassed Brit operator! So let the British and the DEA ask him.' 'What about our involvement?' had brought a more civilised response. 'A watching brief, from a distance. No contact. Special Projects have a man in the field waiting for a bird to break cover. It's all tied up.' Great. Hargreaves had seen this sort of operation before. Nobody knew who was who and what was what. A guaranteed fuck-up! But not to worry – the British liked fuck-ups, it was something they were used to, they wouldn't know where they were if the day didn't start with a fuck-up.

Tony Cobbold of MI6 moved away from his self-imposed isolation at the middle of the table and joined the huddle round at the top end. He glanced down at his briefing notes and stuck his finger on the paper where his doodles had blocked out a section of text. 'The DEA and the CIA already have working groups in Burma and Thailand – it says here . . .'

'They don't work together,' said Hargreaves quickly. 'We don't overlap—'

'That wasn't what I was aiming at,' said Cobbold. 'What I was going to say was if you have two groups already active in the area isn't it going to get a wee bit overcrowded with another lot pitching their tents there? And if we at Six come in with you and we move our resident into your sphere, who is going to point out friends and friends?'

'We thought we'd make it a free-for-all,' said Hargreaves.

But Cobbold didn't see the funny side. 'We'd get in each other's way,' he said seriously. 'And how would we share the resources?'

The DEA cut in, 'Our people would stand aside and watch if MI6 went in on a definite trace. We'd be there, but on the sidelines waiting for the call to join in.'

Hargreaves said, 'Read me the bottom line. I've only got

as far as MI5 and Six going into Thailand and the DEA carrying out their normal, uninspiring activities on the narcotics front. What are you expecting of me?'

'You've already said it, Jack, a watching brief. We do the groundwork and bring this Jim Logan out into the open. We look at him, hurt him if necessary, or be very kind to him and ask him the questions about money from London, opium from Burma, heroin to the States and the price of gin and tonic in the Oriental . . .'

'You got anybody on the spot?'

'We have.'

Chapter 7

Thailand, December 1974

Mark Hagen established himself in a modest, out-of-the-way hotel in the west of the Thai capital and indicated his location with the 290 grouping in Washington under the joint code-word for the operation – DROGHEDA. He'd barely had a shower and changed his sweat-soaked shirt before he received a coded brief through this source. The originator code was CONTROL-SR. It took no stretch of his imagination to penetrate Sam Reilly's thin disguise. It read: *The British have put a man in the field in your region to work with the DEA on the Logan subject. Identify and isolate from your primary target. Don't acknowledge.*

Aubrey St Clair Smith was an agent of the old school. Impeccably polite to everyone, he went about his business with a calm efficiency. He had never been known to lose his temper. Tall, thin, sybaritic, he had pale blue eyes, a sharp beak-like nose and a clean-cut David Niven moustache that sat comfortably over shapely, almost feminine lips. The effect was the perfect English gent; a caricature that was known to raise a titter of amusement behind his back and a controlled expression of disbelief to his face. But underneath the elderly Bertie Wooster veneer was a hard, sharp and calculating brain; that of a senior and resourceful agent of the British Secret Intelligence Service – MI6. St Clair Smith had nothing to prove. He'd done it all, and was ready to do it all over again.

He'd established himself in Malaysia in the early fifties when it was still colonial Malaya. There'd been a lot of his sort about then. They ran the police, the civil service; they were floor managers in Robinson's, whisky importers, bank managers and, of course, the army. St Clair Smith fitted in. He'd had an interesting war – his description – Grenadier Guardsman at Dunkirk and commissioned shortly after. He spoke French, not fluently but sufficient for those who spoke it even less to send him by submarine to the South of France to look at the Germans in occupation. He lasted quite a time, but it eventually ran out and the Germans picked him up, bashed him around and then lost their tempers with the local populace when they helped him escape. He was awarded the Military Cross for that and a free trip out to India. Force 136 beckoned and he was dropped into the Burmese hinterland to join up with the Kachin tribesmen in the hills who made a nuisance of themselves to the Japanese for the next three years. The powers that be gave him a bar to his MC and, when the guns cooled down, an invitation to join SIS. He rather fancied the idea of Whitehall and trips to shadowy capitals but it didn't quite work out like that. They'd got all they wanted of that sort – good schools, old regiments, generals' friends' cousins' chums who had nothing to do now that the shooting game was over. These were Whitehall warriors. There was no place among them for ex-Grenadier Guardsmen, even if they'd had a good war and done well. And, of course, the name didn't help very much. But there was Empire, and somewhere out there was always a place for a man used to mud and loneliness.

'We need a man to dig himself in in Kuala Lumpur – that's in Malaya, you know . . .'

And why not? Smith sent himself to a red-brick university somewhere in the north of England as a mature student in engineering and in record time sat for his AMI mech. E, got it with flying colours, changed his name to St Clair Smith, and with meagre financing from the SIS accountants set up his business, and cover, as a civil engineer and structural consultant in Kuala Lumpur.

That was a long time ago. He served his masters at MI6

well and his business, by his own efforts, prospered. In 1970 he gave his company away and retired with Malaysian citizenship. He watched his p's and q's and paid his taxes and dues and bribes without argument. He was the perfect expatriate. And the perfect undercover agent.

A large but sparsely furnished colonial-style house overlooking one of the many new golf courses sprouting up like mushrooms around the once-wooded suburbs of Kuala Lumpur was Aubrey St Clair Smith's main base. To satisfy his love of the spectacular, and to justify his freedom of movement, he bought a sixty-eight-foot English-built trimaran and had it modified to his own specification. Renamed the *Claudia* after one of the great loves of his life, she cruised happily at seven to eight knots on a Perkins 4.236 82hp diesel. She had the lot. And a lot of things she shouldn't have had, among them a 400-watt SSB radio, a thirty-six-mile Furuno radar and a VHF transceiver. He had every sail known to man but rarely used them; he felt very much at home with the dull throbbing of an engine under his feet. Those who would keep track of his movements would find him, as the monsoon seasons dictated, in either the South China Sea or north of Malaysia in the Andaman waters off Thailand.

The sun poked its nose over the brow of the sixth fairway and peered into Aubrey St Clair Smith's bedroom as it did every morning punctually at ten past seven. Smith was already up and sitting on his verandah overlooking the approach to the sixth green. Everything was lush, deserted and, except for the occasional high-pitched complaint from a small gang of gibbons relegated from all that was left of the expansive jungle of their forebears – a patch of untouched rainforest behind his house – the peace and quiet for St Clair Smith was total. If the arrival, at very short notice, of MI6's Senior Liaison Officer from the fleshpots of Singapore disturbed his routine, he didn't show it.

Wearing an eye-dazzling batik kimono and a bedraggled, wide-brimmed straw hat, he sat under the awning of the bungalow, sideways on from the rising sun, and sipped pleasurably from the long, slim glass in his hand. The SLO

91

preferred tea – weak and sweet. He didn't look half as comfortable as Aubrey St Clair Smith. But he wasted no time in getting down to business. No shilly-shallying, no social chit-chat.

'What do you know about a bloke called Logan working out of Bangkok?'

'James Logan?'

'That's the one.'

'Yank. Does a good line in boat engines and motors. Well connected. Plenty of money. Good guy, by all accounts.'

'D'you know him personally?'

'I've met him.'

'Could you meet him again?'

'That wouldn't be a problem. Why?'

The SLO told him. And when Aubrey St Clair Smith stopped thinking and reached for the bottle of chilled fizzy stuff and refilled his glass, their eyes met. St Clair Smith's were blank but thoughtful; the SLO's were tired and hot with little globules of warm sweat tricking over his eyelids and, in an orderly queue, rolling down his cheeks. He interrupted the procession with an absent wipe of his forefinger – a good, long, clean, refined, bureaucratic finger. 'Is he a bachelor?'

St Clair Smith smiled casually. 'You mean is he gay? No. Forget that approach, it's out of date . . .'

'He's married?'

'He was – to a Thai Chinese girl. Very pretty girl, most attractive. One child, a daughter, even prettier than Mum was.'

'Was?'

'Someone tried to slot him back in 1968 and killed her instead. It was accepted at the time that he'd been marked by a group of Vietnamese for punishment in retaliation for Johnson's unleashing the American Air Force on Hanoi—'

'Why? Was he involved?'

'Only to the extent that he was a high-profile American in the Far East and anybody fitting that description at the time was in line for problems – still is, come to that. He went in for very serious precautionary measures thereafter. Ordinary mortals can't get anywhere near him. Even after

92

seven years you still need a very high set of credentials and testimonials to rub shoulders with him.'

'You can do that?'

'Sure. But tell me, it doesn't sound quite right that the Americans would willingly call us in to help out in what is, after all, their area of influence. We carry no weight; we carry nothing in Thailand. You said the Drugs Enforcement character wants Logan laid out and filleted. OK. But how is that going to improve their track record of controlling the importation of narcotics into the United States?'

'They have to start somewhere.'

'They started a long time ago. The DEA has been sniffing heroin, if you'll pardon the expression, for a couple of years now. There were a couple of people died a short time ago – Americans, male, fit, healthy, young. Crashed their motor car, would you believe? Killed outright. What do you think they were looking for in Bangkok?'

'James Logan?'

'I've no idea. But even if they were it wouldn't have got them anywhere. If Logan's involved he should be left where he is and watched. If they had tried to do something silly and taken him into a back-alley garage for a chat, all he could have done for them was confirm that a bloody great mountain of opium is moving regularly from Burma, under military supervision, after being brokered in Thailand – specifically Bangkok. Logan, if he's involved, will be a very small cog. He won't be the guy conducting the orchestra.'

'What are you getting at?'

'I'd have thought it speaks for itself. The Americans have found that large sums of dirty money are being shipped from the US to London. They've known it for a long time. The Yard knows it, Special Branch knows it, and MI5 knows it. You didn't need the Yanks to tell you that. What you haven't said is what Jack Hargreaves was doing there and what part the CIA's playing in this.'

'They're just holding a watching brief. They say they've got enough on their hands out here without trying to do the DEA's work as well. According to Hargreaves, they've invested all their resources in Vietnam. They feel their backs are up against the wall and they haven't got time to piss around with piddling things like opium shipments. Maybe when things are over and dusted down in Saigon and Cambodia and Laos, and Christ knows where else they'll help out in the drug wars. But until then, like the man said, not interested. But they'll help us if we get in too deep and start feeling the pinch.'

'Still not good enough.'

'OK, then, I agree with you. I've got a feeling, just a little one, a twinge, maybe, about Hargreaves's compliance in the CIA plucking second fiddle to the DEA. It's not like them, and it's certainly not like him. I think Hargreaves has got more to do with this than he shows. If it's straightforward and the DEA are making a ground plan of narcotic and finance movements between here, the US, London and the clean stuff arriving back here in Asia, then the CIA have no position. I'm surprised an Intelligence bloke like Hargreaves is trying to pull something out of it. I think it's something deeper. I think the CIA are using the DEA, and through the DEA, us. We're being taken for a bunch of pillocks.'

'Well, you and yours went along with Hargreaves's wishes. So did Tony Cobbold, and he didn't fall out of the tree yesterday. D'you want to know what I think?'

'Yes.' The SLO listened carefully.

'The Americans have got a very hot operator out here. They've had him on the go for years. It's said that this fellow, and no one knows what sort of fellow he is – Chinese, Yank, Frog, Aussie, anyone's guess – is running one of the deepest infiltration jobs ever known to the game. He's protected. Christ knows by whom or what. Certainly not the Americans themselves, although, as it's told, they enjoy exclusive rights.'

'How d'you know all this? And why haven't I heard about it before?'

'I know all this, old boy, because it's my business to know. I live out here and over the years I've learned to put two and two together. The fact that it usually comes out at five is neither here nor there. Let me tell you a little something . . .' He broke the contact with another brief, absent-minded sip from his glass. 'Just off the Thai coast is a scruffy little shit house of an island called Phuket. Just north of the main town, if you can call it that, is a small, naturally protected bay called Chalong, and Chalong is the rendezvous for every boat-owner who sails this part of the world. Sailing around these countries and islands is not only the most convenient but also the easiest way of running intelligence-gathering units. Everyone goes there, ostensibly to clean the barnacles off their boat's hull, or fix a new aerial to their concealed VHF, repair or change engines, or just drop off dhobi and have a bowl or two of freshly made *thom-yum* and a couple of reasonably cold beers. And if you anchor or moor there long enough someone will have to come aboard and let you know what he thinks about things. You can pin it together if you like. The Yanks have a big man and it's hinted that he could also be big in Bangkok. You've heard of Cong An Bo?'

'Nope – I'm the new boy on the block.'

'A nasty bunch. But don't worry, they probably haven't got Singapore on their visiting list – yet. Cong An Bo is the Vietcong's personal intelligence service, and they've got enough on their hands at the moment not to bother you. Nothing to do with North Vietnam, who've got their own stuff. But these Vietcong are the dangerous bastards and they're after this American. They've got a team in the field and they want him. If they get him they'll take him back somewhere and grind out of him everything he's told his control since he started. Not only that. He's supposed to have infiltrated, and placed plants in, every major military and government administration in the Far East. That includes here – Kuala Lumpur. The man's a walking bomb to his sources and a living disaster to his dependants. Listen. The DEA want this man Logan to help them with their narcotics problems. OK. I go along with that. That's all they're interested in. But why is Hargreaves there? I'll tell you why Hargreaves is there. He's there because he's worried that the DEA, with the help of the old chums, might disturb the nest their man has built for himself . . .'

'You think this Logan is their big source?'

Aubrey St Clair Smith shrugged. 'Hargreaves is worried he might be. If we, urged by the DEA, bring Logan out into the open and he's what Hargreaves hopes he's not, then the poor bugger's going to have Cong An Bo cutting up lengths of rattan to make a basket for him; there'll be S021—'

'Who's that?'

'Nokorbol, Pol Pot's Khmer Rouge hatchet men. Pol Pot's about to move on Phnom Penh, and he'll take it. He knows about the American infiltration of Lon Nol's administration. When he walks into Phnom Penh he'll hang that poor bugger Nol from the rafters, then he'll want to go for all the people who helped Nol run Sihanouk out of the palace in 1970. He'd like this American gatherer of intelligence hanging from a hook on the shit-house wall and spewing out the names of these people, so S021 will be somewhere around waiting for him to be brought into the open.'

'So we can expect Hargreaves—'

'Not Hargreaves. Hargreaves is London – he's done his part of the job by getting us involved. He would have been instructed by someone big in Washington; that same someone big will be controlling things out here. Count on it – men in dark suits and button-down collars without the slightest tainting by principles will be homing in under guidance from Langley . . .'

'To protect their asset?'

'Hardly. They'll be coming to make sure they get to him before the rest of the vultures. That includes me—'

'What does Langley do if this man Logan turns out to be the CIA's star turn?'

'They'll have somebody standing by to kill him.'

'Why?'

'If any of these agencies that he's upset bring him out of the shadow all his suppliers of intelligence go up the spout. Those who are not actively affected will find themselves with new masters; those who are affected will get the bullet-in-the-back-of-the-head treatment. America loses, if not all, most of its high-grade intelligence. They could just do with a CIA wipeout in Vietnam at this minute, couldn't they? The bloody Vietcong, being shoved from behind by the North Vietnamese, are breathing down their necks and are getting the flags unfurled for flying over Saigon, and America suddenly finds it doesn't know what the bloody hell's going on. At the moment they do – and still they can't do a fucking thing about it. Just imagine having their eyes and ears plucked out just as the nasty man's bringing his foot back to deliver a full frontal into their bollocks. They've got to get out with some credit. And they can only do that if they know what's in the enemy's mind. You understand what I'm saying?'

'Can't they just pull him out of the way and put their own heavy mob in to take care of these killer squads?'

'You've missed the bloody point. The Americans don't know who their man is.'

'Oh, Jesus! How on earth did they get into that state?'

'You're in a glasshouse, mate. Be careful where you bung the bricks!'

'What's that in English?'

'I've got half a dozen blokes in different locations. I know them only by their code-names. If somebody wants to castrate me to get their names I'd just have to lie still and let them get on with it. I couldn't save myself. In that way I couldn't drop them in the shit. Understand now?'

'I thought that sort of thing only happened during the war.'

'What the fucking hell d'you think's going on now? It's a damn sight more intense than it was in '44.'

'Any idea what they call this American hotshot?'

'Contractor.'

'Well, it's a start, innit!'

Chapter 8

Bangkok, December 1974

While Aubrey St Clair Smith was sailing through the troubled waters between Penang and Langkawi Island, James Logan was fastening his seat belt and making himself comfortable in the first-class section of the Malaysian Airways flight from Kuala Lumpur to Bangkok. He sat back and relaxed and closed his eyes for a moment.

It was finished.

When the aircraft landed and he descended the wheeled stairs, he caught his breath and felt his feet sink into the soft, melting tarmac of Bangkok's Don Muang Airport. After more than twenty-five years of living in an unrelenting ninety degrees of temperature with the humidity of a bath-room sponge, it still hit him, after the relative cool of the aircraft, like a blast of raw heat from the opening of a furnace door. He loosened his tie at the neck, felt his shirt clam to his back and chest like a poultice, and walked the twenty yards to the waiting electric-driven bus. As the only first-class traveller, he sat in solitary splendour and read his newspaper until the other passengers had struggled down the steps to wait and sweat for the last man off the plane.

Don Muang was hot and untidy. He didn't hurry. That was what the highly perceptive, gaudy, military-uniformed and bemedalled airport staff were waiting for. A hurrying European was guaranteed to receive the cold eye and the peremptory jerk of the black oiled head, but Logan did nothing to draw attention to himself and moved easily across the vast expanse of shiny concourse.

His driver stood unobtrusively by the main exit point. He didn't call out or wave. He just stood there, solid, inscrutable, defying the ill-conceived impression of the idle, workshy, happy-go-lucky Malay. This was a hard man who'd been through a hard school; a tough killing soldier from the bloodletting fields of Thailand's gentle neighbour, Malaysia. Johari was a Malay exceptional. He'd shown the British SAS how to fight terrorists in the jungle until a burst of terrorist .303 smashed into his groin and stomach and took him out of the war. His friendship with Logan went back a long way. Johari was English-orientated. He'd done all his fighting and most of his living with Englishmen; but he found this American a very good substitute and the American accepted him as a friend and equal. Americans were like that. It didn't disturb Johari, who preferred the casual but deeply rooted discipline of the English. To him loyalty was not a commodity, it couldn't be bought. Johari was sparing with his – but, within a very short time, he gave it unstintingly to Logan. And Logan trusted him with his life. He didn't glance at the Malay as he walked past him to the car.

Johari remained where he was for another minute or two, studying the other passengers who filtered out of the airport's main entrance in Logan's wake. If he saw anything that troubled him he didn't say. As he slid behind the wheel of the big Mercedes, he met Logan's eyes in the rear-view mirror and gave the briefest of nods before starting the engine and slipping the gear into drive.

Logan had seen them too. They were good. They fitted into the surroundings as their friends had done in Kuala Lumpur. Not Thai, probably not Thai Chinese – probably not Chinese at all. Logan had slotted them as Vietnamese. He removed his lightweight jacket, sat back into the soft seat and allowed the fierce air-conditioner to do its work on his shirt. He met Johari's eyes once more and then allowed his eyelids to drop. But he wasn't sleeping; there'd be plenty of time for that when the crunch came. And that it was coming he had no doubt.

It was nothing tangible. A few seemingly unrelated incidents and an unerring instinct for the sniff of danger persuaded James Logan that he was coming to the end of his run; he was convinced that he'd not only been blown but severely compromised. Worse. He felt the chill of a pointer from his own people in Washington. No doubt about it, it was time to get out. His eyelids flickered as he resisted the temptation to open his eyes and turn round in his seat to study the road behind. He relaxed again and studied the back of Johari's short-cropped bullet-shaped head through his eyelashes. Dependable and reliable. Logan hoped so. He let his eyelids close, secure and relaxed in the knowledge that he had a dog who could both bark and bite.

The broad tyres of the gunmetal-grey Mercedes hissed on the hot concrete road and its powerful V-12 engine ignored all traffic regulations on its way into the centre of Bangkok. When you had important friends – particularly important friends – status, money and a big, powerful, new imported German car, regulations in Royal Thailand weren't for you. Logan had all this but it wasn't going to help when a hard-faced American with a sanction note from a Langley special projects committee sticking out of his top pocket came knocking at the door. Behind his closed eyes, Logan took a silent, deep breath. It had been a long run. Far longer than he'd had reason to expect.

He came out of his reverie when the car pulled smoothly into a side road and stopped.

'Americans,' grunted Johari without looking round. He had an instinct. He knew when Logan's mind had gone on a trip. He knew now that he was back.

'Say again.'

'The team at the airport looked Chinese but weren't local,' said Johari. 'Not Khmer, maybe Viets.' Johari met Logan's eyes in the rear-view mirror and gave a rare smile. Good teeth, even and white, and his face like a ten-year-old boy's – smooth and hairless – but his eyes were like two black diamonds. Those eyes had seen a lot, not much of it pretty, but the smile was real enough. Logan didn't smile back. Johari watched him for a moment then said, 'Whatever they were they were new.' He shrugged. 'It's getting crowded.'

'Are they still with us?'

'They're still trying to find their way back onto the highway at Chatuchak.'

'You said something about Americans?'

'Two, a woman and a man, in a grey Volvo; Thai number plates, woman driving. Left the airport before us but rejoined behind the Chinese at Bang Khen. They didn't get lost, not until just before I stopped – so they're professional . . .'

'How d'you know they're Americans?'

'I know.'

Logan knew better than to argue with Johari. If Johari said they were Americans, that's what they were.

'See what you can find out about them.'

Johari nodded and started the engine. No questions, no queries; Johari didn't need lengthy instructions – find out about a couple of Americans who are acting curious was sufficient. And that's exactly what he'd do. Logan had no fears about dirty play as far as Johari was concerned. If there was one man in Bangkok who knew how to take care of himself in any form of back-alley rough-house, Johari was that man.

Johari continued exploiting his knowledge of the city's back streets until he was certain he'd left his followers behind before gliding the Mercedes through the electronic guarded entrance of Logan's townhouse. Modest by rich man's standards, but with some of the best security features in the business, it was tucked down a small, neatly tree-lined road off Soi Ruam Rudi behind the select diplomatic enclave near Lumphini Park. A short while later, dressed in his going-to-mosque *seluar*, *sarong pendek*, *baju* and black velvet *songkok*, Johari left the compound in a small, middle-range Toyota. He looked like any one of ten thousand Thai Moslems moving about the streets of Bangkok on a Friday morning.

He drove with all the care and attention of a man who wanted no argument with the beautifully turned-out traffic police already collecting for the forthcoming Songkran Festival. They'd be out in strength today. He crossed the Chao Phraya river by the Taksin Bridge and then headed west through Khlong San. Traversing the busy Thanon Somdet

101

Phra Chao Taksin, he continued west into Thonburi, parked his car in a small street near the railway line, and made his way on foot to the imposing edifice of the Suanphlu mosque.

Suanphlu was more than a mosque. It was a meeting place of a like-minded group of men, men who'd formed a bond of friendship during the wars on Thailand's borders. Johari's friends, all senior military, police and civilian and military intelligence figures, had the common factor that drew men together. They had all seen fighting in various stages of intensity. Johari's nearest friend had, like himself, spent many years with his feet rotting in swamps and communist bullets hissing round his ears on the Malay/Thai border. They had formed a close bond of friendship. And friendship had obligations. When you wanted information about shadows who smoked Lucky Strike and chewed gum, you came to your friends and told them your problems. This was the strongest form of freemasonry – bonded with blood and love of a fellow warrior – and the fact that the fellow warrior was now deputy director of internal security, where one of his responsibilities was the upkeep of the register of foreign residents and visitors, and additions and deletions to the diplomatic establishment, was purely coincidental. Johari knew how to pick his friends.

General Damrong Kamprakorb held up his hand after Johari had explained his request. 'Johari, there are hundreds of Amis in Bangkok like these you describe. How can I pick out two such shadows and give them names?'

Johari looked his friend in the eye but said nothing. This was normal routine. Like a couple of comedians standing in the middle of an empty stage with no one in the auditorium to watch their act. The Thai's face clouded for a second and his eyes hardened. But only for a second. Then it cleared and his eyes opened wide and he burst into laughter. 'We are both crooks, old Johari. You, a Malay, and I, Thai, are Chinese crooks! But we love each other!' He became serious again. 'How do I trace your two Americans out of thousands?'

'Car number?'

'Possibility. What else?'

'Ask your brother the police commissioner.'

'You don't mind if I mention your name?'

'We're old friends.'

'Your Yankee friend, Logan, is attracting a lot of strange interest of late. We already have marked three of the Viets' Cong An Bo who are looking for him . . .'

'That's three, my friend, in addition to the earlier two who never came back from their fishing trip, makes five. A formidable team. I still need to thank you for that.'

'My dear Johari, you have no need to thank me for anything. Say the word when you want these three spoken to.'

'Not just yet. I want to see who they know. They're square heads; specialists at the take and run. They don't want to kill Logan, they want to take him. They're easy to watch if they're not on a killing spree. I shall be very happy if our friendship allows these people to be continually watched but not hindered.'

'Take it for granted. What about the other team, the dark men from Hanoi? Are they killing or watching?'

'Watching. They did all their killing when they destroyed Mrs Logan—'

'Ahhh! That was bad.' General Damrong Kamprakorb touched the back of his bald head in reverence at the memory of Logan's wife's murder. It was admitted, and agreed by those who knew these things, that the blowing up of Logan's car was not an error but a deliberate and successful assassination by a top team from Hanoi's allies in the South – the dreaded Cong An Bo, secret people who could teach Pol Pot a thing or two about method. It was broadly put out that Logan had been the target. Wrong. They knew what they were doing. The murder of Logan's wife, Yik Mun, was punishment. They'd blown Logan's cover, but they didn't want his life, not yet; it was his brain and memory they wanted, and when the time came they'd have them. But first must come the sufferering. They took away one of his most treasured possessions, his wife, and threatened the other. Logan's punishment was that he lived until they could find him and remove him to the bamboo cage that was waiting in the notorious punishment cells in Hai Douong prison, east of Hanoi. Following Yik Mun's murder, the 'mistake' theory was allowed to germinate. But

103

Logan knew, and Johari and his friends knew – and so did the Cong An Bo, who rarely made mistakes. This is why Johari and his friend wanted no action against the Vietnamese team; they could see them and they could watch them. Kidnapping was a much more difficult project than a straightforward murder. But Americans flitting in and out of Logan's screen was something else.

The following day Johari again met General Damrong Kamprakorb, who told him exactly who the Americans were and what they represented.

'What is DEA?' asked Johari.

'It's a Washington agency concerning itself solely with drugs, and in this instance opium, or when it gets there, heroin, morphine and its other forms. It is called the Drug Enforcement Administration and was formed at the end of last year to take over the CIA watch on the movement of merchandise. I'm informed that many of them are former members of the CIA. They are some of the best and I'm told their standard is of the highest. In addition, there exists in America a very large pool of hard men coming from the Vietnam battlefield. America is fortunate. They are going to need these men when their country begins to sink under the weight of imported narcotics. But that's not our problem at the moment, although everything is being taken seriously by us. Already meetings are taking place and there is ministerial discussion of official co-operation with this DEA.'

'It's going to be a problem?'

'In time it will become one. It is known that the Americans have been recruiting among our people and sending them into Burma on spying missions, a very dangerous business both militarily and politically. And the repercussions will fall upon us. But this DEA has no choice. A white face would stand no chance; there are many mounds of earth on the sides of the road leading to Ho Mong containing the remains of such people who thought they knew how. Most of them, to discourage others, were thrown into the hole as they lived and breathed. A salutary warning, my friend. There surely can be nothing worse than trying to suck air out of several feet of compressed earth.'

Johari clicked his teeth. There was no thought of horror in his action. Horror didn't come into it. It was the way of life, and when life went wrong feelings played no part in the disposal of a nuisance. 'So what about these two American faces? Do we know what they want with Mr Logan?'

'Oh, yes. They want evidence that he is involved in the marketing, the buying and the movement of heroin. Their masters in Washington believe that Logan is the spider and everything else in this interesting triangle is his web . . .'

'They're CIA?'

'No, they're what I told you they were, drug enforcement people, nothing to with the CIA – if anything, they are against the activities of the CIA in this region. There's no friendship there, Johari, and when you have no friendship you have no trust and no co-operation. By beating each other round the head to prove that one is better than the other they're allowing foreign elements in.'

Johari passed his friend a cigarette and the two men sucked noisily for a few moments before Johari asked what he should have asked in the first place. 'How is it they were happy to tell you these things?'

'They weren't.'

Johari sucked his teeth again.

'Will there be anything for Mr Logan to answer to?'

Damrong Kamprakorb tapped Johari's arm again. 'I don't think Mr Logan can in any way be answerable for two Yankees who, drunk, and not knowing their way among the treacherous roads of this country, drove their car off the road at Ayuttaya and burst into flames.'

'They died?'

'Sadly. The American ambassador has been informed and is very upset. The evidence submitted to him by my department indicated that this man and woman came into the country under false identities. The ambassador has been advised that they might be involved in illicit drug dealing. He's apologised to the Minister of the Interior.'

'At what stage did you learn of their true activity?'

'That's not a good question. Perhaps it might be suggested to Mr Logan that he wastes no time in contacting his friend Liu Zhoushiu to tell him of this development. In the meantime I shall continue to take great interest in the comings and goings of healthy-looking young Americans visiting our Bangkok sights – certainly for the foreseeable future . . .' He stopped and met his friend Johari's eyes and smiled. It was a deep, genuine smile. 'But I'm not sure how many nice motor cars we can afford to roll over the clifftops before people start noticing things!'

Jim Logan and Johari sat in the shaded garden and smoked a cigarette; Logan drank a large glass of whisky; Johari sipped iced mango juice through a plastic straw as he told Logan what he'd learnt from his friend at the Ministry of Internal Security.

Logan listened impassively. When he'd finished, Johari sat back in his chair and studied Logan's face. He offered no suggestions and no comment. The dry facts were enough. Logan lifted his glass and took a mouthful, holding it without swallowing then swirling it around his mouth meditatively. It helped the thought process. He was, and always had been, aware that he would eventually attract the usual hunting teams from the different sources in the area; he was not flattered to be now a name in his own country's list of drug marketeers. By the sound of it the DEA were serious operators; one indiscreet move and they could upset the whole delicate balance that had kept the Contractor project in place for so many years and the US Government with the most effective intelligence-gathering apparatus in the Far East. But now the ice under Logan's feet was paper thin. It was no more than a coating over a bottomless lake of intrigue. When it gave way there'd be no rush to help pull him out, unless . . . He forced his brain to go over the arrangements he'd just finalised in Malaysia. Where was the loophole? Had he covered everything? Had he missed some vital element? Was there enough tucked away to bring the firemen rushing to the broken ice to haul him out? Think, Logan! For Christ's sake, think!

It was all there. It had to be. The insurance policy. But, insurance or not, you trusted no one in this business; you took no one's word and you never turned your back on the man who had just held your hand in friendship; there was no friendship, there was only what's in it for me – and me was number one, first, last and always . . . And don't you ever forget it. He hadn't. Not from the first step into conspiracy with the upholders of his country's moral and physical wellbeing. The price had been right at the time. Would it always remain so? Not in Logan's thinking. One day it would end; one day somebody with more morals than those of an alleycat would take charge and rip the whole thing wide open. Logan didn't need to stretch his imagination to realise that this wasn't all that far off. Vietnam and its filthy bloody little war had given birth to conspiracy; Vietnam's final victory would put it all right again. But it would have to be goodbye James Logan; goodbye Contractor, you know too much; and goodbye Liu Zhoushiu and your free ticket to peddle dope across the United States.

He'd put it away as it happened. The insurance folder. The ground rules had been simple; nothing under Chinese management – Touming Guanxi was everywhere. It had to be near, but not as near as Don Muang . . . Singapore? Too Chinese. Hong Kong? Same. Bangkok? It was owned by Touming Guanxi. What did that leave? Kuala Lumpur. No chance of Logan's insurance policy going astray here.

He first established a residence in Malaysia. And, he decided, if he had to have a place in Malaysia, make it safe and make it cool. He bought a European ex-rubber planter's retreat in the fresh, invigorating air of the Cameron Highlands. This was a good reason for regular visits – less than one hour by air from Bangkok to Kuala Lumpur; he had a car garaged at a small workshop in Petaling Jaya and available at the flick of the airport telephone exchange. He had it all worked out. KL's traffic problem solved all his tail problems. He knew his movements were logged by Touming Guanxi from the minute he boarded the small Fokker Friendship at Don Muang until he stepped out of immigration and customs at Subang. And then *their* problems began. With a traffic build-up every mile it would have taken ten times the Touming Guanxi team to hold onto him. If anyone got that lucky they wouldn't last a traffic light in the centre of Kuala Lumpur, and by the time Logan arrived at the carpark near the Bank Bumiputra it would have taken a genius to stay the course. He could afford to relax in the vaults of the Malay-run bank. The nearest Chinaman, or any non-Malay, was four levels above him. His safety deposit box was combination and key, no second party. He could add to its content at his leisure, on his own, unwatched and unsupervised.

There was no need to leaf through the papers already there. He knew exactly what they meant; he knew what he was doing – he hoped. There was sufficient literary dynamite in the neat files in the box to destroy any hopes the CIA might have of wiping clean the Contractor slate without prior discussion with Contractor himself. The 290 Committee would realise that. Logan had pre-empted Graver and Reilly's thinking – or the other way round. He knew they dare not introduce a special projects operator into the game without first discussing what sort of back-up Contractor might have laid on. They'd expect to find exactly what he'd laid down – names, beginnings, progression and the role of the senior names in the Agency. These were all neatly and concisely listed; Contractor's own agents, under CIA coverage, throughout the Far East were named and detailed; compromised politicians; compromised military leaders; compromised intelligence organisation officers, operatives and controllers – they were all there.

Over the past few years he had converted the bulk of his liquid assets into the local gem, the highly negotiable Thai sapphire, along with as much cash as he could filter out of his legitimate dealings. All this he stashed in a separate, easier-to-get-at vault in the bank. In this separate box also went details of the administration, location and extent of the Thailand Tongs grip on the narcotics supply and distribution throughout the world, details of the known narcotics dealers in the Far East, the names and positions of people he had turned on behalf of Touming Guanxi's quest for a free-running swipe at the bottomless US narcotics pit. His haul included officials in Western government and military departments whom he had compromised and, as an added bonus for the backs-to-the-wall US planners in Saigon, a summary of the current South Vietnamese administration showing that nearly thirty per cent of the entire government were preparing to desert to the Vietcong at the first movement towards final US disinvolvement in the country.

But his plum document, he considered, was a list of the names of some twenty-five thousand Americans, among them Congressmen and government officials who had privately and secretly taken an anti-war stance and had worked hand in glove with the organisers of *Rampart* and other anti-war publications in a subversive attempt to bring an early retreat from the war. Logan, like the rest of his CIA and DIA colleagues, was well aware of the damage to future American morale these revelations would cause. Only he had a complete list and it was here, in his box of tricks in an untouchable box in an unreachable vault in an uncorruptible bank. Its compilers – the Central Committee for the withdrawal of US troops from Vietnam, a US organisation funded secretly by the Russian KGB to undermine the people's faith in the justice of their cause. It was the most secret document of the subversive war and revealed how successful *Rampart*'s campaign had been. This list of activists and moles had been passed to him through one of his agents within the North Vietnamese Intelligence Service. He had no doubt of its veracity and knew that both the CIA and the FBI would give their front teeth to run their eyes across this list of names. This was his bargaining chip for the final hand; there'd be no hiss from a suppressed .22 behind the ear while this document remained out of circulation, and there'd be a lot of blood being peed in Langley's executive washroom while they waited to hear that some silly bastard had shot him before getting him to unload the big stuff; or worse, that the goddamn Viets or one of the other Chink look-alikes hadn't picked him up to squeeze their own problems into the open and pick up this little bomb before they had time to neutralise the situation. But it didn't worry Logan what was going to happen in Langley; the only thing worrying him was what was going to happen in Bangkok and thereabouts over the next few weeks or so. According to Johari the signs were already there. It looked as though the eighteen-year-old bubble had burst; it appeared that he'd had a cross drawn on his forehead by his friends in Washington.

He stopped thinking. He'd had enough, and watched as Johari waggled the plastic straw about among the ice debris at the bottom of his glass searching for the last drop of tasteless watered-down juice. The gurgle as he sucked among the ice fragments sounded obscenely loud. It didn't concern Johari. He didn't even notice it, and neither would Logan have if he hadn't been so tense.

'D'you want to tell me how you found out about this DEA business, Johari?'

'No.'

'Any more of these people around?'

'Not yet. But there will be. You have nothing to worry about, though. Everything as far as you're concerned is covered. But are you disturbed by American interest?' Johari didn't wait for a reply. 'I can see you are. No man likes to be considered a subject for watching by his own people. Have you spoken to your "relations"?'

Logan didn't respond.

Chapter 9

'Contractor has become a liability,' said Liu Hongzhou, having allowed his father a full two minutes to digest the details of the opening up of the San Francisco pipeline, its local consequences and the results of the meeting of the 290 group of the Contractor Committee that had been deliberately leaked to him.

The younger Liu had none of the sentiments of men who had grown old together and had fought shadows in their nightmares. He was the new generation. There was nothing that had to be fought to be put in place, just the necessity to hold everything together that had so far been achieved. Liu would kill his brother if he threatened the existence of Touming Guanxi.

'A liability to whom?' asked Liu Zhoushiu sceptically.

'The Americans consider he's a liability to them, which means he's also a liability to us. They are worried about what he can tell. We should be too, I suppose, but I have no problems with liabilities – I unload them.'

Liu had been brought up in the States; with a good American education and a fertile brain, he'd made Phi Beta Kappa, UCLA, and went straight to the top table of Touming Guanxi with responsibility for narcotic exploitation in the United States. He was very American in his forthright manner. In Liu Hongzhou, American materialism and the philosophical fatalism of the Chinese made a formidable combination. He didn't have to work the gutter. He could

111

have been anything and gone to the top; the law, politics –
it was all at his fingertips. But his heritage gave him no
choice – that was made for him because he was his father's
son.

'You want to kill Contractor?' The elder Liu understood
American as well. 'Have you thought of the problems that
could bring down on your head?'

Hongzhou saw it differently. 'There's nothing left to worry
about once the lid of the coffin's securely nailed down. If
the Americans take him back to the States, as they want,
they will extract everything the man has in his head. He's
been inside the Tong – you want that known to the CIA?
The operation you and he and the Touming have been
running for the past twenty-five years, you want the nuts
and bolts of that laid before the CIA?' He didn't raise his
voice. He dared not. He kept his face as impassive as
his father's, his voice remained calm and reasonable; he
could have been a partner in a law firm outlining his tactics
on behalf of a client with a minor traffic problem. 'I have
made a deal,' he admitted after receiving no response from
the old man. 'I have made a deal with the American you
negotiated with in the first place.'

'Graver?'

Hongzhou nodded but didn't stop talking. 'We retain the
help of Graver's people until the Americans withdraw from
Vietnam. We keep our apparatus for military intelligence
matters intact on their behalf and they will remain non-
operative against our organisation in the States. I estimate
the Americans have a year left in Vietnam, probably less.
During this time we can intensify our organisation in the
States in such a manner that we won't need Graver's help.
But we do need that year.'

'Then what's your problem?'

'The problem, Father, is as I've just said – the Americans
want to replace Contractor. I don't want Touming Guanxi
and its arrangements with an American government agency
made the subject of Congressional, or any other, investigation, and that's what will happen if Contractor is taken
back to the States and decides to bargain with his own
people.'

112

'Do you not suppose the Americans are thinking along the same lines?'

'I don't follow you, Father.'

'Anybody can go along to the American Department of Justice and say I've just concluded a twenty-five-year-old arrangement with the CIA and these are the laws I've broken. The man who did that would be sent away for psychiatric treatment. But the man who contacted the same department and said "I have in my possession documented evidence of a large-scale conspiracy that I have been instrumental in carrying out on behalf the Central Intelligence Agency" would receive considerable attention. You agree?'

'Of course. But where is this getting us, Father? We're moving further away from the problem and into hypothesis. I want agreement to deal with Contractor – I want him taken out of the situation and I want it done immediately.'

'Want, want, want! You do not want, want, want with me.' Cutting words. But still no anger. A father chiding an eager son, his expression unchanged. 'Have you considered that Contractor would have such evidence as I have described? Do you not think that if his life was in danger he would use this evidence to bargain for that life?'

'Of course I do. But, Father, have you ever met a man who would die of most excruciating pain rather than tell his tormentor where he keeps such evidence?'

Liu Zhoushiu looked his son in the eye for several long moments. 'I know such a man.'

'Contractor?'

'Indeed. Your evidence will only surface if his life is taken. This is why you must keep him alive. The Americans do not think my way. They think yours. They will kill him and when his death becomes known a large packet of irrefutable evidence will arrive at one of the most responsible newspapers in the United States, either that or a reputable publisher, and copies will be sent to the US Department of Justice.'

'You think he could get away with that?'

'You think the man is a fool?' hissed the old man. 'The Drug Enforcement Administration has already sent people to look at Logan. That would have been sufficient warning even if, up until then, he had made no provision. I deliberately put the two together – the Drug Administration and Logan – not the CIA and Contractor. Two separate organisations with two separate ideas. The DEA would want him for connections they might have made between him and Touming Guanxi; the CIA, as you yourself say, want him because he knows too much about CIA business that doesn't conform to its mandate. If Contractor dies without revealing the extent, and location, of his insurance scheme, then everyone loses. Therefore, he must be kept alive, he must be protected from what you must consider as inevitable, a contract of killing against Contractor by the CIA and an attempt to run him down by the Drug Enforcement Administration. In addition to that you must consider the Cong An Bo teams from Vietnam who want to take him to Hanoi and the Nokorbal people—'

'We dealt with those. They don't send any more.'

Liu Zhoushiu shrugged this aside. This was small stuff. 'Just keep Contractor alive – and keep him here, in Bangkok. Don't let him run loose.'

'I'll do as you say, Father, but if your assessment is out in any sizeable degree I must insist that my method be given a chance.'

'You're a young man, Hongzhou. You may be clever but you are not wise. This comes with age. You've a long way to go yet. You want to hurt him. I know what's going through your mind, but remember, inflicting pain is a means to an end, not a means of pleasure. Don't forget Contractor is my friend.'

'You have no friends, Father – only family.'

'The cynicism of youth! Watch him, but don't hurt him. If he makes any attempt to leave Bangkok, stop him. That applies also to his daughter—' He stared hard at the paunchy young man. 'Don't let anything happen to his daughter.'

Liu Hongzhou made no reply or acknowledgement. There were no rules in this business, no safe passages; to achieve an end everyone was a participant. Theresa Logan had no immunity, not in Liu Hongzhou's agenda.

Chapter 10

Liu Hongzhou supplemented his normal team of watchers on Contractor with a specially selected crew of his own. Young, ambitious, anxious to please, they answered only to him. This was where their future lay – with the younger element of Touming Guanxi. The old men held their respect, the young man their loyalty and lives.

They were very good at their work, but it didn't take Contractor, or Johari, long to realise that a new element had moved in. Contractor had no doubts, either, that the increased watch was not a friendly one; not there for his safety, they were waiting there for him to make the wrong move. These people were in position as warders. He decided to try them out.

Instructing Johari to drive the Mercedes in a businesslike circuit of the city, he left his house by its bolthole, cut through to Soi Ruam Rudi and slipped in the vestry door of the Holy Redeemer Church. It was empty. He wouldn't be followed; both Chinese and Thai were far too polite to enter another man's area of religion. But if he had been followed they would have no need of entering; there were only two doors to watch. He sat in a back pew and went through the motions for ten minutes before moving down the aisle on his toes towards the altar. He gave a quick bow and crossed himself, just in case, and left by the same door he'd come through.

Nothing suspicious. No grey, hairless faces watching from

a distance; no car down on its springs with a full passenger load and a suggestion of movement through the smoked windscreen. It was a normal morning in the exclusive Pathumwan district. Hot, humid, sunny, quiet, and discreet. Without appearing evasive, he cut through to the Polo Club, ordered a cup of coffee on the verandah and called for a taxi. Still nothing. Nobody interested? He doubted it.

The taxi dropped him at the entrance to the international terminal at Don Muang Airport and, without looking behind or around, he made his way to the Thai Airways International ticket office. He went to the counter, then took a seat and waited. It wasn't long in coming. He'd been right. They were good. Very good. And he had spotted him, once, or thought he had. And then he was there standing above him.

'Sorry to trouble you, sir. Mr Liu would like to talk to you. I have a car waiting. If you don't mind, sir?'

No argument. He unwound his long frame from the low armchair, noted the other part of the foot team standing near the departure lounge, and followed his new Chinese friend out through the exit and into the carpark. There was no conversation; the report must have been made by telephone at the airport. Scrub the airport. From now on they'd have that covered at all times; Liu Hongzhou's young Turks in addition to the senior immigration, customs, and tax inspectors who were sure to be on income supplement from the Touming Guanxi.

There was no exchange of conversation between the two Chinese and the Thai driver until they turned into a modest, tree-shaded bungalow set back off the road and surrounded by a five-foot spiked-top wall. The only access was through a wrought-iron gate that operated on an electric motor activated from somewhere in the bungalow. Two other cars were outside the building. They had been manoeuvred to catch as much of the shade as was available and their drivers, stocky, serious-looking young Thais, squatted together, each with a cigarette smouldering lazily between his fingers, forgotten for the moment while they stared with interest at the new arrivals.

Contractor gazed out of the side window and met the

eyes of one of the squatting Thais. It was the briefest of meetings. The Thai broke contact immediately; there was a scent in the air of something that smelled of trouble, even danger, and he didn't want to know anything about it.

Contractor was greeted at the door by the younger Liu. An honoured guest. He didn't feel it. The expression on Hongzhou's face was far from welcoming; it was an expression that had been put there for those outside to see; a question of face, again – this time Contractor's face. He was going to get his backside spanked; he knew it, Liu knew it, and the men outside waiting to drive their masters home knew it – but for the time being Contractor's face was to remain intact.

He followed Liu down a corridor lined with clusters of miniature bells made of paper-thin terracotta. The passage of their bodies, causing the slightest movement of the air, set up a discordant tinkling which, by the sheer number of bells, sounded like a herd of cows wandering willy-nilly over a Swiss mountainside. It must have been hell to live with. At the end of the corridor was the bungalow's major room. It was much larger than it had at first looked, and sitting by the closed French window, a cigarette held pinched between his thumb and forefinger, sat the elder Liu. He didn't stand up. Nor did he turn to face Logan. He continued gazing at nothing through the large window.

'Hello, James.' He still didn't turn round. 'Some tea?'

The ritual. No response was required. Within a few seconds a tray of tea and three thimble-sized bowls were placed on the table beside the old man's chair, and the scalding-hot, weak liquid was poured. It had all the appearance of a gathering of three old friends. There were no explanations, no questions, just a quiet sipping or slurping of boiling-hot Chinese tea. The pleasant ritual lasted for five minutes or so. And then it began.

'Hongzhou says your life is in danger, Jim.'

Logan's gaze shifted to the young man. There was no friendship there, no amity. Logan had known him since he was a child; then he'd been a nasty-looking, pretentious little bully. He hadn't liked him then and the still-nasty-looking, pretentious little bully had done nothing since to make him

117

change his early impressions. The feelings were mutual. Hongzhou's eyes hooded over when they met those of Logan. Logan managed to keep the cynicism out of his voice. There was nothing to be gained by needling a man whose balls were itching with new-found power.

'Zhoushiu,' he said easily, 'my life's been in danger since 1941, so what's new?' He was addressing the old man but looking into the eyes of the young one. 'Has the boy gone into the insurance business?'

Hongzhou got fed up with locking eyes with Logan. He crossed his legs and raised his bowl to his lips and breathed across the top of it. 'What does that mean, Mr Logan?'

'It means you sound like an insurance collector getting ready to increase the premium on my life policy. Forget it. We're all in danger, son, some more than others – you're in danger, your father's in danger, all your friends are in danger, everyone who crosses the road's in danger. What's the sudden panic?'

'That's a good way of putting it, Mr Logan. But there's no sudden panic; this is a panic that's been building up ever since the Americans took an interest in the American businessman Mr James Logan; ever since they started sending Drug Enforcement Administration officers into Bangkok to find out what Mr Logan has to do with the narcotics business. Ever since—'

'Just a minute!' Logan stared hard at the side of the old man's head. Liu Zhoushiu seemed to be miles away; he could have been sitting on the back of a blue-and-white Chinese plate sipping his tea in a willow-patterned garden. Logan hadn't seen him for some time. He seemed to have faded. Where was the warlord Liu Zhoushiu? The young man bit his sentence in half. Logan didn't give him a chance to start again. 'Have you retired, Liu Zhoushiu? Why is this boy doing all the talking? Is he showing us how well he's picked up an American accent or does he really have anything to say about our business – yours and mine?'

'Tell him, Father.' The young man took it all in his stride. Logan felt a chill near the base of his spine; the lead dog was lying on his side exhausted and the young pup was shrugging into the harness. This was when the trouble

118

usually started, when the balls of power began to itch and the old were elbowed into the dying rooms.

'Tell me what?'

'Jim.' The grey head finally turned and faced the two men. Liu placed his little bowl gently on the ornately etched brass tray and looked up into Logan's eyes. 'Hongzhou is in charge of all American operations. This means that all the arrangements and deals you and I made are now in his hands and there is some very disturbing news coming from over there. Give the boy a chance. Let him speak. He has your welfare at heart as well as mine and the Tongs'. He is his father's son; he won't let anyone down.'

Logan's gaze slid back to the young man. He didn't have to look too deeply. This inscrutable Chinaman wasn't being as inscrutable as his culture dictated – he was allowing his triumph to show. It was brief, it was fleeting, but it was there in his eyes.

'May I continue, Mr Logan?' Always respectful. But he didn't wait for permission. 'Four US drug people have been killed here in Thailand. Two of them, a week ago, died on our doorstep in Bangkok. These people, Mr Logan, US Government agents, were investigating you. You knew about that?'

Logan nodded. These two Chinamen had just made his decision for him. It was time to go. Time to get lost. But not time to show impatience. 'People, Hongzhou, have been trying to find out what I'm all about for twenty-five years. I know the tricks. I was running with my head up my ass when you were being dropped off at kindergarten by your governess . . .'

'Of course you were. But during that period how many American agents have you counted dogging your footsteps, with your name at the top of their list and a mandate to take you back to the States?'

He'd got him. Logan knew the cunning little bastard had got him. But, just a minute, who were they talking about here – James Logan, marine engineer, or Contractor? He held Hongzhou's gaze steadily. 'You're talking about anti-narcotic agency people. The arrangement I have with your father and the Touming Guanxi is another matter, a personal matter that is between just him and me. Opium distribution is not the bedrock of our agreement—'

'Oh, but it is. The agreement you made with Mr Robert Graver and the CIA—'

'Jesus Christ!' Logan swung round in his chair and hissed at the old man. 'You've told him *everything*?'

Liu nodded expressionlessly. 'Jim Logan, this is my son. Why should I have secrets from him? He is my successor. How can he succeed me if I have secrets of our business that I keep from him? I trust him, so therefore you must. Listen to him.'

'Fuck it!' Logan wasn't in the mood. For the first time since he'd set up business in the Far East, a third party was there with a ready finger to point him out. Contractor could only survive with anonymity. Liu Zhoushiu had thrown that away. And he trusted this sneaky little bastard with the American accent as far as he could throw him. He shook his head and stared out of the window.

Hongzhou went on comfortably, 'Graver wants you killed. Not you, James Logan, but you, Contractor. He thinks, and he's probably right, that you know enough to blow the CIA sky high. He thinks you are the only man who could expose the deal that he and my father made in 1957. Nobody in the American administration would want to talk to Liu Zhoushiu, grand master of the Touming Guanxi, or take notice of anything he said. And, of course' – the young man almost smiled, but his teeth didn't show – 'there is no question of that ever happening. But Contractor? An American agent of the CIA in position in the Far East since the end of the Second World War? Now, *he* would be listened to, and imagine how Graver would react as Director of Central Intelligence when Contractor turned out to be James Logan and had all the documentation to support his allegation that such a deal had taken place?'

Logan knew exactly how Graver would react. He'd spent time with him in Kuala Lumpur in '57. He'd read the little man's tea leaves. He was a hard bastard under those choirboy spectacles. He'd do exactly what had to be done. 'Has he made arrangements?' said Logan.

'Graver? Yes, but I don't know what. I would say there

is at least one specialist here and another in reserve. Not more than one at a time. They would get in each other's way, and if one falls so does the other. One man, is my guess. That's the Contractor side of it. You going to run?'

'I don't think that comes into it.' Logan tried to sound convincing, but didn't, not even to himself. The elder Liu was sufficiently interested to pour himself more tea and watch him. There was a rapt expression on his grizzled old face. 'How did the name Contractor surface in Washington' – Logan locked onto Hongzhou's eyes – 'in your presence?'

'I was invited by Mr Graver to consider the intelligence-gathering facility that we have with the CIA through you. Uhuh!' He waggled his finger without moving his hand from where it was resting on his chubby thigh. 'Before you ask, the name James Logan wasn't mentioned in this context. Mr Graver feels that our agreement has not much longer to run. Apparently the co-operation of the CIA in return for an intelligence network in Vietnam, to name but one country, was jeopardised by an incident in San Francisco. It's a long story—'

'Tell me. I'm interested.' Logan was. It was always simple error, over-confidence, greed or just plain stupidity by a minor player that complicated well-laid plans and caused deep operations to founder. This one sounded a real dooly.

The young Liu looked at his father, who nodded, and related to Logan the events that led up to his being invited to discuss the future with Robert Graver. When he'd finished Logan shook his head. He was right. That a conspiracy, not to put too fine a point on it, could endure for the best part of a quarter of a century and fall flat on its face because a skinny blond guy waggled his tight little ass in front of a randy Chinaman! It was a pity he didn't feel like laughing.

He caught the elder Liu's eye. 'Sounds to me as if Graver's gone over the top on this one. Contractor hasn't been compromised and James Logan is only a shot in the dark by the DEA. What are they playing at, Zhoushiu?'

The old man was slow in coming forward, but Logan made no attempt to push him. Strange that the young thug was interested in his father's opinion as well. Perhaps he hadn't fully considered all the points. Although that was very doubtful. Here was a smart little bastard who'd need to cover every aspect before he even went off for a crap. Logan glanced at him out of the corner of his eye and got no reassurance from his expression.

'Frightened men do strange things,' said Liu, at length. 'I would feel that with the coming of your country's defeat in Vietnam the American people, who've never suffered the humiliation of coming second in a war, will want somewhere to place the blame. Graver is afraid that in the explosion of recrimination the CIA will be exposed to more than intense scrutiny. There are many things they can explain that were done for the good of their country and would be accepted. Patriotism is a thing that can be stretched in any direction; Graver's the sort of man who would know how to do the stretching, but you cannot stretch the deal he made with us into patriotism. What he did, and what I did, was, according to your constitution, not only illegal, but immoral. Its disclosure would result in a total closing down of the one organisation that your country will need in its hour of recrimination.' He paused and dampened his mouth with an almost infinitesimal sip of the cooling tea. Neither of the other men interrupted. He replaced the little cup and breathed heavily. 'Defeat does more than humiliate, it exposes the soul of the defeated people. There are in your country, as in any other, people who are waiting to exploit this . . .' He stopped again.

'Communists?' suggested Logan.

'More likely Americans who would never gain the people's support for their own attempt at government. But communists too – you must never discount the communists, even when they are tapping their little glasses of wine against yours and swearing undying love.'

'As if that's ever likely.'

'Jim, none of us is gifted with foresight. But when I said Graver and I were guilty men, I should have added you as well. Put all three of us together and work out who is the most vulnerable; the one least culpable and the one who has the least to lose?'

Logan didn't have to turn his head to feel the broad smile that illuminated the younger Liu's face. Its glow burned the side of his face. He looked directly into his old friend's eyes. 'Tell me, Zhoushiu.'

Young Liu had worked it out. So had Logan, but he wanted his friend to pronounce the death sentence.

'You, Jim. You are all three.'

'And I have the least to lose?'

'You lose only your life.'

Logan half turned. He expected to see the other Liu on his feet with a long, silenced barrel pointed at the back of his head. Liu had just pronounced the end of their friendship; he'd stopped short of issuing a death sentence, but there was a promissory note in there somewhere. The young Liu stared at him blandly. He turned back. 'Whilst we're beating around the bush, Zhoushiu, isn't there a Chinese saying about it being possible for dead men to speak from the grave?'

'I don't think it's an old Chinese proverb, Mr Logan.' Young Liu had taken over the meeting again. He answered for his father. 'It sounds too theatrical for us. It's probably American. Hollywood, or Poe. Why don't you explain exactly what you mean?'

'I know what he means, son,' said Liu Zhoushiu sadly. 'I was inviting him to tell us.'

'Mr Logan?' prompted Liu.

'This dead man . . .' began Logan.

'Speak in the first person, Mr Logan,' interrupted young Liu, 'make it easier for us simple people to understand. Put yourself in this dead man's shoes.'

'OK. If I thought someone wanted to put a bag over my head I would take precautions . . .'

'My father has just put a bag over your head. Tell us about these precautions you have taken.'

'Sure.' Logan had begun to feel much more comfortable. The earlier fear-sweat around the base of his spine had dried and left a gentle, cool feeling. He thought he could see a pinprick of light. His voice, which had never cracked, now rasped with confidence. 'I've got a fairly thick envelope stashed away. In it is all that documentary evidence you mentioned earlier. It's not only the sort of stuff that would make Mr Graver take a turn for the worse; I've made it my

123

business to include the structure of the organisation you and I, old friend' – he offered the old man a weak smile – 'built up over the years. A number of very interesting names; names that would go straight to the wall in Hanoi, Saigon, Rangoon, Phnom Penh, and even here in Bangkok – want any more?'

'Go on,' pressed the young Liu.

'Then there's the, er, Family – the Silent Relations. Its structure, its leaders, its senior operators throughout the Far East and enough of the US structure to keep the FBI and DEA busy rounding up for the next five years. Enough?'

Logan paused long enough for the two Chinamen to exchange glances, then added, as an afterthought, 'There's a bit for Graver as well.'

'Such as?'

'Domestic stuff. I don't think you'll be interested.' Logan shook his head mockingly at the young man. 'Jesus, Hongzhou! Haven't you got enough there to chew over without helping yourself to some of Robert Graver's domestic titbits?'

Hongzhou wasn't going to allow himself to be riled. He glanced at his father again and received back an expression that said 'I told you so – you thought the man was a fool!' But Hongzhou hadn't finished with Logan. As far as he was concerned, Logan had just started the round of betting. 'Where is this envelope?'

'Is he kidding, Zhoushiu?'

The old man shook his head. 'No, Jim. He's giving you the chance to save yourself a lot of pain. He'll pull it out of you tooth by tooth, finger by finger. You know him. You've watched him grow up. He enjoys inflicting pain; he doesn't want you to tell him, he wants you to dribble it out of an empty mouth like a skinned monkey. Tell him what he wants to know.'

'Well, now,' said Logan comfortably, 'I'll tell you what – I'll tell you what's going to happen while you're skinning this monkey and pulling its teeth out. First, the person who's looking after the packet needs regular verbal reassurance from me that I'm still alive.'

'That can be taken care of.'

'Don't you believe it, sonny. Your imagination is running ahead of you. You can see me spitting blood down a telephone telling my contact that all is well? You know whether I'm using the right words? What d'you think I am, you crummy little bastard? I've been doing this sort of thing all my life. D'you think I'd leave a gap that wide? Oh – and I forgot to mention, the envelope is addressed to the editor, the *Washington Post*. I guarantee he's not one of your brethren, and you try bribing him! You still think that can be taken care of?'

'I'm prepared to give it a go.'

'You mean you're prepared to gamble. Ask your father whether he is.'

'Not necessary. I'll ask you once more . . .'

'Fuck off!'

'Have you considered Theresa's welfare?' The old man thought he held the really big card. He knew it was a dud the minute he said it. Logan's eyes told him so. He ought to have known better than to try one like this on a man he'd known for the best part of thirty years.

'Of course I have,' replied Logan, easily. 'Before I started considering my own. One sideways glance at her from Hongie here, and no questions, no arguments, no delays, the envelope's on its way to Washington. You can chop my fingers off on that one. I promise it.'

'I accept that, Jim. But I think the gamble will have to be taken. You might think you can hold out. You won't. Take that advice from an old friend.'

'And there's one more thing—' Logan reached carefully into the top pocket of his shirt. 'This—' He held his fist out to the old man, then opened it. Nothing dramatic; he could have been reaching out to shake hands. Liu stood up and stood at his shoulder and studied what looked like a foil-wrapped toffee in his open palm; the old man leaned forward.

'What's that?'

'It's for you. Send it to your friend in the lab and ask him to analyse it for you.'

'What is it?' The old man unwrapped the paper and held the small capsule between his finger and thumb. He brought

125

it to his nose and sniffed then, without a change of expression, held it up and showed it Liu Hongzhou.

'You asking me, Father?'

'No – I'm asking you, Jim.'

In reply Logan tilted his head, opened his mouth and with his forefinger tapped one of the back molars. 'The same thing is in that.' The words were distorted by his finger but understandable. 'A light covering, but I can break it quicker than you can blink. What is it? I don't know what name your guy in the lab'll give it, but the one I've got is a ricin-based problem solver.' He clamped his jaw shut. 'Forty micrograms. Takes about ten seconds – stone dead. It's brand new, no antidote.' He turned his head and looked the young Liu in the eye. 'You try pulling me about, sonny, and before you even start getting a hard-on you have a dead man on your hands. No pain. Better than a bullet in the head. Fancy that with all its consequences?'

'I think he's bluffing, Father.'

'Then see me,' said Logan.

Liu Zhoushiu stared hard into Logan's face. 'He's not bluffing,' he decided. 'Jim, I think you and I had better talk privately about this, two old friends solving a problem over a glass of good brandy. OK?'

'And the boy?'

The two Chinese exchanged glances. There were no words, no arguments, no recrimination. The younger Liu understood that they'd been pushed up a cul-de-sac and accepted his father's intercession. His time would come later. But he had one more contribution to make. He made it standing up. 'Why were you running for the airport, Mr Logan?'

Logan didn't turn round in his chair. 'Curiosity, Hongzhou. It seemed a good idea at the time. I wanted to see why so many people were interested in my movements, and exactly who. I wondered about my friend Zhoushiu. You've confirmed my wondering. Your people were quite good, but just not good enough. You'd better go and break a finger or two for shoddy work.'

'I would like to see the ticket you bought at the airport.'

'No ticket. But you can see this timetable for next term's TAI flights to Europe.'

'Very clever, Mr Logan. I think you were doing a dry run. Don't try a real one' – the chubby Chinaman smiled mirthlessly – 'because you'll need luck to make it and I hope you remain lucky for many years to come – but I doubt it. Goodbye, Mr Logan. We'll meet again.'

The old man waited until his son had left the room before he turned to Logan and said, 'That wasn't very clever, Jim. You shouldn't rile him, he's a very dangerous man, and a dangerous man makes a very bad enemy. Now come over here and let's talk about this problem you've got . . . By the way – that thing about your tooth? You were bluffing?'

Logan's face remained impassive. 'There's only one way to find out.'

'Then we'll forget it.' Liu gave a rare smile and showed that he still had all his teeth, white, crisp and clean. 'Be careful how you eat the crackling of your suckling pig! Right, to business. I'm a simple man. I believe everything you say. But I can't condemn you for it. I would have done the same thing myself.' He looked at Logan seriously. 'I warned him. I warned him you would cover yourself and he under-estimated you. Young people can't see as far ahead as we old can. So, it now remains to make a few rules. You have ideas where you want to go from here?'

'Let's hear yours first.'

Liu didn't hesitate. He sounded as if he'd had it worked out all along. He probably had – since 1957. 'We can keep you alive for a year. After that you're looking after your own destiny. You must not leave Thailand and you must not go out of Bangkok without letting me know. That way we can keep you covered. This applies also to Theresa. Listen well to what Hongzhou told you. The Americans have a top specialist in the field to expose you and then eliminate you. You will probably not have time to tell him of your security plans and your little tooth thing won't be needed.' He stopped and tilted his head. 'You have sufficient money?'

'For what?'

'Ah – you're thinking of buying your life? Oh, no, nothing like that; there's not enough money in the coffers to buy your life once the year's up. I mean ordinary money; money to enjoy the last year of your life.'

'Your concern is very touching, Zhoushiu.'

'But you have lost confidence in me? I feel it, Jim. There's a certain coldness between us. Understandable.' He allowed his smooth features to crinkle into a quizzical expression. 'But, of course, I was forgetting – you've been converting money, haven't you? You've been turning your liquid assets into stones – and you don't look surprised that I know? You must have been very confident, Jim.'

'Sure. Well, we've sorted out my financial affairs and you've arranged my domestic routine. I'm cutting out from middleman. You make your own arrangements with Graver from now on. He's given you a year, has he, before he turns the tap off in the States? D'you trust him?'

'I trust no one – you should know that, Jim. I have my contingencies. In less than a year Touming Guanxi in America will have no need of Graver or his CIA, and by the same token he will have no need of us. We can go back to being natural – natural enemies of the Americans in general and the CIA in particular. That's how it will be. But you'll be dead, Jim, your little packet of papers and disclosures will be outdated and worthless – as will be your life. Sadly, because I have enjoyed our friendship. Now unfortunately it has come to an end. Always a sad thing, Jim, when two old friends say goodbye. I shall not see you again, but you will be well looked after. Don't look for Hongzhou's people, just let them be there. You won't notice them. Keep your vigilance for your own kind; they are the ones who are a danger to you. Beware a friendly American. That is my last advice to you. Goodbye, Jim Logan.'

Liu didn't stand up. There was no handshake, no touching, no regret in his dark, almond eyes. He just turned his head away from the American and with that simple gesture ended twenty-eight years of association and friendship.

Chapter 11

Four days after slipping his mooring at the Klang Club, just outside Kuala Lumpur, Aubrey St Clair Smith rounded the island of Ko Lone and steered *Claudia* into Chalong Bay on the eastern edge of Phuket island. Nothing unusual. *Claudia* was well known in these waters. Almost as well known as her eccentric owner.

St Clair Smith picked up his regular mooring and, half an hour after his arrival, he was dropped off at Pan's Lighthouse by his Malay crewman, Junit. Over a well-diluted Gordon's and Indian tonic, he used the Lighthouse's transceiver to contact Ban Yit, a small, decrepit, inlet across the water on the far side of Chalong Bay.

The Lighthouse bar was packed. The usual. Unshaven, unwashed, scruffy, noisy, drunk yachtees doing the oriental Hemingway bit – writing their book from life. But none of them ever did. They got to like the missing civilization, where no one seemed to care about anything except drinking as much cheap beer as the day, and night, would allow them until they ran out of money and had to look for some gullible tourist to hire their boat and to listen to their life story, until they got enough money to get back to the Lighthouse and start all over again. A sprinkling of Australians, but most of the real characters were Americans. They'd all done 'Green Berets' in Vietnam, so they said, and, with conspiratorial winks down the side of the bottle hanging out of their mouths, they were all on, you know what . . . can't

129

talk about it – but it begins with a big 'C' and ends in a big 'A'.

Aubrey St Clair Smith was for some strange reason treated with enormous respect by the regulars – drunk or sober. There was something under the swirling current about St Clair Smith that they couldn't quite fathom; if he'd been dirty and noisy and smelly and drunk they would have understood and spent a happy evening or two taking the piss out of him. But he wasn't, and they didn't. Even when, after two days and nights sailing, he would stroll, cleanly shaven, into the scruffy attap-roofed bar in his pristine trousers, straw hat with its Guards Club ribbons and navy blue shirt. And, as usual, it was disbelief from the newcomers and 'Hiya, Auby, old boy, have a drink!' from the regular bums. And that was the way he liked it. Always polite, the eccentric Englishman, harmless in every respect.

Silence descended when he picked up the microphone of the radio transceiver, held down the transmit switch and, without preliminaries, began talking. 'Jack – it's St Clair Smith . . . Are you open for business?'

'Hiya, Smithy! Jack here – over.'

'Jack,' continued St Clair Smith, unruffled, 'I've got a little problem with the generator . . .'

'Bring her across, Smithy and I'll take a look. When're you coming? Over . . .'

'St Clair Smith still here.' Aubrey intoned his version of radio-speak. 'Right away, Jack – say, half an hour?'

'OK. I'll meet you in the bay and point out your mooring – see ya.'

There weren't many people who called Aubrey St Clair Smith, Smithy. Jack Krislov was one. But then Jack Krislov was an American negative version of Aubrey. An eccentric in his own right, he was everything Aubrey wasn't, and he didn't give a damn for man or beast. But he had a great affection for Aubrey, even if he didn't show it. Krislov was a chain-smoking, genuine ex-Marine Special Forces; genuine ex-capital 'C' working off his penalty points, not that he gave much more than a damn about it. Nothing about Jack Krislov showed that he was one of Sam Reilly's 'names in the book'. He ran his small marine mechanics workshop

130

in the tiny, deserted and scruffy bay opposite the more active Chalong. He dressed like a beach bum and was covered in skin cancer. He treated the cancer with a mixture of contempt and compressed Freon-12 blasted through a modified hypodermic needle. It delayed the process of death; he was going to be eaten up by it anyway and it was going to kill him eventually, but he didn't seem to care much either way. Taciturn and uncommunicative, he had no sense of humour. He was married to a Thai woman and spoke fluent Thai. His children, four of various ages, ran wild, except the eldest daughter who with her mother ran a sort of waterside restaurant accessible only to the yachtsmen approved by her husband. The food, Thai only, was very good, but the menu limited.

Behind the lean-to restaurant was Krislov's office. Any uninvited guest looking through the window would leave with the impression that it hadn't recovered from the battering it had received in the last heavy storm. His real office was in a derelict, beached Chinese junk which seemed to be slowly giving in to the flotsam-choked waters that lapped around its battered hull. Stacked on its deck, in profusion, were broken air-conditioners, dead diesel engines and an assortment of rusting marine bric-à-brac. Under this lot, in a concealed air-conditioned chamber, was the latest in the new computer technology, high-frequency radio links and high-speed cypher machines routed through another disguised floating wireless centre cruising in and out of the hongs that abound in the Andaman Sea.

Thai customs and police officials, if they ever took the trouble to come all the way from Phuket to Ban Yit, were treated openly and with courtesy and the odd bottle of duty-free whisky and cartons of smuggled cigarettes. They never bothered the yachtsmen in the bay.

'Heard you were coming up this way, Smithy,' said Krislov after they'd moored *Claudia* to her buoy out in the small bay. *Claudia* was one of St Clair Smith's minor indiscretions. She was the only trimaran in the vicinity; everything else in Ban Yit as well as the larger Chalong was single-hull yachts or cruisers. Sometimes a charter catamaran moored, but not often. His distinctive boat caused him a little discomfort.

131

But he managed to live with it. Here at Ban Yit she stood out like a flaming beacon.

'Where did you hear that, Jack?'

'Whispers, Smithy. A word here, a word there. Enjoy Langkawi?'

Aubrey took it all in his stride. It was Krislov's way of telling him he was on the network; he was being logged, but torn fingernails and burning matchsticks wouldn't make him give any more. He might like Smithy, he might even respect him, but he was still a limey and he was still suspect. Langley had said so, several times in the past, but no one had seriously marked his card – a 'possibility of involvement' was as far as anyone would go.

'Any new faces around?' asked St Clair Smith. This was the way the game was played – a bit of innuendo, a bit of this, a bit of that. Someone asked a simple question; it was never replied to but it showed each knew what the other's business was and they'd tell you if they thought you ought to know.

'Don't think so. Cobber came in day before yesterday. Picked up a crate of Mekong and fucked off again – Christ knows where, and nobody gives a fuck anyway!'

'Anyone else?'

'The Kraut with a couple of chorus girls as crew. Then there's Dixie. He thinks he's got a nasty packet, could be worse than that. Whatever he's got he's got it bad. Looks like death and is pumping himself full of something or other in the hope it'll go away. Spends a lot of time on the air.'

'Who with?'

'Anybody who'll listen. His people have disowned him. Too unreliable, likely to shoot his mouth off in the wrong direction.'

'Anyone from his part of the world to look after him?'

'Nah. Those bloody Aussies're as hard as concrete. If a bloke falls by the wayside the only thing they'll do is send someone to roll him into the ditch. Give it a bit of time. But my advice, Smithy, avoid visiting him, it might be contagious!'

'Thanks, Jack. Got any gin?'

Krislov lit another cigarette from the butt of the one

he'd just finished, turned his head towards the back of the ramshackle open-fronted café and bellowed. An answering shriek came back in Thai from somewhere. He flicked the finished butt into the water that lapped below them and shook his head. 'No gin. D'you want a cold beer?'

'No thanks. It gives me reason to go into Phuket!'

'You need reasons?'

'It salves my conscience. Let me have a verdict on the auxiliary when you've looked at it. If I needed a new one, where would be the best place to look?'

'Not in Phuket. Price sky high and usually reconditioned – badly reconditioned. A wire or call to Logan's in Bangkok's the best bet.'

'Right. D'you know him?'

'Logan?'

St Clair Smith stared innocently into the grizzled American's face. There was nothing to see. But it was a good start.

'Nah – not my style, Smithy. Neither's Bangkok. D'you want me to try a contact there?'

'Have a look at the generator first – it might only need a washer!'

Krislov rubbed his bristly chin thoughtfully as he watched St Clair Smith's dinghy bend in and out of the few moored yachts, zoom past his own, the *Claudia*, and then open the throttle when he'd cleared the last buoy to head across the bay towards Chalong.

'Bring me a beer!' he bellowed over his shoulder, and grabbed the little half-naked girl who brought it and swung her up onto his shoulders. Allowing her to grip his hair and hang on like a little monkey, he trotted down to the derelict junk and, ignoring her screams, dumped her into the warm clear water that lapped the white strip of gritty beach. That was her ration of fatherly love for the day. Swigging from the condensation-covered bottle, he picked his way across the debris on the deck of the hulk and made his way down into its bowels. It was cool. As he switched on the single bulb overhead the low hum of air-conditioning rose abruptly, then resumed at a higher pace; the effect was almost instantaneous and the soundproofed cabin became as cold as a meat chiller. He pulled a switch on the main generator, sat back in the wicker chair and up-ended the cold bottle in his hand. He wiped his lips, rubbed his hands on his shorts and picked up the handset on the bench.

'C'm'in, Dixie,' he murmured.

'Oo dat?' Dixie sounded everything Krislov had said he was. His voice was weak, no substance, watery and painful. Whatever it was that was afflicting Dixie wasn't very nice.

'Jack K, Dixie. Take it easy, mate. Can you give me a blanket for a few minutes?'

'You've got it.'

Krislov eased in the switches of a small attachment to the large Edison VHF and touched the direction-finder. He switched on the main charge. The speaker let out a long unbroken howl. He moved the DF through the howl until it broke through into clean silence. He spoke evenly into the handset. He spoke openly. He know he couldn't be heard by anyone except the person he was addressing; Dixie had done his stuff, simple stuff to Dixie, highly complicated for anyone with a tracer. It was the Club.

'You wanted to know about anyone mentioning the name Logan out of context. Over—'

'Go on.'

'There's a limey guy, name of St Clair Smith, runs a sixty-foot-plus tri. Regular two-or-three-times-a-year guy. Well known around here. Sails out of a north Malayan club. Over—'

'Go on.'

'Asked if I knew Logan. We were talking about auxiliary motors. He said he might want a new one. That's how the name came up. Over—'

'Did he raise it, or did you? Did he press you on it? Did he make it personal?'

'Come to think of it, he didn't even mention the name – it was me. Negative on the other two. Over—'

'See ya. Thanks.'

Aubrey St Clair Smith booked his usual room in the Pearl Hotel in Phuket town. After a long cool bath, a tray of tea followed by a large whisky and iced water, he lay naked on the bed and allowed the overhead fan to cool his long, thin, pale body. Then the phone rang. He was expecting it.

'London, for you, Mr St Clair Smith.'

He waited a few seconds while the plug in the switchboard was pulled out then announced himself.

London sounded a bit tinny; a long way off, cold, gloomy and damp. 'Century House.'

'Aubrey St Clair Smith for the Director-General, please, darling. Are you well and enjoying life?' Her day was made.

'Thank you, Mr St Clair Smith. I'm very well – nice of you to ask. I'll put you through to Sir Edward.'

'Aubrey?' said a new voice.

'Hello, Teddy. I'd like to have dinner at the Bangkok embassy. Can you arrange it?'

'I'll have a word with Arthur. Anything special?'

'Well . . .' St Clair Smith paused for a moment to swallow a mouthful of whisky and water. The clink travelled.

'Cheers, Aubrey!' said Sir Edward.

'A bit too early for you, Ted. Our man in Bangkok?'

'Is this going to be bad news?'

'No. Just a little rearrangement of his social diary. I was thinking a sort of reception, a little collection of Bangkok expatriates and things and then dinner for, say, a couple of dozen. As soon as diplomatic niceties permit, please, Teddy, and I'd like to be sitting next to a Mr James Logan, who's an American businessman resident in Bangkok.'

'I've always admired people who know exactly what they want. I don't suppose there's any point in my asking for details.'

'None whatsoever, Teddy. It'll all end up on your desk in due course. Ask His Excellency to send my invitation care of the Pearl Hotel, Phuket. Goodbye, old chap.'

Chapter 12

Bangkok, January 1975

Detaching himself from conversation with the second secretary at the embassy reception, Aubrey St Clair Smith made a beeline for Logan's daughter.

Theresa Logan was guaranteed to attract him; he couldn't help himself, she was everything he found pleasing in life – female, beautiful, young, intelligent, alive and vivacious, and with a figure revealed in its perfection by an exclusively designed dress in a rich yellow Thai silk. He was hooked the moment he set eyes on her. That he was old enough to be her father and she was the daughter of his target was neither here nor there. For Aubrey St Clair Smith a woman was a woman. Age didn't come into it.

And James Logan watched the play, surreptitiously, as he listened to the goings-on in ambassadorial Bangkok from the pouting over-rouged lips of the Spanish commercial attaché's wife. She didn't mind. She could see she hadn't gripped Logan's balls tight enough to hold his complete attention, but she ploughed on regardless, puffing from an azure-blue-papered cocktail cigarette with a gold tip and mixing its ordinary-coloured smoke with a mouthful of Heidseck between every sixth word or so before swallowing it. She paused to take a smoked-salmon canapé from the Thai waitress. She bit the postage-stamp-sized titbit in half and popped it into the mixture already brewing in her mouth before following the direction of Logan's eyes. A quick glance was all she needed. She knew everybody and everything about them. Her eyes gleamed.

'You know that man?' she hissed.

'I think his name's Aubrey Smith, isn't it?'

'*St Clair* Smith. Lock up your daughter, James Logan.' The Spanish lady regained Logan's full attention. She considered a father's feelings for a fraction of a second then discarded them. 'He is – how do you say it? – not too much the gentleman with attractive young girls . . .' She turned her head and gave Theresa another sly glance. It was a glance of experience that took in everything. She corrected herself with a coy smile. ' . . . young women.'

'What does he do?' Logan had a good idea what Aubrey St Clair Smith did but it was never politic at embassy gatherings to display too much of what one knew, or thought, about visiting guests. Leave it up to Spanish women; they'd confirm, and elaborate, any wild guesses.

'He has a large yacht that enables him to go where he pleases. He lives in Malaysia. What he does—?' She shrugged her bare shoulders experimentally and exposed the frilly lacework at the top of her dress which just covered the nipples of her large breasts. She watched Logan inspect them for a moment then, gratified, returned to her subject. 'People whisper odd things, but personally . . .' She lowered her voice to a husky undertone and glanced conspiratorily to her right. ' . . . I think he puts these things around to make himself more interesting to the young women – I think he smuggles things. I wouldn't be surprised if he was in drugs.'

Logan held her eyes. 'Let's hope no one ever repeats it to him and says where they first heard it.'

Her eyes widened in horror. 'You wouldn't!'

Logan didn't let her off the hook. 'He's coming over to talk to you.'

She composed herself with another long drag from the coloured cigarette and a full tilt from the glass of Heidseck. She made her right hand available automatically for Aubrey St Clair Smith to touch to his lips, but before she could fully develop the seriously-available-mature-woman pose she was whisked away by the embassy staff official whom Smith had briefed for the job. He held his hand out to Logan.

'I think we've met before.'

'Never known to have forgotten a face,' replied Logan. He pretended to search his memory. 'Aubrey St Clair Smith.' He smiled genuinely. Two men, similar but totally different; same attitudes, same school of underhand, lying and cheating. They recognised themselves in each other. But it wouldn't go beyond that. 'My name's Logan,' he said without easing the smile. 'I'm the father of the girl you were trying to seduce.'

'I know, she told me. She didn't believe it when I told her I'd seen her in nappies.'

'And when was that?'

'About twenty years ago, when you were getting your marine business off the ground. I used to know Bill Donovan. He introduced us.'

'You've got a great memory, Mr St Clair Smith—'

'Please – Aubrey.'

'OK – it's Jim. As I was saying—' He held Smith's eyes. 'How well did you know Bill Donovan?'

'Casually.'

'Meet him in the war?' *In other words, were you in the same line of business; and you're not going to tell me—*

Logan was right.

They had both unconsciously moved towards the edge of the room so that, standing face to face, they could talk quite openly without fear of eavesdroppers. Not that these two were going to say anything that would interest an eavesdropper; they were both much too old at the game. And Logan had spotted the gentle cordon of protection – the two young men who spent all their time discreetly intercepting anyone who felt like joining in their conversation. They were very good at their job. St Clair Smith had clout – that was pretty obvious. Logan studied them surreptitiously as he and St Clair Smith established by their actions and words to each other that they both played similar games. Logan wasn't taken in by the accident of meeting; St Clair Smith wanted something and he made it fairly obvious that he was in the market for an exchange of ideas. He wasn't at all surprised to find himself sitting opposite St Clair Smith when the reception ended and the selected dinner guests sat down.

Logan reckoned he'd worked it all out between the prawn cocktail and the angels-on-horseback. He dropped into the seat beside Aubrey St Clair Smith when the ladies had left and the port began its journey round the table. He helped himself and took his time over lighting one of the ambassador's finest selected Burma cheroots, then shuffled his chair back at an angle and crossed his legs. His head was close to St Clair Smith's so that he didn't have to whisper or lower his voice. The ambassador was in on the game. Logan noticed that he kept the attention of most of his guests and showed that he'd done this sort of thing before by tossing the odd inconsequential remark to the two men at the foot of the table. Logan went along with it. The Englishmen could have been playing his game for him.

But he was the first to open the bidding.

'When are you sailing for Malaysia, Aubrey?'

St Clair Smith studied the end of his cigar. 'You want a lift?'

Logan left it at that. 'I wouldn't mind having a look at this boat of yours while it's sitting in Phuket. Multihulls have always interested me – they don't fall about as much as single hulls. I might consider buying some time in the future.'

'Then come and look before you leap, James. I'll be anchored at Phuket until my new engine is sorted out—'

'New engine, Aubrey? What the hell are we doing sitting here talking like a couple of old women when there's business to be done. What's this about an engine?'

St Clair Smith transferred his gaze from the ambassador's opening and shutting mouth and glanced sideways at Logan. 'It's only an auxiliary, James. Not in your league. I wanted something second-hand – didn't think you'd be interested.'

Logan forced a broad grin. He could have written the script. 'Jesus, Aubrey! That's how I made my business. Christ! I wouldn't turn down the sale of a box of nuts if it was a cash deal. Tell you what—' It looked as though the idea had just struck him. It didn't deceive St Clair Smith, who turned round in his chair, faced him, and waited. 'Come down to my place tomorrow and have a look at what we've got. If I can fit you out I'll come down to Phuket, help your guys fit her in and kill a couple of sparrows with the one engine – I'll have made some money out of you, used you to show me what a tri can do and had a bit of a break into the bargain. What d'you say?'

St Clair Smith played it casually. Logan watched him control his response. It was good acting. He drew on his cigar and studied the length of ash as he allowed the rich blue smoke to filter gently from his pursed lips. He sipped his brandy and then, carefully, smiled. 'When did you last lay your hand on a hot, greasy engine, James?'

Logan evaded the question. 'Gimme a date, Aubrey.'

St Clair Smith looked into space and considered it, then said, 'OK. You can sell me an engine tomorrow; get it to Ban Yit in a couple of days and follow it down. Say, what, four to five days?'

'Make it four.'

'You sure about this?'

'Never been surer, Aubrey. One more thing, though—'

'Go on,' said St Clair Smith, casually.

'I'd like to bring Theresa. She needs a bit of sea air—'

'I couldn't possibly object to that!'

Chapter 13

Bangkok, January 1975

Logan opened his eyes. The sun hadn't even started to hurt. It was early. The thin mosquito-proof curtains cut out the immediate threat but diffused Johari's outline so that, standing with his back to the main window, he looked ten feet tall and shapeless.

'Tea, sir . . .'

'I wasn't asleep.'

Johari was hovering like an old nanny. 'You worried about these Americans, sir?'

'Their being killed?'

Johari coughed. It was a sort of rebuke for a silly question that he couldn't put into words. 'That they've come to look for you?'

Well, now that you mention it, old pal! Logan was surprised that his head wasn't thumping worse than it was. He was feeling a lot better after a night of sweating and tossing and turning and bringing up the past and studying it like a sick man inspecting the bits of tomato skin that he hadn't eaten floating in the vomit. Sure he was worried. Up to now he'd got the Cong An Bo – and for Christ's sake don't bring up Yik Mun's mangled body with the rest of the vomit. We've got over that. We don't hook onto the nightmare as often as we used to, and we don't wake up in the morning any more screaming for the need of her young, tender and eager body. Jesus! So we've got our own people muscling in on the carcase now. But who do they want? Logan or

Contractor? Or have they finally cracked it and put two and two together and made one? About time. 'Yes, Johari, they frighten the fucking life out of me! They're my own people. And, if you didn't know it before, they've got some of the hardest bastards in the business on their books. Viets I can take – Chinese, no problem, I don't mind. But I draw the line at having a bead drawn on the back of my head by a freckled-nosed kid from Milwaukee. D'you follow me?'

If he did Johari didn't answer. 'Drink your tea, sir.'

Logan sat up and swung his feet onto the floor before lighting the inevitable cigarette. Coughing his way through the first half-inch, he began sipping the hot sweet tea.

It brought him back to life, back to the problems, back to the decision that he'd been avoiding. To make a break, run for it and dig a hole deep enough to last to the end of his years. Where? Where in the world would you dig a hole so that a Chinaman wasn't just around the corner? Sweet Jesus! The world was smothered in Chinamen. They were on every street corner in every Western civilised village with a population of more the ten grown-ups. Chinese takeaways, Chinese restaurants, Chinese laundries. Didn't they know? Didn't the people know – they'd been peacefully invaded by the Touming Guanxi. Logan coughed over his cigarette again. It was meant to be a laugh, a derisive laugh, but all that came was a cough and a nasty cold chill where his stomach ground against his bladder.

He picked up his watch to see what day it was. He stared down at the dial. Christ! Forget the bloody day – what goddamn month is it; what year are we in? Calm down, Logan, drink your tea, stub that goddamn thing out and get yourself sorted out. OK. It's Saturday; it's January. He brought the watch closer to his face and studied the tiny bubble on the dial – and it's the third. OK. And the time's ten past seven – as if it mattered any more.

It was nearly eight o'clock when he finished his shower, shaved and dressed. He went back and sat on the edge of the bed again and picked up the phone. He held it to his ear for a few seconds and listened to the dialling tone. It was always there, the almost inaudible click that joined in after a few seconds; one that wouldn't be heard over the thud of the numbers being sprung. There was no point trying to find out who was locked onto his system. It was one of those that was never going to give up its secrets. Whoever it was, he could, without thinking or giving himself another headache on top of the one he already had, offer three different likelihoods as to who was operating an outside trace. They could be anywhere within a mile with a high-frequency beam and the knowledge of how to use it. It might even be Thai Government sources – successful American businessmen were as much a curiosity as unsuccessful American businessmen with unlimited funds. But this sort of call wouldn't help anyone in plotting his thinking.

'Did I wake you, honey?'

'No.'

'Listen, d'you want to have lunch with me?'

The pause was infinitesimal. 'Love to.'

'See you, then. Usual arrangement. Half past twelve suit you?'

'Perfectly.'

''Bye, darling.'

Johari dropped him at the Oriental and went off round the world to pick up Theresa, who lived two streets away. That was the way they decided it was always going to be the minute she no longer wanted to live under his watchful, if benevolent, eye. The death of her mother, Yik Mun, had made all the difference to Theresa's future. A security flat in a security complex that overlooked the startlingly green Lumphini Park, arranged by Liu Zhoushiu, of course, with a little help from his friends the Commissioner of Police and the Minister of Internal Security. A tank might get at her, but not much else. She had missed out on the normal happy-go-lucky existence of the rich kid of an ultra-rich American businessman. She had done the proper schools – England, Switzerland and all points west, all under watchful eyes, until, at eighteen, she'd moved in, gracefully, to the good life in Bangkok. But there was always going to be a drawback. If you called a perpetual security screen of Liu's best middle-aged stranglers a drawback. Not the young ones. Liu wasn't silly. An outstandingly pretty girl who was going to be an outstandingly attractive woman didn't need horny young

143

Chinese Turks watching her every move. Middle-aged Turks harboured the same feelings but they were old enough to foresee the consequences. The man who tried the first experimental probe with his fingers between Theresa Marie Liu-Logan's extremely shapely thighs was going to end up without any. But Theresa learned to live with it.

The heads turned, as usual, as she walked through the Oriental Hotel's main luncheon restaurant. Tall, slim, she was dressed with a simple elegance; Theresa Logan didn't need expensive boutiques to illustrate the magnificence of her figure. Her dark hair was uncomplicated and folded into a short roll just above shoulder length; her eyes were a gift from her mother, dark, a suggestion of a slight almond shape, and concealed in their depths a hint of sensuality that she reserved for no one man in particular. She was twenty-three. She was probably a virgin. And she would stay one as long as Liu Zhoushiu dictated. No man dared think about it. And to those men who knew about these things it showed in her expression. She was a sensual woman. She needed love. She was used to the eyes studying her. It had no effect on her as she followed the slim waiter to her father's table by the window.

Theresa had a great appetite. Logan envied her but tasted nothing from his own plate. He could have been lifting fried sawdust on the fork to his mouth, and waited only until she'd finished before he could get to the serious business of drinking a very large Remy Martin.

'Why don't you light a cigarette—' She studied him seriously, while he gratefully lit up, then leaned forward and rested her elbows on the table. 'And tell me what's troubling you.'

It didn't surprise him. One thing about Theresa Logan was that she didn't beat about the bush. When she had something to say, she said it. He was about to trot out one of the trite old responses about being tired, overworked, needing a rest, but he knew it was both pointless and fruit-less. Theresa would pry it out of him somehow. He knew that – she knew that. At least he could be honest and get most of it off his chest. But where do you draw the line? She thinks her daddy's a good businessman who's done very

144

well in the boat business. What's she going to say when he tells her her father's a spy, and has been since he was her age himself; and that because Father's a spy they killed her mother, and they'd do the same to her if they thought she knew a fraction of what was tucked away inside Jimmy Logan's tired brain. *Oh no, Theresa, the line must be drawn, you must be told something otherwise you won't be frightened and run as fast as me. But did you know, as well, that your old man betrayed his country? Well, not really betrayed, not then, quite the opposite. It looked a dead cert that we'd made a bountiful bargain for our country. Maybe we did. But I don't think the same charitable view will be taken today – or tomorrow, or the day after.*

Logan waited until the waiter had cleaned the table and brought the coffee. He controlled the snatch he'd prepared for the Cognac and made it into a casual movement of the hand. He needed it. He needed it badly and, looking straight across the table into his daughter's shrewd eyes, he sipped the brandy and held her gaze.

'Trouble, Theresa? Sure, I've got some of that. I'm not sure you want to be bothered with it, though.'

Her eyes didn't move. 'Try me.'

'Pour the coffee.'

It was so easy once you started. It was a sort of religious ritual, sliding into the confessional and sensing the too-close presence of another heavy breather. Logan reached for his Cognac and leaned forward on the table. She joined him in the middle. They looked like an elderly lover and his young mistress planning what they were going to do to each other after lunch. Logan lowered his voice. This was breaking the rules. The unwritten ones; the ones that saved not your life but theirs. It was the first, like the Commandments: thou shalt not tell anyone, not even your wife or children, nor your friends – never, never your friends – that you are involved in secret things. Never, never, never. But it felt as good as absolution, telling this beautiful woman who came from his loins that his life was a secret one – or, until now, had been. When he told it, it sounded as if he were talking about someone else. In a way he was. But he didn't mind – it was therapy. He was cleansing himself. He was never going to be purified by baring his soul and beating his chest, but this way he could feel already the dreadful loneliness of the years slipping away. And he'd got a willing listener – not a captive one, and it made all the difference. Theresa was sitting listening to her father's past being raked before her eyes because she wanted to. Jim Logan studied her features. The eyes were the important thing; there was no condemnation there, that he couldn't have stood; there was no rebuke, no contempt. Love – yes, and beneath that, admiration. Silly girl, he almost said. There's nothing to admire in a man who sold his country down the road.

But you didn't sell your country down the road, Jim, you brokered an arrangement that nearly saved its bacon in one of the nastiest little wars in the history of nasty little wars. So maybe you and Graver conspired, if conspired is the right word – and conspiracy in a national context is a very emotive word, not to say action. Definitely a hanging word in earlier days. Now—? A lifetime of staring at the sky through four-inch-wide bars and eating dinner off an aluminium tray until your teeth drop out. And that's the up side. The alternative is the one where you cut and run; pick up your overnight bag and your lovely daughter and run – run like hell!

'How did you know what was going on in Washington and in people's minds?' asked Theresa. She had listened, totally absorbed, not interrupting and not taking her eyes off her father's face throughout his lengthy discourse. Only when he stopped talking to pour more coffee did she break into his chain of thought.

He stirred sugar into the coffee, tasted it and said, 'There's nothing clever or sleight-of-hand in knowing the reaction to certain events when you know the sort of people who are going to perform them. When I told Langley I wanted a father confessor I knew exactly what they'd do. It's like a goalie on the wrong end of a penalty kick; he's made a study of the guy who's about to try to put one past him. Very often it's the speed that beats him, but nine times out of ten the kick goes exactly where he knew the guy would put it. And that's the same as putting something in the hands of people like Graver and his masters – they're always going to do the same thing.'

'So you guessed all that!' Theresa said accusingly.

'Oh no, not all of it. Graver came and saw what he wanted to see and heard what he didn't want to hear but feared the worst. He got more than he feared. But he couldn't afford to turn his back on it.'

'And that's all gospel?'

'More or less. As I said, somebody in Washington who mattered sent Graver to Malaysia to see what it was all about and he agreed to Liu's ultimatum.'

'You didn't say it was an ultimatum before.'

'Liu is the best poker player in the world. It started off as a little bit of give and take, but as he kept drawing the right cards he kept raising the stakes. Graver wasn't a poker player; Graver was a CIA desk man destined for high office. He hadn't learnt the tricks of those of us who normally work in the gutter. He saw things at their face value and bought what he saw.'

She waited a moment, but the curtain had come down. She studied his eyes; there were going to be no more revelations. He was regretting it already, like a convert to a strange sect. He'd converted to the sect of people who tell things to each other and don't have to think of alternatives to the truth. But there was one more, and he couldn't refuse her that.

'So, when did it all go wrong?'

In for a penny . . . Logan didn't stop to think what he was doing, he knew what he was saying, and he knew that Theresa was now in almost as deep as he. But he needed her to be. She was going to be the other runner, and when you're running there can be no secrets between two runners with their ankles bound together – it has to be go right! go left! go stop! go nowhere! No time for why? why? why?

'About six weeks ago,' he said, and told her what had happened to break the seal in San Francisco.

She listened in silence until he finished. 'I don't believe it! San Francisco—?'

'Believe it, honey – just believe it.'

She stared at him with her lips parted. He tried a gentle smile but it didn't work. And then she shook her head. 'OK, I believe you. I don't like it, I don't like it one little bit—'

'I understand,' he tried.

'No you don't. But tell me – how're we going to get out of Bangkok from under Hongzhou's nose, give these Americans who want to kill you the slip, and collect all this stuff from Kuala Lumpur . . .?' She shook her head again, but there was love of memory in her eye. 'It all sounds like one of those fairytales you used to whisper to me when I wouldn't sleep.'

'I don't think you were ever told anything like this, sweetheart! OK, but this is no fairy story – that guy Aubrey St Clair Smith who was making a heavy pass at you last night—'

'I liked him,' she said quickly. 'And he wasn't . . . But I wouldn't have minded if he had,' she added, aggressively.

'He's old enough to be your father. Christ, child! He's older than me!'

'And what makes you think you're not attractive to twenty-year-old women?'

'Forget it!'

'All right,' she said eventually. 'So what was it you were going to say about Aubrey St Clair Smith?'

'I'm going to use him.'

'Very nice!'

'Cut it out! It's not easy. I don't need sarcasm. I said I'm going to use him. I don't have to tell you but I will and you're going to do exactly as I say.' He fixed her with a tight expression. 'Lives could depend on your doing this properly . . . I'm going to use him to get you out of Bangkok and then out of Thailand. He doesn't know it yet but you're going to sail with him to Malaysia. I've already done the groundwork—'

'I thought you were worried about my being seduced by him!'

'It was concern, not worry, and you're old enough to brawl with anyone you choose to. If you want a bruising from a fifty-three-year-old who's forgotten everything you're ever going to know about sex, then be my guest. At the moment, Aubrey St Clair Smith, like me, has got other things on his mind, and very shortly he's going to have another – you. So just sit there, don't interrupt and listen to how it's going to happen.'

Chapter 14

By the third time Mark Hagen made contact with Jack Krislov they'd sorted themselves out into chief and Indian. Krislov had been led by the nose. The first sign of encroachment into his territory had resulted in a sharp reminder of his status to Langley. He'd got an even sharper reminder of his status from Samuel Reilly, GS18, threatening something slightly worse than castration unless he co-operated with the bearer of the code-word DROGHEDA and did everything, short of carrying his gun for him, that Mr Hagen required. Krislov got the message but, in time-honoured fashion, didn't make it easy for Hagen. Hagen helped him with the conversion and the partnership settled down. Hagen was used to getting his way.

'Jack,' he said over the phone, 'tell me if this means anything to you? An oldish but healthy-looking guy, about six two, silver top, smooth, limey. Well connected British embassy-wise Bangkok. Ring any bells?'

'In what connection?'

'Logan.'

'Yeah. Aubrey St Clair Smith.'

'Who's he? And why?'

'Second time somebody's raised this guy's name in a week – same connection.'

'Tell me more.'

Krislov told him what he knew about Aubrey St Clair Smith. 'But I wouldn't get excited,' he concluded. 'He's been

149

trundling these waters a couple of times a year for as long as anyone can remember. As far as I know he's harmless, no known involvement in anything remotely serious.'

'So how come he's joined in conversation twice in a week with the guy I'm interested in?'

'He's got a broken auxiliary motor in his big trimaran. He's looking for a replacement. He wouldn't find that here in Phuket. The only person who could help him out there is the Logan Maritime in Bangkok. You gonna try and make something out of that?'

'He was at the same do in Bangkok with Logan. He was last seen trying to work his hand up Logan's daughter's skirt in a watering hole in the city.'

'Forget it, Hagen. The guy's harmless, he's an eccentric, thinks he's still a lad with the girls.'

But Hagen didn't want to forget it. 'Are you anywhere near where this guy parks his boat?'

Krislov's wince could be heard quite clearly. 'Near.'

'Go and have a look and see whether this engine he's so worried about really is kaput and get back to me as soon as you can.'

'You're wasting your time.'

'It's my time, I'll waste it any way I like. See ya!'

He waited a moment, lit a cigarette, then picked up the phone again. He dialled international, then 1, and 703 482 1100. When the Langley operator answered he said, 'Two nine zero,' and was put straight through to Sam Reilly. 'I'm not sure Logan's our man, sir.'

'Is that what you rang to tell me?'

'It's the prelude, sir. By all accounts he's a straight-forward, well-heeled American who runs a prosperous business in Bangkok—'

'That's what *I* told *you*.'

Hagen waited a second for the echoes on the line caused by Reilly's interruption to die down, then went on, patiently, 'In two weeks he hasn't put a foot wrong. Done everything according to the book. But—'

'But what?'

'There's something I just can't put my finger on. Something

150

that makes me want to duck whenever I take a look at him. I think he's being covered—'

'He is. The DEA's covering him – they're logging every move. They've fallen in love with him; they've decided he's the Man and they're going for it.'

'The DEA got Chinese operators?'

Reilly thought about that one for a few moments and couldn't come up with anything. 'What're you saying, Hagen?'

'Logan's got a close screen of serious-looking Chinks. He can't take a crap without one of 'em on his tiptoes looking over the top of the door. Could be just the drug scene, or could be something more flexible. If you'll pardon the question, sir, has this business I'm on been discussed with anyone of an oriental disposition?'

'Say what you mean, Hagen.'

'Have you mentioned your fears about Two nine zero with any Chinese contact in the States?'

'That's nothing to do with you. You just watch your back when you're dealing with anyone whose eyes are not completely round. Get my meaning? Is that all you want?'

'Meaning got, sir. No. Could you have someone put a trace on a limey named Aubrey St Clair Smith and see whether he's got any background. He's what you might call an old China hand – been out here for centuries. Nothing concrete – he intrigues me.'

'OK, Hagen. Pick up the flimsy on the limey, if there is any, from Krislov. But get on with it!'

The phone clicked and went dead in Hagen's ear. He dropped it in its cradle, picked up the cigarette he'd left in the ashtray, shook off the three-quarters length of ash and stuck it between his lips. There was nothing left to smoke. Hagen spat it out in disgust and absently lit a new one. His mind wasn't on it. It was all being done by instinct as his mind trawled through Reilly's half-admission that the stupid asshole had discussed the whole operation with what sounded like, from the tone in his voice, a member of the Chinese Cosa Nostra in Washington. Just what was needed! No wonder their man Logan had more Chinese faces looking after his welfare than Ho Chi Minh. So, what about Logan?

Hagen was just as wise. Drugs or spying? Could be either. Or both. Or none.

He dressed himself in his GI-on-rest-and-recuperation-from-the-battle-front-in-Vietnam kit – white T-shirt, skin-tight jeans, taut body and scared-looking eyes – and walked out of the Mahanob Hotel and onto the sweaty, humid, noisy streets of safe Bangkok. They were everywhere, the battle-shocked kids who'd been netted by the draft and would never be the same again. And they all looked alike – young and innocent, they should have been lounging around the campus and hanging out around the drug-store whistling at the girls. But they were good cover. Unless someone took a closer look at him and saw that his eyes hadn't the same haunted look as those of his fellow recuperees.

He caught a tuk-tuk outside the hotel, had it drop him on the edge of the Nakhon Kasem market and disappeared on foot into the heart of Chinatown.

Chapter 15

Logan made his move four days after meeting Aubrey St Clair Smith at the British embassy.

'Bring the Merc round the front, Johari. No hide-and-seek, all in the open. And wait there with the engine running. I'll tell you where we're going in a minute.' Johari nodded. There was nothing in his face; if he was suspicious he didn't show it.

Logan remained sitting in the main room until Johari had left, then got up and stood to one side of the front window and waited until the Mercedes drifted round the drive from the garage at the rear and pulled up at the front door. He watched Johari get out of the car and open the front gates. He didn't need to strain his eyes; there'd be several other sets watching the proceedings.

He ran quickly up the stairs and tapped lightly on Theresa's door. She was ready. But she was indignant. Just a shoulder handbag! Logan swept her protestations aside. 'Quick! Natural and casual. You're going shopping and then you're going to meet me at the Oriental for lunch. Make it obvious, buy the sort of things you'd buy normally. Don't stock up with masses of bags. No new outfits, keep it light. OK! Give me five minutes then join me in the car.'

It looked right. The hand phones hummed and buzzed as the Mercedes made its way across Bangkok and two sets of watchers controlled each other's movements. They saw the Mercedes pull into the side of the road at the junction of

153

Ratchadaphisek Road and the elegant Thanon Sukhumvit and watched Theresa alight and disappear into the Harrods look-alike set just off the main thoroughfare. The Mercedes pulled away. The hand phones hummed again. There was no problem with priorities; Logan was the target and Theresa was his daughter. Liu Hongzhou's watcher teams knew that Logan wouldn't be running anywhere without his daughter. Leave her. Concentrate on him. 'Where's he going?'

'Looks like the Oriental.'

'Very normal. No problem. One team follow, one team go direct and watch inside.'

And Logan did exactly what they expected.

Theresa strolled round the store then left by the same entrance and walked aimlessly along Thanon Sukhumvit, every so often, as she had been diligently primed by Logan, turning in her tracks to reassure herself that there wasn't something in a shop she'd already passed that she urgently needed. It all seemed a bit of a game, and would have been if her father hadn't been so serious. She took her lead from him and did exactly as she'd been told. She continued in this manner, strolled past the entrance to the Landmark Plaza Hotel, stopped at the traffic lights at the junction of Thanon and Soi Sukhumvit, and when they turned green moved across quickly with the other pedestrians. Halfway across she changed her mind. She'd forgotten something. She turned suddenly, bumped into an American GI behind her, smiled apologetically, and darted for the pavement she'd just left.

Hagen smiled to himself philosophically. She'd done all the right things at the right moment. There was nothing he could do except cross the teeming Thanon Sukhumvit, wriggle his way through the milling crowds and try to pick her movements up on the other side of the road. He knew he'd lost. She'd vanished. He carried on walking, crossed the road again and joined the crowd on the other side of the street. He waited in the shade of a shop entrance. There was no point in trying to pick her up again. In this place she'd be gone for ever; she could have gone anywhere and he'd blown it anyway; she'd smiled at him; she'd know him next time she saw him and by the way she'd behaved along the shopping centre and at the road crossing she wouldn't accept coincidence as a logical factor if she bumped into him again. You might as well piss off, Hagen, and go back to square one ready for the next move. He smiled ruefully to himself. Hagen was like that; he held no grudge, only faint praise for a lucky break and a natural physical liar. Somebody had been at her. She'd learnt the moves like a pro. Maybe she was. He caught a passing tuk-tuk and went through the motions himself. As with Theresa, if anybody had been interested in him they were now very disappointed people.

Theresa had only gone back as far as the Landmark Plaza. Without looking round she went straight into the main entrance, collected the small suitcase from the cloakroom which Johari had deposited the day before and booked a room for one week.

Comfortably installed, she waited an hour then rang reception. 'I'm expecting a friend,' she told the receptionist. 'Has anybody asked for me, or been looking for me, please?'

'Just a moment, please.' A pause. There was nothing in the book about a receptionist pausing to check. Then, 'No. Nothing for you. Sorry.'

Relief. Theresa was experiencing the right emotions – fear followed by relief – for nothing tangible. She'd become a player in the Game. 'Thanks. I want to hire a car while I'm here – can you arrange that?'

'No problem. When would you like it? Any preference of car or company?'

'I'll leave it up to you. Please book it for the week and put everything on my bill. I'd like it here as soon as possible. Will they deliver?'

'No problem. Shall I ring you when the representative arrives? He'll want to see your documents.'

'Perhaps you'll send someone up for them?'

'Of course.'

Hertz wasted no time. Within half a hour a light grey air-conditioned Volvo was parked in a shady spot in the hotel carpark and the key delivered to Theresa's room. Hertz liked it like this. The hotel bore the responsibility – no risk, no problem! She lay on the bed in cool comfort and at exactly twenty minutes past two picked up the telephone and asked for an outside line. She dialled the Oriental Hotel and asked for Mr James Logan to be paged to the telephone.

Logan was waiting for it. It came when he was halfway through his main course. He waited a couple of minutes for his watchers to absorb the situation, then walked casually out of the restaurant to the foyer telephones. Liu Hong-zhou's inside men were content and relaxed. Logan's plate was still full, his tall glass of chilled lager waiting for his return and his napkin lying in a heap beside it. They considered all options. Sit quiet and wait; no one leaves in the middle of his meal. And if one of them got up to follow he was quite likely to meet him halfway. They both fiddled with their food without raising their heads.

'Half an hour, Dad. I'll be in the carpark at Sathorn. Everything all right?'

'Sure. Did you do what I said?'

'Of course.'

'Anybody interested?'

'Not a soul. I'm disappointed.'

'It's no joke. See you at the Sathorn landing.' Logan kept the receiver jammed against his ear for a couple of minutes after Theresa had hung up and talked to himself until the operator told him his party had disconnected. But he'd had long enough to check his surroundings and confirm that his watchers hadn't followed him. He replaced the phone and turned right towards the men's toilets. He stopped at the entrance for a moment, confirmed that still no one had followed him, then carried on past the toilet entrance, into the small foyer, and stopped by the bookshop. Still alone. He carried on, turned left and headed for the river-view bar where he walked through the open window, out onto the verandah overlooking the Chao Phraya river and, stopping briefly to light a cigarette, made his way down to the water-taxi landing. He mingled with the mixture of tourists and locals, bought a ticket to the Sewetchat Temple, downriver and on the opposite bank to the Oriental, and squeezed his way onto the flat-bottomed boat. Once aboard he sat down quickly with his back to the landing stage in the first bank of seats beside the ramp.

An American woman wearing a pristine straw imitation coolie hat with a black string tied tightly under her chin, in true coolie fashion, tried to make conversation, but gave up after a few seconds of non-response by Logan. He had other things on his mind. A chattering woman he needed like a hole in the head. He pulled on his cigarette and scowled. It was enough for her. She hadn't come to Bangkok to be scowled at by a bad-tempered foreigner. She left him alone and then they were in the middle of the river. It was a ten-minute trip to the next landing, but to Logan it seemed an eternity before the boat's engines frothed up the mud as the driver thrust the screw, with a nerve-jangling howl, into reverse and bounced the vessel hard against the Tha Sathorn landing stage. More people boarded. They crowded around the ramp and pushed the stragglers further into the body of the boat. The barefooted coolie in charge of the barrier leaned his back into a fat Chinese and shoved. It was all good-humoured.

Just as the the long boat began to move away from the jetty, Logan pushed himself up, trod on one of his companion's red bunions and, ignoring a howl of agony, squeezed and shoved his way to the entrance, lifted the worn barrier and jumped the narrow gap between the departing floating bus and the wooden landing. He was alone. But he didn't linger. He cut through the ticket collector's barrier and made his way under the Thonburi bridge to the carpark.

The Volvo's lights flashed briefly in the sunshine and, after a quick look round behind him, a survey of the surroundings and a glance at the empty cars in the park, he walked briskly towards the car and slipped into the passenger seat.

'Good girl!' He patted Theresa's leg as she started the engine. 'Any problems?'

'None. I haven't seen a single suspicious-looking American. I hope you know what you're doing.'

It wasn't worth a reply. He kept his eyes about him as she manoeuvred the Volvo out of the parking lot, took the Bantab road and then joined the east-going Thonburi bridge road. On the far side of the bridge, Theresa filtered left and joined the traffic moving out of the city, heading south for the main trunk road to Samut Sakhon. Once out of the main stream the traffic thinned and Logan began to relax. Theresa had never been anything but relaxed; but then Theresa hadn't been running with her head back to front for thirty-five years, and she didn't realise that the end of the road really was, for him, the end of the road. He dropped his eyes to the map on his lap. It was a long way to Phuket, over four hundred miles, and there wasn't much choice. It was a straight run, good road, bad road, and the good road was fairly indifferent. He studied his watch. Liu's men in the Oriental Hotel restaurant would, by now, be contemplating suicide. They wouldn't have lost their heads yet; they'd be combing the hotel, checking, checking and double-checking and asking discreet, and not so discreet questions, and eventually they'd end up on the water-taxi landing and discover that their man had gone to the other side of the river. And then they'd find that he hadn't, he'd only gone one stop and then alighted. Logan had disappeared.

An hour later, when the watchers finally accepted that they had nothing to offer Liu Hongzhou, they returned for their medicine. They took with them Johari, whom they had found in the hotel carpark, like them, waiting for James Logan.

'Johari, where's Logan gone?' Liu Hongzhou's anger was well controlled. Johari, who had never had trouble bending the truth in any direction his interrogators would like it to take, had no difficulty with the truth as it was. Hongzhou believed him when he told him he knew nothing of James Logan's plans.

'Where's the girl? Where's Theresa?'

Johari had to shake his head again. But there was a certain feeling of admiration tickling around in his mind. Logan had done the job; he'd run and by the look of it he'd run clear. But where to? Johari had no idea, he couldn't even begin to think, but one thing was for certain – if he'd managed to lose some of the best people in the business he would have done it properly. He was out of Bangkok, was running free, and Johari would have bet his life on the fact that Theresa was running with him. Johari was philosophical; he knew what was going to happen and he and Logan had often discussed it in the past. A good Muslim, was Johari – death was inevitable, it was nothing to be afraid of, it was just another step on the journey to everlasting paradise. He wasn't worried; he knew the journey was about to start.

They sat him down and worked out of him Logan's thoughts and actions over the past ten days. They didn't spare themselves. They held nothing back and made him suffer as only Chinese watchers who'd been made to look foolish could make a man suffer. Somebody had to pay for the loss of face – and their own forthcoming punishment.

The fact that Johari had nothing to hide wasn't going to help him. Logan hadn't asked him to delay or lie on his behalf. That gave his deeper sense of loyalty absolution, and he told them openly what he thought. It didn't help. They managed to work off some of their frustrations with small, sausage-length, leather-covered, sand-filled coshes. Johari's face remained untouched so that he was able to continue talking. Former peasants, they had no feelings; they were masters of the pain-inflicting business; they could extract words from a dead man.

Johari's body, when they'd finished, looked as if it had been pushed off the top of a ten-storey building. But it made them, if not happy, satisfied that he'd given them the hour-by-hour timetable of Logan's activities. When they found there were no unbroken bones left in his body, they threw him into the back of a truck and took him with them to one of the isolated opium-refining stations at Chiang Mai in the mountainous Tanen range on the northern Thai–Burma border. This was to be their exile, a minor punishment, and they would stay here until they had purged their inefficiency. It usually took about four years.

Johari's exile was shorter.

As soon as they arrived they threw him off the truck and, whilst the others watched impassively, one of them tightened a length of piano wire round his throat and throttled him.

159

Chapter 16

Phuket, January 1975

Logan sat on the ledge in the diminutive hip bath in the Pearl Hotel in Phuket and, as the hot water worked its way into his muscles and joints, revelled in a sudden light-headedness. He'd slipped out of the constricting chain mail of obligation and his naked, skinny body was once more his own. He drank a cold beer. It didn't stay cold very long but it was ambrosia, and it was his third. There was only one more thing to do, but that could wait. After a two-day road trip another half an hour wasn't going to break the bank.

He swung his leg over the side of the bath and pulled himself out. It was cramped; it was built not for six-foot-plus Americans but five-foot-nothing Asians. The room was similar. Everything seemed in miniature: a miniature bed, out of the end of which his feet stuck out a good foot and a half; the only armchair was about the same size as the one in the doll's house he had bought Theresa when she was four. God! What a bloody long time ago that was.

He dried himself, finished another miniature cold beer and then reckoned he was ready for a serious ten minutes. To help him he poured a miniature whisky into a miniature glass and topped it up with slightly cool water from the mini-bar. He lit a cigarette to go with it and rang the number Aubrey St Clair Smith had given him.

'Krislov.' It was an American voice.

Logan put the phone down.

He finished his whisky in one gulp, padded across to the mini-bar for another and redialled the number.

There was no improvement. 'Krislov,' said the same voice.

Logan put the phone down again without speaking. The feeling-good factor he'd had in his little bath slid away like the sweat down his back. But what was he worried about? He studied his face in the mirror as he pulled on his pants and a shirt, stopping every so often to interrogate the tired, worried-looking grey eyes that stared back at him. So an American voice answers the phone? So goddamn what! Every fucking American in the world's not after your balls. Sort yourself out, Logan – and quickly!

The brief self-lecture did some good. His brain felt lighter and more agile as he sat on the edge of the bed and pulled on his socks and shoes. He waited a few minutes then lifted the phone off its hook again. He didn't dial. He asked for Theresa's room.

'D'you fancy a bite to eat?'

'No,' she snapped. 'The only thing I fancy at the moment is twenty-four hours' sleep.' She relented briefly. 'I'll join you for breakfast.'

'Sure. Goodnight, baby.'

He walked down the back stairs rather than use the lift. It was only four flights but he was beginning to feel the paranoia creeping back into its receptive slot in his mind again; paranoia and claustrophobia, endemic among agents on the run. He knew the symptoms – everyone was suspect, everyone wanted to kill you, even anonymous American voices on the phone. The symptoms spelt fear. It was a disease he'd never mastered, and he'd never met an honest man yet who hadn't felt its gut-wrenching, liquid clutch. He knew he'd got it and there wasn't much he could do about it. He lit another cigarette, pushed open the doors opposite the small lounge, sat down and calmed himself by watching the gentle motions of the caged fishes that surrounded the area. A smiling young Thai brought him a bowl of peanuts and a card with a list of about eight different local beers.

'Whisky, please.'

'Local?'

Heaven forbid! Logan suppressed a shudder. 'Scotch.'

'Large?'

'Treble.'

When the drink arrived, Logan refused the chit and paid in cash. He tipped the boy generously. 'Have you got a moment, son?'

The boy's smile bent slightly but he didn't run.

Logan took a quick sip from the glass. It was good Scotch. 'How do I get to Ban Yit?'

The boy thought for a moment. He stared about him for inspiration but nothing came. 'Ban Yit?' he repeated to himself. It was a good sign for Logan; it sounded like isolation. The boy gave up. He knew where all the whores were and where the twelve-year-old massage girls sharpened their toenails; he knew Phuket like he knew his own top lip; but what happened where, beyond where the dirty yellow standard lamps ended he neither knew nor cared. 'I'll ask the manager,' he said after a moment. 'He knows everything and everybody around Phuket. He'll know Ban Yit.' Which was exactly what Logan didn't want. The circle was large enough; it didn't need widening with hotel managers and his friends. But he was too late. The boy had gone in search of Mister Manager.

He was a mixture of Swiss and Indian; he had the colouring of a Swiss but the accent and mannerisms of a Bengali. It might have been better the other way round. He glided towards Logan with both hands held stiffly to the seams of his trousers which, for anyone other than a hotel manager, would have thrown him off balance. He halted and bowed, his eyes centring on a point halfway down Logan's nose. 'You want to get to Ban Yit, Mr, er . . .?'

Logan didn't help him out. 'Yeah. I didn't realise it was that hard to find.'

'It's no problem.' The eyes shifted fractionally to meet Logan's then departed again. 'May I ask whether you're meeting someone there?'

'You may.'

He got the message. 'I'm sorry, sir, but it's only yachts that use Ban Yit and I know most of the regular users. I wondered whether I might know your—' He tailed off. 'I can arrange a taxi for you. Not many will go there.' He dry-washed his hands and replaced them down the seams of his trousers. 'A bad road, bad people and accidents—' He tightened his lips over the word 'accident' to indicate that he used that word for want of a more descriptive one. 'There's nothing at the end of it except Mr Krislov's place. It's used as a landing stage by a few boats – friends of Mr Krislov. Not many come here from that direction. You'd be much better advised to go to Chalong where you'll find many Europeans in the Lighthouse and I'm sure somebody there will be able to help you find your friends.'

Logan ignored his advice. 'You said you knew most of the people who berth around there?'

'They all come here at some time or another.' He raised his eyebrows and smiled for the first time.

Logan didn't smile back but relaxed his features. The man was doing his job. He was trying to please a taciturn, bad-tempered American. 'D'you know of an Englishman named Smith?'

'Mr Aubrey St Clair Smith?'

'You know him?'

'You're in luck, sir.' He studied the face of his watch then compared his findings with the main clock over the reception desk. 'Mr Aubrey St Clair Smith comes in every day when he's at Chalong. He collects his mail – he uses this address. Excuse me one moment.' He turned and searched the foyer with his eyes. He found what he was looking for and, with a limp-wristed downward wave, summoned a short, dapper Thai in a suit that had been cut from the same bolt of cloth as his own. 'Has Mr Aubrey St Clair Smith been in today to collect his mail?' he snapped.

'No, sir.'

'Thank you.' He dismissed the little man by turning his back on him and readdressing Logan. 'I should imagine he'll be here any time now. If he hasn't already looked in he'll come for dinner. I'll direct the hall porter to bring him across the minute he arrives. Will that suit you, sir?'

'Thanks. The name's James.' Logan raised his glass to his lips and drained it while the manager considered how to disengage. The empty glass guided him.

163

'Very well, Mr James.' He clicked his fingers at the young man in charge of drinks. 'Look after Mr Aubrey St Clair Smith's friend.' He lowered his voice so that only the boy and Logan could hear. 'And bring the receipts to me personally.' He turned back. 'Thank you, Mr James. If there's anything you need, please come directly to me. I'm at your service.'

'Thanks.'

Logan was only halfway down the first of his free whiskies when Aubrey St Clair Smith entered the small lounge. Not a bead of perspiration, every silver hair in place, immaculately dressed as if for a light dinner at Claridge's, there was nothing about Aubrey St Clair Smith to indicate that he'd just come twenty-five miles from a gap in the hills via an unmetalled, dusty road in a temperature of between eighty and ninety degrees.

There was a certain hesitancy in his manner – initially. But he recovered quickly. 'Evening, James,' he said as he lowered himself into the armchair beside Logan and reached for a handful of peanuts. If he was surprised at seeing Logan, nothing showed. 'I was rather expecting you to call. We could have done better than this for you.' He gestured with his hand as if the hotel's lack of international opulence was all his fault. 'Why didn't you warn me you were coming?'

'And thereby hangs a tale,' said Logan through a mouthful of nuts. 'Have a drink?'

'Scotch.'

Logan waited until Smith's Scotch had been placed in front of him and the waiter had retreated to his place in the corner of his small bar, wondering how far he could go with this Englishman. He studied his face as he took the first taste of his whisky. St Clair Smith seemed to have infinite patience. He'd accepted Logan's presence with hardly a raised eyebrow; now he sat calmly savouring his drink and so far hadn't posed a single question. Ingenuous? Or canny beyond the realms of normal British behaviour when presented with a possibly awkward situation?

'I'm going to be brutally frank with you, Aubrey.'

St Clair Smith met his eyes. Logan read nothing in them. 'I've got an ulterior motive for coming here—'

St Clair Smith picked the ball up. 'I had rather thought something along those lines, James. Driving from Bangkok to Phuket overland is not the recommended route by those who know. Who're you running from?'

'It's a long story.'

'Turn it into a short one.'

'Sure—' Logan relaxed into his lines; it was going to be fairly easy. He emptied his glass and nodded to St Clair Smith. 'But first, Aubrey,' he said causally, 'how about putting our cards on the table?'

'Go on, then.'

'No, not me – you.'

'I haven't got any cards, James. What you see is what you get – an elderly expatriate with a boat who likes cruising these waters.'

Logan stared into St Clair Smith's eyes and tried to see behind them. There was nothing there.

'Have you got any accreditation?'

'Jim, I don't know what you're talking about. I don't know what you mean by accreditation. Tell me what your problem is and I'll see if I can help.'

Logan couldn't help but admire Aubrey St Clair Smith – he not only looked the part, he talked it. He moved on to the other part of his script. 'OK, then, Aubrey. Let's forget that, for the time being, and talk about me. I'm running, as you put it, from an affiliation in Bangkok that's gone wrong. I've got onto the wrong side of a bunch of Chinese who run a sort of Mafia-type ring. They control all business—'

'You mean you've upset the Touming Guanxi.'

'You know these people?'

'Jim, I've been cruising and walking these areas since Pontius was a trainee pilot on a little river boat. Of course I know the Touming Guanxi – and I know who sits in the big chair at the top of the table as well—'

'That saves a lot of explanation.' Logan would have been surprised if the conversation had taken any other route. 'They want my ass pinned to a wall—'

'Hang on a second.' St Clair Smith ordered two more whiskies. The hotel manager was going to have to reassess his gestures of friendship at this rate. When the drinks were

165

set on the table, St Clair Smith didn't allow Logan to continue where he'd left off. 'Just to clear the air, Jim, the Touming Guanxi's main preoccupation, as it has been for quite a few years, is opium and all its little derivatives. They own exclusive rights to its production, marketing and distribution, and they control everybody who's as near as a sniff to the business. I hope you're not going to tell me you're involved with that lot?'

Logan allowed himself a brief mental glance at the script. It was OK so far.

'First question. Are they working on your case together, the Chinese and the Americans?'

'I doubt it.'

'Can you be sure?'

'OK. I'm sure they're not working togther.'

'Question two – the obvious one; you knew about this when we met in Bangkok. That was five days ago. You haven't been hiding in a back street since then so why haven't you been killed by the Touming?'

Logan nodded, thoughtfully, again. 'Way back in the late forties I was introduced into the society by a person of influence who they trusted. They accepted me as a good guy and I played along until I realised they had penetrated an official US Government agency. Christ knows how they did it, although . . .' Logan leaned forward, held Aubrey St Clair Smith's eyes with a sincere, worried expression and lowered his voice confidentially. He was almost whispering. ' . . . when the deal is drugs on a scale undreamed of there's enough money sloshing around to buy huge patronage in some very high places. This is what's been done. People have been bought.'

'You haven't answered my question, James.'

'About being killed in Bangkok?' Logan shrugged his shoulders easily. 'I've insured myself against sudden death, Aubrey. The Chinese know this, it's been carefully explained. I've got enough material stashed away to blow every Touming outlet in every little corner in every country in the world. I could close them down for the next ten years. I could stop their revenue, I could stop their deliveries, I could do everything except stop the goddamn stuff growing. They

166

don't want me dead, Aubrey, they want the stuff that I've got. They blocked every exit to me; I've had a tail as long as your arm for the past couple of months. I couldn't even start my car without a half-dozen of 'em crawling out of the garage wall—'

'Which poses another simple question.'

'Go on—'

'Why have you done a runner now – and more importantly, how did you do it?'

Logan gave a mental sigh of relief. He'd sold the pup. Aubrey St Clair Smith had bought it. It showed in the Englishman's questions. Logan couldn't have been more relaxed. *But careful, Jimmy . . .* 'Two good reasons here, Aubrey,' he said easily. 'I ran because I want to get Theresa out – for obvious reasons, and . . .' He paused as if debating the wisdom of revealing his plans, then decided, and hoped Smith had noticed the hesitation. ' . . . so that she can recover all this documentation. I want her out of the country and this is where I go down on my hands and knees.' He gazed with all sincerity into Aubrey St Clair Smith's pale blue eyes. 'Am I in a position to ask a favour of you?'

The pale blue eyes didn't alter. They offered no commitment. But then neither was there outright refusal.

'A really big favour—'

Logan accepted St Clair Smith's blank expression as a 'go ahead – try me' and said, 'I'd like you to take Theresa out of Thailand and land her in Malaysia. Secretly. No immigration, no formalities. I'm asking you to smuggle her to safety.'

Aubrey St Clair Smith smiled without showing his teeth. His eyes remained set, slightly cold. 'And yourself, James?'

Logan drank from his glass again and kept it in his hand in case he was going to need it quickly. 'Nothing for me, Aubrey. I stay and then take the dogs with me, back to Bangkok. That'll give Theresa a free home run. Whaddya say?'

'Why d'you need to go back to Bangkok? Why not make a run for it with Theresa?'

'When I said I gave the Chinese the slip in Bangkok it was partly wishful thinking. I know this game well enough

167

and I know the Touming Guanxi. Put yourself in their position. They've got me in one place, and paperwork that'll blow their business sky high in another. What would you do, Aubrey?' He didn't give St Clair Smith a chance to help out. 'You'd let me run in the expectation that I'd lead you to the paperwork and then you'd lift it. If I appear in the Oriental having my lunch the day after tomorrow they'll assume it was a dry run or a no-go . . .'

'You're still thinking wishfully, James. They'll miss Theresa.'

'By which time Theresa'll be on her way to either Langkawi or Penang – if you're prepared to go along with it.'

'No reason why I shouldn't,' said St Clair Smith casually. 'But they won't stop once they know she's bolted.'

'But they won't know where or how. When she's got the stuff into the States I'm home and dry. They'll have to negotiate an agreement that leaves me and mine alone, or better still, an agreement that makes sure me and mine are left alone and Jim Logan and his daughter Theresa live happily ever after.'

'And what about Aubrey St Clair Smith? What does he get out of it?'

Logan looked surprised. He hadn't thought about that one. 'You want money, Aubrey?'

St Clair Smith shook his head with a sad smile. 'I've got plenty of that, thank you, James.'

'Then what do you want?'

'Why don't I present you with a bill when Theresa's home safe and sound and your little packet of insurance is out of harm's way?'

Logan studied St Clair Smith's suggestion with suspicion. It left a lot of holes for him to exploit; surely Smithy wasn't that dumb? Maybe he was. 'That sounds fair, Aubrey. Let's call it a deal.'

'Right,' said St Clair Smith. 'Let's assume you've brought the Touming Guanxi to Phuket and play it by ear. You can explain yourself at Ban Yit by helping to mount my new engine. No one'll query that. You could even be a friend down for a couple of days. Let's leave it like that.'

'Suits me.' Logan drained his glass and placed it carefully

on the table and got ready to stand up. St Clair Smith didn't move.

Logan subsided back into his armchair and raised his eyebrows.

'One other thing,' said St Clair Smith, ingenuously.

'Sure.'

'You said the CIA had sent a couple of people to look you up. How did you hear about this?'

Logan flipped his mind over a page of script. 'The Touming Guanxi warned me. I told you, they want to keep me alive until they can get their hands on the documents; they weren't sure what form the CIA contract took, but if I know the sort of boy who's carrying special-project credentials nowadays he's likely to kill first and worry about the details after. But there's no way I've got a CIA tail, Aubrey – that's one thing I'd bet my ass on. I might hallucinate Chinks but there's no fucking way I'd miss an American watcher – no way at all!'

'Well,' said St Clair Smith cheerfully, 'thank God for one bit of good news. D'you want to tell me what your CIA are getting out of a deal with the Touming Guanxi?'

'I told you – money.'

'Must be something else, James.'

'Nothing I can think of. It's pure "look the other way" for a numbered account in Geneva. You wouldn't even know where to start counting the noughts, Aubrey. Big money – Jesus! Don't even try to work it out.'

'OK, I won't. Where's Theresa now?'

'In bed, fast asleep.'

'Leave her there. Let's go and eat and we'll move out in the early hours.'

Logan nodded his head enthusiastically. He was happy to hand the controls over to Aubrey St Clair Smith – more than happy. Things had gone much more easily and smoothly than he'd expected, but there was one more small thing. 'I said I wouldn't let an American face within a mile of my back. But what about American voices?'

'The two usually go together, old chap. What's your problem?'

'When I rang that number you gave me it was answered by an American—'

'They call it paranoia, James. You've got it. The man you spoke to—'

'I didn't speak to him, I slammed the phone down.'

'—is a miserable bastard named Krislov. Runs the little workshop where I tie up my boat. He didn't arrive last week looking for you, James, he's been there for years. Now, are you going to leave the arrangements to me?'

'I've no choice, Aubrey,' said Logan with feigned reluctantance.

'OK. I'll arrange a car to take us round the back road to Ban Yit. That way we'll avoid the mob pissing it up at the Lighthouse at Chalong—' He broke off and waggled his fingers at the barman again. 'Please take Mr James to the restaurant and arrange a table for the two of us. James, tell me something.'

'Go on.'

'You've been around this part of the world for a hell of a long time. Have you ever come across an American called Contractor?'

Logan's expression didn't alter. 'What's his Christian name?'

'No idea. It was just something I'd heard. Chap I'd rather like to meet.'

Logan shook his head. 'The name doesn't ring a bell. What does he do?'

'No idea.' St Clair Smith stood up. 'It's not important. Let's go and eat.'

Chapter 17

The hired car St Clair Smith had arranged turned off the badly rutted road and crept down the gravelled, bumpy track that led, according to a crude hand-scrawled wooden sign in a sort of English, to 'Ban Yit Marine Workshop & Thai food eatery'.

St Clair Smith, sitting in the front beside the Thai chauffeur, tapped him on the knee and told him to put out his lights. The driver complied without answering and, in bottom gear, bounced the two hundred yards or so to the bottom of the slope. Half past three in the morning and it was as it should be – as quiet as the grave. It was deserted, the dim overhead lights barely showing the new arrivals another rough board with the word 'Footpath' scrawled across it in dripped black paint pointing between the boat yard's main, ramshackle tin building and Krislov's office. Higher up on a semi-cultivated slope was the living accommodation. Equally ramshackle, it was in total darkness. Somewhere at the base of it a dog gave a tentative instinctive growl but abandoned the temptation of a full-blooded howl remembering the last time he had woken up his master.

The car waited until the three figures had disappeared from the lambency of its dimmed lights then, with the back wheels skidding in search of traction on the uneven surface, the driver turned and disappeared back up the way he'd come. Silence descended once more. The place went back to being a midnight grave; not a person had stirred. Krislov

171

had a philosophy. If anyone wanted to rob him they were welcome to what they could find; if they came anywhere near his bedroom they'd be blown in half by the short-barrel Remington automatic twelve-bore beside his bed – no questions asked.

Aubrey St Clair Smith's inflatable with its powerful Johnson outboard waited for them on its bed of firm, clean sand about twelve metres from the lapping water of the incoming tide. It took the three of them a good few minutes of sweating and grunting to reach floatable water, and one by one they piled in. The moon had dropped behind the hills. It was pitch dark, like a black wall in front and with the dim outline of the semi-illuminated boat yard behind, but St Clair Smith seemed to know where he was going and for the first hundred yards or so he balanced himself on the stern and propelled the boat with a long-handled oar. When they reached deep water he started the motor and, keeping it to a gentle purr, headed slowly out into the bay. The heavy rubber dinghy made little wash. Nobody spoke and the engine sounded like the beating of feathers. Everywhere else slumbered.

But not Junit. In front and to the right of the dinghy the outline of the big trimaran loomed under a dimmed deck light hanging from the stern of the *Claudia*, and the shadowy figure of the Malay boat boy appeared on one of the stern fins ready to guide the dinghy alongside. No words, no greeting, no orders, no commands – everything was done as if in broad sunlight. Junit made fast the dinghy and reached out a hand for Theresa. Logan and St Clair Smith made their own way on board and within minutes everyone was below decks and everything except the riding light extinguished.

The cabin was large and airy and with the blinds down the night-light gave an eerie, ghostlike form of illumination. 'Anyone for a drink?' St Clair Smith dropped into his stance of urbane host quite naturally. 'Theresa, would you like Junit to prepare a little something for you in the microwave?'

'The only thing I want is more sleep, please, Aubrey.'

'Help yourself from the bar, James.' St Clair Smith took Theresa's hand and led her up the companionway, across

172

the deck and down into the port hull. It was a luxury compartment; bathed in pink light, she could have been standing at the door of one of *Canberra*'s more exclusive staterooms. 'Sorry it's so basic,' he murmured with concern. 'I really must do something to make it a little more comfortable. Can you manage until then?' It was all show. It was the sort of thing he did best. He was riding his eccentric Englishman pose to the full, and she loved it – as they all did.

In reply she turned, and on her bare tiptoes kissed the side of his face. He felt her full, unsupported, firm breasts through his thin shirt. His loins stirred. If it hadn't been for the fact that Dad was only a few yards away her little bare feet wouldn't have touched the deck! 'It's lovely, Aubrey,' she whispered. It was all promise, but no substance. Theresa was like that – she could have been a female Aubrey St Clair Smith. 'I'll manage. Goodnight, Smithy.'

It was the first time a woman had called him that and he liked it. The next time he heard it was early the next morning, and it came from a rough American accent below the *Claudia*'s stern.

'SMITHY!' Jack Krislov balanced himself gingerly in a barely adequate, much-battered narrow fibreglass dinghy and, with his hands cupped round his mouth, desecrated the quiet morning air with another round bellow. 'Come on! Move yourself, you dickhead! Some of us've got work to do!'

Logan got there first. He poked his head out of the stern hatch and glared around the otherwise peaceful bay. 'What's all that goddamn noise?' It came naturally to Logan, and the two men studied each other, one glaring, the other staring, with interest.

'Mr St Clair Smith about?' Krislov lowered his voice, instinctively, not respectfully. He wiped the curiosity off his face before St Clair Smith appeared.

'Good morning, Jack.' St Clair Smith wore one of his outrageous psychedelic kimonos; even having just been rudely awakened, his hair was immaculate, there wasn't a trace of sleep in his features, and it looked almost as if he'd shaved between being woken by Krislov's bellow and appearing on the stern of his boat. 'Do we have a problem?'

'That must have been you, then, Smithy, making all that

goddamn racket first thing this morning! Four o'clock, I made it – what time d'you call that? Wait until I tell Dad!'

'Did you come to say that, Jack?' St Clair Smith, still excessively polite, ignored Krislov's curious glance at the head poking out of the stern hatch. 'Or was it something less important?'

'You kill me, Smithy!' Krislov gave him a broad, unshaven grin and removed the smouldering cigarette stub from between his grizzled, blistered lips. 'Can I come on board?'

'Absolutely, Jack. Approach!'

'Aye aye, sir!' Krislov threw an exaggerated salute, retained his balance and manoeuvred his flimsy craft alongside the large trimaran. 'My God, Smithy!' He shook his head in feigned wonderment. 'You look so goddamn beautiful I could eat you! Where would I get a dress like that?'

'Thank you, Jack. How can I help you?'

'What about this auxiliary that's sitting in the workshop. I can bring it over but I can't start on it yet. I had a look at yours with young Junit. I wouldn't advise putting to sea with that one, it's going to pack up any time now.'

'Thanks, Jack. I'll come ashore and see about it later this morning—' He gave the American a broad but humourless smile. 'When I've woken up and had my toast and marmalade . . .'

'See ya, Smithy!' Krislov gave himself a push off from the *Claudia*, dropped into the bottom of the craft and tugged the cord of the engine. It spoke volumes for his skill as an engineer. The tiny outboard looked as though it had stopped functioning at about the time of the Iwo Jima landings, but it started first pull and, with a healthy thump, lifted the flimsy craft's bows out of the water and carried Krislov in a wide arc back to his bit of beach.

Aubrey St Clair Smith watched Krislov weave his way in and out of the moored yachts for a few minutes before giving Logan a sad but slightly cynical smile. 'That, by the way' – he jerked his chin in the direction of the departed Krislov – 'is the voice that spoilt the taste of your whisky last night. See what I meant? Can you imagine him crawling around in the gutter with an AK47 looking for a guy who hasn't paid his income tax!'

174

Logan didn't see the funny side of it. 'Stranger things have happened, pal. How long before you can get out of here? I want to see Theresa on her way—'

St Clair Smith returned his gaze to the sandy beach below the ramshackle café where Krislov was busy securing his dinghy. His expression was thoughtful. He appeared to have other things on his mind than Logan's problems. 'Junit tells me Jack Krislov came and had a look at it while I was in Phuket. According to Junit he pronounced it dead. I was going to help him install the new one but you heard him say he couldn't fit the time in just yet. He works like that. Some days you can't see his body for sweat, he's all over the place doing this and that, and other days he's lounging around the sand with nothing to do. I wonder how he found the time to trot over here and look at my auxiliary?'

'Is it of consequence?' Logan turned his eyes to the shore, crinkled them against the sun as he picked out Krislov's departing figure, then searched St Clair Smith's face. Paranoia was infectious.

St Clair Smith made no response.

Settling himself in front of his radio, Krislov lit another cigarette and pressed the button. 'Dixie?'

'C'm'in.'

'Jack K. Gimme a blanket but don't go away, I wanna talk to you in a minute. OK?'

'Y'got it, mate.'

Krislov turned the dial until it reached the minute pencil mark on the screen. This was Hagen's contact slot. There'd be a permanent voice watch on stand-by.

'C'm'in, Sentry,' Krislov said softly.

'Go on.'

'What's the target look like?'

No questions, no queries; Sentry described James Logan as he'd been described to him by Mark Hagen.

'He's on Aubrey St Clair Smith's boat,' pronounced Krislov.

'You sure?'

'I only saw his head, but it's him. Arrived with St Clair

175

Smith by car early this morning. Don't know where from – could have been the airport or Phuket town. Roger on that?'

Sentry didn't say. He checked his notes. 'What about the engine?'

'Definitely kaput. St Clair Smith's bought a new one. It arrived day before yesterday from Bangkok. He won't be leaving before the new one's in and I've told him I'm too busy to do it at the moment.'

'Anything else of interest?'

'That's it.'

Krislov flicked the switch to stand-by, sat back in his cockpit and beat a few drum rolls with his fingers. He was going to break a rule, and Hagen wasn't going to like it. Fuck Hagen! He went back to the radio, switched to a preset frequency and waited ten seconds. Clear as a bell. He turned down the sound. 'Sierra two one,' said a crisp, comfortable American voice. S21 – Central Intelligence Radio Relay Center, Saigon.

Krislov squeezed the tit on the handset. 'DROGHEDA,' he said into the mouthpiece.

'Wait a while—'

He waited, but only a few seconds while the comfortable American voice looked up the code-name.

'OK, DROGHEDA. Talk to me.'

'I want a trace through DROGHEDA source on HOTEL-ALPHA-GOLF-ECHO-NOVEMBER.'

'OK. Cut out now. I'll come back. I've got your twenty.'

Krislov lifted the switch for a count of five then dropped it again, went back to his chair and picked up the finger-drumming where he'd left off. He didn't have time to finish the tune before the red light on the radio set flicked twice in quick succession.

'OK,' he announced.

'Bangkok,' said the easy-going voice. 'That's brackets, zero, two, then two, two, six dash zero, one, nine, nine. You want a repeat?'

'No thanks. Out.'

Krislov picked up the ship-to-shore phone and waited for a connection.

Hagen watched the buzzing telephone like a mongoose

watching a swaying cobra. This wasn't good news. It couldn't be. The only contact with this number was the last man in the world he wanted to hear from. Eventually he picked up the phone and listened to the silence and waited for the blunt voice of Sam Reilly to spoil the rest of his day. A strange voice was even more disturbing. He'd rather have had Reilly.

'Bangkok number two, two, six dash zero, one, nine, nine?'

'Yeah. Go on,' he said gruffly.

'Maritime radio telephone station, Pattaya,' the voice said in barely recognisable English. 'I'm relaying a call from three, bravo, bravo, tango; international code – tango, hotel, one, seven. Connecting.' The clear tone was replaced by the sound of a running tap, and through the hissing and crackling came, to Hagen, an unrecognisable voice. He said nothing but listened carefully.

'Krislov here,' he made out. 'Your man is in Phuket. I suggest you make tracks right away . . .'

Hagen removed the mouthpiece and stared at it. Then he stuck it back against his ear. 'Are you fucking crazy?' he hissed.

Krislov wasn't having it. He'd already broken a couple of primary rules, and the first of them was a finger-breaker at the best of times – never contact an agent in position without arrangement. Tough on Hagen, but he'd have to live with it. 'You've got no time to waste bollocking about on the phone, and you've got no fucking time to sit around waiting for Sentry to work through the system. Get your ass down here immediately. Airplane to Phuket, taxi to Chalong. Contact me over Pan's Lighthouse radio link. My call sign: three, bravo, bravo, tango. I'll pick you up. Now fuck off yourself!' Krislov slammed the phone back into its bracket and Hagen was left listening to the water sloshing around in the bottom of the bucket.

But he wasted no time. Before the sweat had dried on the phone's earpiece he had packed his few pieces of kit, rung down for his bill and ordered a taxi. Three-quarters of an hour later he was on the domestic flight to Phuket Airport.

Chapter 18

Ban Yit/Chalong, January 1975

Pan's Lighthouse had started life as a small shed on the edge of the Chalong Bay where the local fishermen would sit and chat and smoke and complain about the lack of amenities. Then it became a large shed and now it was a larger shed where local fishermen wouldn't be seen dead, and alien yacht owners, beach bums, drifters and the debris that had filtered in from different sections of the Vietnam War now sat and chatted and smoked and complained about the price of good smack and the lack of amenities. But it was a meeting place; one with a pointed tin roof, like a miniature mosque, the heat on the tin roof being absorbed by a straggly and motley layer of attap that had turned dark brown, not only with drying out from the heat but by the assault of about three-quarters of a ton of nicotine and tar. Everyone smoked. It was as if dying of lung cancer were the yachtsmen's ultimate ambition. In the Lighthouse the food was good, expensive and plain, and the beer was always plentiful and cold.

By half past three in the afternoon the tin roof of Pan's Lighthouse was bouncing off its beams with the volume of noise hammering against it from thirty or forty beer-laden voices shouting into each other's ears. It was a normal Tuesday afternoon. The yachtsmen and women were in the middle of their usual daily social. Nobody listened, everybody spoke at the same time. But they liked it. It was an escape from the rat race. They were all modern Gauguins,

178

escapists. It was what they'd come halfway round the world to do.

Nobody noticed Hagen's arrival. If they did, nobody was interested. He made his way to the section of the bar that held the till and the VHF radio. 'Beer,' he bellowed into the young Thai woman's face, and when she brought it he pointed to the solid radio transmitter with an elongated microphone on a bent metal stand. 'Does that thing work?'

'Who you want?'

He lowered his voice automatically – it was habit – and studied his neighbours. They weren't interested. 'Three, bravo, bravo, tango.'

'In the bay?'

Hagen stared at her. *Was it in the bay? How the fuck would I know?* 'I think so.'

'What's name of boat?'

Fucking hell! 'Can't you just scream out the call sign?'

'Who're yer trying to reach, mate?' A friendly Aussie turned on his elbow and offered his advice. Hagen didn't want it. He didn't want a fight either. 'A friend. Krislov . . .'

'E's aht in the flaming bay – on 'is boat.' The Aussie put his other bare arm on the bar and bellowed at the young Thai woman. 'Forgit the flaming call sign – just ask for the *Sara-Louise*.'

'What's that?' asked Hagen.

'Name of 'is boat, mate – go on, yer silly cow, get on with it!'

'Thanks,' said Hagen.

'No probs.' The Australian had done his turn. He turned his back on the Yank and picked up with his mates where he'd left off. The girl muttered into the microphone, turned up the volume on the speaker and handed the mike to Hagen. Krislov's voice boomed out of the receiver.

'Watcha, Jack, boy!' Hagen's new friend and his mates near by bellowed – it was part of the joke, all part of the atmosphere. But not for Hagen. He winced and reached across the girl's body and turned down the volume. 'Krislov?' he muttered into the microphone. 'Come and get me out of this fuckin' madhouse.'

'On my way. Don't go away.'

The Chinese who'd travelled from Bangkok on the same aircraft waited until Hagen entered the Lighthouse then turned away and watched from a distance. When it looked as if the wait was going to be a long one he took off his jacket, shirt, shoes and socks, rolled his trousers halfway up his substantial calves, meandered along to one of the local stalls on the hard bit of road leading to Chalong village and bought himself a chipped enamel plate of fried mee. He sat down at one of the broken wooden tables shaded by a large, dirty blue-and-white umbrella advertising Rothman's King Size cigarettes. He ate his mee slowly, without taking his eyes off the entrance to Pan's Lighthouse. He fitted in. In Bangkok he'd looked like a businessman; in Phuket he looked like a local Chinese with a good pair of trousers.

When Krislov and Hagen came out of the Lighthouse, the Chinaman left his package of clothes on the table with the unfinished mee and walked aimlessly along the untidy beach. Then he turned back and watched one of the Americans climb into a heavy rubber dinghy while the other pulled it off the sand and into the water. With a roar of its outboard, it stuck its rubber nose into the air and, almost skimming the mirror-like surface, hurtled off across the bay. The Chinese had glanced casually at the name on the dinghy. As he walked back to his table his head was down and he absently kicked the sand and bits of drift as he muttered to himself the unfamiliar words, 'Sara-Louise . . . Sara-Louise . . . Sara-Louise . . .'

Chapter 19

Bangkok, January 1975

It wasn't in Liu Hongzhou's nature to smile or show pleasure, but if this was the first time in his life he did both at the same time he made a good job of it. He replaced the telephone and went back into the sitting room and rejoined his father.

'I think the Americans have found Logan for us, Father.'

'He shouldn't have been lost in the first place,' said the old man. 'And what does "think" mean?'

Liu went on unabashed. 'Peng Soon was watching an American who was watching Logan. The American then switched his attentions to Theresa. He wasn't obvious, he wasn't stupid, he was very good at his job . . .'

'And that was?'

'We think CIA. New face, very gifted in moving himself about. But Peng Soon was his better . . .'

'Was it not Peng Soon who lost him?' responded Liu Zhoushiu sarcastically.

'One of those things, Father, when all the accidents happened at the same time in the enemy's favour. Likewise we lost James Logan and Theresa. But all has come well.'

'And you're determined to tell me how clever everyone has been.'

'Not only determined, Father.' Liu smiled again. He'd have to be careful – it could become a habit. 'But with pleasure. Peng Soon should have joined his brothers in

Chiang Mai but he debased himself and pleaded for the chance to restore himself . . .'

'How did he manage to crack into your non-existent good nature?'

'He offered me both his hands if he did not find Logan . . .'

'And he hasn't yet found him. He's found some American that you think may be a CIA agent. When's he going to give us these useless hands?'

Liu Hongzhou listened with respect to his father but, nevertheless, continued without acknowledging what he'd said. 'Peng Soon waited at the airport for two days and nights. And then he was rewarded. The man he'd lost came in hurriedly and took an instant ticket to Phuket. Peng Soon went on the same aeroplane and followed him to a boat harbour at Chalong. There the American was picked up by another American and taken to a boat on the other side of the bay. The name of the man who took him was Krislov. He owns the yard at Ban Yit and has a boat the name of which is *Sara-Louise*.'

'You believe that Jim Logan will be there too?'

'He has to be, Father. Why else would this experienced watcher leave Bangkok to join up with another of his kind in a place like Phuket?'

The old man shook his head slowly and studied the long nail on his little finger. He always did this when something was bothering him. He was murmuring to himself as he stroked the fingernail. The younger Liu stared at the bowed head and listened.

'Why would Jim Logan stop at Phuket?' asked the old man. 'Once he'd broken our ring round Bangkok he could have continued. What happens at Phuket that he should waste his time when he should be fleeing? Has he hidden his confession and fortune there . . .?' He looked up into his son's eyes. 'You're taking personal charge of this business? You're going to Phuket yourself?'

'Of course.'

'What arrangements are you making?'

'I think you can safely leave those up to me, Father. I

want—' He corrected himself quickly in the face of his father's sharp glance. 'We want Mr Logan alive and unharmed and we want any information he has hidden. It's as simple as that.'

Chapter 20

Hagen hadn't moved for the last half-hour. Since early dawn he'd remained below deck on Krislov's *Sara-Louise*, a pair of high-powered binoculars glued to his eyes as he studied every movement on the *Claudia*'s deck.

'That's definitely Logan's daughter,' he murmured without moving the glasses from his eyes, 'and the bozo with the snow-white thatch is St Clair Smith? He doesn't look like the guy I saw in Bangkok.'

Krislov studied the back of Hagen's head. 'What's he wearing?'

'What the fuck's that got to do with it?'

'Well,' growled Krislov, 'for one thing it saves me getting up there and joining you with the binocs, and secondly I don't want attention drawn by too much movement. If we start moving ourselves from one side to the other of the slammin' boat it'll jump up and down like a fucking roller-coaster. You want everyone looking across at us? Just tell me what the guy's wearing.'

'Some fancy blue trousers and the same colour shirt with a white collar. What is he – some sort of faggot?'

'That's definitely Aubrey St Clair Smith. He wouldn't be seen dead on board his boat in any other sort of clothing. Not the shorts-and-singlet type.'

'OK,' said Hagen, 'so that's St Clair Smith and the girl is Logan's daughter. So where the hell is Logan? How do we know he's on that boat?'

184

'I should imagine if the daughter's there so is Logan. He was there yesterday, I definitely saw him, or at least I saw his head, going by your description . . .'

'Shut up a minute!' Hagen touched the tip of his finger on the focusing knurl, threw everything out of focus, then started again. He got a needle-sharp image of Junit. 'Who's this, then?'

'Whaddya see?'

'Young guy. Dark brown. Looks in good shape, dressed for the weather and the job – shorts, bare feet and a shirt.' Hagen watched Junit talking to Aubrey St Clair Smith for a while then, in case he was missing something, quartered the large trimaran's deck again.

For Hagen, a non-seaman, Krislov could have done better, he could have put his boat much closer to the *Claudia* and made life much easier for him. But Krislov had his reasons. He had moored the *Sara-Louise* on the most northerly buoy without losing the protection from the weather of the bay itself. By doing this he had shielded them from observation from St Clair Smith's boat. In between them were half a dozen other yachts of different sizes, shapes and nationalities. He wasn't expecting company, neither was he expecting trouble, but when you've been running with your head back to front for as long as Krislov had you did things always with the escape route in mind. And when you've got guys of Hagen's calling moving in on you, trouble, ducking and weaving, and hard running usually went hand in hand. Krislov reckoned he was ready for all of that.

He'd been on board the *Sara-Louise* with Hagen since before first light. Ostensibly he was working on the boat's main engine but, so far, he hadn't dirtied his hands. He sat comfortably in the cabin looking at the back of Hagen's head and up-ended his fourth beer of the morning. He removed it from his lips, replaced it with an unlighted cigarette and said, 'The young guy's named Junit. Indonesian. Tough bastard but not in your league – not in your game either. Works Smithy's boat for him, been with him for a few years, looks after him as though he was his dad.' He lit his cigarette from an old petrol lighter, blew smoke at the back of Hagen's head and coughed out what had started as a chortle. 'Might even be that too, except he's the wrong colour.' Still talking, he brought the chest-racking cough under control and smothered it with a grin. 'You can count him as a nuisance, not a threat.'

Hagen lowered his binoculars and turned his head to frown into Krislov's eyes. 'I can take your word on that, can I? And St Clair Smith too, I suppose? Fuck-all to it, is there?'

Krislov let Hagen's quietly hissed sarcasm slip over the top of his head. Without malice he stared hard at Hagen as if looking for a crack. But nothing showed. Hagen was being himself. Krislov reached over and opened the cooler and took out another cold can. He pulled the tab and shoved his mouth over the opening without losing a drop. 'Don't get yourself into a sweat worrying about Aubrey St Clair Smith, pal, he's just a fucking rich limey. There's no background of spookery. It's my bet he'd run a mile if someone crept up at night-time and said "boo"!'

'I'm not worried about St Clair Smith,' said Hagen. 'I'm worried about getting this Logan guy off his boat and onto ours without starting a fucking war. Do people like St Clair Smith carry weapons?'

'He's probably got an old bird-scarer on board in case he runs into pirates. But even that's unlikely.'

Hagen considered every option. He tried not to under-estimate his enemies, but this one was out of his range. For once he had to rely on others. He'd no experience of taking out people on the water, particularly in public. He'd got a large audience if anything went wrong. He wasn't worried about an old man like St Clair Smith – he'd studied him carefully for the past two hours. It was young men in shorts with sturdy thick thighs and shoulders like those of middle-weight boxers that worried him.

'So, what d'ya reckon?' He shifted his glance back to the *Claudia*, silhouetted against the early sun as she wallowed imperiously on the thick, rippleless water of the small bay. 'What's the method of taking a guy off another boat?'

'Like you said, in this sort of society, with this number of boats hanging around, if he doesn't come quietly and of his own free will it's more than likely to start a war. I think the best thing we can do is hang around until he goes ashore and take him then – in fact, that's the only way.' Krislov removed the can from his mouth, belched and put the can back in place.

'Which doesn't advance us a fucking inch.' Hagen was fast running out of patience. He'd never been a sit-around-and-wait-for-it-to-happen man; he hadn't the temperament for ambush. 'So how do we get him to go ashore?'

'Could be fairly simple,' grunted Krislov. 'I'll bring him ashore.'

'You'll what?'

'St Clair Smith's got an engine waiting to be installed. It'll take more than just Smithy to help me get it there. If I persuade this Logan guy to come ashore with me you can give him the good news while my back's turned.'

'Won't that look suspicious?'

'What, for me? I don't give a fuck. D'you think I'm going to sit in the corner and bawl if Mr Aubrey St Clair Smith cuts up rough and tells me he won't never use my mooring again because one of his guests got his head stove in? Don't make me laugh!'

Hagen looked at Krislov anew. 'OK,' he said, 'let's assume you've persuaded Logan off the boat and onto the sand. What are the others going to be doing – lining the edge of the boat and waving their handkerchiefs at him?'

Krislov's patience ran out. 'Listen, schmuck—' He wasn't intimidated by Hagen. He'd seen boys like this before; big heads, big words, sometimes big balls, but it always came down to what they had up top. And he'd seen that too, he knew what they had inside their heads, he'd seen it spread around enough in the dirt after they'd practised what they preached. *His* head was still intact. He intended keeping it that way. 'You want me to wrap this baby in cotton wool for you so that you start tweaking his fingers? I've already solved half the problem for you. I said I'd get him ashore. I'll do that. Then *you* can do something. That's what you're here for, to pick that guy up, not to come round here telling me to do it for you – got it, asshole? Just keep out of my fuckin' face!'

Hagen watched the red light flashing for a moment and then nodded. 'OK.'

It took Krislov by surprise. 'What's that supposed to mean?'

'It means OK, I'll sort it out myself.'

Krislov tipped the can into his mouth and gurgled until there was no more there. He lowered the can. 'Sure. OK, then. Just don't fuck me around, asshole, and don't talk down at me!'

'OK, Jack.' Hagen smiled disarmingly. 'Let's start again. Make a suggestion. It's your land, you know the place and you've got the brains. You've done this sort of thing before?'

'I was standing behind trees getting fuck shot out of me when you were wondering what that zip in the front of your short pants was for.'

Hagen didn't take offence. He'd read the signal – and he wasn't stupid. Krislov the ugly was the key. 'OK, tell me how you think we ought to do it.'

Krislov hadn't worked himself into a lather; his performance was superficial. Inside he was as cool as an ice cube. He accepted Hagen's invitation, but first said, 'Are you sure the guy we're handling is the one you want? There's no profit in going through this routine and finding at the end of the line something you didn't want.'

Which was an interesting point. It wasn't lost on Hagen, but he wasn't going into details, not with this scab-covered punk. 'Sure it's the right guy. I wouldn't be here otherwise, and anyway, it's fuck-all to do with you what's on the end of the line. If I don't like what's there I'll throw the fucking thing back. All you've got to do is prepare the ground and then forget it. Get on with telling me how to do this thing.'

Krislov shrugged. 'It's on your head.'

'Sure – but get on with it.'

'OK – we'll play the game at night. There's a three-quarter moon so we'll be able to see something, or at least you will. I'll arrange from St Clair Smith's boat that the guy – Logan, you say . . .?'

Hagen nodded.

' . . . comes ashore in St Clair Smith's dinghy on his own. Simple. You do what you want, tap him on the head, break his legs, whatever, just as long as you make no noise over it.' He stopped for a moment to light a cigarette and reached for another can. He washed the smoke down with a couple of mouthfuls of beer. 'About the noise—'

'What about it?'

'I'll cover it for you. I'll tell Phipop—'

'Who's he?'

'A kid, a nutcase, attached himself to me; does odd jobs for his feed. I'll tell him to start up the pick-up and give it a few revs, just in case there's any screaming and shouting . . .'

'There won't be,' said Hagen knowingly.

'Just in case,' repeated Krislov.

'OK. I'll go along with that—' Hagen stopped abruptly and thought about it for a moment. Krislov waited. Hagen's eyes narrowed. 'Can this guy, Peepop, drive the pick-up?'

'After a style,' said Krislov. 'Why?'

'What if instead of just revving the motor he took it for a ride?' Hagen lowered his head, glanced out of the starboard porthole and studied the hillside above the bay. 'That road,' he said without turning his head into the cabin. 'I followed it through with the binocs. It runs right round the bay above where Logan's friend's boat is. If your Peepop made enough noise and flashed his headlights around, it could be thought later that Logan had been taken out of the area. Could be anywhere. One place he couldn't be is on this little old tub.'

Krislov stared into space for several seconds, running the idea through his head, looking for snags, then he raised his gaze to Hagen. 'That's a good one,' he said simply.

'We'll do it,' said Hagen. 'That's it. You make whatever arrangements are necessary. I'll get round the back of the scenery out of the way while you sort it out and move in when you reckon the time's come. OK, Jack, it's all yours. You bring 'im in and I'll take it over when you touch sand.' He allowed the suggestion of a satisfied grin to touch the corners of his mouth. 'And you'll tell this boy of yours when to run the motor.'

'I won't be here to tell him. I'll be on the boat fixing the fucking engine. You'll have to tell him yourself.'

'Does he speak English?'

'He doesn't even speak fucking Thai. He's dumb, he's got no tongue.'

'Jesus Christ! Just what we need—'

'But don't worry. I'll instruct him. The minute he sees Logan go down he can do his thing with the pick-up. Don't you try to tell him anything.' Krislov's eyes bored into Hagen's. 'You'll only confuse the poor fucker. So? You happy with that, then?'

'Sure,' said Hagen. 'What time's all this going to take place?'

'Fucked if I know!' Krislov showed his tar-coloured broken teeth in his version of a smile. His face wasn't used to it; it looked more like a grimace, a snarl. 'You can't set a deadline on a thing like this, but I'll tell you what, get yourself into position about eleven and stay there until it happens. That's the best I can do. Once I've talked the guy into coming ashore it's all up to you. From then on I'm out. I know fuck-all about it and if you screw up get out of here and keep running. I don't want to hear the name Jack Krislov mentioned in connection with a dickhead who's killed some poor innocent old fucker on my beach. Got it? OK?'

Hagen up-ended a bottle of Singha beer and stared at him down the side of it as the contents gurgled down his throat. He removed the neck of the bottle from his mouth, belched, wiped his lips on his bare arm and said, 'The only time your name will be mentioned, Jack, is if everything your end goes wrong. Bear that in mind and make sure it doesn't.'

'Go screw yourself!'

Chapter 21

Ban Yit, January 1975

The sun suddenly dropped as though its string had been cut and disappeared in a blaze of orange, yellow and red streaks into the trees on the crest of the ridge that gave Ban Yit bay its protective weather shield. The water glistened like a wet mirror, and across the bay through the distant reflection of Mrs Krislov's waterside café could be seen a million mosquitoes hovering just above the water, waiting for their dinner. Apart from the gentle hum of the insects and the unaggressive slap, slap, slap of the water, disturbed by the movement of small craft somewhere out in the main bay, reaching *Claudia*'s hull with its last gasp, Ban Yit was enveloped in a deathly quiet.

Aubrey St Clair Smith came on deck with a large whisky in one hand and a cigarette in the other, stood at the stern of his boat and breathed in the peace and quiet. He glanced down, through the window into the cabin. Logan sat with his feet up and like himself clutched a large glass of whisky in his hand. Theresa sat opposite, poring idly through one of the boat's many paperbacks. It seemed as good a time as any. Without rocking the boat he made his way to the crew's quarters and tapped with his roped-sole shoe on the hatch. Without waiting for a response, he lifted it, propped it open and sent a solid shaft of light soaring into the clear sky like a searchlight with nowhere to go.

'Come and hold a torch for me in the engine room, will

you?' he called down. He spoke in a normal voice. It was surprising how it echoed off the still water.

Logan hadn't missed the movement on deck, nor the voice. He remained still in the cabin, listening, but there was nothing more for him to hear. He made a casual move towards the companionway as if the desire for a spot of night air had suddenly come on him, then, with a natural cough, surfaced on deck and strolled towards the stern.

'Did I hear the word engine?' he said lazily, and was just in time to notice the exchange of glances between St Clair Smith and Junit. 'I know my way around an engine room if it's any help to you, Aubrey.'

'Ah, James! Just the man.' St Clair Smith took Logan by the arm and walked him up to the bow. He stopped above the netting where the deck ended. Across the water the ridge of trees stood out against the darkening sky like a charcoal drawing, highlighted against dull silver contours showing where the moon would shortly appear. St Clair Smith leaned on the safety rail and lowered his voice. 'Don't be deceived by the air of peace and tranquillity, Jim. It could be a bloody hotbed out there—'

Logan studied the blurred outline of St Clair Smith's face and wondered whether he'd given the Englishman too much of an impression of vulnerability. Did he think he was shitting himself? He said nothing.

'Which is why I must warn you again about keeping yourself out of sight. I don't want any of the smartasses on these boats here to get a sight of you and I can't guarantee anonymity if you are seen too much on deck.'

'You serious?'

'Of course I'm bloody serious. Out there are Chinese in every crack you can find; Chinese from Hong Kong, from Taiwan, from Singapore, and you can't tell the difference between any of them, and those from Bangkok . . .'

'You trying to tell your old granny how eggs should be sucked, Aubrey?'

'James, I'm telling you something that you should be telling yourself. You will have been missed by now. The dogs are out for you. You didn't go by air and you didn't go by

192

boat or train – they've covered all those. So how did you go?'

Logan shifted his gaze from St Clair Smith's face to the flickering reflections of the lights from across the bay at Chalong. He must be kidding! 'Aubrey,' he grunted, 'I'll grant you Phuket, anything could have happened there. Compared with this place that's the centre of the universe. But Ban Yit? Come off it – nobody's coming to Ban Yit to look for Jim Logan. It's the last place in the world, Aubrey. Bangkok won't know anything about this.' He looked around him again. 'Jesus, how the fucking hell could anybody find me here?'

St Clair Smith studied the American's face by the light of the mast lamp for a few seconds. He'd deliberately kept the deck lights off, but he knew that if anyone was interested in activity on the *Claudia* they wouldn't need deck lights to know about it. But his main object was to show his innocence and the innocence of his boat and crew; not to show that he was suspicious of every little ripple on the pond and that he was prepared for most eventualities. He must be exactly as people wanted him to be; exactly as he'd always been – harmless, a non-eventer in any sort of game or race. 'OK, James,' he said at length. 'Let's see if we can all get infected by your unbounded optimism. But I must, again, insist on that one thing—'

'What's that?' asked Logan aggressively. Aubrey St Clair Smith's big-brother attitude was beginning to cloy. He must be tired. He felt irritation rising, and getting irritated with the guy he'd put most of his money on wasn't going to pay any sort of dividend. He took a grip on his attitude and looked attentively at the Englishman.

'That you don't show yourself too much in the daylight,' said St Clair Smith. 'Words travel faster than the speed of light around here. One word about strange Americans and you'll have the whole Chinese fleet converging on us. Stay quiet, stay out of sight and beware of strange Chinamen . . .'

'Fuck the Chinese, Aubrey! I can handle those. It's strange Americans that give me the shits; they're the guys that worry me. I can talk and make reason with the Chinese, but not these bastards. The only thing they want is to do the job

193

and get out.' He stopped and stared at the stars for a moment. 'Unless the system's changed a lot since I was running wild . . .'

'Forget Americans for the time being, James. You just concentrate on keeping out of sight in daylight and I'll keep my eyes open for strange Americans . . .' Aubrey St Clair Smith's teeth showed in the dark. 'And the only strange ones you'll find in Ban Yit, my friend, are ordinary, straight-forward, crazy American yachtsmen. But enough of that. Go and tell Theresa what I said about keeping out of sight. It'll probably only be for tomorrow. If I can make that bugger Krislov get a move on we could be on the move by first light day after tomorrow. You won't change your mind and come with us?'

Logan shook his head. 'We've already been over that. Let's leave things the way we agreed.'

Chapter 22

Krislov arrived at the *Claudia*'s mooring at four in the afternoon. The water was almost lapping the gunwales, and as he passed on her port side he called out and did a wide sweep to draw up to her stern. He grabbed hold of the ladder of the starboard hull, hung on against the movement of the tide and shouted again.

Junit accepted the line he threw and made the overloaded dinghy fast. 'Smithy about?' Krislov nipped lightly aboard and headed for the engine room.

'Hello, Jack.' St Clair Smith cast his eyes over Krislov's overloaded dinghy. 'What've you got there?'

'Stuff to get started on dismantling and replacing that motor of yours. Got held up over there.' He didn't say where or point; it was 'there' and that was all Smithy was going to get. 'Got a couple of hours to spare . . . OK with you?'

St Clair Smith glanced at his watch. It wasn't necessary; he knew the time down to the last second. It was surprise. And with surprise, in St Clair Smith's world, always went suspicion. But that was part of the business. He recovered before anything showed. 'Bit late to start, isn't it, Jack?'

Krislov allowed the tone of St Clair Smith's voice to go over his head. 'Nah, I've brought some strobes. I thought I might leave it till tomorrow but there's a guy just arrived with a kaput main engine. I'm going to be on that for the next three days. So—' He offered his take-it-or-leave-it look and waited for St Clair Smith to make up his mind. He helped him on a bit. 'Be nearly a week before you can get out of Ban Yit if I don't start now.'

'I reckoned a three-man job, this,' said Aubrey. 'How many can you muster?'

'Well – there's me.' He stared hard at Junit. 'You know mechanics, son?' he said in Malay.

A barely perceptible glance at St Clair Smith, a slight hesitation, and Junit shook his head and offered him one of the cold beers he'd brought up from below.

Krislov ran his eyes over the stocky, tough-looking Javanese as he burst the lid off the can of Fosters. It confirmed his first impression. This boy was tough. He hoped Hagen had listened hard to his physical combat instructor. He took a long swig from his can of beer and, without another glance at Junit, touched the condensation-covered can to St Clair Smith's arm and said, 'Well, he can hold the light. Smithy, you're handy with a spanner – I'll try and find another pair of greasy hands and we'll have it finished in no time. Whaddya say?' Krislov looked Logan up and down incuriously. 'You know anything about auxies, pal?'

'You hum it, I'll play it,' said Logan, straight-faced.

'The world's full of fuckin' comedians,' commented Krislov as he descended into the engine room and stared around him in the artificial light. 'Let's have that stuff in here . . .'

'By the way, Jack,' said St Clair Smith, innocently, 'would you try and remember we have a lady on board?'

'I should have worn a tux?'

'Your language, Jack. Keep it down.'

'OK, Smithy, just for you.' He turned to Logan. 'Come on then, smartass, let's get this fucking engine out of its bed.'

It was well past one in the morning before the *Claudia*'s auxiliary engine was finally changed over. There was no time for chat, just a quick beer each, and Krislov, on edge, returned for the second load. 'I'm pooped,' he told St Clair Smith. 'That was a helluva goddamn day's work. How much stuff is there left to take?'

'Why don't you leave it till the morning?'

'It's already fucking morning, Smithy. I don't want to see any more friggin' morning until tomorrow!' He threw an appealing look at Logan. 'How about you taking the next load ashore? My dinghy's not up to a wanked-out engine block. It'll have to be yours, Smithy . . .'

'OK with you, Jim?' said St Clair Smith.

'Sure thing.'

'Go with him, Junit. D'you want some cash, Jack?'

'Never say no, Smithy. Hey, sonny!' Krislov watched Logan and Junit manhandle the solid engine casing into St Clair Smith's rubber dinghy and broke off to give his version of a stage whisper to Junit. 'Try not to make too much noise when you land this thing. Stick it in the back shed, metal door, round the back. Just in case some thieving bastard sneaks up and pinches it . . .'

'I hadn't got you down as a worrier, Jack,' said St Clair Smith, seriously.

'It's all bubbling underneath, Smithy. It's having had so much shit thrown at me that it's stopped showing!' Krislov sat back and accepted another can of beer from St Clair Smith. The new engine was working nicely. Everything was cooling down, and with the deck lights off they sat in a sort of suspended limbo on a lake of black shimmering tar. The three-quarter moon was at its zenith. It should have been one of the most peaceful little corners of this little wet paradise. The two men conversed in hushed tones as they waited for the return of Logan and Junit. They'd been gone for twenty minutes. They should have been back five minutes ago. But nobody panicked. Aubrey St Clair Smith should have done.

'OK, Junit,' said Logan as they approached the beach in front of the café. 'I'm lifting the screw. Time to get your feet wet.'

The Javanese slid over the inflatable's bulky rubber side and found himself up to his thighs in the cooling water. He slung the painter over his shoulder and hauled Logan and the boat over the last of the rocky outcrop and onto the sand. Logan leapt out onto the dry and helped drag the dinghy as far up the beach as it would go. The discarded engine

197

weighed a ton and, grunting and groaning with the effort, they hauled it out of the bottom of the dinghy and onto the sand.

They both straightened up simultaneously and peered around them. The moon chose that moment to slip coyly behind a thick bank of cloud and the two men stood staring at what looked like a huge black wall. 'Over there,' said Logan, 'that's where the guy said.' He jerked his chin, Asian style, into a patch heavier and blacker than its surroundings. 'Feel your way round the end there. He said the door's just at the back. It's got a light switch inside the door.'

Junit's bare feet glided over the soft sand and up the shallow slope. He paused for a second to establish his bearings and laid his hands on the tin side of the café and vanished into the blackness. He found the door, edged it open and ran his fingers up and down the inside of the frame searching for the light switch. But his hand never found it. Instead, an iron-like grip fastened onto his wrist and he was jerked forward into the Stygian blackness of the shed. The beam of a powerful flashlight, inches away, hit him squarely in the eyes. He was off balance as another hand, fingers outstretched, crawled over his face, searching, then slid down over his chin and found what it wanted. The fingers dug into his windpipe and tightened. The bright beam continued to burn into his eyeballs and he tried to bellow in pain with the pressure on his neck. But nothing came out except a guttural bark and in desperation he hit out blindly. He made contact only with air.

There was still no sound except the howling in his throat and the laboured breathing of the man holding him. Nothing was said.

He tried to throw himself forward away from the blinding light in his face and the throttling grip on his neck. His wrist was released and he heard a swish as the air against his right ear was displaced, and then a resounding thwack as something hard smashed into the side of his face. His knees gave way and he hit the floor. Groggily, he forced himself up onto his elbows, shook his head and then heard heavy breathing, a rasping of breath and a far-off voice. 'Drop, you bastard! And stay there!' It was an American voice. The silence, a pause, and he thought that was it, it was over, he was alone. He brought his knees up. Wrong. He didn't feel the second blow but knew all about it. A blinding yellow streak flashed across his eyes and before he could feel the pain everything cut out. Jet black.

Hagen rested his foot at the base of the unconscious man's spine and pressed down with all his weight. There was a faint whistle as the air left Junit's lungs but no other noise; no grunt, no suppressed hiss of pain and surprise. That was good enough for Hagen. He wasn't concerned whether the man was alive or dead – either would do, just so long as he wasn't going to interfere in the next bit of the script.

Hagen left the tin shed and waited in the darker shadow for his eyes to readjust. After a moment, less than a few seconds, he turned his head and strained his eyes for movement.

There was nothing at first. And then a sliver of the moon suddenly poked out of the side of the cloud, then more, and within seconds the beach and everywhere around it was bathed in a silvery blue light. Hagen could see Logan quite clearly.

He was standing staring out into the bay, studying the scattered masts of the boats at anchor against the white puffy background of cloud as he waited for Junit's signal. He didn't move when the area was floodlit by the moon's appearance and he didn't hear Hagen walk casually across the sand towards him and stop a couple of metres away. He was still admiring the scenery when Hagen half turned and flicked his flashlight towards where the Thai mute was waiting in the cabin of the pick-up.

And then everything happened at once.

The pick-up's engine roared into life; the moon went back into its slot behind the puffy silver cloud; and Logan swung round to find Hagen standing three feet away from him.

Hagen held the gun out for him to see. It was almost like a wax tableau. Neither man moved or spoke for several seconds.

It was Hagen who spoke first.

'Browning,' he said conversationally. 'Hi-Power. Thirteen

rounds, one up the spout. You can have as many of 'em as you like – it's all the same to me.' His teeth gleamed phosphorescently in the shaded moonlight; the rest of his face was a pale blur. 'Or you can walk across this strip of sand in front of me and end up all square. Don't say who are you – that comes later. Your turn.'

The howling of the pick-up's tortured engine almost drowned out the words, but Logan knew the form. He bracketed him immediately. CIA, possibly Special Projects – a killer and a pro. If he wasn't he certainly sounded it. That was enough for him. You didn't play the fool with professionals; the only time they counted up to ten was when they were counting the bullets going into you.

'Which way?'

'See over my right shoulder? Do a circle round me, stay about a yard away, put both hands by your side, palms facing backwards. OK?'

'Now?'

'Yeah. Move carefully.'

Logan did exactly as he was told. He trudged across the sand and didn't look round. He didn't need to. When he arrived at the far corner of the café he stopped and waited for more instructions. He strained his ears but said nothing and did nothing.

'Now carry on down to the water inlet. Stay in the shadow.'

'Here?'

'That's it. Don't say anything more.'

'OK.'

'Get in and start the engine.'

'We'll have to push out a bit. Not deep enough here to lower the shaft.'

Hagen considered it. It didn't take long. 'OK, do that. I'm right behind you. Find your depth then start the engine when you're ready. Don't rev it, just start it. And don't bother about trying to make a noise—' It was an unnecessary warning – the entire bay reverberated to the howling and screaming of Krislov's probably ruined pick-up engine. Hagen leaned forward, tapped Logan lightly on the shoulder with the Browning and said, 'OK, start walking the boat.'

When they arrived at the *Sara-Louise*, Hagen reversed the process. Him first, awkwardly backwards, the heavy Browning never wavering from Logan's body. He switched on the deck lights and, with his outstretched hand on Logan's shoulder, guided him down the companionway and indicated a chair in the cabin below. The *Sara-Louise* settled back into the water after she had been disturbed. Her mast righted itself and she was bathed in a harsh glare of yellow light reflected down from halfway up the mast. The cabin blinds were closed; the riding light illuminated her name. She had nothing to hide. She now looked like all the other boats that had been disturbed in the middle of the night. Some of the moored yachts began to stir and here and there deck lights came on as bleary-eyed faces peered into the night to see what all the commotion was about. Hagen leaned forward, turned his head fractionally and glanced out of the cockpit windshield. The pick-up's headlights lit up half the hillside as it roared round the bend in the road and, without straining his ears, he could hear Krislov's disembodied voice raging and bellowing and echoing across the bay and bouncing back from the range of hills.

Chapter 23

Ban Yit, January 1975

'Jesus Christ! What the fuck's going on!'

Krislov angrily threw his half-empty can of beer into the bay, jumped to his feet and scampered to the other side of the boat. The roar of the pick-up's engine sounded like a bomb going off. Even with its engine over-revving, St Clair Smith and Krislov could hear quite clearly the squeal of rubber on loose gravel.

'Hey!' Krislov let out another yell, then turned to St Clair Smith. 'That's my fucking pick-up!'

A few seconds later the lights of the pick-up described a series of quick, jerky movements. One minute the lights pierced the black sky, the next minute they thudded down to the ground as the truck bounced up the narrow track before levelling out on the road and, increasing speed, hurtling off into the night.

Krislov let out half a dozen more ripe oaths at the top of his voice as he watched the lights of his pick-up zoom round the side of the hill above the bay and disappear round the corner. The whine of the overstretched engine continued to disturb the peace and tranquillity for some time, but before it finally faded Krislov had scampered down the companionway and thrown himself into his flimsy dinghy. By the time the little engine putt-putted into life, St Clair Smith was in there with him. He'd taken a quick detour to his cabin. Tucked in his trousers under the back flap of his shirt was a large, warm .45 Colt automatic, cocked, safety on, and as he carefully balanced himself in the flimsy craft he stuffed a fully loaded spare magazine down the front of his trousers.

'That broad's jumping around the deck,' snarled Krislov. 'I don't want her in this fucking dinghy . . .'

'Go round again, quick!' ordered St Clair Smith. He raised his voice over the tiny outboard. 'Theresa! Go below! Go into your cabin and lock the door. Don't move until you hear my voice . . . OK, Jack, fast as you like to the shore!'

'Screw you, Smithy! You'll sink the goddamn thing!' hissed Krislov. 'It won't take two. I didn't invite you to come. It's my goddamn truck that's vanished up the hill, not yours – and where are those two guys of yours? Fucked off in my truck, by the sound of it. I never did like the look of that smart bastard. He's a fucking wrong 'un, Smithy!'

'Stop talking, Jack, and concentrate on what you're doing. I don't want to have to swim ashore. And it's not your fucking truck I'm worried about—' Krislov's narrowed eyes tried to pierce the moonlight and stare into the pale smudge of St Clair Smith's face. Smithy must be upset. He'd never heard the Englishman swear before, not like this. Krislov was more worried about St Clair Smith than he was about his truck. He'd seen the heavy magazine being stuffed into his trousers. That meant he had the rest of it somewhere on him. If that crazy fucker, Hagen, hadn't done the job properly there was shortly going to be some very heavy metal flying about in Ban Yit bay. He still couldn't see St Clair Smith's face, but he mentally kicked himself when he remembered telling Hagen that the most he'd have was a scatter-gun and that he'd duck if anyone said 'Boo!' It didn't look like it from where he was squatting.

'Speed it up, Jack.' St Clair Smith's voice was ice calm. Krislov had never heard this before; he didn't like the sound of it – a hard nut with a cold voice and a heavy piece of weaponry tucked somewhere in his trousers. Hagen was going to be very pleased if he heard that banging around his ears.

Ignoring his passenger, Krislov ran his dinghy in as far as it would go and grounded it on the sand. He leapt out into ankle-deep water and ran into the wall of blackness and disappeared. St Clair Smith took a more leisurely route.

Leaving the grounded dinghy, he swept the area with the powerful beam of the flashlight. It came to rest on *Claudia*'s inflatable some distance along the beach. He lowered the beam and approached it openly. The replaced engine block was lying solidly where it had bedded itself in the sand. The other stuff was still in the bottom of the dinghy. He directed the beam onto the sand. Footprints, several pairs, but no sign of a scuffle.

Krislov appeared out of the blackness. 'They've taken my fucking pick-up!'

'Who?'

'Your fucking pal and that fucking Malay boy of yours!'

'I wonder why they would want to do that?' St Clair Smith was quite casual about the missing truck. It didn't go down well with Krislov; he was acting his ass off but he wasn't enjoying it. He glanced out of the corner of his eye in the direction of the *Sara-Louise*. She was still shrouded in darkness and her riding light, high on her slim mast, waved ever so gently. Krislov daren't look too closely; he daren't study the dunes to the side of his wife's café which led to the inlet in case the whole fucking show had turned plum-shaped and that smooth Hagen bastard had dropped Logan and the Malay. He searched the area with his eyes without moving his head. It looked right enough. It all depended on St Clair Smith. He kept his head straight and hoped for the best. It was out of his hands; it was all down now to the gullibility of the Englishman. Krislov finally turned and brought both his eyes to bear on St Clair Smith's face. He couldn't tell how he was taking it; the reflected light of the flashlight's beam showed a flat, featureless shadow where the expression should be. But there was nothing in St Clair Smith's demeanour to show that he was unduly disturbed. He hadn't even brought that piece from under his shirt.

Krislov turned his head and tried to pierce the dark wall behind him again. As he turned he noted that most of the boats had lit up. 'Look's like the circus has come to town,' he muttered. 'The bastards have all woken up to watch a couple of performing clowns!' But it gave him the opportunity to note that the *Sara-Louise* had joined the crowd. She too was nicely lit up. It looked like Smartass had made it. There was relief in Krislov's thinking; it looked as though he'd made it, that he'd got his man and, fingers crossed, he'd got the mother stacked away out of sight on the boat. He could relax, nothing was coming his way – but Jesus! What about the boy?

'Bring your light up here, Smithy.' Krislov scuffled across the sand and stopped by the corner where the shed started. 'Let's get some proper light on the subject.' He was fully recovered and sounded like the normal, taciturn, bad-tempered man of few words that St Clair Smith knew him as. Guided by St Clair Smith's flashlight beam, he moved round to the door. He knew he was going to find something there. He didn't know what – it depended on how clever Hagen was on dishing out the rough stuff.

He jabbed angrily at the light switch and stared for a brief second at the Malay's curled-up body. Jesus Christ! He's croaked the poor fucker! He bellowed, 'Smithy! Come 'ere! Quick!'

Aubrey St Clair Smith squeezed through the opening of the shed, glanced briefly at Junit's body, then moved into the depths of the barn-like building and searched round it, lighting up the shadowy corners with his torch. He hadn't expected to find Logan, but then he hadn't expected to find Junit crouched in a ball in this shed either. He came back and felt for the boy's jugular. There was a strong pulse. He ran his hand over his head. Blood, lots of it. He gingerly felt the sticky mess. There was one deep cut that had opened the scalp down to his skull, and another lesser wound at the back of his head. But there was no soggy give around the wounds. The skull was intact. St Clair Smith smiled thinly to himself. Bloody good job whoever had clouted Junit hadn't aimed at something vital!

'He's alive,' he said to Krislov. Krislov didn't seem too worried either way. 'Got a doctor around here?'

'You must be fucking joking, Smithy! Doctor? Around here? Don't make me laugh! Phuket town – that's the nearest you'll find anyone who knows anything about medicine.'

'Tough on the lad, then. Dr Aubrey St Clair Smith'll have to get his first-aid kit out.'

'I didn't know you were a doctor, Smithy . . .'

'I'm not, but I know how to sew up a hole in my sock.'

'Jesus Christ! The poor fucker!'

St Clair Smith wiped the blood off his hands with the flap of Junit's shirt and gently felt the back of the boy's neck. That felt all right as well – solid, slightly stiff, it didn't feel as though it was going to waggle off his shoulders. 'I don't think there's anything serious – neck's not broken.' St Clair Smith stood up. 'Come and help unload that junk out of my dinghy and we can get this chap back to the boat – give me a hand.'

'What about the other guy?'

'What about him?'

'That's what I mean, what about him, what're we going to do about him?'

'Me, Jack? Nothing. He was just a guy I met. *You* might have to do something about him. After all, it's your truck he's buggered off with. I'm taking this fellow back to my boat and then I'm going sailing—'

'I'm not following you, Smithy. Your friend's nearly broken this guy's head in two then he's fucked off with my pick-up and you say you're doing nothing, you're going sailing? Come on, Smithy, what do I do; what's the fucking game?'

Aubrey St Clair Smith finished making the unconscious Junit comfortable in the bottom of the dinghy then, pulling the boat into deeper water, clambered in beside the engine. Krislov, ignoring the water flapping around his knees, followed him. 'Is that it, then, Smithy? You're going? You're fucking off? What do I do about my truck?'

'Go and tell the police.'

'But where're you going?'

'Home. See ya, Jack—' The roar of the Johnson drowned out the last of his words and left Krislov standing up to his thighs in water with a totally mystified look on his face. This somehow didn't seem right. This wasn't what he had envisaged would happen, but when he racked his brain for what he did think was going to happen he realised he'd never considered the aftermath at all. He stood where he was, the muck and debris lapping around his legs, listening

206

until the dinghy's engine slowed down, then stopped. He lit a cigarette, narrowed his eyes into the bay and waited for St Clair Smith to return and talk some more about his missing friend. The moon was still playing hide-and-seek – every so often he could make out the shapes of boats and then they vanished as if a curtain had been drawn over the bay – but after a full cigarette had been smoked Krislov heard the *Claudia*'s main engine throbbing across the water, and after a few more minutes the rattle of the anchor chain. That had to be it. He was doing what he said he was going to do. The fucker was going sailing. Krislov spat the remains of his cigarette into the water and turned his back on the bay. This was it? It had to be the anticlimax to beat all fucking anticlimaxes.

He walked slowly towards his derelict junk, climbed aboard and went below, locking the door after him. He grabbed himself a bottle of Singha beer, wrenched the top off it and sat down in front of his VHF. But he didn't switch it on. He sat there, in the semi-dark, drinking local beer and smoking local cigarettes, and waited for Hagen to come and talk to his masters.

Chapter 24

Logan sat on a hard chair in the cabin of the *Sara-Louise* and stared blankly at the other man sitting comfortably in one of the softer chairs.

Hagen stared back. He nursed a chunky tumbler of Scotch in one hand and a lighted cigarette in the other. There was nothing for Logan. But it didn't disturb him. So far there had been no threats, just introductions and stilted conversation between two members of the same race, possibly the same persuasion, and, more than likely, the same employer.

'Logan,' said Hagen after the brief silence. His expression remained unchanged, one of mild curiosity, nothing friendly for another American, just an expression of a man considering someone whose luck had just run out. This one wasn't going to get any help. Quite the opposite. 'Your limey friend's taken a powder. He's up-anchored and pushed off with your daughter. I thought you'd like to know that.' He paused and studied the effect. There was no reaction from Logan. It surprised him. 'Just in case you expected him to come charging across the water and dig you out of the shit.' He waited, still studying Logan's manner. 'No? Not interested? OK – think it's time we had a look at each other's cards. I'll put mine down first so you can see how deep your particular patch of shit is.' Hagen mulled it over in his mind for a second or two, then clarified the statement. 'And I think you'll find it's shit like you've never been in before – it's called terminal shit! You ready?'

Logan looked at him and shrugged. It was all he felt like doing; he could see it was all Hagen needed. Logan knew the type: hard, remorseless, no feeling, and could be a very heavy bastard if things didn't go his way. He had killer's eyes. Logan could tell they were killer's eyes because he'd seen the same telltale signs in his own when he'd been this boy's age. They were eyes that appeared flat, not lifeless flat but flat without the gleam that normal people's eyes had.

The shrug did nothing for Hagen's attitude. The glass remained stuck to his lip, his eyes remained cold and searching. There was no give. He wasn't particularly enjoying himself, he was just doing a job of work. The next phase should be: pick up the Browning, flip off the safety, stand up and walk casually behind the sitting man and blow a hole in the back of his head. Simple. Clean and antiseptic. Contract ended, let's go home. But he had a feeling it wasn't going to go like that.

'My contract says you die,' he said. Simple as that.

'So what's holding you up?'

Still no change of expression from Hagen. He stopped playing with his whisky and drank it. He gave a tight grimace.

'I'm supposed to electrify your balls or something; give you some pain, old-fashioned stuff. The contract was drawn up by your contemporaries, Logan, it's got all these old-fashioned things in it, like make him tell you this, and make him tell you that. Not my style. I reckon inflicting that sort of pain went out with Adolf Hitler and his crazy assholes. So, we'll do it the American way, the modern way – I tell you what I'm going to do and you tell me what the Friends in Washington, DC want to know.'

Logan uncrossed his leg and squared his back against the wooden chair frame. He appeared quite at ease. 'You haven't said anything yet,' he said evenly; there was certainly no panic or fear here. It caused a slight pinching just above Hagen's nose. 'You're like the rest of your breed, full of piss and wind, all mouth – you talk a lot but you say fuck-all.'

Hagen lowered his glass and stared into his eyes. Logan didn't flinch.

'Don't get too cute, Logan. I can think of a lot of ways

of knocking the piss out of you before I blow your head off. You can have it any way you like, it's all the same to me. You're going to die. That's something I've said that's more than fuck-all.' He almost smiled but didn't quite make it and, instead, stuck the cigarette between the gap in his lips. Logan waited. Hagen hadn't finished. 'Whatever the outcome that's the certain thing about this, Logan. I don't know what's going to happen tomorrow, but you do. You're going to be dead and have no more problems like me. Can I start asking my questions?'

Logan decided it had gone far enough.

'Throw me one of those cigarettes.'

'Sure.' Hagen flipped a Lucky Strike out of the packet and tossed it across the room. It landed in Logan's lap. He held it up and raised his eyebrows. Hagen's lighter followed it.

Logan sucked greedily on the cigarette, blew the first mouthful of smoke upwards and brought his head down to Hagen's level. 'Let's get this straight, Hagen. Whether I satisfy your curiosity or not you're going to kill me – have I read it correctly?'

'Spot on.'

'So, there's nothing I can do to save my life?'

Hagen shook his head. 'Absolutely nothing, pal. You either go to hell screaming in pain or you go Pullman. As they say, it's nothing to me, I'm just the bloke with the sanction note.'

'OK,' said Logan, calmly. Hagen met his eyes. Something wrong here. Hagen looked hard. Definitely something wrong. The man wasn't afraid, not in his face, not in his eyes; his legs weren't pressed together, his feet were firmly on the floor, he wasn't fidgeting, his arms were folded across his chest and his hands were steady. There were none of the signs of a worried man. He should be grovelling – forget the pride, man! It's your fucking life – plead for it. 'Ask your questions.'

Hagen's expression didn't change. Any surprise he might have felt at Logan's sudden co-operation he kept well to himself. It was understandable to Hagen; he'd probably have done exactly the same thing himself. Very understandable.

Maybe the poor fucker had lost it – although he didn't show it – but either way he obviously didn't like the thought of checking out, Pullman or otherwise. He threw it at him without preliminaries.

'What d'ya know about Contractor?'

'I am Contractor,' said Logan simply.

That shook Hagen for a second. He had to think along a new tack.

'Why does Washington want you on ice?'

'I didn't know they did.'

Hagen drew very heavily on his cigarette; the smoke went almost down to his toenails. 'There's something about your attitude that worries me, Logan. You should be shitting yourself. You're not. You're sitting here as though everything's going your way. Is it?'

'I think so. But tell me why Washington wants me dead.'

'It doesn't get you off the hook, but OK.' Hagen's face hardened. 'First of all you covered yourself so well they didn't know who the fuck you were. Apparently they were happy that you were doing a good job of work, but then suddenly they decided that you might know too much about things that other people know nothing about. Do you get my meaning?'

'Yeah, sure.' Hagen had left him an opening. He slipped through it. 'But without going into specifics, surely if Washington thought I was a danger, mouth-wise, shouldn't they first ascertain whether there's been any insurance taken out on the possibility of, er, inadvertent revelations?'

Hagen took the message on board and gave it a quick run through. The roundheads at Langley had read it perfectly. Reilly's Irish voice boomed out of his subconscious – how had he put it? . . . *First you find him, then you ask him if he's got any stuff tucked away that he's saving for his memoirs; if he has, you trace it and destroy it – without reading it. Then you put him quietly out of his misery* . . . Couldn't be clearer than that. Hagen continued staring, unseeingly, at Logan; Logan reckoned he had a bloody good idea what was cruising through this young executive killer's one-track mind. It looked like roll-up-sleeves time and a bit of old-fashioned ring work. Hagen's eyes had blanked over. But now he was back again.

'Correct,' he said. 'And you're going to tell me that such a policy has been taken out – the, without specifics, cover against . . . how did you put it? Inadvertent revelations.'

'You got something right for once, sonny! And another little thing. Just bear in mind that the closer you get to me the greater risk you become to the shiny domes at Langley. They're not deep thinkers, those guys. They see only the wave that's breaking at the time, and if you're surfing across the top of that wave with your hand in mine your name'll go on the contract as well. Take a tip, pal – don't ask any more questions. You've done your job. You've brought me in, you've exposed my cover and the minute you did that you became a runner yourself.'

That didn't worry Hagen. 'You have a jaundiced view of life, Logan, but I grant you you have a very interesting way of putting things.'

'Then let me help you out with some more interesting things.' He didn't wait for Hagen's approval. 'Get on the horn and tell your controller what you've got here and mention the word insurance. That's my advice.'

Hagen said nothing. Logan gave the boat a little push.

'It's good advice.' He waited on Hagen's change of expression. It would have been a long wait. He decided to keep the chummy conversation going. 'Who's running you on this one?'

Hagen came out of his meditations slowly and still thoughtfully. 'No can tell. D'you know anybody in the Company who could help us out of this quandary?'

Logan hesitated for a second, then said, 'Graver – Bob Graver. He might be interested in the fact that you've opened up Contractor – yeah, try him. I reckon a Langley number, don't you?'

Hagen didn't like it. He didn't like it one little bit. He felt as if he'd launched himself off the highest diving board in the county and all he could see below was a damp sponge. There was only one way to go now. But he waited a moment and threw up all the options. Only one stuck out. After a few moments he plucked that one out of the air and, with the gun still pointing casually at Logan's ribcage at unmissable range, swung sideways in his chair, leaned forward and threw the switch of the RT. It was almost as if Krislov, in his dark tomb, were waiting for it. 'You still awake, Jack?'

'Come and have a beer.'

'Good idea.'

Hagen stood up and tucked the Browning into his trouser band under his shirt. He wasn't going to need it, not for Logan; Logan had almost taken charge, and one thing Hagen wasn't going to do was shoot him. 'OK, Logan. You drive the dinghy, I'll sit in with you. Head for the place you were picked up, OK?'

Dixie never seemed to sleep. Krislov reckoned he was going to get all the sleep he could handle in the not-too-distant future. In the meantime he was seeing as much of this life as he could. He sounded wide awake when Krislov asked him for cover.

'You got it! Nothing going on this time anight, anyway.'

'Make sure about it, Dixie.'

''Kay – enjoy your beer! And out.'

'Sierra Two One,' intoned Krislov into the hand microphone.

'Sierra Two One,' it repeated, then, 'Gotta word?'

'Is it still DROGHEDA?' asked Krislov over his shoulder.

Hagen nodded without taking his eyes off Logan.

Krislov spelt the name out. It made the operator in Saigon happy. 'You've got it,' he hummed. 'How can I help?'

'Langley Central, Green. Then clip it.'

'Gotcha. Hang on a second.'

It was no longer than that. 'Langley,' said the clear voice. 'Department?'

'Give it here.' Hagen nudged Krislov to one side and sat in his chair. 'Two nine zero,' he said, 'specific—'

'Specify, please.'

'Graver.'

'Hold, please.'

The line died to a fizz, then, seconds later, came alive again. 'Reilly here—who's asking for Graver?' Hagen almost smiled at the gravel voice that seemed to fit in so well with

213

darkened rooms and clandestine radio hook-ups through a war-torn city in Vietnam from a placid, silent bay on the other side of Thailand. He couldn't be bothered looking up the time in Washington, but he hoped it was early in the morning.

Hagen touched the button and said, 'Contractor. Personal. He specified Graver.'

'Tell him to talk to me.'

Hagen grinned happily. 'He insists on the specific.'

'The specific's fast asleep in his goddamn bed. I'll handle this.'

'Then wake him up and connect this call to his bedside.' Hagen held the phone slightly away from his ear. He valued his eardrums. But he needn't have worried. Reilly might be many things, but he was no fool; he knew the voice and he knew that voice wouldn't insist on Graver if it wasn't the highest possible priority. Reilly gave in with good grace. 'Hold.'

'Holding.' Hagen leaned back in the chair and fumbled in his shirt pocket for a cigarette. He flipped the packet, dragged one out with his lips and tossed the rest of the pack onto the bench. He turned to Krislov and flicked his thumb and forefinger under the end of the cigarette. Krislov pulled out a lighter, but before he could bring it to life Bob Graver's voice, sleep-laden, came through the speaker.

'This better be good.'

'Sir,' said Hagen. He made no introduction; Reilly would have done all that. 'Would you recognise the voice of Contractor if you heard it?'

There was a lapse of time sufficient for Graver to pull himself out of bed and flop into the armchair by the telephone. 'Who else have you got there?'

'There's just a guy who says he's Contractor, and me, sir.'

Hagen flicked his finger under his cigarette again and when Krislov lit it he pointed to the door. Krislov understood. There were things not for his ears. He didn't want to hear. It sounded high brass. He left the room, collected another beer on his way out and went on deck.

Down below Hagen handed the microphone to Logan and indicated for him to speak. 'Hello, Bob,' said Logan, clearly.

214

'The last time we met was in Kuala Lumpur in '57. We had gins and tonic in a place called the Griffin and met a Chinese Tongmaster in a used-tyre store on the outskirts. Is that enough? Can we get down to business?'

It was the identification procedure. Even if Graver didn't remember the voice he'd remember at least one or two of the locations.

'Put Hagen back.'

'Sir?' said Hagen.

'What's the story, Hagen?'

Hagen told him. There was a long silence, long enough for Logan to help himself to one of Hagen's cigarettes, light it, and raise his eyes at Hagen's cocked-finger demand. He threw one on the table just as the speaker came to life again.

'Hagen, d'you believe him?'

Hagen turned his head sideways to meet Logan's steady gaze. 'I fulfilled part of the contract but I'm not inclined to close it until you give the word. Contractor has insurance. It's not my business to believe or not to believe. I was contracted for one mission. There was no mention of my being his confessor. Bearing in mind that secrecy was the name of the game and in order that secrecy be maintained, I would rather you spoke to Contractor and confirmed that he is the man designated and that you understand the implications of his insurance.'

'I asked you a question.'

'Sure. Yeah – I believe him.'

'Where is this insurance policy kept?'

Logan shook his head in disbelief. Hagen almost laughed. 'I think you had better ask him yourself, sir. He doesn't look the sort of guy to me who's going to start weeping over a broken arm.'

'Let me talk to him.'

Logan accepted the handset. As he did so he met Hagen's eyes. There was sympathy there, a sort of mutual understanding, the sort of glance that two old footsloggers exchange over the head of the beautifully turned-out brass hat. 'What sort of a deal are you asking for, Contractor?' Gone was the camaraderie. No more Jim – it was Contractor. It was down to business, serious business.

215

'I'm asking to come in,' responded Logan. 'And I want you to call off the dogs.'

'I didn't hear mention of an insurance policy.'

'You won't. The only time you'll hear mention of it is if the policy-holder's life is at risk or if he dies. Otherwise it stays in limbo – nobody sees it or hears about it. And before you ask, it's secure and in unassailable hands. The way things stand at the moment – and I mention this gorilla of yours standing with a gun at my head—' He exchanged glances again with Hagen. Hagen hadn't taken umbrage; he hadn't taken anything. He'd relegated himself, for the time being, to interested bystander. But it didn't mean that at his master's voice the serious piece of hardware he had in his trouser band wouldn't come out and do its work. All was well for the moment. '—is that the package in question is being brought out for review – if necessary.'

'I don't think I like the sound of that.' Graver's voice had risen slightly; there was nothing wrong with his imagination. Packets of documents brought out for review did nothing for his blood pressure. 'And I don't think the question of review arises. I would like you to return here to the States and meet me in a fitting and proper manner where we can discuss the ins and outs of this business. But I must ask for total security of the principal. If its present location is impregnable to outside forces it should stay there. There should be no attempt to, as you put it, bring it out for review—'

Logan butted in. 'In the meantime?'

'What in the meantime?'

'My security.'

'You have no fears from us.'

'Does Hagen understand that?'

'Do you understand that, Hagen?' said Graver.

'Yes, sir. May I request that a copy of the relevant section of this tape be placed before General Reilly?'

The pause that followed was significant – and indicative. 'You've got it. Your contract is closed and you've been reassigned. You are to return to Washington in the company of Mr Logan.'

'You'll call off all other sources so that I know who's friendly and who ain't?'

'You've got it.'

'Including the DEA?'

'I said you've got it, goddammit!'

Hagen exchanged glances with Logan and got a blank response. 'Roger all that, sir,' he said into the mouthpiece. 'May I close down?'

'Make sure he gets back here.'

Hagen didn't bother with procedure. He just pulled the plug out and swung round in the chair to face Logan. He held his hand out.

'No hard feelings?'

Logan looked him in the eye. His stomach had stopped churning, the fear bubbles had subsided. This good-looking, arrogant bastard had frightened him. No hard feelings? Like fuck there weren't. He kept his hand by his side.

'Go to hell.'

Chapter 25

Liu Hongzhou's right-hand man Peng Soon and the two eager young Touming Guanxi apprentices waited until the peak of midnight before clambering into the inadequate Thai fishermen's clothes and slipping into the water from the stern of the deep-sea Thai fishing trawler. They swam silently to the shore and picked up the long *perahu* they'd stored there earlier. Swimming with the tide, they hung onto the sides of the wooden craft and gently steered it to a position some two hundred yards from Krislov's boat. Concealing the *perahu* in a small tree-shielded freshwater inlet, they crawled through the undergrowth and took up position opposite the *Sara-Louise*. Totally invisible, they sat and watched.

They had plenty to keep their minds off the crisp night air.

Peering through night glasses, Peng Soon watched the activity that had woken up the slumbering bay; he carefully observed the arrival of Hagen and Logan; then, after a wet, chilly half an hour, when everything had quietened down again, Peng Soon made his move.

Stripping off the few clothes he was wearing, he crawled into the water and struck out silently for the *Sara-Louise*. Hanging onto her stern line, he trod water and listened as his night-accustomed eyes searched the deck of the yacht. Satisfied, he came closer and finally, with infinite patience, eased himself onto the stern deck. Inch by inch, fearful of

218

rocking the boat or causing any movement, he crawled on his belly to the main cabin housing and stuck his ear to one of the curtained windows. The voices came through very clearly.

But he'd left it too late.

The two men in the cabin were on the move.

Lying flat in the shadow on the deck, he watched Logan and Hagen clamber into the inflatable dinghy and head across the bay.

Taking advantage of the lapping of the disturbed water against the hull of the *Sara-Louise*, the solidly built Chinaman edged his way round the cabin superstructure until he found a gap in the curtains wide enough for him to study the interior. There was no one there. He went below and thoroughly searched the yacht then, still cautious, he climbed up the companionway to the deck. Once there he studied the shore where the two Americans had gone. There was no sound, not a light to be seen. Silence. Grave-like, the night had settled back, everybody had had another drink and gone back to bed. Krislov's place was in darkness.

Peng Soon, flat on his stomach, crawled to the other side of the yacht and gave a low whistle. It was returned. Then he made a sound like a grunting frog. It carried across the water and within a second was repeated from the under-growth. The shadowy outline of the long *perahu* appeared and, gathering speed, it came silently towards the *Sara-Louise*.

When it arrived at the side of the yacht, one man pulled himself round from the stern and scrambled over the rail and up onto the deck of the *Sara-Louise*. The other man remained with the boat and, after whispered instructions from Peng Soon, he manoeuvred the empty *perahu* close under the yacht's weather side, tied its painter loosely to a cleat and lay down in the bottom of the boat in the shadow of a large fish trap secured between the thwarts. The other two Chinese flattened themselves onto *Sara-Louise*'s deck and waited.

A gibbous moon, casting thin, insubstantial shadows across the water, sent a ghostly glow over the deck of the yacht when Hagen and Jim Logan came out of the bowels of the floating radio centre. Krislov was standing by the dinghy, its painter held loosely in his hand.

'Everything OK?' he asked.

'Sure. Anything going on around here?'

'Nothing happens here this time of the night – although . . .'

'Although what?' snapped Hagen. Changes of plan, changes of people's status; he'd got a friend where he'd had an enemy, someone to keep alive whom he'd come to kill. It put him on edge. He wasn't yet used to the change of game.

'Nothing. Just the night playing tricks. We used to get that in 'Nam—'

'Fuck what you used to get in 'Nam, Jack. Did you see something or didn't you?'

'I thought I saw something move about on the deck of the *Sara-Louise*. Just a shadow. Something dark. Probably imagination. Forget I mentioned it. What d'you want me to do now?'

'Go to bed. I'll see you in the morning after our new friend and I've had a good think about what we're going to do.'

Hagen and Logan pushed the inflatable out into the water and, without worrying too much now about noise, Logan opened the throttle. It was too noisy to talk. Before the engine caught up with the throttle they'd arrived at the side of the *Sara-Louise*. Logan cut the engine and allowed the way on the dinghy to carry them to her side. Hagen stepped aboard first and took the painter, motioning Logan to pass him.

'I think you and me's got a bit of talking to do,' he said, softly.

Logan wasn't interested. It had been a long day.

'Let's leave the talking till morning. Is there a spare bunk below for me? Hang on a second . . . ! What's that fishing boat doing alongside?'

The tide, reaching its turning point, had swirled between the *Sara-Louise*'s side and the bows of the narrow Thai *perahu* and had just edged it out of the yacht's shadow. No more than a foot. But it was enough.

220

'What fucking fishing boat?' Hagen stiffened. The Browning, with its long silencer, appeared in his hand, the safety catch automatically flicked off. 'What the fu ... ! Logan, get—'

The warning wasn't necessary. Logan had seen the shadow unwinding from behind the raised cabin structure. He threw himself backwards over the guardrail. There was an almighty splash as he hit the water.

Hagen spat the surge of vomit from his mouth, recovered immediately and, spinning out of the companionway, fired one shot at a shadow that came flying at him, then received a tremendous thump on the side of the head. He staggered forward and put out his hands to save himself from falling down the companionway, regained his balance, turned to fire again, and received another crack, straight down on the top of his head. His eyes closed for a fraction of a second. He felt movement just in front of him and fired two shots blindly. He didn't hear the thud of them hitting but heard a groan inches from his face and a body, naked and wet, fell onto him. Another crack across the forehead and he went down on his knees. He didn't feel the final blow that landed on the back of his neck.

Peng Soon ignored the dying man who lay in the scuppers. He'd fixed the priorities. He'd allowed for at least one death. 'Make the boat fast and bring the basket,' he hissed to the shadow that had appeared on the other side of the deck. 'Quick!'

The two Chinese up-ended the trap; it stood about four feet high, two feet across and bulged in the middle like an old fat pig. They picked up Hagen's unconscious body and jammed him into it; upside down, first head and shoulders, then legs and feet bent as far as they would go. Hagen was stuffed tight like a pig going to market. He couldn't move. His head was bowed, his knees were pressed hard into his face and his hands were lost somewhere between his thighs. They tied the rattan lid securely and rolled the cage across the deck to the stern and threw it overboard. The shorter of the two men followed and recovered it, turning the floating cage over so, by the light of the descending moon, he could see that Hagen's face was out of the water – for most of the time.

Peng Soon lowered his now-dead team-mate over the side and went with him, cuddling him like a child and working his way, one-handed, round the *Sara-Louise* until he met the other man. They'd planned it beforehand; Peng Soon was an old hand at the killing-and-abduction game. But this was a new one and so far it had gone like clockwork. They strapped their dead friend across the bows of the fishing boat and tied Hagen's cage by a rope to the stern so that his head was just out of the water. Then they both climbed aboard and, with paddles and the help of the tide, they left the *Sara-Louise* and headed down the bay towards the dark, brooding trawler moored outside the limits of the yacht harbour.

Chapter 26

Hagen was still unconscious when the two naked Chinese, watched by Liu Hongzhou, tumbled the bamboo trap onto the trawler's deck.

They tied a rope to the cage, threaded it through a pulley at the extreme end of the mizzen boom and, with the two of them hanging onto the rope, raised the cage with its prisoner off the deck so that it hung free, level with Peng Soon's face. He stood and stared at the man curled up inside the cage. There was no expression on his flat features. There was nothing unusual in this presentation; this wasn't the first time a body had been suspended in front of him for his inspection.

The young Tongman, now in baggy, calf-length fisherman's pants and a loose-fitting top, squatted on his heels below the cage and from somewhere down below had produced a bundle of green bamboo sticks. He split them with the kitchen chopper, then split them again, turning them into a small pile of quarter-inch-thick splinters. With a sharp pocket knife he sliced rapidly until each tip had a razor-sharp point. He stood up and handed a couple of them to Peng Soon.

Liu Hongzhou moved closer and rested his chubby arm on the stern guardrail, a slight dribble running from the corner of his lips. He ran his tongue over it and concentrated on the contents of the basket.

After he had studied the American for some minutes,

223

Peng Soon spoke. 'Wake up, Yankee!' His English was quite good; it had an American accent. 'Wake up!' he repeated, and touched the nearest bare patch of Hagen's skin with one of the pointed bamboo slivers.

The patch of pale skin was the side of Hagen's face pressed hard against the bamboo mesh. It was just a tickle. A testing touch to make sure the victim was awake and suffering. Hagen made no response. No move. Peng Soon spoke again, the same sentence. He touched the same spot of Hagen's skin again with his bamboo and jabbed.

This time it broke the surface of Hagen's face and, like an electric shock, reached his nerve centre and jolted him to life.

He tried to open his eyes but one of the bamboo struts was pushing down on the lids. He moved fractionally and one eyelid popped open. The deck light cast a dim yellow glow, enough for him to see a naked Chinaman staring into his one open eye. The shock seared through him like a red-hot poker and sliced deep into his bladder, and he felt the warm liquid crawl over his groin. The humiliation did the trick. In a flash he was wide awake and up to date. The fear flooded into his open eye. It was not lost on Peng Soon, who looked up and met Liu's interested eye. Liu gave a brief movement of his hand – a movement that said wait, and let the victim enjoy his awakening. The youngster stood up and joined the two men by the stern rail and the three Chinese, expressionless, watched closely the agony that followed Hagen's realisation that he was curled up like a boiled prawn, helpless and entrapped.

It almost brought a scream of horror to Hagen's throat. But he held it back. The claustrophobia of it almost sent him wild in panic. He tried to kick his way out, to move his arms, to move anything, but he could move nothing; he was jammed in his cage as tight as a surgeon's finger in a rubber glove. He was freezing with cold, but even though he shivered uncontrollably the sweat bubbled out of his forehead and forced its way through the water dripping off his face.

Peng Soon withdrew the bamboo splinter, threw it over the side of the boat and put his face closer to Hagen's eye. 'What is your name?'

'Go and screw yourself!'

'What is your name?' Peng Soon seemed to have infinite patience. Hagen's liquid, almost incoherent mumbling had no effect on him. Perhaps he didn't understand. But Liu did.

'Hurt him,' he whispered, wetly.

Peng Soon glanced down and selected another bamboo splinter. He chose with care, tested the tip of his thumb on its point and held it just far enough away from Hagen's eye so that he could focus on it.

'What is your name?' he repeated. He didn't wait for a reply. The needle-sharp bamboo touched Hagen's eyelid. The eyelid closed automatically, but even Hagen, racked in excruciating pain, with every joint howling in agony, knew that there was only the thinnest membrane of skin between the needle-sharp stick and blindness. He'd heard of this one. There was no second chance. Unless it was the other eye.

'Hagen,' he mumbled.

'Again,' said the Chinaman. He didn't remove the bamboo.

'Hagen,' repeated Hagen, louder, more clearly. 'Hagen.'

Peng Soon removed the point from Hagen's eye and threw it over the side with the other one. His expression still impassive, he moved away from the cage and stood on the side of the afterdeck and gazed down at the water. Liu Hongzhou joined him and they both stared at the slowly moving dark water; their heads were close together.

'This is definitely the man you followed from Bangkok?' said Liu, without taking his eyes from the water.

'Yes.' Peng Soon had covered his nakedness, with a thin towel wrapped sarong-fashion around his waist. His well-built shoulders and muscular chest remained bare. He sweated profusely, although the night air brought with it a crisp edge of chill. He turned to face his master. 'He' – he jerked his chin fractionally in the direction of Hagen's cage – 'had been interrogating Logan.'

'Serious interrogation?'

'I couldn't hear. He might have got what he wanted because when they returned this man no longer held his gun to Logan's head. I allowed Logan to escape, as you had ordered. This man' – he jerked his chin again – 'will tell us what he wants from Logan, what he talked about, and what was discussed on shore to make him lift his guard.'

Liu continued staring at the slowly moving water. 'Find out everything about him. Find out what he proposed doing with Logan; where he was going to take him – and then kill him.'

Peng Soon glanced at the side of Liu's head for a second or two, then moved over to Hagen's cage and prodded him to life again. This time Hagen groaned and tried to move his tortured limbs, but he was wasting his time. There wasn't a fraction of empty space in the cage. The groan of pain was wasted. Staring blankly at the apparition, Peng Soon said to his master, 'May I suggest we leave him in place for some time and allow him to think about his position? It will save time if he arranges his mind for us. Why don't we go and eat our meal in comfort and leave him to contemplate his future?'

Liu shifted his gaze from the slow-moving water to the man in the fish trap. He studied him for several moments then moved towards the basket and searched for Hagen's eye.

'Look at me,' he commanded.

Hagen forced his eyelid open and stared into Liu's face. No detail; all he could make out was a white, misty blur like an old-fashioned out-of-focus black-and-white photograph. But he'd never forget the voice.

'Think about Logan,' said Liu without passion. 'And very shortly you will talk to me.' He turned away without another glance and said to his compatriot, 'We'll do as you suggest.' He clicked his fingers at the apprentice killer. No words were necessary. The young Chinaman squatted on his haunches with his back against the wheelhouse and turned his head so that he could watch Hagen in his basket swaying gently, backwards and forwards, like a baby in a cradle in time with the movement of the boat rocking on the slow-moving tide.

Half an hour later Liu and Peng Soon returned on deck. Liu Hongzhou prodded Hagen. 'Have you had some thoughts about James Logan?'

Hagen groaned, but said nothing comprehensible. Liu stood staring at him for some time then said, 'Bring him to life.'

'Water?'

'That's what he needs.'

It was a different language altogether. They both spoke it; they both understood what water meant. The third man loosened the rope from the cleat holding the basket and, taking the strain, swung the boom so that it hung over the stern. Peng Soon joined him on the rope and with a nod they both let go at the same time, allowing the rope to spin through the pulley. The cage hit the water with a smack and then went under. The two men stood with the taut rope in their hands and watched the bubbles arrive on the surface. Liu lit a cigarette, belched softly and, leaning on the after-rail, joined the other two men in their study of the frothing, disturbed water.

Chapter 27

After he'd thrown himself over the side of the *Sara-Louise*, Logan stayed under water until he felt his lungs were about to burst. Then he surfaced, steadied his breathing, turned and, treading water, faced the boat he'd just left in a hurry.

He was about twenty yards away, and the yacht stood out in stark silhouette against a lumpy moonlit sky. She rocked and bucked, and across the water he could hear an ominous thud that sounded like someone chopping wood. Then two heavy but muted explosions. He continued moving away on his back as he recovered his breath and waited for signs of a chase. He had no idea who'd carried out the ambush. He suspected Liu's people, but it didn't fit; it was him they wanted. He was the target. When they saw only Hagen they must have known that he had escaped. Why hadn't somebody come overboard after him? Perhaps they hadn't seen him. Of course they'd seen him; he'd looked directly into the eyes of the naked shadow. He stopped thinking. His feet touched the sandy bottom and he turned over, pulled himself to his knees and dragged himself up the shallow beach.

His face pressed into the gritty sand, spitting water, his chest whistling and heaving as he fought for breath, he didn't hear the light footsteps that approached him over the sand. Too late he sensed the feet near his head and tried to pull his shoulders off the sand. Then something hit him across the head and his arms collapsed. His face smashed back

228

into the wet sand. He tried to spit the sand out of his mouth but before his mouth could react he felt another meaty whack on the side of his head and it didn't matter about the sand in his mouth any more.

When he came to he was lying face down on concrete, shivering, soaking wet, with his hands tied behind his back. It was pitch black. He couldn't see a thing.

All he could remember was hitting the beach and crawling over the sand. Then it came back with a rush. The blow on the back of the head – the stars of red, and the black mist. He'd been there before, but that was a long time ago. He struggled with the knots binding his hands but gave it up very quickly. The rope was sodden and it had been applied by an expert. The wet had tightened the knot and he was doing no good pulling on it. His feet were tied too, but it didn't matter; there was nowhere he could see to go. He lay still for a while and listened. Nothing. Silence. He sniffed. A faint smell of oil and . . . that was as far as he got. He stiffened at the squeal of metal as someone put his shoulder to a tin door. The light went on, blinding him. He clenched his eyes tight then slowly opened them. The first thing he saw were the two scruffy deck shoes he'd seen when lying on the beach just before the lid slammed on his head. He craned his neck and looked up. He should have known. Krislov.

'I wouldn't've thought you were capable of that,' growled Krislov. He didn't move, he didn't kneel down to untie his bonds. There was anger in the slow drawl.

'Capable of what?' managed Logan.

'Wanna tell me what happened?'

'Knock it off, Krislov. There's fuck-all to tell. Just get this fucking rope off me . . . Whatever it is, you've got it wrong—'

'I'll be the judge of that.' Krislov still made no attempt to release Logan. He moved away a few feet and slammed the tin door shut. Then he lit a cigarette. 'Talk yourself out of it, then.'

Logan told him exactly what had happened. He couldn't tell him much except that they'd been jumped by people already on the boat and that he'd thrown himself overboard.

He thought he'd heard a couple of suppressed shots from Hagen's automatic but apart from that he'd seen nothing.

'I heard those. Couldn't make it out for a moment,' said Krislov, partly to himself. He was barely on speaking terms with Hagen, but he was coming round. 'Long time since I used a silenced gun meself. But then there was a lot of thumping going on. The next thing I saw was your head in the water and I waited for you to land. Then you got it.'

'Why?'

'Hang on a second. Let's get you on your feet. I'm beginning to believe you.' He stuck the cigarette between his lips and bent down to grasp Logan's elbows. He heaved him to his feet as if he were a bundle of cornstalks and propped him face up against the wall. As he worked on the wet knots he continued talking, inhaling every so often from the cigarette and blowing the smoke around Logan's head. 'They've taken Hagen away, probably goin' to tear the poor fucker's arms off, but in the quiet somewhere. I've seen some Chinese tricks in 'Nam. Some of the things they did to our boys don't bear thinking about. Poor old Hagen. Such a cocky fucker too!'

He finished unravelling the knots, turned Logan round and stuck a lighted cigarette between his lips. Logan hung on to it like grim death, his shivering and shaking threatening to throw not only the cigarette from his mouth but remove his head as well. 'W-here d-did they t-take him?' he stuttered.

'I followed them from the top road,' said Krislov. 'Could just make them out with the moon on its downward path. They were going into it. I could see their silhouette . . .'

'So w-where did they g-go, for Christ's sake?' Logan was recovering. He began stripping off his wet clothes and rubbing his blue body with his hands.

'Hang on, I'll get you something.'

'No t-time.'

'What d'ya mean, no time?' Krislov stopped on his way to the door and stared at the naked man. 'No time for what?'

'You're going to tell me where they, whoever they are, took Hagen and you and me are going to get him.'

'You're fucking crazy.'

230

'Sure I am. Where'd they take him?'

Krislov found a strip of old sail and handed it to Logan to dry himself. 'There's a Thai fishing boat anchored outside Chalong, near the Esso place along the bay. I don't know who it belongs to but it hasn't been there long – it's not a regular anchorage for local boats. Could be a hired job brought round from Gipsy Bay. Don't know who'd wanna do a thing like that though.' He stubbed his cigarette out and lit another. 'But you would, wouldn'tcha?'

Logan threw the lump of sailcloth into the corner. 'And what the fuck is that supposed to mean?'

'It means that you're the frigging problem. It's you everybody wants, ain't it? Hagen wanted you and he came down from Bangkok to get you – you must have brought the Chinks with you . . .' He stopped and watched Logan dragging his wet clothes back on again. After a moment his eyes narrowed. 'Was the limey in on this with you?'

'What limey?'

'Smith – Aubrey St Clair Smith.'

'No. He's just what you said, a limey with a boat. Got any ideas about that fish boat?'

'I'll help you, if that's what you mean. 'Aven't *you* got any ideas?'

'Beyond sinking the bastard – no.'

'How're you going to do that, for Christ's sake?'

'We'll work it out on our way. Let's get out to your boat and see what demolition kit you've got tucked away.'

'I can tell you now, before you start looking – there's fuck-all in the demolition line.'

'We'll see.'

While Logan hauled up the anchor and got the *Sara-Louise* under way, Krislov went below and busied himself turning out old forgotten lockers and corners crowded with bits of radio and miscellaneous junk. After a moment Logan came below and joined him.

'Found anything useful?'

Krislov didn't look up. 'Just keep your eyes on the goddamn boat! Half an inch either side and you'll have the fuckin' thing on the mud. There ain't much water here. Get back to the wheel and keep 'er in the middle of the

231

channel until you see the first of the Esso lights, then put her in neutral and I'll take over. The Thai boat is just round that headland where the light is. We can tie up to the mud there.'

After a short time Krislov sidled up to Logan at the wheel. His breathing came in hoarse, cough-like barks. After a moment, when he'd recovered, he lit a cigarette and rasped, 'Gimme the goddamn wheel. I'll take it from 'ere.' He spat the barely touched cigarette over the side and peered into Logan's face. 'There's fuck-all down there to sink my old dinghy, let alone a friggin' sea-going boat. 'Ave you thought of anything yet?'

'What are you like under water?'

'No problems.'

'Have you got any gear on board?'

'Sure. Got the lot, bottle recharger as well. I've had a good look around in case I'd tucked something away and forgot about it. Nothing. Fuck-all. No sticky bombs or hole-makers, but I know a little gimmick that might pull the fisher boat down without making any noise. Wanna give it a try?'

'It's all we've got at the moment. You mooring here?'

'Yeah. No noise now. Whispers only, no smokes, no lights, OK?'

'Let's get that stuff on.'

Logan spat on the glass of his mask and before pulling it on to his head touched the dark shadow beside him. 'OK, Jack, basic plan, but if things start going wrong it's improvis-ation. I'll go for Hagen, you see what you can do about the boat. OK?'

OK? Krislov had shrugged off about twenty years. This took him back a bit, he was enjoying every moment, but he barely nodded an acknowledgement and allowed the adrenalin free rein.

The two men avoided the mud that continued out from the shingle and made their entry into the water via the freshwater inlet. As soon as they found enough depth they lay in the water and propelled themselves out into the bay. After about fifteen minutes' heavy paddling they approached the fishing vessel from the bay side and stayed together until they touched the bottom of the vessel. They looked at each other and parted, Krislov moving cautiously towards the bows, Logan to the boat's stern.

They'd only just parted company when there was a tremendous explosion in the water just beyond the stern as something smashed into the water in a mass of bubbles and air and silt. Krislov turned and came back. He thrust his mask close to Logan's, his eyebrows going up and down like a pair of live caterpillars.

Logan indicated for him to go back to the plan and pulled himself along the hull. By the time he'd got to the disturbance the water had cleared and he could see what had caused the explosion.

It was a fish trap. And in it, screwed up into a tight ball, was Hagen.

Logan moved closer and stared in horror.

He could see Hagen's face quite clearly. His eyes were closed, his mouth pursed, his lips glued tightly together but unable to prevent a minute stream of bubbles from escaping to shoot upwards in a straight line. Hagen's cheeks bulged with the effort of hanging on to what little bit of air he'd managed to retain, but it was a futile effort.

The picture had no sooner impressed itself on Logan's brain than, with a swirl of bubbles, Hagen's lungs exploded and ejected the last of his air.

Logan fumbled desperately with the catch that held the knife strapped to his leg. He was unable to take his eyes off the cage, but just as he managed to free the dagger another great explosion of water threw him backwards as the cage was hauled upwards, smothering him in a cloudy deposit from the disturbed silt at the bottom of the anchorage.

He moved back, inch by inch, towards the stern of the boat and, finding a handhold on the starboard side of the wooden hull, turned himself on his back and peered upwards. He could see nothing. They must have pulled Hagen on board.

He waited, undecided, for several minutes, and then felt his flipper pulled. It was Krislov. His thumb was stuck up out of a fist and over his other shoulder he carried a sharp-pointed two-pronged anchor. His thumb waggled urgently and, straightening himself up, Logan turned towards him. He peered over Krislov's shoulder. Trailing behind was the entire length of the anchor chain; it was still attached to the anchor and the other end hung loosely suspended along the length of the boat and disappeared up into the anchor port.

Logan took the weight of the anchor from him while Krislov pulled on the chain until a length of it trailed straight down to the bottom below them. Krislov pointed upwards, then allowed himself to float gently until he reached the shaft of one of the boat's screws. Logan, seeping air into his jacket to compensate for the weight of the anchor, joined him, and between them they hoisted the anchor so that it was hooked over the propeller shaft. They eased it gently back until its points rested on the hull where the shaft housing protruded from the engine room.

They couldn't talk. Logan couldn't tell Krislov what he'd seen; all he could do was point to the stern, then upwards, and shrug his shoulders and hold his hands out. It meant nothing to Krislov, who shook his head and turned to go back to the bow again. Logan indicated for him to wait and the two men hung precariously under the boat, dispersing the bubbles from their masks as best they could by breaking up the flow with a gentle wave of the hand. Logan had no idea how long he and Krislov had been hanging under the boat's hull when the earlier explosion of water was repeated.

Logan grabbed Krislov's arm as the disturbance settled and once again the fish trap hung suspended in front of their faces.

This time the clear water around the cage turned to colour as broken clouds of red heavier-than-water liquid spread and streaked thickly towards the surface. Krislov struggled under Logan's grasp, but finally gave in when he realised there was nothing he could do.

But Logan had other ideas. He pointed to the bottom of the inflatable, riding on its painter at the front end of the boat, and drew his finger across his throat. Krislov frowned behind his mask for a moment, then got the message. He floated underneath the dinghy, held onto the boat's hull with one hand and stuck his razor-sharp knife into the thick rubber. Praying that everyone on board was enjoying the fun at the stern and not looking over the side at sinking inflatable, he ran the blade along the side, opening it up from one end to the other. There was an initial whoosh, a froth of bubbles and the big Johnson outboard dragged its stern down below the water so that the deflated dinghy was hanging from its painter like a burst balloon. With two hard kicks Krislov was back at Logan's side. Logan could see Krislov's teeth, gripping the air valve. Krislov was trying to smile. It wasn't a pretty picture. With another hand signal, Logan pointed to the stern and the two men scurried into the disturbed water. Logan grasped the rope holding the suspended cage and hacked below his hand. The cage floated free, but before it could move upwards he manoeuvred it with his feet towards Krislov, then put all his weight on the loose end of the rope and, keeping it taut, urged Krislov away. Hagen could have been dead by now, but it didn't matter to Krislov who grasped the cage by its bamboo bars and thrust himself under the other side of the boat and towards the shore.

Krislov made a rough estimate of the distance he'd pushed the basket. His instincts told him it wasn't enough. He dared not surface, not yet. He'd have to push on under water and Hagen would have to take his chance. He'd be better off drowning among friends than with those fucking Chinks. Krislov's reasoning was always uncomplicated. He carried on, thrusting his flippers vigorously behind him.

He stopped again and worked his way round the basket to study Hagen's face. He didn't like what he saw.

Hagen had been under the water for the best part of two minutes. There were no bubbles escaping from his slack lips; his eyes were open but not seeing. Krislov removed the mouthpiece from between his teeth, partially emptied his lungs then filled them again, fully, from the tank on his back. He jammed the fiercely gushing mouthpiece through the cage and rammed it into Hagen's mouth. A mass of swirling bubbles covered Hagen's head then something found its way into his lungs and his teeth tightened on the rubber and he drank down the air as if it were liquid. Krislov had to force the mouthpiece from between Hagen's fiercely gripping teeth with both hands. He'd given Hagen another couple of minutes of life. But that was all he was going to get.

Blood was still discolouring the water but he pushed as fast as his legs and flippers would allow him. Eventually he brought his head above the water and stared across the choppy surface.

All hell was breaking loose on the trawler.

Hagen's first dunking by the Chinese had been a mere preliminary, a little sampler of what would happen if he didn't realise very quickly where he was going. That he would be going there anyway, at the end of the meeting, and for ever, was without dispute. It was, as Hagen had himself remarked earlier to Logan, a question of whether you wanted to go in comfortable style or have the life drawn out of you inch by agonising inch.

When Logan was studying his face under the water during the first trip, Liu Hongzhou, up on the deck peering over the side with the other two Chinese, had no doubt of the outcome. He looked up from the bubbles, nodded for the others to join him on the rope, and slowly they pulled Hagen out of the water.

He was not quite unconscious. Liu had decided to take over the physical part of the interview and had timed Hagen's journey to perfection.

Once the fish trap was back in its suspended position, he picked up a handful of the little sharpened bamboo sticks and, with the concentration of a surgeon's assistant choosing a scalpel, selected a pair of them. He twisted the cage on its swivel until Hagen's half-face appeared and stared with interest into his glazed eye.

Hagen's breath was coming and going in deep heaves and whooshes as he tried to settle his straining lungs. All he could hear was his own heart beating as it went up gear by gear as oxygen poured into him. But Liu was talking, and he could hear. But he could feel nothing.

Liu studied Hagen's form in the basket and discovered his leg. He clicked his fingers and made a cutting motion. Peng Soon handed him a knife and, without testing the blade, Liu stuck it into the material of Hagen's thin trousers and slit it as far as it would go. Hagen didn't notice it.

He then placed the bamboo lightly on Hagen's hairy calf, just below his tautly bended knee, and pushed. Hagen's bellow of anguish was muted by the pressure of the bamboo cage strands on his mouth; nevertheless, all the agony he'd endured for the last hour or so was encapsulated in that one cry of release.

'Talk to me about your interest in Logan. What does the name Contractor mean to you?'

Before Hagen could take another breath, another bamboo went into the gap below his knee-cap. Another scream. They didn't want any answers now; they wanted their pleasure, their reward for all the trouble they'd taken. They enjoyed themselves, and when they were ready for the answers he told them everything he knew about James Logan and about Contractor. He kept nothing back, and it was with relief that he dropped into merciful unconsciousness. His last thought was 'Please ask me more questions, and then, for pity's sake, kill me.'

Liu and Peng Soon looked hard into Hagen's unconscious face.

'Put him in the water again,' said Liu, 'and then we'll see if he's missed anything out.'

The same procedure, another loud splash, and the three Chinese Tongmen gazed down and watched Hagen's life-blood rush to the surface and disperse in the flowing water. They straightened up. The bubbles and blood stopped. Liu nodded and the other two pulled on the taut rope. Their combined strength dragged it out of Logan's hands. The severed end hurtled out of the water like a released spring.

Peng Soon recovered first. 'Go and look!' he snapped to the third man and, as he pulled himself upright, he watched the youngster throw himself into the water.

The young Chinaman went straight down where the basket had been dropped. He had no idea what to expect. What he got was the last thing he saw or felt. It was pitch black and he saw nothing except the dark mass of the boat's hull and nothing but deep shadow underneath. He groped around and went deeper, trying for the bottom. Nothing.

His lungs bursting, his eyes closed, he turned and headed for the surface. Just as his outstretched hand touched the hull of the boat something made him open his eyes. But he had no time to register a human shape as he received Logan's knife in an upward thrust below his rib case. Logan held onto him, ignoring the thrashing of arms and legs and the blood that pumped out onto him, and struck again. It wasn't necessary. The first blow had killed him; the second sliced across his neck artery and added to the rush of the confused mixture of water and blood on the surface.

Liu Hongzhou and Peng Soon, leaning over the stern, exchanged quick glances, and Peng Soon, first off the mark, dashed round to the side of the trawler and leaned over as he tried to penetrate the cauldron below. He saw them first – Logan's flippers which broke the surface as he released the dead Tongman and turned to swim for the middle of bay.

Peng Soon switched on the trawler's powerful working spotlight which pierced the early morning darkness and mist like a fully blown searchlight and weaved around like a lost soul until, steadying it and controlling its direction, he began sweeping the beam across the surface of the inlet to the bay.

Liu Hongzhou, cool, calm and outwardly unfussed, moved lightly on the balls of his feet to the weather side of the boat and stared across the water. He studied the erratic movements of the light.

'How many?'

'I saw only one—'

Liu picked up a small Uzi machine-pistol from its bracket just inside the main cockpit cover and cocked it. 'The dinghy!' he hissed urgently to Peng Soon. 'Make the light fast – leave it on and get the dinghy. Quick!'

Liu kept his eyes fastened on the circle of the light thrown onto the water by the spotlight and saw, quite clearly, a thin line of air bubbles moving away from him and out into the channel.

'Quick, Peng Soon!' he hissed loudly and urgently again.

But Peng Soon was already moving as fast as he could. Scrambling over the main cockpit housing, he slipped down the other side and ran along the deck, picking his way through the darkened side of the boat until he was able to grasp the dinghy's painter.

He had already untied it when he realised there was nothing floating below.

He threw the rope down in disgust, ran back to the cockpit and pushed the boat's main engine starter button. It coughed once, then roared on over-throttle and nearly died again when he revved the powerful engine to maximum. He leaned out of the cockpit window and shouted at Liu over the top of the thudding roar, 'Take the light while I bring up the anchors...'

He searched the unfamiliar dashboard in the poor night light, found what he wanted and pressed the anchor winch engine button. The engine whined and with a rattling of wire and chain along the boat's side, the port anchor glided out of the water, shook itself dry and clicked snugly into its home. He changed gear for the lighter starboard anchor and pressed the winch button again. The engine howled, the anchor chain tightened. The boat juddered and rattled but nothing came out of the water.

Peng Soon leaned out of the window. 'Anchor fouled!'

He slowed the engine, waited a second then revved again. The screw churned up water and mud behind them. Once again the chain creaked and strained, taut almost to breaking point. But the anchor still refused to budge. He shook his head and appealed to Liu. Liu's equanimity slipped. He turned from Peng Soon's efforts in the bridge, shaking his head despairingly, and ran his eyes again over the now calm unruffled waters of the channel. He saw nothing. On his tiptoes he danced to the other side of the boat and peered over the stern at the muddy disturbance made by the frenetic churning of the propellers.

Here was something.

The shout of triumph was strangled in his throat.

It was the body of the third man, the young apprentice murderer, rising and bouncing against the hull where one of his limbs had been trapped in a projection. Liu turned away in disgust and joined Peng Soon in the bridgehouse.

His eyes scanned the control panel and then he tapped Peng Soon on the shoulder and pointed to the main engine

239

emergency anchor winch. Barging Peng Soon to one side, he opened the throttle as far as it would go. The anchor chain, already strained, tautened like a steel bar and shuddered as if it had been electrified. The links of the chain squealed and howled and for a second it felt as if the boat were trying to pull herself apart.

Peng Soon, under Liu's urging, kept his hand on the juddering throttle lever. His startled eyes appealed to Liu but, before he could get a response, the whole structure of the boat suddenly shuddered as if she'd been hit by a torpedo. She almost leapt out of the water and, with a grinding and creaking, the rotten timbers under the engine room were dragged away from the hull. There was a sudden explosion. The engine stuttered. Then it coughed and died.

The silence almost burst their eardrums.

But it didn't last.

As the two Chinamen stared at each other, the brief silent interlude was shattered by a great gurgling noise as the fishing boat, her bottom ripped out by the anchor, the engine shuddering itself loose from its fractured mountings and all life cut from it by the inrush of water, rapidly filled up.

The boat tilted backwards with a lurch and the stern peeled open like a sardine tin.

When she began to slip stern first under the black water, Liu Hongzhou and Peng Soon threw themselves into the bay and, surfacing close together, turned to watch the rusty, barnacle-encrusted bows of the boat hang for a second then, shaking herself like a wet puppy, she plunged straight to the bottom of the bay.

The two Chinese swam the short distance to the bank of the inlet. The *perahu* that Peng Soon had used on his expedition was still where he'd hidden it after loading Hagen's body onto the trawler. Between them they floated it and worked it, silently, out into the water until they met the current and allowed it to carry them into the bay. Once clear of the sunken trawler, Peng Soon started the motor and, with Liu huddled on the bow thwart, they made their way round the headland. Before the chilled night mists were cleared by the threat of the sun lighting the skyline in the east, he cut the engine and crept silently into one of the Relations' boat yards off Phuket town.

But for Liu Hongzhou it wasn't all doom and gloom; he didn't consider the operation, so far, a total failure. In fact there was an enormous up-side to the night's work. The American had known more than he'd expected him to. He now knew where to find James Logan, where to find Theresa Logan, and he had a good idea where Logan had cached his assets. Altogether not too bad a night's work – if you could discount the loss of the American, who should, by now, have been well established at the bottom of Chalong Bay with a fairly serious set of anchor chains round his ankles. But Liu Hongzhou was always going to see the philosophical side to a lost pawn. The man who called himself Hagen was back in the game; that meant he had a face and had been drawn out of the shadow. If he remained in the action he was there for all to see – a face with a very short future.

'Peng Soon—' He took the hard Chinaman to one side. 'Go to Malaysia. Activate a team in Penang and other points on the west coast where foreigners might try to land unnoticed. You know what to do?'

'Tell me.'

'Find the man we've just lost. He'll lead you to Logan. Then you kill him.'

'I'll look forward to that—'

'I'm sure you will, my friend. But only after he's led you to Logan. Then you allow James Logan to lead you to his daughter, Theresa, and she will be brought back to Bangkok with Logan and the stuff she collects for him. Is that fully understood?'

'I know the girl only fleetingly.'

'Her father will lead you to her. She is to be taken and brought back. She's not to be hurt.'

Chapter 28

Chalong, Monday, 0330 hours

Clear of the bright area created by the trawler's lighting, Krislov surfaced and, resting his weight on the loaded fish trap, peered across the surface of the water.

But he could see nothing.

He thumped the side of his head to dislodge the water from his ears and listened. All was quiet. The inlet and bay were now shrouded in white mist and silence after the din of the trawler's howling engine and the cumulative racket as the boat crumbled and cracked apart on its way to the bottom of the bay. He turned his back on it and concentrated on keeping Hagen's mouth out of the water. He was fortunate that the basket was of bamboo and floated; anything else and he'd have been in trouble.

Now he began to worry about Logan. He paddled for another ten minutes in the silent blackness, then stopped again and searched and listened. Still nothing. He looked at the gauge on his air supply. The needle was in the red. Logan's would be the same. And still no sight or sign of him. Write the bastard off! Krislov's action philosophy – he'd lost more partners than he'd had hot dinners. No point hanging around in the wet waiting for a body to float by. He remained on the surface and consulted the luminous arrow-head of his wrist compass. He altered his direction so that he would miss the shallow water on the edge of the jutting headland and, remaining in the channel, edged round and approached the *Sara-Louise*.

She rocked gently at her mooring and her pure white superstructure stood out in a ghostly outline against the black wall of tropical undergrowth. He waited in the water and watched. It was that peculiar night-time chill – warmer in the water than out. His adrenalin was still coursing. But if he didn't get Hagen out of this goddamn cage and straightened up, and the water pumped out of his lungs, the whole thing would have been a waste of time. Yet he still refused to hurry. He pushed the cage very slowly towards the rocky outcrop at the tip of the headland and then manoeuvred it down, towards the *Sara-Louise*'s bows, and stopped again.

It all looked very innocent. Still no movement; nothing suspicious.

And where the hell was Logan?

He'd barely given birth to the thought when a faint sound of a guarded cough trickled across the water. He strained his eyes. Nothing. But again the gentle restrained cough. And then a delicate splash. His eyes zeroed in on the sound. He watched the ripples of water approach and die against the beach, and then he saw it. The glimmer of a white circle, the reflection from the glass of a mask shimmering just above the level of the water. He watched it approach the landing area and crawl on its belly to within twenty yards of the yacht. He gave a silent sigh of relief. It was Logan. He croaked like a frog and his face, now relieved of tension, broke into a grin as he watched the figure flatten itself even more into the sand and remain still.

'I bet that made you crap your pants!' Krislov whispered.

Logan let out the breath he was holding. 'I'd be obliged if you didn't do things like that!' Then he too grinned. It was relief. The adrenalin went back to its usual place. 'You stupid bastard!'

They wasted no time on more pleasantries; with no conversation, they quickly cut open Hagen's cage and, with a gentleness foreign to their type, carefully eased the cramped body into the open. Hagen was unconscious but there was a pulse and, with his ear jammed to his mouth, Logan could hear a rumble of erratic breathing. But Krislov was running out of patience. Elbowing Logan to one side, he lifted Hagen into a sitting position, threw him over his shoulder and, bow-legged, broke into a fast trot, signalling Logan to go in front.

Drawing the knife from the sheath strapped to his leg, Logan dragged himself over the *Sara-Louise*'s guardrail and, crouched double, the knife held in front of him in his outstretched hand, he quickly covered the whole of the deck. Krislov didn't wait for the OK. As if it were a bag of potatoes, he dumped Hagen's body under the lower rung of the guardrail and pushed him aboard. By this time Logan had searched the main cabin and instead of the knife he now had Hagen's much more reassuring heavyweight Browning clenched in his wet hand.

But it was still not finished.

One by one he checked the sail lockers and then the engine room and stowage holds. Only then did he relax. There was no one on the boat who shouldn't be there; everything was as they had left it – no naked Chinamen skulking in the scuppers. That wasn't going to happen again – not on this trip. He poked his head down the companionway. 'You OK down there?'

'Sure.'

'Hagen?'

'He'll live.'

Logan had a brief glimpse of Hagen's body, now naked, white and lying face down on the main cabin floor. Krislov was bending over him, a large towel in his hand, the first-aid box by his knees. Logan didn't linger. 'I'm starting the engine and moving fast. We're getting out of here. OK with you?'

'We'll talk about it later. Watch out for people in the water who shouldn't be there ...'

But Logan had gone and a few moments later the *Sara-Louise* shuddered as the pistons in the big Liston turned once, coughed throatily, then roared into life, quickly settling to a healthy throb. Logan jumped onto the soft shore, cast off the yacht's moorings and with the water above his knees dug his heels into the sand, pushed her away from the bank and pulled himself aboard. Within a few minutes and with minimum revs, the *Sara-Louise* was safe in the middle of the channel. A couple of minutes more and they sailed out of the inlet and into the main bay.

The sun, rising on the other side of the headland, broke the darkness into a misty, wishy-washy grey as Krislov mounted the companionway stairs. He looked up for a moment and studied the sky, then said in a low voice, 'Go down and finish sorting out Hagen. He'll be ready to start swearing any second now. Get the whisky bottle ready and keep that gun out of his sight – he's just as likely to want to go looking for those fucking Chinks!'

'I can manage here,' said Logan.

'Not as well as I can,' growled Krislov. 'I don't need light, I don't need radar. I can find my way around this bay as well I can find the door to my shit house. Now get below!' They changed position. But before Logan reached the top of the companionway Krislov said, 'Where we goin'?'

'Anywhere, far away from here,' retorted Logan. 'Just keep going south until the sun comes up and then we'll talk about it. You all right leaving your place?'

'It can take care of itself.'

Chapter 29

Aubrey St Clair Smith approached the Malaysian mainland in the late afternoon and anchored in a small isolated lagoon behind a headland just north of Kuala Kedah.

'Come over here,' he told Junit when he came on deck. He glanced quickly over his shoulder at Theresa. She was well out of earshot in the bows of the boat where, in the clear water below, a pair of frisky porpoises hunting a shoal of small fish kept her fully occupied. But it wouldn't have mattered anyway; Junit and St Clair Smith spoke only in Malay when together. They had a very easy-going relationship built up over many years – ever respectful, never familiar, they were more friend and equal than boss and worker, except when it really mattered, and then both accepted their status. 'How's your head?'

'OK.' Junit made light of the punishment he'd received from Hagen but spoke in a hoarse, whispering voice as if he'd got a severe case of laryngitis. 'My head's a coconut. It doesn't worry me. This is different—' He pointed to the damp cloth around his neck. 'This hurts. I would like to talk to him about it some time.'

St Clair Smith didn't join in Junit's weak grin. He admired his cheek and his large white teeth. Someone was going to have to pay for the lad's pain. But Junit shrugged it aside. 'You reckon it was the girl's father who did this?'

'It had to be.'

'I left Mr Logan on the beach; my lights went out immediately I went through the door. There was no way he could have got into the shed before me. I heard an American voice and it wasn't Mr Logan's.'

'Junit, my friend, you weren't in a position to tell one way or another. You were getting your head bashed in. You could have imagined all sorts of things.' St Clair Smith offered him a gentle smile and left it at that. The smile and the silence concealed his disquiet; he hadn't considered second parties, not as quickly as this. He'd assumed Logan had taken the opportunity to carry out his earlier-conceived plan of getting Theresa to do the running while he played the hare. They'd been too quick for him. They? Exactly! Who were 'they'? Something was very wrong for their trail to have been picked up so quickly. But Junit had said an American. An American talking American to another American? Christ! How many bloody people were there looking at Logan in Ban Yit? And who had got him now? 'You were confused,' he said at length.

Junit wasn't going to argue. It was none of his business what these Americans got up to. But what Aubrey St Clair Smith got up to was his business. 'Do you think whoever it was will be happy now that he has Mr Logan ...?'

'Mr Logan's gone back to Bangkok, Junit,' insisted St Clair Smith. 'There was no one else.'

'If you say so,' responded Junit patiently, 'but if there was and he wanted more than just Mr Logan – his daughter, for example, as well – wouldn't someone like Krislov tell them where you're heading?'

Good point.

That's two things, St Clair Smith told himself, he hadn't considered. 'I don't think Krislov would have suffered any treatment on my behalf. None of his business. If he was asked nicely where I was making for he'd tell them. I have nothing against him. It's common sense. Why should he get a dose of what you got when all he had to say was "He's gone to Penang. He always goes to Penang from here – never known to do anything different—" '

Mark Hagen, sitting on the main cabin superstructure of the *Sara-Louise*, was not the happiest of men. Every bone in his body felt as though it had been twisted in different directions; his chest ached with trying to hold his breath under water and the deep bamboo wounds hurt more now than they did before being crudely stitched together by Jack Krislov's horny fingers. Sleep had hastened the recovery and the large glass of neat whisky clutched in his hand was consolidating it.

'How're you feeling?' said Krislov from the deck wheel.

'I've felt better.'

Hagen studied the tied edges of the rough stitching job on his various wounds. He wasn't complaining, not even to himself. This was par for the job, this was what he was paid to do – and accept. Getting drowned in the process, too; he wasn't a water man, he hated the bloody stuff, but being shoved in a fish trap and thrown into the deep, now that was a different story. Nothing to do with being put through the wringer; this centred on the indignity and the humiliation of being taken by a bunch of gooks and trussed up like a fucking chicken. It went deep.

Throwing the whisky down in deep gulps, he coughed and could still taste seawater. He spat it out onto Krislov's nice clean deck and moved into the shade. There was nothing to look at, nothing moved; they were alone as far as the eye could see.

Logan came up out of the forward compartment and spread himself lengthwise beside Hagen on the superstructure roof. He'd found an old baseball cap and pulled it forward so that it covered his eyes and, moving his body until it settled in a comfortable position, rested his head on the mainsail boom.

'Feeling OK?' he asked Hagen.

'Knock it off, will ya. I've just been through all that with Krislov. Forget how I'm feeling. Tell me what's happening next.'

'Krislov saved your life.'

'I'll try and remember that when his turn comes.' Hagen remained staring at the horizon. His lungs wouldn't accept a cigarette yet; he'd tried when he'd woken up and nearly died again. Instead he chewed on a matchstick stuck in the

248

corner of his mouth. 'Krislov said they were Chinks. What sort of Chinks are you running from, Logan?'

Logan didn't alter his position. 'None of your fucking business, Hagen. Graver's given you a job, concentrate on that and leave me to worry about what sort of Chinese we're playing with.'

'Let me put it another way, then.' Hagen didn't feel well enough to lose his temper. 'That will perhaps make it my fucking business. Those Chinks, whatever sort they were – I told 'em everything they wanted to know.' He glared accusingly at Logan. 'Have you got some fucking argument with that?'

Logan didn't respond for a few moments. He didn't even turn his head towards Hagen; he just continued lying there soaking up the sun with his eyes closed. 'What exactly was it they wanted to know?'

Hagen spat the chewed-up match from between his lips. 'It was all done by a little, fat, ugly bastard who was running the show. He wanted to know where you were going. I said to the States – eventually. He asked how. I said you'd be flying out of KL. Then he wanted to know where your daughter was. I said she was on a boat with a limey. What limey? A limey named St Clair Smith. Going where? South, probably Malaysia. But I had a couple of questions. They didn't give me a chance to ask them, they were too fucking busy hammering nails into me and doing a slow water job—'

Logan opened his eyes briefly but saw only Hagen's head in silhouette. The sun was scorching down but appeared to be affecting only him and Hagen. Jack Krislov, stripped to the waist, clad only in a pair of purple jockey shorts, was in his element. He remained at the wheel and made no attempt to keep his melanoma-covered body out of the sun. Logan closed his eyes again.

'What did you want to ask them?'

'Whether they were gunning for Logan or Contractor. What say I ask you the same question?'

'Again, it's none of your business. But as you're a smart young bastard who thinks he knows it all, I'll tell you something that's grating on my fucking nerves. Whatever sort of Chinese they are, somebody led them to Phuket, and then to Ban Yit. And they knew enough to equip themselves with hired boats. They didn't come with me. That means they were on to you.' He gave it a second to sink in, then added, 'How well d'you know Krislov?'

Hagen made no reply. He was busy thinking. *How could he have been blown in Bangkok – a single agent, no control, no runners, one man on his own – how in hell's name did he not spot a tail? Krislov? He didn't know him at all. Reilly in Washington reckoned he did. But how well? The scabby little bastard knows the Thai Chink and speaks it – could he have called them into play? Krislov's doubling? Could be, it's a logical sequence. OK – Krislov's working the Chinks. Why, then, you smart fucker, would Krislov help Logan push them off the track and dig you out of a bamboo cage? Forget it! Forget Krislov! Play it as it comes.*

But he had one of his own for Logan. 'You happy with what Graver said about your future? You trust him to make no move on you provided you keep your stuff under wraps?'

'Nope.'

It was Hagen's turn to raise himself on his elbow and study the man lying beside him. The complacent bastard looked comfortable and relaxed. You wouldn't think so, by what he'd just said.

'So why are you going through with this thing; why are you handing him your cards before he's paid to see 'em? Why don't you leave 'em where they are and tell him he doesn't get a sniff until you've been made bomb-proof? Surely, when everything stops dead in 'Nam, whatever you've got on Graver comes to an end anyway. The people you've got in place around the East will've outlived their usefulness once the Langley paymaster stops paying into their secret accounts. They won't work for nothing. No reason why they should. So why don't you keep the stuff under wraps until then and then go and shake Graver's hand and say, How about a bit of back pay and a bonus? And go and settle yourself in the warm somewhere?'

'Thanks for the advice. You can stuff it!' Logan had had enough. He knew the game and he knew the rules governing how it was played. He didn't need advice or comment from a cocky young bastard who'd been crawling across the floor in diapers when he'd been arguing with real people in a real war. Logan knew he was now way out of date in his approach to all things shadowy, but he didn't intend changing – not yet. 'All I want from you, Hagen, is cover for my back. I don't want conversation, advice, or suggestions. I'm collecting in Kuala Lumpur and the whole lot's going to the States. End of subject.'

Not for Hagen it wasn't. 'Why the hell would you do that?'

'Because that's the way I've planned it. You're not part of those plans. You've been sicked on to me and I'm stuck with you, so you just stick around, do fuck all, and keep your goddamn mouth shut – OK?'

Hagen absently reached for one of Logan's cigarettes lying on the deck beside him. He even lit it absently and drew a lungful of smoke into his throat. Just in time he realised what he was doing and threw the unused cigarette overboard where it fizzled into the cool, green water. He coughed for a few moments, and when he'd recovered said, unabashed, 'Personally I'd leave these papers where they are. Where only you' – he paused – 'and Theresa know their hidey-hole. The CIA can't touch bank vaults in Malaysia, or anywhere else – in theory – but they've got an awful lot of keys to places where others wouldn't even get as far as the teller's grille.' Hagen snorted. It cleared his damaged nasal membranes and brought water to his eyes. He blinked it away. 'I don't know why I'm spouting all this at you, you know better than I the powers the CIA's taken unto itself. National security, or an imagined threat to it, will have your little insurance packet out of its supposedly safe deposit box in the US and on Graver's desk before you can say "fortune cookie – very fine thing!"'

Logan said, 'Yeah – like I said, it's none of your goddamn business. Drag yourself up onto your feet and tell Krislov we're going to Penang – and, Hagen . . .'

'Yeah?'

'That's all you tell him.'

Junit gazed, unseeingly, across the flat water at mainland Malaysia for several minutes without speaking, then shifted his gaze back towards Aubrey St Clair Smith. He very carefully cleared his throat. 'Krislov is a strange man.' No criticism, but simple Malay-style statement that a man was not to be trusted. 'I wonder if Mr Logan told him he was coming down with the new engine?'

Krislov.

St Clair Smith stared at Junit for several seconds as he ran through his mind the activities of the last few days. Krislov – he'd been in it since the beginning. Forget the engine, he'd seen Jim Logan on the *Claudia* the morning after they'd arrived. He couldn't have helped noticing Theresa either. Krislov, ex-US Special Forces, Vietnam – and where else? Washington? And old Special Forces operatives never died; neither did they fade away; they simply got themselves recruited by the CIA.

He concentrated his mind on how Krislov could have worked the system and snatched Logan with as professional a job as he'd seen in a long time. It seemed there had been no planning – they hadn't had the time to plan or rehearse – it was just a straightforward piece of one hundred per cent improvisation and it had been one hundred per cent effective. Whoever they were, Krislov's team sounded like people who really knew their business.

Aubrey St Clair Smith continued studying the distant horizon as it came and went through the heat haze building up around them, the gentle eastern breeze bringing with it the approaching evening. Krislov was the CIA's contract man? Unlikely. But then what wasn't unlikely in the games they played?

'Be back in a second,' he said to Junit abruptly, and went below. He closed the door of the chart and wireless room behind him and lifted the screen off the large British military VRC.322 set he'd had secretly installed. He checked Dixie's ASIS frequency; this would be an exclusive between Dixie and his Australian paymasters. St Clair Smith didn't mind the Aussies listening to what he had to ask; he didn't want Krislov listening in.

Dixie's voice, as usual, betrayed no interest, and he wasn't surprised when St Clair Smith announced himself on the exclusive Australian intelligence frequency. Nothing fazed Dixie. 'Hiya, Smithy! You move in mysterious circles!'

'Dixie, is Jack Krislov's boat still anchored in the bay?'

'Negative, mate!'

'Is Jack in his shack?'

''Ang abaht, I'll see if he's in business.' It took about four minutes. 'No response, mate. 'E must have gorn with the *Sara-Louise* – charter job maybe?'

'When did she leave?'

'No idea. She wasn't here when the sun got up. Haven't heard Krislov singing either. D'ya wan' his call sign?'

'Thanks.'

'Three, bravo, bravo, tango – you'll have to change frequency. He hasn't got anything on the boat that'll accept this.'

'Thanks, Dixie.'

'Shit happens, mate!'

St Clair Smith moved over to the normal here-it-is-for-everyone-to-see VHF set and picked up the mike. He clicked in to maximum power, positioned the manual aerial and put out the *Sara-Louise*'s call sign. The response came immediately.

'Three, bravo, bravo, tango, c'm'in.'

It was a strong signal, at least strength seven. St Clair Smith raised his eyebrows – now he'd got two more problems. The *Sara-Louise* wasn't hovering around the Andaman on a charter job within sight of Phuket, she was just on the other side of a bloody big wave; she was well within a sixty-mile band covered by *Claudia*'s VHF and, as if that wasn't enough, it was Krislov's voice. St Clair Smith said nothing and laid the microphone down. His face showed no expression as he plotted the position of *Sara-Louise*'s signal.

'What's the matter with that?' grunted Hagen when Krislov in agitation flicked the channel switch up and down on the VHF before banging the handset back onto its hook.

'Somebody looking for a chat, by the sound of it. Got us but then tracked off. Could be out of range.'

'Is that normal?'

'What, someone calling on VHF? Nah – probably someone mixed up his bravos and his tangos – it 'appens.'

'Will that call tell this guy who doesn't know his ass from his elbow exactly where the *Sara-Louise* is?'

Krislov moved over to the cockpit wheel and studied the autopilot setting; then he checked it with the compass before returning to the armchair he'd vacated to answer St Clair Smith's probing call. He looked searchingly at Hagen. 'Not exactly. Only in a certain radius within the limit of the strength of the signal . . .'

'Will it tell what direction we're heading?' persisted Hagen.

'Hagen,' grunted Krislov scathingly. 'You're straining your bladder trying to read a problem into a simple radio call. Why don't you stick your nose on that radar screen? Have a good look. There's nothing coming up our ass and nothing in front. Stop wetting your pants. Do us all a favour and go and have a look.' He jerked his head towards the navigation equipment. 'There's a bit of traffic tight on the Malaysian coast, but that's always so. Alor Star at times is as busy as Penang. If you wanted something to worry about you should be looking there.' He pointed over his shoulder with his finger. 'That's where we left the trouble – and that's where it'll be coming from. Not from someone Christ knows where, fucking up my call sign.'

But Hagen still wasn't happy. He wanted to live a little bit longer. He'd tasted death, at very close quarters, and discovered he didn't fancy it. His survival glands had inflamed and they did nothing for his frame of mind. Hagen was a loner, and that was how he preferred things to be – crowds of people around him directing and suggesting didn't suit his temperament. He wanted to make his own decisions.

'Anyway . . .' Logan joined in the conversation, turned his head and studied the chronometer over the chart table. 'In less than five hours it'll be daylight and we'll be just off the north tip of Penang. Anybody near enough to see us dodging into the traffic there'll be close enough for us to see them. These are my problems, Hagen. You haven't got any, so for Christ's sake relax.'

'You relax, Logan, I'm happy as I am.' Hagen's flat

expression shifted to Krislov. 'You know all about these waters, Krislov. You got it all worked out how you're going to put Logan and me ashore?'

Krislov was tired too. 'Like the man said, asshole, relax and leave it up to us who know what we're doing.'

'Go on, then, I'm relaxed,' grunted Hagen. 'Tell me about it.'

Krislov looked into Hagen's face for a few seconds and then shifted his eyes to Logan. Logan gave a slight nod. 'OK. Just before first light, when the screen shows we're all alone and the island's about half an hour's run in the dinghy, I'll slip into an inlet at the north end of the island and drop you two off. Then you'll be on your own and'll have to make your own way to wherever you're heading. When your feet touch sand that's my day finished and I fuck off back to the peace and quiet until another smart asshole like you comes riding out of the sun to upset my routine.' He turned his craggy face to the other two. 'Unless either of you want to come back with me?'

Logan and Hagen stared back at him.

'I didn't think you did! I was joking – OK.' Krislov's humour was short-lived. 'I'll sail back to Phuket waters – I can creep into Ban Yit and carry on life as normal. And if anybody asks – never heard of you two bastards in my life!'

'Sounds OK to me,' said Logan. He shifted his gaze to Hagen. 'You got an argument on that?'

Hagen shook his head.

The dinghy, loaded with three men, their fishing rods and gear there for all to see, moved slowly on its engine round Penang's Muka Head and followed the coastline to Batu Ferringi. The men landed openly on the sandy beach near the Lone Pine Hotel. They pulled the dinghy out of the water and onto the sand and tied it to a small concrete block. They left their rods and gear in the dinghy as a sign of good faith and scuffed their way across the sand to a table on the grass outside the Lone Pine. They attracted no attention. Europeans had funny habits. They sat in their little rubber boats and fished for fun; they got burnt by the sun, and then they came and sat in the blazing heat and ate eggs and beef-bacon and drank gallons of black coffee.

Krislov pushed his plate away, lit a cigarette and drank the remains of his coffee down to the dregs at the bottom of the cup. 'I'm off,' he said abruptly. 'Back to Ban Yit and pray like fuck none of you people ever come back again.'

'Amen to that,' said Hagen in a rare moment of reverence. 'If I never see you or Thailand ever again I'll be a very happy man—'

'OK, now that you've both got that off your chests let's get on with it,' said Logan, and stood up. 'You' – he nodded at Hagen – 'go down to the dinghy with him and help him into the water, then make a show of saying goodbye. I'll pay for this and go and get a taxi. Meet me out front. So long, Krislov. Be seeing you!'

'Hope not!' No warm handshake, no thanks for everything, just 'be seeing you' and 'hope not.' Theirs was a game completely without feeling.

Chapter 30

The Malacca Straits, Tuesday/Wednesday

Junit studied Aubrey St Clair Smith's face as he came back on deck. The news didn't look good.

'I think you're right about Krislov, Junit. He's followed us. He's somewhere out there' – he jerked his chin towards the open sea – 'and not very far away. I think he's finished with Mr Logan and now wants his daughter.'

'For what purpose?'

'For things, my friend, that it might be better you didn't know. Logan has something that both the Thai Chinese and his own people want from him. I believe he must have been pretty badly hurt by these people for him to tell them where his daughter is going and how she is going to get there . . .'

'You know this, or you think this?'

St Clair Smith didn't answer for a moment, then, after lengthy consideration, he said thoughtfully, 'I'm fairly certain that these people, Junit, are professionals, very serious American professionals. They don't leave many pieces on the board when they pass through. I've got in their way; so have you. They've marked us both so I'm going to put you and the girl ashore and try and get you a head start . . .'

'I'd rather stay with you.'

'I know you would but this is something I've got to do on my own.' He stared hard at the Malaysian coastline in the distance; it stood out stark and clear in front of the

257

dropping red sun. But it wouldn't last for long. He called Theresa to join him below and left Junit on deck.

Theresa rested her body against the chart table and offered St Clair Smith her innocent little-girl look. If St Clair Smith was deceived it didn't show. This was business; innocent little girls didn't come into the equation. 'OK, Theresa, the favour I offered to do your father has expired. You know all about the favour?'

'I'm not sure—'

'OK, so you know. He wanted you brought to Malaysia and turned loose. I don't know where he is or where he's going but I presume the two of you arranged all that before this game started.' He cocked an eyebrow. 'D'you want to tell me the next move?'

'I'm to go to Kuala Lumpur and wait.'

'For what?'

'For him or someone to get in touch with me.'

'Where did he tell you to stay?'

She hesitated. Her newly acquired lying and cheating attributes took a second to move into gear. Long enough for St Clair Smith to get ready to discount anything she was about to tell him. 'The Ming Court . . .' She paused. 'Jalan Ampang?'

'That's where it is. What name?'

'Theresa Logan.'

'He said that?'

She didn't reply. 'All right,' he continued pedantically, 'I'm going to arrange for you to be taken to KL and then I can wash my hands of the Logans.' He smiled kindly to show it was the last thing in the world he wanted but that was how it was to be. Whether she took it all in was another thing. It didn't bother him. St Clair Smith was quite capable of tossing several balls in the air at the same time and making each one appear the genuine article. 'Junit will take you to Alor Star and there you will meet an Englishman who knows all about taking people into Kuala Lumpur without the necessity of a brass band to announce your arrival. Once he's dropped you off at the Ming Court you'll be on your own – until, that is, your father makes contact and decides his next move.' He stood up. 'Before I sort this

258

out is there anything you want to ask me—' He waited for a moment. Nothing came except a long appraising look with no movement of the lips. '—or tell me?'

Still nothing.

'Then perhaps you'd give Junit a little hand with the dinghy?' He closed the cockpit door behind her and locked himself in the chart-room. He removed the screen again from the VRC.322 and set the scanner on a tour of the dial until it stopped by a designated band. St Clair Smith fine-tuned the wavelength and waited a second. An English voice came into the small cabin. 'Simon. Go ahead, Aubrey.'

St Clair Smith responded quickly and economically. He finished with ' . . . Go along with what she intends in KL. Let her book herself into the Ming Court but she won't be staying there more than an hour or so – just long enough for you to say goodbye and head on your way back to Alor Star. Stick with her, though, and cover her back when she moves hotels. I'll want to know who comes calling on her – night or day. OK?'

'Junit?'

'Forget Junit. Just say goodbye.'

'Roger all that, Aubrey. See you in KL?'

'Look forward to it.'

Aubrey St Clair Smith dropped Junit and Theresa on a strip of white sand just out of sight of the club at Kuala Kedah. From there Simon would take over and Junit would fade into the background and make his own way to the prearranged rendezvous with St Clair Smith in Port Klang, west of KL.

St Clair Smith headed *Claudia* out to sea again and set course for a point where he would intercept the Americans' boat as they approached Penang.

But, once again, he'd miscalculated.

After leaving Logan and Hagen at the Lone Pine Hotel, Krislov had motored the *Sara-Louise* round the North Channel to Georgetown and refuelled at the floating Shell station. By the time he worked his way back the light was fading and he reset his course for a long night's sail in the sixty miles of highly unpredictable water between Penang and Langkawi. Had he not stopped for fuel, Krislov would have been home and dry; instead, St Clair Smith spotted him leaving the North Channel just before turning west to cut the *Sara-Louise* off on the course for the western tip of Penang he had erroneously predicted for her.

St Clair Smith was out on all counts. He was wrong about *Sara-Louise*'s original position when he'd made radio contact and his timing now was out even further. He couldn't believe his eyes when, just before dusk, he spotted the distinct sail formation of the *Sara-Louise* through his high-intensity glasses. She was hull down and creaming across the light seas, heading for what he thought was the west coast of Penang. He nodded his approval. This was exactly the course he would have set himself to land people who didn't want their presence announced. He was happy with that, but, for St Clair Smith, it wasn't just a question of landing people; that was a foregone conclusion. The question was – what people? Krislov himself? Sure. He'd already shown whose side he was on. But who else? The guy with the heavy hand and the American voice who'd put out Junit's lights? He'd got to be there with Krislov. But who was he, and where did he fit into the board game? St Clair Smith seemed to be getting nowhere, but he stuck with it; how about a one-man hit-team from Langley contracted on Logan? Or was it more than a one-man team? For Christ's sake – how many, then? St Clair Smith finally gave up. He stopped thinking of the intangible and concentrated on what he'd got – *Sara-Louise*, as far as he was concerned, was on course for the West Approach, the extreme west tip of the island, and St Clair Smith calculated that Krislov, who knew these waters like the back of his hand, wouldn't consider doing anything else.

But in fact Krislov was on his way home. When St Clair Smith sighted him he had battened down, set the autopilot on a course for Langkawi and gone to sleep. He knew if he didn't get his head down before he hit the treacherous crosswinds and turbulent waters between Penang and the island it would be a good twelve hours before he got a rest.

He didn't spot *Claudia* sitting on his beam, and at first light in the morning St Clair Smith had approached to within three-quarters of a mile of him. They still hadn't reached the section of rough sea. But it wasn't far off.

Handing over the *Claudia* to the autopilot, St Clair Smith made his way below deck and moved through the length of the boat to the forward cabin. Shutting the door behind him, he clambered across the covered mattress to the large mirror on the bulkhead. He removed the two screws on the right-hand side of the mirror and pulled it away. It was hanging on two finely balanced hydraulic hinges, and behind it was a narrow shelf with small piles of money of different currencies, various documents and some small items of silver and jewellery. He swept all this onto the bed and reached his hand inside and upwards and slipped a small catch in the top corner of the recess. Forcing his fingernails into a shallow inset, he pulled gently, allowing the entire back of the recess to slide out of sight. Where the back had been was a large rectangular cupboard lit by a glowing humidifier. The dull bulb illuminated a small arsenal of weapons, racked neatly and ready for use.

He took out a compact Heckler & Koch 9mm machine-pistol and laid it on the bunk with two spare thirty-round magazines. Next, four standard British Army L2 hand grenades with three-second fuses and, finally, with a grunt, a well-used, late-model Bren with four magazines loaded with .303 mixed ball and tracer. St Clair Smith was getting ready for battle.

He replaced the cabinet and mirror and stood at the door and studied the bulkhead. Nothing of the secret recess showed. He put one of the green oval L2 grenades in each of his trouser pockets and picked up the Bren. He clicked one of the magazines in place and, balancing the other three in the crook of his arm, climbed up to the deck and took a quick look at the radar. The distance was closing – just under a thousand yards and no activity on the *Sara-Louise*. But this didn't concern him. His object was to stop the boat or slow it down, and he knew exactly how he was going to do it.

He clicked down the Bren's bipod and rested it on the cabin superstructure. It raised him well above his own boat's deck level, and getting down beside the Bren he set its sight, initially, for a thousand yards. Cradling the solid wooden stock in his shoulder and gripping with his left hand, he raised his head and studied the movements of the *Sara-Louise*.

Not bad.

She was riding up and down with the swell, but he had a good platform with his three hulls under him. He decided to give it a barrel-warming burst.

Grasping the butt and allowing his forefinger to settle naturally on the trigger, he rested his cheek on his left fist, settled the fore and back sights on the sail and squeezed. He gave four bursts of four rounds and could just make out the tracer line as it appeared to rise and then dive in a shallow curve behind the *Sara-Louise*. He lowered the sight fractionally, readjusted the stock in his shoulder and emptied the magazine in controlled three- to four-round bursts. He changed the magazine and waited, unmoving.

Before the first round hit his boat, Krislov hurled himself out of his bunk.

'Fucking pirates!'

He didn't panic. Already fully clothed, he threw himself across the cockpit, lifted the lid off the lowest step and brought out the South-East Asia yacht traveller's standard weapon – an old, well-worn AK47, the ever-reliable Kalashnikov, and cocking it on the run threw himself up on to the deck and squeezed the trigger. Anywhere would do – frighten the fuckers into putting their heads down while he sorted himself out. He was just in time for St Clair Smith's second load, which cracked and buzzed around him, and, with the sound of rattling tin cans, a burst of ball smashed into the aluminium mast. It was all luck for St Clair Smith. The mast wavered like an overextended metal tape-measure then crashed forward from the bullet-torn gap, strewing the deck with torn and ripped sail, aerial wire and bits and pieces of radar equipment, before slithering across the cabin roof and smashing through the guardrail into the water. It hung there, half on and half off, until the weight and drag of the sea cleared it. Krislov changed the AK47's magazine, raised his face from the deck and stared across the water.

He saw the unmistakable three hulls of the *Claudia* rising gently with the swell.

'Smithy?' He blinked in the inadequate light. The sun was only threatening; it hadn't yet pierced the horizon. But there was no mistaking the *Claudia*.

He laid the Kalashnikov down and leapt to his feet and waved.

'Smithy!' he bellowed at the top of his voice. 'What the fuck—'

He threw himself down again as another series of short bursts clawed towards him, and he lay with his hands over his head as he tried to press his body into the woodwork of the deck. This time the heavy .303s were thudding into the boat's structure with a cracking of wood and the smashing of glass, and then, after a solid metallic thud and a splash of liquid, Krislov smelt petrol. Just then, in the sudden cold silence, he heard St Clair Smith's voice echo across the water.

'Tell the others to come on deck!'

'There ain't no fuckin' others, you mad . . . Fuck it!' He raised his head and prepared to move.

There was a brief pause while St Clair Smith changed magazines. Krislov seized his chance and scuttled to the stern. Mistake. Wrong way. But he was rooted to the spot when, with horror, he saw petrol spurting out of holes in both the five-gallon petrol tanks hanging on the stern rail, for refuelling the outboards, and gushing across the heaving deck.

'Oh, Christ! Sweet Jesus! You mad motherfucker, Smith! For God's sake keep those fucking tracers away—'

He turned to run and his bare feet skidded on the wet deck. The smell of petrol was overpowering, but before he could scramble to his feet the next burst found the side of the hull and thudded into the *Sara-Louise*'s guts; the first of the next four-round burst bounced off one of the stainless-steel windlasses, the second slammed into Krislov's chest and turned him over, the third, the tracer, found the petrol tank again and in the same instant the whole rear of the *Sara-Louise* went up in a great ball of fire. The fourth round thudded into the base of Krislov's spine and hurtled his blazing figure over the side and into the water.

By now the *Claudia* was within four hundred yards of the burning *Sara-Louise*. St Clair Smith stood up and coldly studied his handiwork. His face betrayed no expression; neither satisfaction nor pleasure, nor sadness at the destruction of a fine boat. He picked up his binoculars and studied the burning vessel, then turned his attention to the water. He frowned. 'Where the bloody hell're the rest of 'em?' Not a sign. He'd seen Krislov. 'Now where's he gone?' He was quite at home talking to himself. It often solved a lot of problems.

But not this time.

Sara-Louise was still moving through the water. Very slowly, but definitely moving. And how long was it going to take for someone to spot a burning yacht?

He secured the Bren, picked up his .45 Colt and tucked it into the back of his trouser band. He pushed out the inflatable, dragged the engine into life and approached the *Sara-Louise*. The heat was stifling. He studied the boat professionally. The flames were nowhere near the main fuel tanks; it was going take her a long time to go down.

And then he saw it.

The object floating about twenty yards behind the *Sara-Louise* raised an arm. It was the shape of an arm – it looked more like a leg of roast lamb. St Clair Smith brought the Colt from under his shirt and rested it on the wooden slats at his feet, then, with the engine barely turning over, he made for the figure in the water.

Krislov was alive. Barely. It might have been better had he not been. In the brief moment before he'd been hurled overboard his face and body had been completely engulfed in flames. He'd been cooked all over down to a depth of half an inch; either of the two bullets that had hit him could have proved fatal – eventually – but Krislov had been chosen for the hard way. Perhaps the salt water had helped. St Clair Smith didn't know or stop to find out. He brought the Colt up and rested it in his hand on the rubber freeboard.

'Why, Smithy? Why?' The words came out of a hole in what should have been a face. It had no mouth, no lips; it

264

was a hole filled with little bits of tooth. But Krislov's voice was firm even though it came from the back of his throat. 'I know you've gone fuckin' mad, but why, for Christ's sake . . .?'

St Clair Smith didn't tell him.

Krislov's brain was screaming. There was only one thing left. He focused through the mist and red pain on St Clair Smith's face and saw nothing there to help him. He wasn't going to know why either. 'Thanks, you motherfucking limey bastard! Go ahead – finish the job . . .'

St Clair Smith leaned away from the smell of burnt flesh. 'What've you done with Logan?' he asked.

There was no response. Krislov's eyes were closed. But the hole where the mouth should have been was still open and still working. St Clair Smith tried again. 'What've you done with Logan?' This time he raised his voice to a shout. The cultured English voice was loud enough to be picked up by the breeze which bounced it across the waves into another oblivion. It sounded like something out of a horror movie. But Krislov got it before it vanished.

'I'm telling you fuck-all, you limey shit—'

'OK, Jack,' said St Clair Smith, calmly. 'See you—!'

'Hey! Fuck you—!'

'Sure.'

But St Clair Smith made no effort to go.

'Smithy – finish me off . . .'

'OK. What did you do with Logan?'

There was a long pause. No eyes; no mouth; no face – nothing. St Clair Smith thought Krislov had gone. But then it bubbled out of the hole. 'He's with Hagen – landed at Penang – going for the daughter and something . . . Oh, Jesus! Get it over with, Smithy—'

'Who's Hagen?' St Clair Smith didn't expect anything more. The burnt object was just floating, going nowhere, like a bit of driftwood.

But there was more. 'CIA – he's gonna kill him—'

'Who, Logan?'

'—and everybody else! They're all going for Logan . . .'

'KL?' urged St Clair Smith.

'Come on, Smithy, ya bastard, finish the job! Get the fucking 'ammer back – and I'll tell you.'

St Clair Smith cocked the Colt in front of Krislov's eyes. 'Yeah. They're all going for the girl—'

St Clair Smith kept his promise. Krislov's unseeing eyes stared into his as he eased back the hammer and held the Colt two inches from Krislov's wet, oily, cooked forehead and squeezed the trigger.

No prayers. St Clair Smith put the Colt away, turned the throttle on the Johnson and steered the dinghy towards the receding *Sara-Louise*. Going as close alongside as he could bear, he matched her drowning speed. Steering with his elbow, he took both L2s from his pocket, rested one in his lap, pulled the pin on the other and tossed it into the middle of the boat, aiming, as near as he could judge, for the companionway. He didn't hang around to admire his work. He opened the outboard's throttle all the way and veered off in a smooth arc in the opposite direction.

The explosion from inside the *Sara-Louise* almost lifted her out of the water, and bits and pieces of woodwork and metal splattered around the dinghy like lethal snowflakes. But it wasn't an instantaneous death. She was a solid vessel; she didn't want to go and settled back in the water, the flames roaring and cracking. She was badly battered and bruised, but still afloat.

St Clair Smith approached her again, very cautiously. He studied the dying boat for a second, then tossed the other grenade into the centre of the holocaust. The explosion broke her back and breached her main fuel tanks. There was a huge bang, an enormous cloud of black smoke, flame, debris and hissing steam, and then everything cleared and all that was left of the *Sara-Louise* was a collection of flotsam that, even as Smith watched from a distance, dispersed into smaller and smaller elements.

It was if the *Sara-Louise* had never existed.

Chapter 31

Simon had acquired the art of wandering in and out of places, particularly hotels, without being noticed. He managed this in spite of Theresa, and the pair of them managed to look like any other young couple booking into the Ming Court Hotel. Theresa's one small holdall gave them an air of respectability and her gold Amex card the wherewithal for preferential treatment. The highly painted and over-effusive American-trained Chinese receptionist took it all in her discreet stride when only one room was booked and for only one person. Simon said a friendly, if polite, farewell to the package he'd escorted down from north Malaysia and left the hotel.

But not for long.

He waited a few minutes in the busy Ampang Road, then removed his tie, pulled his shirt out of his twill trousers and returned to the foyer. Nobody gave him a second glance. He took up a station near the large, ever-crowded foyer and made himself comfortable in one of the plush armchairs. His wait, as Aubrey St Clair Smith had prophesied, was a short one. Shorter even than that. He'd barely sat down with the in-house magazine before Theresa, changed into a dull-coloured trouser suit, booked herself out of the Ming Court and into a taxi.

Simon followed her to one of the smaller, cheaper hotels on Bukit Bintang, gave her ten minutes to book another room, then entered the hotel and walked purposefully up to the desk. The reception area was deserted. The Malay girl behind the desk smiled a toothsome welcome.

'My friend asked me to wait here for her,' he said easily. 'She just booked in—'

The girl's smile continued unabated. 'Miss Chapell – shall I ring her room for you?'

'No, please don't bother. She knows where I'll be. Thanks.' He returned her smile, backed out of the hotel and sat at a table outside one of the all-purpose cafés that proliferated on the pavement. By the time his sweet, thick coffee arrived, Theresa had left the Royal Kuching Hotel by its rear entrance and was booking into the Equatorial on Jalan Sultan Ismail.

Chapter 32

The night mail train from Butterworth to Kuala Lumpur pulled into Tapah Road station and waited in the still night air while the empty platform echoed to the noisy humming of the huge diesel as it wound itself up for the long run into the capital.

Hagen and Logan stood just out of the arc thrown by the gloomy orange overhead lamp at the top end of the now empty platform and smoked a cigarette. When the station-master gave the signal for the train to leave, Logan flicked his half-smoked cigarette into the gap between the platform and the train and climbed onto the steps of the first-class carriage.

'Going to the john,' he said over his shoulder to Hagen, and disappeared into the carriage. Hagen remained on the platform until the train began its ponderous move out of the station, then ground his cigarette under his heel and mounted the first step. He remained, hanging onto the side bar with the door wide open, studying the solitary figure of the stationmaster as he made his way back along the deserted platform until the station's details blurred to just an orange glow in the blackness of the Malaysian night.

Hagen went back to his place in the over-chilled, dimly lit first-class carriage, settled his head on the reclining seat's headrest and closed his eyes.

The train was already roaring through the Perak jungle when he realised that Logan hadn't come back from the lavatory. He didn't flap, he didn't make a scene; he just sat with his eyes closed and remained still.

After several minutes he got slowly to his feet, stretched, and walked towards the rear of the carriage. The skinny young Indian stewardess with matchstick arms and legs waiting at the buffet for something to do gave him a tentative shy smile and then looked away in embarrassment when all she got back was a non-seeing blank scowl.

Out of the air-conditioned area, he lit a cigarette and, using his hand to shade his reflection, peered out of the window. There was nothing to see. It was pitch black – and there would be little else to see even in broad daylight as the train thundered through the cutting made into the dense, uninteresting jungle which was now, for want of maintenance, beginning to encroach back on either side of the track. Every so often the train, forever gathering more and more speed, flashed past tiny villages that seemed to have no connection or contact or access to the world beyond the straight metal lines that carried with regular monotony the clackety-clacking of twenty or so wagons or coaches that disturbed their night and day. Hagen lost interest within minutes. Only when he was halfway down his cigarette did he turn away from the window and make a pointless examination of the toilets. Both were empty, as he'd expected. He went back to the Tamil girl at the buffet. She didn't bother smiling this time. He wouldn't have noticed if she had.

'When does this train stop again?' he asked her.

'Sorry?' He'd made no concession to his accent; she hadn't got a clue what he was saying.

'Oh – never mind. Gimme a cup of coffee.'

This she understood. 'Shall I bring it to you, sir?'

'OK.'

He went to his seat and carried on where he'd left off – eyes closed, head on the back of the headrest. There was nothing he could do. Logan, for reasons best known to himself, had pulled a fast one at Tapah Road station. Even if this thing had stopped again a hundred yards down the track, he'd never have been able to find him in the bleak desolation of a no-town station in the middle of the jungle.

There was only one thing left to do; there was only one thing he could do – go to Kuala Lumpur and play it by ear.

Logan stood in the shadows of the up-line platform on Tapah Road station and watched the tail-lights of the train carrying Hagen disappear into the black wall of darkness where the main line to Kuala Lumpur looped into the jungle.

Avoiding the central ticket office and the subdued air of neglect of the main part of the station, he recrossed the line further down the track where the platform ended, cut through one of the rail workers' vegetable plots and emerged on the road near the run-in to the station carpark. He cut back into the concourse and darted into a telephone kiosk and, with his back to the door and his head bowed, dialled a Cameron Highlands number. A Chinese voice answered.

'Order me a car,' he told the voice. 'Your name. Tell the driver to collect a Mr Rapisada at the Tapah town rest-house and take him to the Smokehouse in Tana Rata. Tell him Mr Rapisada is Italian and doesn't speak English. As quick as you can, please.'

He dropped the phone into its holder and backed out of the booth, then walked at a half-stoop out of the station, crossed the road and persuaded a half-asleep Chinese taxi driver to drive him the half a dozen or so miles to Tapah town. Telling him to stop in the deserted main street, Logan stood and watched the taxi disappear to the end of the road and turn into a side street. He walked the rest of the way to the old rest-house, ordered and paid for a cold, sinus-jolting Anchor beer and a plate of sandwiches. He went and sat in the shadows on the verandah and for the first time in several weeks felt the great tiredness from the raising of the siege his brain and mind had undergone since the long run from Bangkok. It was a good tiredness; a good sign. He ate his sandwiches and drank his beer like a normal man; the burning in his gut had stopped and the unwinding was almost complete. When he saw the hire car cruise through the gate, he moved out of the shadows and walked down the wooden steps. The rest-house behind him was deserted. There was

271

no one to say goodbye to as he stood at the foot of the steps waiting to be picked up.

'Mr Rapisada?'

Logan nodded and climbed into the back seat. Not a word was exchanged. Nobody had seen him climb into the car and without any fuss the hired car traversed the parking area, left the rest-house and, after negotiating the semi-deserted streets of Tapah, joined the south highway and headed up the 59 towards Cameron Highlands.

Logan relaxed in the dark interior of the car and closed his eyes. He was sure he'd done it properly; he was safe, home and dry. Everything was now up to Theresa.

Hagen stepped off the train at Kuala Lumpur and walked out, head bowed, into a gloomy, overcast morning. The air was thick and humid and the clouds, tinted orange from the glow of a million hurriedly switched-on lights, were heavy and lumpy. Swollen with the weight of tropical rain, they hung low and unmoving as if anchored over the brightly lit city.

He crawled into the back of a smelly black-and-yellow taxi, grunted 'Federal Hotel', settled gingerly into the cracked black imitation-leather seat and lit a cigarette.

He'd barely got it going when the sky opened with a clap of thunder and tipped its contents into Kuala Lumpur. As the torrential rain hammered like machinegun bullets on the thin metal roof of the taxi, he found himself sitting in the middle of an unmoving traffic jam where the main road narrowed through Petaling Jaya.

In the taxi behind Hagen, Peng Soon was more philo-sophical. The monsoon allowed his taxi to remain glued to that of Hagen and removed the need for continued vigilance. Like Hagen, he was tired, but unlike Hagen he was not dispirited. His passage to Penang had been less traumatic, quicker, and infinitely more comfortable.

He sat without discomfort, his back settling comfortably into the warm seat; there was no need for him to sit on the edge and stare intently at his quarry. The weather and the traffic were doing that for him. He lit a cigarette. He should have had a smile of contentment on his flat, oriental features, but nothing materialised. Peng Soon's face was never going to smile; not after nearly twenty years of killing and maiming and torture – smiling, like happiness, was for the next generation's children.

He gazed out of the side window of the stationary taxi. This shouldn't take long. Liu Hongzhou had left the Logan problem in good hands; there would be no more mistakes. And so far everything had gone like clockwork. He'd caught the ThaiAir evening flight from Phuket to Penang. His new passport supplied by the Touming-run agency in Phuket showed him to be a journalist from Bangkok and his accreditation with a respectable English-language Thai newspaper was almost genuine. There was no problem for him at Penang Airport, where he was met by another of Liu's people, who had news for him. Logan and Hagen had been identified by Touming agents when they landed on Penang, and they also reported Krislov's departure in the *Sara-Louise*. From Penang, Hagen and Logan were followed to Butterworth, and it was there that Peng Soon had joined the two Americans on the night mail to Kuala Lumpur.

Like Hagen, Peng Soon had been caught out by Logan's leaving the train at Tapah Road station. That Logan was lost again for the time being was one of the setbacks that had to be borne with a Taoistic philosophy. Hagen was the next best thing. Logan would turn up at this man's side – it was written! And, as he puffed at his cigarette, he was quite content sitting in the taxi studying, without discomfort, the back of Hagen's head through the slow, inefficient clanking of the taxi's windscreen wipers.

The rain continued its heavy downpour and the traffic moved inch by inch towards the city centre. Hagen's taxi finally drew into the forecourt of the Federal Hotel and, without a sideways or backwards glance, Hagen walked through the wide automatic smoked-glass doors and up the stairs to the reception hall.

Peng Soon waited until Hagen had disappeared into the building before paying off his taxi and following him into the hotel. He hesitated only for a moment before walking across the wide, carpeted foyer to the coffee room and finding himself a free table where he could watch the activity

273

around the escalator and the stairs without drawing attention to himself.

After he'd waited an hour he went to the telephone, asked for an outside line and rang the hotel's number.

'This is the American embassy,' he said in a passable accent. 'Has a Mr Hagen booked in this evening, please?'

'Just a moment, please ... Yes, he has. Would you like me to connect you to his room?'

'No, I'll send someone round, thank you – er, what room is he in, please?'

'Room Three one five.'

'Thank you. Good morning.' Peng Soon replaced the receiver, waited a few minutes, then rang a Sentul number. In less than half an hour he was approached by a young Chinese dressed in the Kuala Lumpur Chinese businessman's uniform – dark well-cut trousers, white short-sleeved shirt, necktie and clean black leather shoes. He settled comfortably in the chair beside Peng Soon's and listened attentively. After Peng Soon had left, he went to the third floor, spoke to the Chinese *amah* who was responsible for that floor and indicated room number 315. She didn't need to be told what the well-dressed young man was; it was all there, in his face and eyes, for those that knew about these things. She picked up a bundle of fluffy white towels and with the young man smiling beside her knocked firmly on the door.

'More towels, sir,' she said when Hagen opened the door.

Hagen stood aside and allowed her through. The young man stood his ground. Hagen looked at him blankly.

'Under-manager, sir,' said the young man. 'Everything all right?'

'Sure.' Hagen turned his back and allowed the old woman to leave, then closed the door. The two Chinese retreated along the corridor and, without speaking again, the young man went down the stairs into the coffee room and drank coffee and ate little free biscuits while he waited for the the American he'd identified as Hagen to leave the hotel.

Chapter 33

Mark Hagen was in a much better mood after a long bath, a second, more substantial breakfast with half a gallon of good coffee, and the best cigarette of the day. He called for the old Chinese woman and sent her down to the hotel shop for a couple of new cream shirts and had his trousers cleaned and pressed. He felt like a new man. Ready for anything. Anything, meaning just that. He had nowhere to go and nothing to start on. According to Logan, his daughter was somewhere in KL. Christ! It was like a goddamn rabbit-warren; she could be anywhere! Also according to Logan, she'd taken off with the limey with the tri. So – where was the goddamn tri? Where was the goddamn Logan woman? Where was the goddamn limey? And where the fuck was Logan? He lit another cigarette quickly. He could feel his black mood returning. He picked up the phone.

'D'you know the number of the American embassy?'

'They rang you earlier, sir. They said someone was coming round to see you.'

Hagen's tone didn't change. 'Thanks. Something came up. Can you call them back for me?'

He hung on while the operator dialled the number and waited until she'd clicked down her switch. The embassy operator was male, American, and was used to bad manners.

'Gimme Assets Control,' said Hagen.

'You've got it.'

'Simmonds,' said a voice after a pause.

'Yeah,' said Hagen. 'Whaddya know about DROG-HEDA?'

'Nothing – on the phone,' said Simmonds briskly. 'D'you know where the embassy is?'

'I'll find it. Don't tell it on the phone – you may give it away! Is there a record of my being called earlier this morning?'

'Who are you?'

'Good point. See you later, Simmonds.'

He poured himself another cup of coffee, lit another cigarette, stuck his feet up on the table and waited for his trousers to return. Whoever'd stuck the hook on him was good – very, very good. He didn't bother to work out how they had done it. It didn't matter how; the fact that they'd done it was enough. He swore volubly to himself, and then stopped and began thinking laterally. Spilt milk! There was fuck-all use crying over it, but there was another use for it. Somebody had locked a tail onto him. They'd done him a good turn. The minute they showed themselves he could move one step forward. He'd have someone to follow. He was a silly bastard, the guy who tried to find out whether he was staying here. He should have sat and waited – ambushees came to you, you didn't go to them.

'Get me an English-speaking cab, will you?' he said to the Malay doorman.

'A taxi, sir?'

'Sure – gotta speak English, though.'

The Malay beamed happily. He came back from the taxi rank signalling the third taxi in the line to pull up at the entrance. 'Thanks, son.' He gave the doorman a US dollar. He was delighted. He'd remember him.

Hagen climbed into the back of the taxi. 'D'you ever clean these cabs out?' he asked.

'Pardon?'

'Never mind. Take me to the American embassy.' He lit a cigarette and sat back in the corner of the taxi so that, from the corner of his eye, he could see out of the rear window without making it obvious. He waited for a straight stretch of road then, without changing position, said, 'Take the next right.'

'Right, sir?'

'Look, boy, it ain't necessary to repeat everything to me. If I say 'right' go right; if I say 'left' go left. OK? You got it?'

'Yes, sir – right here?'

'Yeah – keep going.' Hagen watched the blue Nissan slow down almost to a crawl, then turn as they had done. 'Do a left—'

'Left, sir?'

Hagen didn't answer. They turned left. So did the Nissan and four other cars. 'Left again—' And they were back on the ring road. 'Now go directly to the embassy.'

The only car that had survived the roundabout trip was the blue Nissan. Hagen made a note of its number and when his taxi pulled up to the barrier he got out, paid the driver and, without looking at his follower, who carried on past, presented himself to the Marine guard and asked for Mr Simmonds.

'OK, Simmonds,' he said, when he'd been taken to the sanitised area between the outside world and the territory of the United States of America – as it said on a plaque on the wall – and told to wait, 'I'm the guy who called you about DROGHEDA.'

'And you are?'

'D'you know the procedure?' asked Hagen, reasonably.

'I know the procedure to use when I've got an awkward sonofabitch on my hands,' replied Simmonds.

Hagen's expression didn't change. 'Good. Well, now that we've established a sort of rapport I'd like to suggest that you go down to the hole in the ground, open the safe and look up the code-word DROGHEDA. Don't bother coming back here to apologise to me. Pick up the dark green phone and ask Langley for the name alongside that code-word. And no, you're not getting my name. Get on with it!'

Simmonds was no fool. He might have been an arrogant bastard full of his own importance, but he was no fool. He wouldn't have been where he was if he had been. He picked up the vibes, but tried unsuccessfully for a few seconds to outstare Hagen before turning on his heel and going off to do what he been told to do.

Five minutes later a messenger collected Hagen and conducted him into the bowels of the embassy. Simmonds handed him the dark green phone. He didn't say sorry. He pointed to the 'No Smoking' sign on the wall and left Hagen on his own.

Hagen lit a cigarette. 'Is Two nine zero still active?' he asked before identifying his listener.

'Talk about it,' rasped Reilly.

Hagen grimaced. Did this bastard never sleep?

'Contractor has broken out. He didn't take to Mr Graver's assurances. He's holed up somewhere here, in Malaysia, and he's sent a messenger to collect the loot. During the trip down he told me he was arranging to have the stuff brought to him, then he'd ship it to the States and negotiate with Mr Graver face to face. It seems to him that somebody's going to slip up and squash him out of the game and he's taking precautions. I reckon he's going to split the stuff and give it up piece by piece as the occasion demands.'

'We don't want that to happen.'

Hagen didn't respond. 'So far I've counted three agencies who've got people in the field looking for him. I have a faint suspicion there may be others. He can buy off the VC with a list of names and keep himself intact. I think, from what I can make of it, he can do a similar deal with the TG. Will he have anything left to buy you off?'

'I told you, no split. You've got to find him again, or find his messenger – who is this messenger?'

'His daughter.'

'OK. You know the form, you take the stuff off her. When you've got control of that you go back to your original mandate. There will be no need for negotiation.'

'Couple of small snags come to mind, sir.'

'Tell me about them.'

'Well, first of all I don't know where Contractor is, and secondly I don't know where the messenger is either.'

'And you recommend—?'

'No recommendations, sir.'

'Well, suggest something, then.'

'Have we any local contacts in Malaysia – police, for example?'

Reilly hesitated long enough for Hagen to read his mind. Sure, he had contacts in the Malaysian police – like he had contacts in every other police force in the world. But they were his contacts. He didn't want them brought out for something less than a national emergency – a *US* national emergency. But would this matter? This was Malaysia, it was on the other side of the world to Reilly's fears. But so had Vietnam been! Reilly coughed down the phone. He had made up his mind.

'Francis Ong,' he said softly, as if someone in the background might hear. 'He's adviser to one of the big private security agencies in Malaysia. Here's his phone number—'

'Haven't we got any real policemen? Someone who can cut paper?'

'This man was head of the Malaysian Secret Intelligence Service before he retired. He has all the contacts in the country. He's a powerful man. He's much more than you'll need, but he's the only authority I've got there. Don't move anything; I don't want him burned – I don't even want him singed around the edges.'

'Thank you, sir. That sounds OK for moving mountains but now I want a leg-man, someone who can fetch and carry for a few days and knows the streets of Kuala Lumpur.'

Reilly was much more forthcoming with this one. 'Tan Soo Lee, American, permanent CIA operative working as a lawyer for the KL branch of Grindle Associates of Baltimore. You make personal contact with the agent in the usual way.' Reilly read out a back-to-front phone number.

'What's his greeting signal?'

'He's a she—'

Shit!

'—and her contact name is Loriane. Anything else?'

'Yeah. DROGHEDA's closed down.'

'Terminally?'

'And permanently.' Hagen removed the phone from his ear and studied it. It had gone dead.

The closing of the line must have set up a signal. No sooner had Hagen turned away from the desk than Simmonds appeared. He was a little more amenable.

'Don't hesitate if—'

'Sure. I left my gun on a boat because they said guns weren't allowed in Malaysia—'

'Someone gave you very good advice – mandatory death sentence.' Simmonds pronounced the words with relish. 'D'you want to take a chance?'

'Yeah. But you'd better give me a certificate of authorisation.'

'Sorry.' Simmonds shook his head happily. 'No can do.'

Hagen didn't move. 'OK. Er, how do I call back that Langley number I was just talking to?'

Simmonds thought about it. 'Would you like me to have a word with the Head of Chancery about a gun?'

'You do that. Put the name Hagen on the form. I want something .45, self-loading, spare mag, a box of shells, no pouch—' Hagen suddenly stopped barking out his requirements as a thought came into his mind. He put on his genial expression. Simmonds looked wary. 'How long've you been in Malaysia, Simmonds?'

'Couple of years – why?'

'If I got off the night train from Butterworth at a place called Tapah Road, where would I be heading for?'

Simmonds didn't have to think about it. 'You'd get a taxi to Tapah town, which is the jumping-off point for Cameron Highlands. That's a hill resort. Very pleasant,' he mused. 'Smoky fires and—'

'Thanks.'

A short distance away from the American embassy, in the Equatorial Hotel, Theresa opened her eyes and for a moment wondered where she was. The lack of movement, the creaking of woodwork and spars and the muted thud of the boat's engine combined with the continual sound of lapping water hadn't been eradicated with one night's sleep in a proper bed on a solid, unmoving foundation. She revelled in a sense of luxury and stretched like an awakened cat before studying her tiny Cartier wristwatch. Half past ten – she'd needed that sleep. She leaned over, picked up her bag from the floor beside her and dug out a tiny leatherbound address book. The number she was looking for was listed under Liew Say Han (manicurist). She put a Cameron

Highlands prefix in front of it and dialled the number. It was answered by the same voice that had answered James Logan the night before.

'Has he arrived yet?' Theresa asked.

'Yes.'

Logan's voice came down the line. It was much more relaxed; the tension in his voice when she had last spoken to him had vanished. This sounded like the old Dad, the real one.

'Did you have any problems getting away from Aubrey St Clair Smith?'

'He's more than you think, Dad. You want my opinion?'

'Sure.'

'He's the same as you. Under that smooth English façade there's a very sharp operator. Do you trust him?'

'I've no reason not to. So, you're in KL? Alone?'

'For the time being. Had you someone in mind?'

'I was thinking about St Clair Smith. Where did he get off?'

'He dropped me on the beach in Kedah and went his own way. He arranged someone to bring me to KL, said I needed looking after—'

'Where is he now?' snapped Logan – too quickly. Suspiciously.

'I don't know,' she said truthfully. 'He said he'd be around if I needed help. He's staying somewhere in KL – he didn't tell me where.'

'OK, listen. Get the stuff. I'll give them a ring to say you're on your way, and then you play it the way we decided. You still quite happy about doing it?'

'I'm your daughter, Dad – I don't have to be happy or otherwise about helping you. Are you all right?'

'Sure – I love you, honey.'

'I love you too.'

She replaced the receiver thoughtfully and ordered breakfast. She looked at the time again. It was eleven o'clock. She changed the order to brunch.

Chapter 34

Francis Ong accepted Hagen's testimonials but only after a short call to the same Washington number Hagen had spoken to earlier that morning. He arranged to meet him in the Coliseum Hotel on Batu Road.

'Old-fashioned, colonial and now a tourist treat,' he told Hagen. 'Nobody you or I ever met would be seen dead in here now. In the old days—' He stopped and allowed the humorous expression to drop into a ready smile. 'Ah – but you didn't come all this way to hear about the old days . . .' The smile receded. 'How can I help?'

Hagen studied his contact closely. It was difficult to get to the eyes; they were well protected from examination by high cheekbones and heavy eyelids. Hagen viewed him with suspicion. It was his accent. He spoke English, not like the waiter in his favourite San Francisco Chinese restaurant, but like the Duke of Edinburgh. It was too good; too English. And Hagen had a healthy disregard for Englishmen, particularly when they looked like Chinamen and spoke like a British guidebook. Short, about five four, his hair almost white; chubby features with shrewd eyes that, at first glance, looked as though they found everything in life amusing – or incredible. He was a man who'd learnt his trade the hard way. He'd started at the bottom of the Malayan police ladder, meeting the communists of the fifties and sixties on their own ground and beating them at their own game. Once the way was clear for promotion by merit, he shot to the top and was the father of the modern intelligence service in Malaysia. As in most other countries, intelligence officers rarely retired. They faded into the background and remained forever there to be shot at – or to be used. Ong was no exception – he was still active. He waited for Hagen's inspection to be completed, then repeated his invitation.

'So, what's the problem, Mark? You don't mind my calling you Mark?'

Hagen shook his head. Why should he? That was the only name the Chink had; they hadn't got as familiar as surnames yet – that only came with trust and respect. 'I'm looking for a pretty, part-Chinese, part-European woman—'

Ong's smile broadened. He didn't allow Hagen to finish. 'Ahhh! You want the old Eastern Hotel – that still doubles as a part-time knocking shop.'

Hagen was thrown for a moment, then shook his head vigorously. 'No, that's not—'

'OK. My sense of humour!' Ong set his features as serious as they'd go. 'Sorry! Go on.'

Hagen started again. 'Some time during the last couple of days this young woman arrived in Kuala Lumpur from Thailand. I'd like your advice on how I should go about finding her.'

'What's her name?'

'I'm not altogether sure.' Hagen could lie with the best of them; it went with the job. 'She's tall, probably more European than Chinese. Slim, nice legs, nice figure, short bobbed hair. Well educated—' Hagen stopped and quickly corrected himself. 'I reckon.'

Ong thought for a moment then pursed his lips. 'I think it would be just about impossible to find a specific woman with a description like that anywhere. I could give you the names of half a dozen in KL who'd come fairly close to matching it—' He stopped, as if thinking exactly where in KL. Hagen waited. Ong shook his head and his lips tightened, not noticeably so, just enough to replace the amount of friendly paternalism he'd set to his features. 'One of the great things I admire about you Americans is that you're so astute, so perceptive – you can tell a woman's education as well as the length of her legs and probably the size of her nipples by just looking at her. Pity you couldn't tell the name by the same instinct.' He waited again. 'You're quite sure you can't hint at a name?'

Hagen submitted. He'd seen Ong's eyes. Briefly. And there was a hard, knife-like edge in the glimpse he'd been given. 'Theresa.'

Ong studied Hagen politely. 'What's her business in KL? Is she here to do some shopping? Some spying?' He smiled fleetingly. 'Looking for a husband? Investments? What's she going to be doing all day?'

Hagen was thinking. But nothing came. Reilly's Malaysian ex-Head of Spies wasn't clairvoyant. Hagen understood. There had to be something, just a grain of sand, to start a landslide – or even a little downhill movement. He side-stepped Ong's questions. 'Got any contacts in the telephone business?'

'You mean the exchange?'

'Are all calls going outside KL logged?'

Ong's eyes settled on Hagen's. 'We are a democracy, Mark. We don't keep track of people's private affairs. Logging phone calls and checking behaviour patterns are appanages of despotism—'

'And the CIA—' added Hagen.

Ong nodded his large head. 'What had you got in mind?'

'I think sometime she will have to make a phone call to the Cameron Highlands.'

'Within the last, say, two days?'

Hagen nodded.

Ong thought for a moment, then glanced over his shoulder at the bar. 'Let's have another beer and then we'll eat.' He stood up ponderously. 'Sit there and I'll be back in a moment. I'll do the ordering. Smoke a cigarette.'

Hagen waited until the Chinaman had gone through the door by the bar which led to the hotel's upstairs rooms, then went to the bar as if to confirm the order. But he went only as far as the door and glanced through it. Ong's ample figure was jammed over the phone. Hagen retreated quickly. So much for people's democratic rights to privacy. He'd lay money that someone in a responsible position would shortly be checking all phone calls made from the democracy's capital to its mountain retreat in the Cameron hills.

Hagen was only half right. The telephone logs were being checked. But Ong was also making another call. It was to a house on the edge of a golf course on the outskirts of Kuala Lumpur.

'Aubrey?'

'Yes.' Aubrey St Clair Smith hadn't long been back in Kuala Lumpur. Junit had taken care of *Claudia* and he had come home to his hot showers and bubble baths. He was busy washing the smell of blown cordite and blood and burnt flesh off his skin and out of his system. The champagne was also helping. 'Hello, Franny.'

'Listen, I'm in the Coliseum with a most interesting person. American. Hardball player – has connections with your cousins. Don't ask me any questions, not yet, but he's looking for an educated girl of Chinese-European mix who's got nice legs and a nice body . . .'

'Aren't we all!'

'This woman came down from Thailand – Bangkok, I think he said – and he doesn't know her name or where she's staying. Looks to me as if he's been following her and she gave him the slip and now the only thing he knows is that she might be making contact with someone in Cameron Highlands . . .'

'Why are you telling me this, Fran?'

'Because you, like my American friend's woman, have just come from Thailand. It's called the connection, Aubrey.'

'A vague one, Franny.'

Ong cleared his throat. 'Don't fuck me about, Aubrey – please. Look at it like this. Aubrey St Clair Smith has just arrived back in town from Thailand waters; so has an Anglo-Chinese girl, and an American hardball player looking for an Anglo-Chinese girl. Neither of them bothered Immigration, which means they probably came to Malaysia by boat. How do you like the sound of that?'

'Reads like a novel, Francis.'

'Good. Come and have a look at my American. He's one of the Langley Light Horse, known as Mark, and he's booked into the Federal Hotel under the name of Hagen.

Probably paper name. You still want to play games with me?'

'What's the woman's name and where's she staying?'

'Mrs Chance. Equatorial, Room Five two six.'

'Thank you, Francis. Are you going to pass this information on to the American?'

'His people help pay my wages.'

'Can you delay him for twenty minutes?'

'Sure.'

Aubrey St Clair Smith joggled the telephone cradle up and down, made sure the line was clear, and dialled the Equatorial and asked for Mrs Chance's room.

Theresa hesitated for a long time before curiosity forced her to pick up the receiver. She expected Jim Logan; instead she got Aubrey St Clair Smith who, in a very brusque and unfriendly voice, told her, 'Don't argue, don't ask questions. Get out of there quickly. Now. As soon as you put the phone down. Don't settle your bill, leave no message, say nothing...'

'And go where?'

'Anywhere. Do it now. Just get out of that place. Ring 605 05300 as soon as you're clear and I'll come and collect you. OK?'

'Yes, Aubrey. But how did you—'

'No questions – just do it!'

Hagen wasn't disappointed with his Coliseum special mixed grill but his mind was on other things. It improved when the waiter returned and asked Ong to the phone. Ong's face betrayed nothing when he returned and sat down. He picked up the ample sizzling pork chop from his mixed grill with his fingers and gnawed into it. Hagen displayed no impatience. After he'd chewed and swallowed the mouthful, Ong wiped the fat from around his lips with a large napkin and met Hagen's eyes.

'It's surprising,' he said, 'how many telephone calls have been made in the last forty-eight hours to such an unexciting place as Cameron Highlands. So far' – he glanced down at his watch – 'that's up to one hour ago, there were thirty-six calls—'

'Oh, Christ!' Hagen stopped eating.

'It's not that bad,' said Ong. 'Only six were women's voices and only two used the English language . . .' Ong attacked the pork chop again. Hagen drank from his glass of beer. 'The one you're looking for is a Mrs Chance who's staying at the Equatorial—'

'It can't be.'

'Why not?'

Hagen didn't know why not.

'Who's the other one?'

'A taster of tea in her late sixties. An Englishwoman. Would she be your slim lady with the nice body and long legs? Let's go back to Mrs Chance – who *is* slim, *does* have a nice body and long legs, and, my informant tells me, *is* part Chinese, and part English or American.'

Hagen's appetite suddenly returned. 'You're very good, Mr Ong.'

'Not at all.' Ong smiled deprecatingly. 'I'm just an old, superannuated ex-policeman with a sinecure in a private security firm. Finish your mixed grill. They do a very good English rice pudding here. You'll like it.'

Aubrey St Clair Smith slipped his car into the rough lot that served as the Coliseum cinema's carpark and cut across the road. Walking briskly in the shaded sidewalk, he slipped into one of the silk and cotton goods shops further up Batu Road. It was exactly opposite the Coliseum restaurant.

He spent some time studying material for shirts. Nobody bothered him after the initial burst of interest, and when Ong had finished his rice pudding and drunk his coffee and Cognac, St Clair Smith had all the time in the world to study the well-built, young and athletic-looking American coming through the swing doors with him.

Ong, seemingly reluctant to part company with his new friend, kept him talking outside the bar. He glanced down at his watch and Hagen grasped his opportunity. He grabbed Ong's hand in mid-sentence, shook it and darted after a taxi passing by with its driver hanging halfway out of his window. Ong glanced across the road and nodded his head as St

Clair Smith emerged from the silk shop. He turned on his heel and went back through the Coliseum's swing doors.

St Clair Smith joined him, and they sat in the far corner where they could both study the door. Ong moved on to Drambuie.

'Still working for our cousins, then?' said St Clair Smith as he sampled his Drambuie. 'Do they pay you by the hour?'

Ong's eyes wrinkled. He liked Drambuie too – there wasn't much with an alcoholic content he didn't like. 'Exclusively, old boy! By the hour? It's a bloody good job they don't pay me by result.'

'How do *we* pay you?'

'You don't. I do it for yours out of love and gratitude!' He smiled broadly. He was telling the truth. 'So – what's your interest in Mr Hagen, and what's his interest in Mrs Chance?'

'I'm not sure. He suddenly appeared in the middle of a little research I was carrying out. A couple of players dropped by the wayside and he's been promoted front-runner. I don't know him, but he's supposed to be leading us to the people who're building up a new empire. Opium – from Burma and Thailand to the States via here and there; dirty money to London, where it's cleaned and brought back into the system. It all starts and finishes in Bangkok—'

Ong tipped his glass up, emptied it and held it in front of his eyes, studying the thick liquid remaining glued to the inside of the small glass. He tilted it, found there was a little more left, and drank that. 'Want another?'

St Clair Smith nodded. 'You were going to say something?'

Ong waggled a hand like a bunch of bananas and then stuck two of the bananas in the air. Two more Drambuies arrived. When they were alone again Ong said, 'I was going to say why are you following an American to lead you to something that I could have told you over the telephone? Is this London's idea? Cobbold's?'

'It came from that direction. And I agree with you. I think Cobbold's been manipulated, I think the Americans are using him. But I don't mind. Little things like this keep me off the streets.' St Clair Smith knew this man so well;

they thought alike and they'd been involved together in one way or another for the best part of thirty years. They trusted each other – a very rare thing in their profession. St Clair Smith decided to take a chance. 'What do you know about a man named James Logan?'

'Ahah! You should have asked me what I don't know about a man named James Logan! Bangkok. He's got a lot of money – a millionaire several times over – deals in marine engines and all sorts of maritime affairs. Was married to a Chinese girl of the Liu family – you know the Liu family?'

'Tongs?'

'A very simplified description. Logan's a member of the Touming Guanxi, the only European to so be, so he's a highly protected man. What about him?'

'That's who Hagen's looking for. He thinks he's somewhere in Malaysia. Mrs Chance is Logan's daughter. He thinks if he can get to the daughter he can get the father.'

Ong wasn't unduly put out. 'But she won't be there any more, will she? You will have moved her away from the Equatorial while Hagen was eating his English rice pudding. I know you, St Clair Smith, my friend. I'm never worried when you accuse me of things after I've told you about them! You too are looking for Logan? Popular man. Does your interest run parallel to Hagen's?'

'No – I think Hagen's working a contract. I think he wants to kill him.'

Ong raised his eyebrows. 'And does Aubrey St Clair Smith have a contract on James Logan too?'

'We don't go in for things like that. You ought to know that, Franny.'

'Of course we don't! Have you found him?'

'Not yet.'

'He's in Cameron Highlands.'

'That doesn't surprise me.'

Ong smiled in agreement. 'I didn't think it would. There isn't a lot that does surprise you, my friend, is there? Mrs Chance rang her father this morning. Mr Hagen's gone to the Equatorial to find out exactly where her father is staying. Then he's going to Cameron Highlands to kill him. He'll probably kill Mrs Chance as well while he's at it. He struck me as that sort of man.' Ong sipped his Drambuie gently this time, savouring its aromatic and heavy cloying taste. He ran the tip of his tongue over his lips in case any had stuck there and centred his gaze on St Clair Smith's eyes. 'I'll tell you exactly where he is if you tell me what it's really all about.'

'Like I said, Franny—'

'Bollocks, Aubrey! There's more to it than London's interest in heroin money; there's a heavy CIA hand in this somewhere, a hand a bloody sight heavier than Mark Hagen's, and it's not drugs.'

'What is it, then?'

'Don't piss me about, Aubrey, we've been too long standing in the next stall to each other for that. Have you ever heard of an operator called Contractor?'

'Yes.'

No more than that.

St Clair Smith kept his eyes glued to Ong's slits.

'You going to tell me about it?'

Ong thought for several seconds, then nodded. 'Many years ago, more years than I care to remember – must have been some time in 1956 or '57 – I'd just started in Special Branch and I was working undercover out in Setapak. You remember what Setapak was like in those days? There were more communist terrorists under the floorboards in and around Setapak than there were in the jungle. It's even worse now.'

St Clair Smith sat quietly sipping his drink and let Ong have his head. He didn't interrupt, he didn't even agree or nod his head, he just sat and watched and listened.

'I'd got a job in a car parts shed. I used to spend the whole day stripping tyres off wheels – that's how I got my magnificent figure! Early one morning there arrived in great secrecy a man called Liu. That was all he was called. I memorized his face because I thought he was definitely red – I thought at least a District Committee Member – but then in the afternoon he was joined by two Europeans. Can you imagine how incongruous two Europeans looked in one of the biggest junk-yards in Malaya, meeting what I'd marked as a terrorist bigwig? But there was nothing I could do. The whole bloody area was sealed off by this Liu fellow's people and supporters. So I had to hang around and bite my fingernails.

'But I got a good look at them – all of them. A couple of days later I managed to get out. In those times we still had the old-fashioned hotel booking-in cards and they were collected every evening and kept for a month in Central Registry. I checked the Merlin first, of course – all foreigners stayed at the Merlin in those days, it was the newest thing in town. But a dead giveaway. I took all the Merlin's cards to their reception, gave them the description of the two guys and they matched one of them to a card in the name of Mr R. Graver, US citizen, a lawyer from somewhere in America. The other one I couldn't find; he obviously had contacts but it didn't take long to see his picture somewhere. James Logan, US citizen making lots of money in Bangkok. I had to be interested, didn't I? Two Americans meeting what I later discovered was the godfather of the Touming Guanxi in a shack in a metal shit house on the bandit-ridden out-skirts of KL.'

'How far did you take it?'

'Nowhere. I just kept my ears and eyes open. D'you know the name of the current head of the CIA?'

'Graver.'

'The same man. So what were Logan and Graver talking about with Liu Zhoushiu in 1957' – Ong pointed one of his fingers at St Clair Smith – 'so that now, eighteen years later, a Mr Hagen whose controller is a General Reilly of the CIA, who's in line to be the next head of that agency, comes to our part of the world to look for Mr Logan. So does Touming Guanxi—'

'Liu's here?'

'If he's not his people are. Sure to be. Logan's a Touming asset. They wouldn't let him roam around Asia unattended. Count on it, Aubrey; everybody's here and everybody wants Mr James Logan – surely not to discuss the price of heroin on the Kuala Lumpur commodity market!'

'So, what was your conclusion?'

'The same as it is now. It's not drugs at all. It's political,

291

and you, the British, have been sucked in by the Yanks to open the way to Logan.'

'What do you mean by political?'

'Don't be naïve, Aubrey, old chap – the man's got something serious on the top people of the CIA, something that was arranged and set in motion nearly twenty years ago by the now head of the CIA and the grand master of the Touming Guanxi and brokered by Mr James Logan, and they don't want him to go public on it. And in answer to your next question, they haven't killed him because he's covered himself and they don't know where or how. They've sent this Hagen to either screw it out of him or negotiate terms.'

'Hadn't we decided Hagen was here to kill Logan?'

'I've just changed my mind! Now, how else can I help you?'

'Why's it all happening now?'

'What's about to come to an end after over twenty years?'

'Tell me.'

'US involvement in Vietnam. That's the root.'

'Nothing to do with the narcotics industry?'

'I didn't say that.' Ong had had enough. He emptied his little glass again and stood up. 'I must go. You know how to get me if you need anything else.' He smiled broadly and held out his hand. 'And I'm sure you will!'

Chapter 35

Kuala Lumpur, Thursday, 1500 hours

As soon as he was out of sight of the squat Chinaman, Hagen tapped the taxi driver on the shoulder, showed him a five-dollar note and held his hand to his ear, thumb and little finger extended. The taxi driver got the message and the five-dollar note and squealed to a halt outside a row of shops. He left the engine running, beckoned Hagen to follow him and darted into a Chinese herb shop. He barked out a mouthful of Cantonese at the girl behind the counter, offered Hagen a toothy grin and pointed to the telephone.

Hagen turned his back on the two Chinese and dialled the number Reilly had given him. It was answered immediately; a private line to a private phone. 'Loriane?' he asked.

'Bit more.'

'Reilly; Snow; cover, seven zero.'

'OK, Snow, how can I help?' It was a gentle feminine voice, no sign of Asian intonation; this one was pure American. She sounded both attractive and intelligent – and quick.

'Can you get to the Equatorial Hotel in less than even time? There's a woman going under the name of Mrs Chance about to leave the place.' He gave the attractive voice a clear description of Theresa. 'I want her delayed until I get there. If you can't manage that follow her until she sits down and then go home and wait for my call. If you want an introduction mention her father, Jim Logan, who's on the run somewhere. D'you roger all that?'

293

'I'm on my way.'

'What're you wearing?'

She paused fractionally. 'Dark blue shirt, long sleeves, dark skirt.'

'See ya.'

'Equatorial,' he told the driver, 'quicker than you've ever done it before.' He needn't have bothered. The driver didn't speak a word of English, but his normal speed with a passenger, a European passenger, was flat out. And he knew his Kuala Lumpur and one-way streets and other minor traffic impediments held no brief for him. The taxi, under Hagen's deaf-and-dumb instructions, pulled up short of the main entrance to the Equatorial in the old Treacher Road. 'You wanna wait?'

The driver was learning American quickly. He pointed to the front carpark; there were no free places but it didn't worry him. The driver disgorged Hagen from his taxi almost without stopping and slipped out of sight. Hagen slowed himself down, strolled casually through the main portico and, without moving his head, surveyed the area as he crossed the floor. Shops on the left, open restaurant on the right, and in the middle a wide staircase that curved up into the business part of the hotel.

The reception area was cool and quiet. A well-dressed Malay chatted with the Malay girl at the cashier's section; a young woman in very short shorts pored over the registration card as she booked in. Hagen's eyes slithered over her good, suntanned thighs and moved on. The place was otherwise empty and the quiet disturbed only by the ping of the lift indicator. He moved to the balcony overlooking the ground floor and watched to see who the lift was bringing down. It wasn't Theresa Logan. He turned his back as the doors hissed together and all was quiet again. He glanced down into the restaurant. Most tables were occupied; Malaysia's capital had no set hours for eating or drinking; this was teatime and it was anything from lamb soup to croissants and coffee. And then he saw the two attractive women sitting at a table against the wall. They were being served tea. Half past four. Very English. He watched for a brief second then drew back. They both looked interested in what the other had to say.

He walked slowly down the stairs and moved in the direction of the two women. The one in the blue shirt had to be Loriane – he knew the other one.

Theresa looked up briefly and met Hagen's eyes. Nothing happened. Not to her. But for Hagen it felt like the holy grail. Theresa Logan had been passing through his life ever since he'd first sunk up to his ankles in the melting tarmac of Bangkok's airport. She'd thrown him a dummy in Bangkok and waggled her body at him through binoculars from Krislov's boat, so he had no fears that he wouldn't recognise her the minute she walked across a shiny tiled mezzanine floor – or raised a fine porcelain cup to her sensuous lips. Mrs Chance! You couldn't disguise that face and shape with city clothes, or a different name. He paused for a moment and ran his hand through his hair as he adjusted his thinking. *And now what, Hagen? Play it by ear. Back to her old man wherever she's arranged to meet and then a threesome back to the States. Sounds good! Sounds simple! Sounds like all good, unrehearsed, prospective balls-ups.*

The girl in blue looked even better than she sounded. Not all Chinese, a bit European, a bit like Theresa Logan, possibly the other way round – Chinese father. But almost as beautiful and certainly as elegant. Somehow there was a lot of similarity between the two women; Hagen didn't try to work out how Reilly's KL resident had effected the miracle. It was enough that she had got there on time to delay the contact; this was the bonus – she'd also made friends. But before he could make his move a Malay boy in a brilliant white starched jacket with a choker collar and shiny brass buttons approached their table and pointed towards the door. Taxi? Or telephone? Whatever it was they both stood up and moved like women with a purpose. To Hagen it looked as if Theresa had suddenly lost her nerve or the word had got through to her that she'd been marked. Who would do that? The fat master spy? Who cared. It had happened. She suddenly seemed in a hurry to get out of the Equatorial Hotel. He branched off before he entered the restaurant area and went into the photographic shop on the main concourse. Ignoring the bored-looking shop assistant, he looked at the cameras and accessories and the laughing, always laughing, posters of highy coloured women throwing highly coloured beach-balls into a highly coloured royal-blue sky and studied the foyer sideways through the shop window.

They were coming across the floor towards him. He moved out ten yards or so in front of them and made eye contact with the girl in the blue shirt. She knew. He allowed his eyes to pass briefly and meet Theresa's. Theresa saw, probably what she wanted to see – a good-looking man; a good strong face, nothing pretty about it, clean-shaven, short light brown hair and honest eyes. Hagen had never had any difficulty injecting honesty and sincerity into his eyes. His teeth were good; so was his colour and his mouth, with the suggestion of a smile, wide and generous. He looked like a clean-living young man with a fun quotient much higher than any she'd met since returning from Europe to Thailand. He wore one of his new cream sea-island cotton shirts, open at the neck, and a slightly rumpled lightweight fawn jacket to cover the Sig-Sauer automatic Simmonds had reluctantly given him which nestled under the trouser band in the small of his back. He gave a slight nod and a 'Good afternoon' – nice voice, pleasantly low and soft, and non-committal American – and then he was past them. Theresa felt a small tickle at the back of her neck; a sensation of déjà vu, of having been or seen before – and not all that long ago. She fought the urge to look round for confirmation, overcame it and walked with her new friend, behind the bell-boy, towards the main entrance and into a waiting taxi.

'Shit!'

Hagen spun on his heel and saw the women's taxi draw out of the portico. He moved quickly. His taxi was standing under the one bit of shade in the parking lot. The driver was asleep, his mouth, full of broken brown teeth, wide open like a specimen model for a dentists' convention. Hagen lost several minutes while the driver sorted himself out, but once he was back in the land of the living he reacted quickly. He was a master driver and tucked himself in within sight of the other taxi before it entered the usual traffic snarl-up inching closer for fear of losing it if the traffic suddenly went berserk and moved. Hagen sat and sweated. He was getting used to the Kuala Lumpur traffic and sat back and enjoyed the placid expressions of the hard-suffering motoring public hanging over red-hot steering wheels. Bored with that side of the unmoving scenery, he shifted his stiffening buttocks to the other side of the taxi. A casual glance behind, and—

'Jesus Christ!'

A controlled explosion of breath as the corner of his eye caught something he'd totally forgotten about. Another quick look from the curve of the taxi's rear window. The dark blue Nissan. Number plate? He leaned forward and studied it from a different angle – check! check! check! Occupants? Driver and one. Wasn't there something about the one's face? He shivered inside as if a cold, wet hand had grasped his entrails. He didn't recognise the feeling; it was primeval, something his brain and body knew about that he didn't. Whatever it was it made his hand search under the back of his thin jacket and touch the old but solid and reliable Sig-Sauer P220. He cursed himself for allowing the fat Chinaman, Ong, to distract him from following up the Nissan. You're getting old and slow, Hagen! This is how you end up in fish traps – or pig baskets and holes in water.

As the traffic inched along he kept his eyes surreptitiously on the Nissan. There was no need to worry about the women – the taxi driver had got them in his sights, he wouldn't lose them; he'd looked into Hagen's eyes and seen what would happen to his investment if he did.

The sudden manoeuvre of Theresa's and Soo Lee's taxi took Hagen by surprise.

It darted forward into a gap, then turned abruptly, right, no signal, cheekily through the no-entry opening in the road separator. But Hagen's driver was equal to it. He waited a second then did the same thing.

Behind them Peng Soon's driver missed the point. His target was Hagen, and he was too late. But he didn't panic. He turned quickly in his seat and watched Hagen's taxi pull up outside a tall building some distance behind another slowing taxi. He suddenly became aggressive and forced his

way into an opening in the traffic and cut up three cars
before he reached the next roundabout. Peng Soon threw
himself into the back seat to follow Hagen's progress and
saw him climb out of the taxi and move in the wake of the
women he'd been following.

'Quick!' snapped Peng Soon. 'Find a place for the car and
meet me in that building. Do nothing that I don't tell you
to do, but be ready. You've a gun?'

The well-dressed, smiling young Tongman nodded
without speaking.

'Let me out here,' hissed Peng Soon.

He crawled out of the back of the car just as Soo Lee,
with a flash of cream thigh, unwound, in front of Theresa,
from the back seat. Peng Soon caught sight of her, and then
Theresa from the corner of his eye, and then quickly turned
his back and leaned into the car as if giving his driver
instructions. But he said nothing and didn't take his eye off
Theresa as she paid off her taxi. She walked round him and
towards the entrance of the building.

It happened very quickly; it could well have gone completely unnoticed. Peng Soon took it all in in a flash. His
quick eyes darted from Soo Lee to Theresa and, after a
brief moment's confusion, all the pieces jiggled together.
The man called Hagen; the woman who was Logan's
daughter. His eyes went back to Soo Lee. Then who was
this? He made his decision. It was Peng Soon's biggest, and
his last, mistake.

He turned and took a step towards Soo Lee, who now
had her back to him. In his hand he had a solid military
Tokarov pistol. It was cocked. He jabbed the safety catch
with his thumb and reached out to grab her. Soo Lee was
quick and snatched at the opening of her handbag. She
fumbled. Peng Soon saw his mistake but before he could
move again towards Theresa, Soo Lee called out.

'Snow!'

It wasn't a shriek, it wasn't even a loud call, but it reached
Hagen and he stopped and looked over his shoulder. It was
like a stalled film. For a second nothing moved; the quiet
call of a name and four people in a crowded city centre road
frozen into a marble tableau. Hagen and Peng made eye

contact. Nothing connected with Theresa; she didn't have time to wonder how he had got there or even notice the intent in Hagen's eye. She looked past him, her face creased into a startled frown which, when she met Soo Lee's eyes, turned into an open-mouth scream of shock and warning when she saw the stocky Chinaman, gun in hand, reaching for her. Still screaming, she moved towards Soo Lee, round Hagen, who had turned, crouched sideways on, and reached round his back for the Sig-Sauer.

For a moment Theresa's body blocked Hagen's view and he heard two heavy thunderous whacks as Peng Soon fired insinctively at the moving figure. Peng Soon recognised Theresa at the last second, realised his mistake and deliberately snatched at the trigger. Both rounds thudded into the wall.

Hagen, still crouched, cool, unruffled, aimed at the gap between Theresa and the shoulder of the man now with one arm on the young Chinese woman's shoulder, and squeezed off two shots. They were much louder than the Tokarov's and the pedestrians on the busy road nearest to the shooting suddenly aware that something unpleasant was happening, became a mass of hesitant ant-like, safety-seeking creatures.

Some, quicker, were already flat on their faces on the hot pavement. Others scrambled and scrabbled away on all fours before gathering themselves into invisible – they hoped – balls of nothing, their faces pressed into the stone sidewalk, eyes tightly clenched as they willed their bodies out of sight and danger.

One of Hagen's shots hit Peng Soon's shoulder with a heavy, meaty thwack and threw him backwards. Hagen moved forward two paces and with his shoulder barged Theresa hard in the back. It lifted her off her feet and, with a flurry of legs and arms and the breath knocked out of her, she crashed in a heap against the wall of the building.

The noisy, busy street resounded to screams and shouts and Peng Soon's driver, still smiling, spread himself across the front seat of the car, reached out of the nearside window and without taking aim fired off five sharp rounds in the direction of Hagen. Hagen ducked, instinctively, and snapped a quick shot at the driver which caused him to fall back inside his car. He then gave the staggering Chinaman with the gun two close-up shots into the thickest part of his body.

As Peng Soon's legs gave way his finger tightened on the trigger of the Tokarov and he kept pulling and jerking as he collapsed slowly onto his knees. The driver took a quick, experienced look at him, pronounced the verdict, and, in one motion, drew himself back behind the wheel, jabbed his foot hard on the pedal and screeched in a zigzag down the road, in and out of the stalled and startled traffic.

Hagen straightened up. He didn't recognise the man lying at his feet, but he knew who it was; he felt the bamboo spikes searing into his flesh; he felt the claustrophobic agony of the dripping cage. He didn't give it a second thought. He looked Peng Soon in the eye and emptied the rest of the magazine into his head, face and neck. The whole thing from start to finish had taken no more than a few minutes.

Hagen turned away from the dead man, replaced the empty magazine, then bent down to help the young Chinese woman to her feet. She was still crouched, like most of the other people on the pavement, with her hands over her ears. 'It's OK, Loriane,' he said, softly. 'It's finished, it's all over. You can get up—'

People were raising their heads and scrambling to their knees, a police car stuck up the road in the jam sat and howled on its siren, but from Soo Lee came not a sound. Hagen loosened his grip and took her gently in his arms and turned her round. All he could see was the blood still oozing from three places high in her back. She was dead. He looked into her eyes; she'd known fear before she died, but it had been quick. It wouldn't have hurt her. But it was no consolation. He placed his hand gently over her eyes and closed them. Then he looked up as a shadow came between them and a man in shirtsleeves pushed him urgently to one side.

'I'm a doctor,' he said breathlessly.

'Nothing you can do,' said Hagen. 'She's dead.'

But the doctor wasn't interested in Hagen or what he had to say; he didn't even look at him, he just went to work.

Hagen, still crouching, edged his way across the pavement

300

to where Theresa lay squashed up against the wall of the building. She was ashen and shaking, her eyes were over-bright; she was edging on hysteria and staring at the still body on the hot pavement lying on its side in a pool of already congealing dark red blood, with the man in shirt sleeves trying hopelessly, and pointlessly, to stem the steady flow. She dragged her eyes towards Hagen.

'Who are you?' She could barely get the words out through her stuttering teeth and tried to edge away from him.

'It doesn't matter,' said Hagen. He pointed with his foot to Peng Soon's body. 'He wanted you. Soo Lee got in his way – deliberately,' he added harshly. 'Now for Christ's sake pull yourself together. I've got to get you out of here ...'

He was being intentionally brutal – it was necessary with a brain-shocked girl; it was the only way he knew to bring her out of the trance she was slipping into. There was another way, but this was neither the time nor the place. He put his arm round her waist to help her to her feet but she stiffened and pressed herself against the wall as if trying to climb through it. It was Hagen she was afraid of now, not Peng Soon.

'I said, who are you?'

'Oh, shit!'

She recoiled.

No time for niceties. 'Listen, you stupid bitch! Snap out of it! I'm the guy who's trying to keep you and your father alive ...' Hagen's self-preservation instincts, and nerve ends, were forcing themselves to the surface. He shouldn't be here wet-nursing a shell-shocked female; he should be on the road, getting out of here as fast as his legs would carry him. This wasn't good enough. He tried to soften his voice. 'Trust me ...'

'Like hell I will!' She scrabbled to her feet, nearly fell and grasped at him to prevent herself going down again. Her knees weren't working properly; they wouldn't take any weight. And as she held on to him she saw again the pathetic, curled-up, unmoving body of the vivacious young girl she'd just been having tea with. She clung to Hagen and shook uncontrollably. He held her tight and with his hand brought her head to his shoulder and neck and stroked her soft hair; he could smell the delicate perfume of her neck and ears and for a moment wished that time would stand still – or better, that they were somewhere else . . . *You stupid, cock-happy bastard, Hagen!*

He was brought back to the hot pavement in the sweltering heart of the Malaysian capital, and the danger around him, when a police car bumped its way through the traffic and screeched to a standstill in the middle of the road. Three policemen poured out, revolvers drawn, all pointing at the doctor on his knees.

'Watch this man,' snapped the doctor, without moving. 'He has a gun. These two people are dead—'

The policemen made no move. 'Stay where you are,' one of them snapped. Then calmly, 'Put your hands flat on the ground. Don't stand up.'

The doctor did exactly as he was told, then looked up into the young policeman's face. 'Don't keep pointing that bloody thing at me,' he said through clenched teeth. 'Do something about this person behind me before he causes any more deaths. He's an American.'

'What man are you talking about?' asked the Malay.

The doctor turned his head.

'Careful!' snapped the policeman, and moved the service revolver fractionally closer to the doctor's head. He turned his body slowly. The crowd was getting cautiously to its feet and gathering around the dead bodies. They watched the tableau curiously. The doctor searched the faces. There was no American there; no one with a gun. Hagen had gone. He shifted his eyes and searched in the other direction for a white face; more crowds, more curiosity, but no one vaguely resembling an American. Hagen had vanished.

When he heard the police sirens getting closer and saw the flashing ice-blue light weaving its way through the traffic, Hagen, still holding Theresa close to him, began inching his way backwards until he was standing on the edge of the gathering spectators. They were concentrating on getting a good close-up view of death, and parted willingly to allow the man and woman to move through. It was the dead they

302

were interested in, not live people who wanted to get away from the sight of blood. Hagen released Theresa from his grasp, moved back into the circle of people and reached down casually to pick up her bag. She seemed incapable of movement; she had ample time to break away but she was still there, eyes glazed, leaning groggily against the wall when he rejoined her. Again, he took her hand lightly. She didn't resist. Clear of the crowd, and without speaking, he led her towards the building Soo Lee had been heading for. Without looking round, he turned and strode up the steps.

'Where was your friend taking you?' he asked gently as they went through the portico.

Theresa was still wary, still tense, still in shock, but no longer frightened. She didn't meet his eyes. 'We were going to her office – here, in this building.' She hiccoughed then recovered, and her voice became stronger, firmer. 'I was about to change my hotel. I wanted to get away from the Equatorial ... Soo Lee was—'

He cut her off. 'Just a minute – we'll talk later.' He continued walking, continued holding her hand; it looked very natural, unhurried, two young people going about their business – whatever that was. They were now inside the main part of the building and Hagen's eyes quickly took in the geography of the place: eight lifts in a bay; stairs going upward; stairs going downward with 'Parking' and 'Exit' clearly signed. 'Down here.' He lowered his voice and guided her down to the vast expanse of the building's underground carparking – acres and acres of new pale grey concrete held together by a forest of pale grey concrete pillars. There was a heavy, pervading aroma of piss; there always was in KL underground carparks. It was an old Malaysian tradition that anywhere out of the sunlight became a male public urinal. He pushed the smell to the back of his mind and made for the opposite side of the concrete forest where there was a green door with a lighted exit sign above it. He pushed the door. It opened onto a narrow concrete staircase.

He let go of Theresa's hand and realised that he was still carrying her shoulder bag. 'You left this upstairs.' She barely glanced at it. 'It's not mine.' Hagen stopped in his tracks and stared hard at the bag. 'Are you sure?'

303

'Of course I'm sure.'

'Oh, shit! Hang on to it and wait here.' He took the stairs two at a time and came to another small landing and another undersized door. Above this one was marked 'Emergency Exit'. He pushed it open, peered out into the broad hot sunshine, glanced right and left and then closed it and signalled Theresa to join him. He opened it again, just a narrow crack, hissed involuntarily, and closed it quickly as a middle-aged Chinese in a jacket and tie crossed the road and headed towards them.

'Quick!' He grabbed Theresa and pushed her against the wall at the top of the stairs. She hissed in pain, fright and then shocked surprise as he thrust his body against hers. 'Someone coming,' he breathed into her ear. 'Don't let him see your face.' She turned her face round to his. His mouth found hers – it was only pretending. A measure of security. Her lips were tight and unyielding, as they should be, her body stiff and unco-operative as he pressed hard into her. He felt rather than heard the door open behind him, a sharp intake of breath, an embarrassed pause, and then 'Excuse me' as the man, his eyes averted, his thoughts about Europeans making love inside an emergency exit to his office building forever his own, brushed past them.

Hagen remained where he was until he heard the footsteps fade and the door below slam shut, then he drew away from Theresa. 'Sorry—' He glanced down at her. She was flushed, her mouth now open as she struggled for breath and composure. She refused to meet his eyes. She said nothing; she made no movement. Hagen opened the door again and looked up and down the road. It was empty. He'd brought them out at the back of the building, in a street that seemed totally unaware of the commotion going on on the other side of the block of granite they'd just left.

He kept her slightly behind him as he stood in the doorway and watched a taxi pull up next to a rickety stall selling grated coconut in ice and syrup. A brief exchange of words between the vendor and the driver was followed by a hand coming out of the driver's window with a coin pinched between its fingers.

Hagen crossed the road and came up behind the taxi and

stuck a ten-ringgit note among the fingers holding the coin and, without a word, climbed into the back seat. He looked out of the rear window and rapidly quartered the surroundings. The street was clear. He leaned across the seat and opened the offside door. As he signalled to Theresa to join him, he met the flat black eyes of the driver.

'Hotel—' he said.

'What hotel?' This boy understood American – he'd already forgotten about his coconut and syrup.

'Any one.'

His eyes shifted to Theresa. He understood – or thought he did – *orang puteh* with someone else's wife. 'Short-time hotel?'

'Why not. Yeah – go on.'

The taxi wriggled its way into Pudu Road and then crawled down Jalan Imbi. The driver stopped the cab on the corner, just beyond the cinema, and jerked his chin over his shoulder. 'Hotel Europe,' he said. 'Clean—'

Hagen followed the direction of the driver's chin. It was pointing at a scruffy grey door set back in a small brickwork arch that looked like the entrance to a public lavatory. Hagen gave the driver another ten ringgit and under his steady gaze walked with Theresa towards the entrance and pushed open the door.

He was hit by a gust of concentrated incense, sweaty body smells and the overpowering perfume of strong pine-scented disinfectant. Nobody approached them. He gave Theresa a reassuring grimace, took her hand again and, guided by memories of Saigon whorehouses, led her down a dimly lit corridor, past a washhouse containing a sopping floor with a bar of soggy soap swimming in it, a smell of disinfectant and a large, genderless, bare backside sloshing water over itself with a metal ladle scooped from an overflowing Shanghai jar. He caught Theresa's eye. She smiled shyly, then giggled. This was better. Much better. Hagen found a way out to the back, through the washing lines and the crates of empty beer bottles, until they came to a ramshackle wooden fence. It had a door in it. Hagen opened it a crack and saw that it led to a narrow alleyway with another wooden fence on the other side. Above the fence and beyond a thick canopy of trees he saw the Federal Hotel building rising up into the steamy pollution that separated Kuala Lumpur from the clear blue sky.

'Fancy a cup of coffee?'

She laughed again, but kept hold of his hand. The sound was light and airy, but the spectre still hung around; there was death and disappearance, and deeper games of intrigue still to be played. One of them was going to have to do a lot of talking and explaining. And all the time she kept Aubrey St Clair Smith's telephone number running through her memory. Where did he fit in with this hard, but nice-looking man? But coffee first.

He led her out of the alley and across the Federal carpark to the rear entrance of the hotel, and walked through the door held open by a polite, smiling, uniformed Malay doorman.

The pure air-conditioning enveloped them like a pair of friendly arms. Taking Theresa's elbow, he walked straight through to the foyer and into the coffee bar. He ordered coffee and watched as she rode the escalator to the mezzanine floor and the ladies' room. He followed her up, and with his eye on the door of the powder room moved to one of the telephone points. He asked for an outside line, there was only one man in Kuala Lumpur whom he knew well enough to be able to confess his sins and ask for help.

'Mr Ong, it's Mark. We had lunch—'

Ong cut in abruptly. 'Yeah, OK, let me guess!'

Hagen told him what had happened.

'Where are you now? Is the girl with you?'

'Yeah.'

'Then you've got a problem.' Ong's voice had a crisp edge to it.

'Don't I know it. Can you move me from here?'

'Go and get yourself a drink or something and ring me back at this number. Give me fifteen minutes.'

Hagen replaced the receiver, darted back down to the coffee room and raised the cup to his lips just as Theresa came down the escalator.

'Start talking,' she said firmly as she sat opposite him. She ignored the coffee and looked him directly in the eyes. He didn't flinch, neither did he oblige. He stood up and grinned lopsidely and pointed his finger up to the ceiling. 'My turn.' He leaned forward across the table so that his face was a few inches from hers. 'Don't make a scene, don't attract attention, and don't forget we're both in trouble. Sit quietly, drink your coffee and try to look invisible. I'll be back in a second.'

He turned his back on her, confident that, if nothing else, curiosity would keep her bottom stuck to the chair. She no longer looked frightened. Wary? Perhaps, but not obviously. He'd already worked out the routine to come – and if lies didn't work, he'd try the truth. He went into the washroom and locked himself in one of the cubicles. He dropped the seat cover, sat down and stripped the Sig-Sauer to its elements. Each piece he wrapped separately in lavatory paper, distributing the small packets around his person. All hotels are the same; they all have a front entrance and they all have a rear. The rear is where the engine runs and the rubbish piles up in big, but manoeuvrable, bins. Hagen followed his nose to the kitchen waste disposal area and, unobserved, distributed his little packets among the messy, smelly trash cans. He went back to the toilet and washed himself.

Leaving his hands well soaped, he shoved them under the hand dryer before rubbing them liberally with the hotel's free eau-de-Cologne. He sniffed his hands. Eau-de-Cologne and soap, but his imagination gave him cordite, blood and the bulging eyes of a Chinese assassin watching his death approach. It didn't worry him – quite the opposite.

He wandered back into the coffee lounge, ordered a glass of iced water to go with his coffee and joined Theresa.

She'd still got the same inquisitive look in her eye, but behind it was something else. Interest? In the predicament – or rather who she was in the predicament with? Hagen wasn't sure; but she looked a lot more agreeable and friendly than she had at their first meeting. He pre-empted her question.

'Your father knows me. I was sent to help him out of Bangkok and get him safely to the States . . .'

'You're CIA?'

307

There was something in her voice that told him the CIA wasn't good news in this instance. He shook his head. 'No. I'm a presidential agent.' It sounded better – legal and clean. He wasn't sure General Samuel Reilly would approve of his new designation but, at the present moment, General Samuel Reilly could go fuck himself. 'I went up to Bangkok but your father had left and teamed up with a shifty limey agent named Aubrey St Clair Smith—' He paused and sipped black coffee, then took a swig at the iced water, allowing Theresa the opportunity to tell him everything he wanted to know about Aubrey St Clair Smith. It worked.

'There's nothing shifty about Aubrey,' she said, indignantly. 'And there was nothing shifty in his desire to help my father and me get out of a very awkward situation...' Hagen continued sipping water and studying her face. She was aware of his scrutiny and felt uneasy; uneasy because, for the first time in her life, she hoped this man liked what he saw. 'Which reminds me,' she said hurriedly, 'I must ring him and tell him where I am—' She stopped again. This time she frowned. 'Does he know you? And what you're here for?'

'I don't think so. You obviously trust him...' He waited. She didn't acknowledge. He went on, 'Your father's in the Cameron Highlands—'

'You asking me – or telling me?'

'Can we not play games, Theresa?' It was the first time he'd used her name. She liked it. So did he, particularly the way her eyes had suddenly changed from slightly hostile to almost friendly. And he hadn't even started the lying game yet. 'We both know where he is. Let's leave it at that. Is this St Clair Smith guy arranging for you and your father to get out of Malaysia?'

She pursed her lips, but said nothing. She kept her head very still.

'Your father has some stuff he wants to take with him – has St Clair Smith got it? Are you going to take it up to him?'

'Mark, why don't you come and ask Aubrey all these things yourself? If you're that keen on helping us I'm sure Aubrey will let you in on his plans—'

'Did you know St Clair Smith's a British intelligence agent and he's not interested in you or your father – he's only interested in whatever it is your father is taking to the States? He's working against your father, Theresa, he's in this game for his own interests and that of the British Government. Once he's got what he wants he'll drop you and your father so quick you'll wonder where the hell you are.'

She smiled. A very genuine smile. 'I presume, Mark, you've met Aubrey and you don't like him. Sorry. But I trust him, my father trusts him and that's the end of the discussion. D'you want to tell me now exactly what your interest is in this affair?'

He tried a smile. It didn't match hers. 'Ring your father and ask him. It was I who helped him out of Phuket and brought him to Malaysia. We got separated. I've got to get back to him . . .'

'That's what you've *done*! Now answer the question – what's your *interest*?'

'I thought that was self-evident. I've been empowered by Washington to bring your father safely back to the States, and I intend doing that. You have now become part of the equation so I have to get you there as well. What more d'you need?'

She thought about it for a moment; it was a moment she didn't really want to end, or at least not just yet. She looked around the almost empty coffee room. There was nothing he could do here. He couldn't kidnap her; he couldn't bundle her up and haul her out of the hotel; and this wasn't a shooting gallery. He'd know that. He looked very serious and as though he knew exactly what to do. She had no doubt that, in different circumstances, she'd like very much to be bundled up by Mark Hagen and carried back to the States. But not this time. That wasn't part of the package. This was—

'I'm going to ring Aubrey St Clair Smith and ask him what I must do. First, though, I'm going to ask him to check your bona fides through his contacts here. If they come up white and pure and you are what you say you are, then I'll

309

contact my father and then you, he and I will work the thing out together.' She met his eyes again, full on. 'OK?'

No, it wasn't. But there was nothing he could do. He went through the same assessment exercise Theresa had gone through and studied the surroundings. His conclusions were more definite than hers. It was a definite no-go. She'd got him stuffed. He nodded his agreement; he'd at least got his Chinese friend Ong to fall back on. If Ong could find a man who got off a train in the middle of the jungle in the middle of the night then he wouldn't have much trouble putting a trace on Theresa Logan.

'OK.' He acknowledged defeat as graciously as he knew how. 'I've enjoyed the afternoon. Thanks. You can contact me by leaving a message here at the reception – collect.'

Her eyebrows rose fractionally. 'Are you staying here?'

He smiled broadly. 'You know the old saying?'

'Which one?'

'Ask me no questions . . .'

Chapter 36

'Are you alone?'

Aubrey St Clair Smith kept the telephone glued to his ear as he shifted his gaze from the window overlooking the course to Theresa. 'It can be arranged.'

Ong read the signs. 'If it's her it doesn't matter. It's the American, Hagen – I'm bringing him over. OK?'

'By all means.'

He replaced the receiver and went back to Theresa. He made no explanation; it was as if they hadn't been interrupted. 'As far as I understand, Theresa, the plan you and your father worked out was that you collect these personal belongings of his and, after you've shaken off the Chinese and the Americans, take them to the Cameron Highlands. Then the two of you make a break for it. Is that about right?'

'No. That was for you, Aubrey. Everything was geared to my getting out of Bangkok, collecting the stuff from the bank and making my way, independently, to the States. Dad expected to be followed and eventually picked up. The idea was for him to attract the attention, giving me a free run . . .'

It made sense. Although he doubted the wisdom of Logan allowing himself to drop into the hands of Chinese Tongmen, or CIA Special Projects operatives – least of all those – for the sake of making a gap for an untrained, and certainly innocent, girl to dart through. But it wasn't working like that.

311

'And your free run ends up with a gun battle in the middle of Kuala Lumpur, two people killed, one of them a totally uninvolved young woman, and you having tea and biscuits and things as large as life in the Federal Hotel with the one person you were running from?' There was no rebuke in St Clair Smith's voice or expression. 'You did know you were running from this Mark Hagen?'

She didn't reply. She looked him full in the face, squarely in the eyes, kept her thoughts to herself and said nothing.

St Clair Smith didn't pursue it. He knew enough about women to know that balanced judgement of a good-looking young thug who'd gone out of his way to make himself agreeable didn't come into it. He took up where he'd left off.

'Assuming that before you got yourself blown by Hagen you had achieved this free run – how were you going to capitalise on it? How were you going to leave Malaysia and slip into America? Your name alone'll bring a posse of Hagen's CIA friends and associates galloping to wherever the immigration authorities are holding you. Had you thought about that?'

She looked up, back into his eyes, and wrinkled her nose. That usually worked.

'No,' she said, hesitantly.

'And how was your father going to disappear, convincingly, from the Cameron Highlands?'

'I don't know.'

St Clair Smith frowned down at her for a moment. Things seemed to be working out quite nicely. His face didn't show it. But there must be a catch.

'A short time ago,' he said, 'I asked you to trust me; to trust me implicitly . . .' He waited for her to nod her agreement, then continued in the same flat voice. 'I think I can see a way for this thing to end exactly the way your father wanted it to, but, I repeat, you must trust me and do exactly as I say.'

She nodded again. 'OK.' She smiled thinly. 'I don't think I've really got much choice – have I?'

He shook his head. 'Not unless you want to take your chances with Hagen. And that I don't recommend.' She smiled hesitantly. He ignored it. 'Let me have your father's phone number.' He wrote it on a scrap of paper, just the number, nothing else.

Francis Ong arrived at Aubrey St Clair Smith's house with Hagen just as dusk was beginning to crawl up the ninth fairway in the wake of the last pair out. Ong made the introductions. Hagen and St Clair Smith studied each other with mutual mistrust. Hagen smiled, unusually, at Theresa, acknowledging her surprise at seeing him in St Clair Smith's drawing room. Only she knew exactly what he thought of the suave Englishman; she doubted that Hagen had any illusions about what St Clair Smith thought of him. St Clair Smith, by expression and attitude alone, made it obvious that Hagen was never going to be one of his favourite people. However, he poured three large whiskies from a bottle of Johnny Walker Black and placed them on the glass-topped coffee table. 'Shall I pour you a gin and tonic, Theresa?'

'I'll help myself.' She removed her eyes from Hagen's face, but not quickly enough for St Clair Smith to read the telltale signs. He didn't like what he'd read. He picked up one of the glasses of whisky and sat down. The other two men followed suit. He kept Hagen well in his sights as he addressed the squat Chinaman.

'Francis,' he said formally, crossing his legs and relaxing back into the sofa, 'you mentioned problems – plural. I can only see one at the moment.'

Hagen didn't smile. He liked the whisky. He let Ong do the work.

'Two people were shot dead in KL this afternoon.' Ong inclined his head towards Hagen. 'He killed one of them. The other, a woman, he says was shot dead by the man he killed. Mark Hagen, by the way, is a special agent of the White House security detail and a representative of the US Government—'

St Clair Smith shook his head. 'Francis, he's nothing of the sort. He's a renegade CIA operative who's the representative of nothing. He holds no accreditation and has no affiliation to anything even vaguely official. He's a dog,

313

Francis, and he's here, as he was in Thailand, on a search-and-kill operation against one James Logan.' He turned his head and studied Hagen. 'How is that so far, Hagen?'

'Cow shit, Aubrey! May I call you Aubrey?'

St Clair Smith ignored the grain of politeness. 'Who was this man you killed?'

'A senior Chinese Tongman who'd been tracking your friend Logan and thought Theresa here was a short cut to re-establishing contact with him. He tried to grab her and I got in his way. I was doing what you should have been doing, Aubrey – looking after Jim Logan's daughter.'

Aubrey ignored the aside but glanced gently in Theresa's direction. She was sipping her drink and deliberately kept well out of the conversation, apart from occasional glances in Hagen's direction. St Clair Smith returned his gaze to Hagen. 'Was the dead girl anything to do with you?'

'No. She was a friend of Theresa's. Her death was an accident. The gook was trying to take Theresa, not kill her.' Hagen made a point of not looking at Theresa. He concentrated on St Clair Smith; he was the one he had to convince. 'The girl got in his way – I happened to be passing by and I happened to have a gun in my pocket. I got lucky – for once.'

St Clair Smith studied Hagen's relaxed features for a few seconds then turned to Ong. 'So what's the problem, Fran?'

Ong's eyes hooded for a moment then narrowed in Hagen's direction. 'Nothing if it's told like that! Except that according to the police the woman who was killed has been identified as a Miss Theresa Logan, an American citizen resident in Thailand who apparently arrived in Malaysia without going through Malaysian immigration formalities . . .'

'Identified?' St Clair Smith's eyebrows came together over his nose. Hagen had forgotten; so had Theresa.

'Nothing spectacular,' continued Ong blandly. 'The contents of her handbag . . .'

'I picked up the wrong bag,' admitted Hagen.

'Stupid bastard! Beg your pardon, Theresa!' St Clair Smith's eyebrows remained fiercely locked together as his head swivelled towards Hagen. Ong defused the situation.

'Not all that bad, Aubrey. According to Hagen here, these two girls have a remarkable similarity from the back. Same bodies, same hair—' Ong paused and let St Clair Smith think about it, then met his eyes, saw that they were thinking alike and gave a slight flicker of warning. He continued, 'But that's something else.' He turned his round face to Hagen and nodded approvingly. 'I've had a long chat with this young man. I think I have a clearer understanding of his motives and I've just had a conversation with his principal that confirms his good intentions towards James Logan—'

'You mean, Francis, he wants to put a bullet in the man's head and walk off with some documents that might be prejudicial to his principal's future prospects!'

'I wonder where you pick up things like this?' mused Ong, more to himself than anyone, but with his eyes slitted in St Clair Smith's direction. Then, aloud, he said, 'I want to talk to you about this identity problem Theresa has just acquired, but first Hagen wants to talk to Logan on the telephone. I told him nothing doing until I'd discussed it with you.'

St Clair Smith considered it. Then, without a word, he learned forward, placed his empty glass on the table, stood up and walked across the room to the telephone. Glancing at the strip of paper, he dialled Logan's number. A Chinese voice answered. St Clair Smith said in English, 'Tell Mr Logan Mr Aubrey St Clair Smith wants to talk to him—' He waited a second then said, 'Please take my message to Mr Logan, then come and tell me you don't know who he is and he's not there . . . I'll hold on.' He remained standing. Catching Theresa's eye, he pointed with his chin to his empty glass, but before she could move he held up his hand. 'Hello, James,' he said into the mouthpiece. 'D'you want *me* to bring *you* up to date; do *you* want to bring *me* up to date – or do you want to speak to one Mark Hagen?'

'How's Theresa?' barked Logan.

'She's fine.'

'Let me speak to Hagen.'

They spoke for about ten minutes, then Hagen handed

the phone back to St Clair Smith. 'He wants a word with you.'

'Aubrey,' said Logan, 'first of all, without letting that bastard know what the subject is, can you tell me categorically that you have Theresa under your wing and that you're looking after her welfare?'

'Certainly,' responded St Clair Smith. 'Have you come to some sort of arrangement with Hagen?' His eyes met the American's across the room; they looked honest enough, from a distance, but so, they said, did John Dillinger's.

'I've agreed to his coming up here,' responded Logan. 'And then we'll come down together under a separate cover. He'll explain. I've grown to trust him.'

'Bully for you, James! I hope your arm's stronger than mine—'

'What d'ya mean, Aubrey?'

He looked Hagen in the eye. 'I trust Mr Hagen about as far as I could throw him!'

St Clair Smith replaced the receiver, accepted the refilled glass from Theresa and gulped from it as if he needed it. 'I gather you've sold your good intentions to our friend, then, Hagen. He said you'd put me in the picture.'

Hagen didn't bridle. 'I'm going to help him and Theresa disappear. That's all. Simple as that. We'll come down from these Cameron Highlands in the dark and fly out from Subang. When we arrive in the States he can negotiate his own insurance policy, on his own terms, face to face with the people who matter. That part of it's nothing to do with me. My job is to see that he' – he glanced at Theresa without expression – 'and his daughter arrive there safely.'

'Was that what you came for initially?'

'What I came for initially, Aubrey, to put it politely, is damn-all to do with you. But I'm going to have to break a lifelong habit and ask for help, your help, with this particular assignment.'

'You have a fine way with words, Hagen,' said St Clair Smith, with a wry smile. 'And I can see you've done the Carnegie course on winning people over to your cause. How can I help you?'

'Two things. A gun . . .'

St Clair Smith looked at Ong, then nodded. 'And the other?'

'A car?'

'No problem.'

'And a map to the Cameron Highlands—'

'That's three things. All totally useless to you.'

'What d'you mean?'

'Tell him, Fran. I'm fed up with people whose imagination stops at about one and a half dimensions. Explain to him in simple American what he's trying to achieve but can't quite see ... Ask him whether disappear means the same in his language as it does in mine. D'you want another drink?' St Clair Smith was tired. Impatience and tiredness, they went with age. He knew it. So did Ong, but Ong understood; he was neither impatient nor tired. He nodded. Hagen emptied his own glass and passed it over. There didn't appear to be any ill-will. Which helped, because he didn't know what the hell these two old fogies were talking about.

'Mark,' said Ong, patiently, 'you've forgotten about the Touming Guanxi.'

'I said we'd make Logan disappear.' Hagen was struggling. He knew there was something he'd missed. But he couldn't quite see it. Ong explained.

'When you're dealing with the Touming Guanxi, disappearing is not enough. People are trying to disappear all the time. You need a body, a dead one, and then, and only then, will a line be drawn through a name. They won't let up. Do you know what Touming Guanxi means?'

Hagen shook his head.

'It means invisible relations. And they are – the Touming Guanxi is invisible because it's everywhere. Where and when you least expect it you'll find an invisible relation tapping you on the shoulder. How are you going to cause a disappearance when the only person you can see and trust is yourself in the mirror? If it is said that James Logan is dead you must produce more than a headstone in a graveyard, because the man who dug the hole in that graveyard is probably Touming Guanxi; the man who made the coffin is Touming Guanxi; so is the doctor who signed the death certificate – all Touming Guanxi, or owned by them, or

bought by them. You do not know! So – no body, no disappearance. And they won't stop looking until death is
indisputable.'

'How do I take that – indisputable?'

'Any way you like. It means the Touming have got to be
one hundred per cent convinced their subject is no longer
living. His head on a plate might convince them – I don't
know! But driving down from the Cameron Highlands in
the dark with Mr Logan and his daughter on the back seat
under a blanket is a definite no-no!'

Hagen looked warily from one to the other as he sipped
his whisky. They stared back. It was a blank wall. 'Got any
suggestions?' he said finally.

Chapter 37

After Hagen had left to find his way out of Kuala Lumpur and up to the Cameron Highlands, Ong sat back in one of Aubrey St Clair Smith's deep-set armchairs and stared moodily at his empty glass. St Clair Smith broke his reverie.

'How far are you prepared to go with me on this one, Francis?'

Ong met his eyes. 'All the way, my friend.'

'OK, let's try it again, then.' St Clair Smith pulled no punches. 'Theresa, I want to use Soo Lee's murder to help get you out of the country.'

Ong studied him unblinkingly for several moments then lowered his glass. 'I've always admired this undoubted ability of yours to impart delicate news with such a heartless brutality, Aubrey. No beating about the bush with you, my friend—'

St Clair Smith didn't hesitate. 'There's no time for niceties. You listening, Theresa?'

'I wish I didn't have to.'

'But you do – you're a major player and this is the game you've allowed yourself be dragged into. So drink your drink and listen, and if you've anything concrete to add, say it. OK?' She didn't answer but held his eyes over the rim of her glass. He turned back to Ong. 'Francis, can you blackmail somebody with the authority to explain that Soo Lee's death is a matter of Malaysian national security? I would like to see a notice of restraint put on all information to the press

319

for the time being, and a warning against publication of any details not issued by the police—' He stopped. Ong offered him the briefest of acknowledgements, the barest movement of his large head. A lot of thought had gone into this in a short time. 'And,' continued St Clair Smith, 'it must be done very quickly.'

Ong was on his feet and standing before the telephone before St Clair Smith had finished the sentence. He dialled, turned his back to the room and, in a voice barely above a whisper, spoke at length into the mouthpiece. When he eventually replaced the receiver, he wiped his large forehead with a clean white handkerchief and returned to his chair. He took a good swallow from his glass.

'I hope Malaysia has things to gain from all this, Aubrey,' he said when he'd settled down. 'I've almost pledged a senior person's blood vessels on the promise of good things to come!' He smiled crookedly at St Clair Smith; he didn't think there were going to be many good things coming Malaysia's way. It didn't quite work that way. But it was worth voicing the thought. 'OK – what's your next trick?'

St Clair Smith smiled his thanks. 'The police have got Theresa's identity in place of that of the dead woman, so it should be routine...' Theresa's melting ice cubes rattled nervously again. Still she said nothing. 'To allow a limited press release that a Miss Theresa Liu-Logan, from Bangkok, was murdered in a KL street and, as yet, no motive has been established. Neither has an arrest been made, although a person, foreign, believed to be from Thailand, was killed at the same time. The investigation continues—'

Ong's equanamity didn't waver; he seemed impervious to surprise. 'I can't control a splash like that, Aubrey,' he decided after a moment. 'A beautiful woman, a Thai gangster, gun battles on the streets of Kuala Lumpur. It'll be like old times! The press'll go to town...'

'Include a suggestion of terrorism; communist terrorism, there's still plenty of that about. Suggest money-raising for the cause – attempted kidnapping for ransom...'

'Ransom for a young American-Chinese woman?'

'No, ransom for the daughter of the Bangkok millionaire, James Logan...' St Clair Smith paused, his expression

320

bland. 'And her bodyguard killed one of the kidnappers. That covers the death of the Touming gangster and tells the invisible relations that they no longer need to look for James Logan's daughter. Remember? It takes a body to cross a name off a list.'

Ong refused to be reminded. But he nodded his approval. 'OK. So what happens to Miss Logan now?'

'She becomes Miss Tan Soo Lee with all the documents to prove it. You'll arrange that?' Ong nodded again. Theresa started to say something but was stopped by a shake of the head from St Clair Smith. 'And she leaves the country under that name.'

'You'll arrange that part?'

'Yes. And now comes the real problem – the disappearance of Mr James Logan, millionaire American businessman from Bangkok, with all its relative publicity.' He paused again, met Theresa's troubled eyes, and quickly passed on to Ong's narrowed slits. 'The crux of this operation, Francis, is to minimise the possibility of Logan being spotted anywhere from the time he's supposed to have vanished until the time we read his obituary notice. There are hundreds of eyes, and they are always looking when you don't want them to. There's always somebody who's going to come forward and say they saw James Logan under a blanket in the back of a car on the Tana Rata road after he'd gone missing, or strolling around the back garden of the American embassy in KL. When he goes he's got to go for good. There must be no likelihood of anyone raising doubt about his death. OK?'

Ong shrugged. 'And you've got an idea how to perform this miracle?'

'No miracles, Frannie, not this time. We're going to have to do it the hard way. Hagen and James Logan are going to have to walk out of the Cameron Highlands – through the jungle . . .'

Ong sat forward in his seat and locked his narrowed eyes onto St Clair Smith's. 'That's got to be a joke, Aubrey. I've done that bit of jungle. It's all up and down and in and out and you're either gasping for breath at the peak of a mountain or pulling your feet out of swamp with both hands. It's a bloody nightmare, even when you know your way around, but for a couple of Americans ...?' He stopped in mid-sentence, then shook his head vigorously. 'Aubrey, don't even think about it – it's not a viable proposition!'

St Clair Smith's expression didn't change. 'If you did it, Francis, anyone can do it!'

'I'm talking about when I was twentysomething and had a stomach as flat as a dinner plate,' snorted Ong. 'I can hardly climb into bed nowadays let alone climb across a mountain – and I'm still younger than Logan. Anyway, that's a non-starter. These are two Americans, one of 'em well over the age of reason. The other's probably got it but I'll bet he's never done one like this before. Christ, Aubrey! Turn them loose in the Kinta Hills and they'll never be seen or heard of again.'

'Might solve a problem,' muttered St Clair Smith.

'That's my father you're talking about!' Theresa broke her silence with an indignant sniff. She stood up, walked purposefully to the Chinese credenza on which the tray of drinks stood and poured herself a stiff gin. She didn't offer to help the two men, but stood with her back to the wall, arms and legs crossed, the glass cradled in one hand, and stared moodily out of the window at the patch of sanitized jungle on the far edge of the golf course. Even tame jungle looked ominous with the sun setting behind it and the mist already rising from its broad canopy. But she couldn't ignore what Ong and St Clair Smith were saying.

'It's got to be the answer,' insisted St Clair Smith. 'There's no way you could get two strange men, Europeans at that, down the road from the Cameron Highlands to Tapah without something going wrong. Christ! They'd only need a bloody puncture and that would be that. That's all it needs, Fran, one bloody sighting, and the whole game's up the spout—'

'Just a minute!' Ong clenched his eyes shut and stroked the back of his head. 'Has your Alor Star man Simon crawled back into his hole yet?'

Theresa looked up sharply at the mention of the name; St Clair Smith raised a single eyebrow.

'What about him?'

Ong didn't pause for breath. 'When he was with Malayan Special Forces Simon commanded one of the jungle forts up in the mountains. Fort Brooke. It's north of the Cameron Highlands, very rough country, bloody awful terrain. You needed to be a madman to last any length of time up there – no contact with civilisation, just the occasional helicopter food deliveries.'

'For a bloke who couldn't do a proper job watching a pretty girl in the middle of an open, civilised city, that sounds right up his street!' grunted St Clair Smith.

Ong ignored the comment. 'Simon became a specialist in working with the Sakai, the Temiar Senoi tribe, tough little bastards who took some getting to know. But Simon did. He spent a lot of time with them. If anybody, other than a Temiar Senoi, knows the jungle around Cameron Highlands, he does.'

St Clair Smith frowned. He didn't look pleased. 'Why didn't I know this?'

Ong threw him a sidelong glance. 'You're not the only secretive old sod in the game, Aubrey. How many people know about all these MCs you picked up in the war?'

St Clair studied the chubby Chinaman; the frown was still in place. 'OK, so we've got a bloke who can walk through the jungle and recognize a Sakai when he sees one. So what?'

'Simon's one of the few non-Sakai who can speak the Temiar Senoi dialect; they'd trust him and believe him; he would take the edge off their curiosity if they came across a party of Europeans in the middle of their bit of jungle.'

St Clair Smith considered it from all angles while he sipped his whisky and water. He nodded to himself. Not that he liked the idea, but it was all they had; there was nothing else on offer. 'Let's get him in,' he said at length. 'Let's go for it.'

'Would he be safe?' Ong, typically, began to pick to pieces the good ideas he had raised.

'What d'you mean, safe?'

'Mouth-wise.'

'Hasn't he proved that? I'd put money on his discretion.'

'Would you put money on Logan's life?'

St Clair Smith turned his head. Theresa was still gazing out of the window. She hadn't touched her drink. 'Theresa, ring your father now and let him know that nothing has happened to you. Tell him I have everything in hand—' He stopped and frowned. 'Do you speak Thai?'

'Of course.'

'Talk to him in Thai – just in case!'

While she was dialling the number, Ong looked at his watch and said, 'I've a lot of convincing of people to do, Aubrey. So have you, I think. Where d'you want Simon?'

'Get him up here by the back door. I think he'd better vanish from sight right away. You'll arrange that?'

Ong nodded.

'Fran—'

'What?'

'Thanks.'

'Oh, you'll pay for it, Aubrey. Count on it. One way or the other you'll get a bill!'

After Ong had left, St Clair Smith spoke to Junit, then got his car out and without a word to Theresa drove off into the orange lights that guided him to the city centre. He turned off Jalan Pekililing and into Ampang Road and then into the lightly guarded compound of the British high commission. Half past six; he had to drag the duty officer from his working perch at the high commission's private bar to gain access to the code-and-communications room. Once there he was left alone with a secure line. It was a good time to contact London – half past ten in the morning and the first load of biscuits were being dunked in the first cups of tea. When the director of SIS's 'E' Branch heard his voice, she bounced out of her chair and locked the door.

'Lyndy, this Logan business is opening up into a major occasion,' St Clair Smith began. 'We're heavily involved but there will be a dividend. I've got a list of things I want doing. Are you ready?'

'Go on.' Lyndy was efficient and brusque. There was no overlap between business and pleasure with her. This could have been two strangers – almost.

'I want a used British passport, date of issue a couple of years ago in Kuala Lumpur. I advise that nobody be involved below the high commissioner himself. I'll go and see him privately and give him full details after you've had the appropriate authority in London whisper in his ear.'

'OK. Anything more?'

'I would like you, personally, to meet this new British subject when she arrives in London. I'll let you have details of passport and flights and things when they are finalised. No special treatment at LHR; just a normal British passport coming through from anywhere East – I haven't made my mind up yet.'

'Are you expecting a backtrack on this item?'

'Sure to be. Can you ensure that everything's catered for; that she's been on an overseas jaunt for a reputable British company in KL?'

'What do you want done with her when she arrives?'

'Hide her for a day or so. She's *en route* to the States. But you'll have to discuss that with her. I think another new passport issued in London. I leave it all up to you once she's left here.'

'What about the original deal?'

'This is all part of it. Keep a tight hold on Cobbold when the news breaks.'

'Oh dear! Is it going to be one of those?'

'Quite! I'll be in touch.'

Chapter 38

It was, as usual, a hot, sultry, humid morning with a large round sun beating mercilessly down on the halfway tee below Aubrey St Clair Smith's verandah. He'd been there for some time sipping his usual pre-prandial glasses of champagne when Theresa joined him.

'I need to go to the bank, Aubrey.'

'Not necessary,' beamed St Clair Smith, 'I have plenty of money here. How much do you want?'

He poured her a glass of well-chilled champagne, but she didn't touch it. 'Aubrey, I came to Kuala Lumpur to do something – it's what it's all about. My father's stuff – remember?'

St Clair Smith hadn't forgotten; he'd been waiting for it. 'Of course. What bank?'

'Bumiputra – Jalan Ampang, I think.'

'I know the one. Leave it to me. Give me half an hour to get ready and we'll go.

St Clair Smith slid the car into a shady slot just near the Bank Bumiputra and switched off the car engine.

'I have to go in by myself,' said Theresa. 'It was part of the deal.'

'Of course. I'll wait inside the bank,' said St Clair Smith, 'just in case—'

They walked in together and St Clair Smith made himself comfortable in one of the no-expense-spared leather armchairs surrounding the indoor fountain. He watched as

Theresa approached the desk and handed over an envelope and, after a few minutes, saw her whisked away by a smartly suited middle-aged Malay executive.

The senior manager addressed her as Miss Goddard and, after studying the contents of her envelope and comparing them with a similar document he took from his own office safe, asked for no further identification; Logan had made the job foolproof. He removed a key from a small hook on the inside of the large Chubb safe and led Theresa through another door in his office and into a lift that carried them soundlessly down two floors.

'Mr Goddard,' he said in a hushed voice that blended with the sepulchral atmosphere, 'has one compartment here that requires the key he has given you plus the one he left in my custody. There is another one on Level three which requires your key and mine to access the area and then the code for you to key in which will allow you to pass through the security grille. The box you are looking for is the last two digits of the year of your birth; and the combination to the box is known only to you and Mr Goddard.' He recited all the arrangements with a set expression, but underneath it there was a controlled sense of pride in the bank's formidable security system. And he had reason. The place that held Logan's life in its hands was as secure as any vault in Fort Knox.

'I'm afraid I can go no further. I shall wait here until you return and we shall deal together with the opening of this box. Please forgive me, I am not allowed in Level three.' For the first time he allowed a kindly smile. 'But don't be worried. I shall be right here.'

She was expecting to find a drawer full of paper, charts, typewritten sheets, files – anything except the neat parcel, the size of a box of copy paper, wrapped in hard brown paper and sealed with plain heavy-duty tape with a clear address written in black marker ink. She stared at it in surprise. It had obviously been weighed; it even had the stamps for ordinary airmail shipment stuck on it. She studied the address. It meant nothing to her. It was going to a Mrs Hilda Goddard in a place called Kendalville in Indiana, USA. Who was Mrs Goddard? Theresa tucked the parcel under her arm and went back to the second landing. The man was standing exactly where she'd left him. He hadn't even moved his expression.

'Let me take that off you.' He removed it from under her arm as though he knew what it was all about. 'The instructions were that this had to be posted from the bank, with the bank's normal routine despatches. It's all part of the account,' he said, which added to her confusion.

'Do you know what's in the other box?' she asked.

'I don't even know what was in the one you've just opened, Miss Goddard. The instructions were as I've just explained.' He walked across the thick carpet to the heavy door that made up one wall and placed his hand on a panel set in the other wall. The huge door opened with a hiss and he removed his hand and invited her through the semi-round opening.

'This is yours.' He stopped in front of a bank of large metal-fronted cabinets. 'Your key goes in there' – he pointed to the lower keyhole – 'and mine here, and, with luck' – his set features relaxed into a smile – 'the door will open.' It did, and he returned to his earlier position, the parcel still clasped under his arm, and turned his back to her as she pulled out the drawer and peered in.

This one held a smart leather Gladstone bag. It had a flap that concealed its lock, but attached by a piece of thin white string to the handle was a tiny but solid brass key. It opened the bag.

The whole of the bottom of the bag up to almost halfway was jammed with thick packets of used $100 and $50 bills. It was an enormous amount of money. Resting on top of the packets were two dozen or more small suede leather pouches; they looked like a job-lot, each the same size and colour, light fawn, about six inches high and as round as a medium-sized coffee cup. She opened one of them. The overhead light glanced into the pouch and was reflected back into her eyes by a myriad of glistening many-faceted transparent blue mirrors. She carefully tipped a few into her hand. Beautifully cut and polished, they were exquisite examples, and, with the slightest movement of her hand the perfect sapphires flashed modestly like soft blue flames disturbed by a gentle breeze. She tipped them back carefully, tied the pouch and placed it back in the bag with the others.

The Gladstone was heavy and the bank executive hurried forward to relieve her of its weight. He placed it at his feet while he dealt with the door mechanism and, loaded with both the parcel and the bag, ushered her into the lift. In his office he placed the bag on the floor and held the parcel in both hands. 'There are no further instructions for this. It will go out tonight with the rest of the bank's mail and that will fulfil the agreement Mr Goddard made with the bank.' He placed it on the edge of his table. She would have liked to have known what was in it, what had caused her to be smuggled all the way from the luxury of Bangkok to the waters of Phuket, the chase all the way down Malaysia to Kuala Lumpur and the death of the girl whose name she was about to assume. But these were her father's instructions and she'd promised to carry them out to the letter.

Aubrey St Clair Smith hurried across the floor of the bank to relieve her of the heavy bag. It worried her for a moment, but then she realised that St Clair Smith would not be interested in money. Her father had already made it quite clear that St Clair Smith was as rich as anyone in that part of the world – another few million dollars in sapphires and used notes would hardly urge him to a life of crime, she thought. And she hoped.

'Were you satisfied with what you collected?' he asked as he drove her round the outskirts of the city. 'Was everything there that you expected?'

She didn't reply; instead she felt in her pocket and took out a small white envelope. 'Dad asked me to give you this after I'd been to the bank.' She held the sealed envelope out to him and he frowned as he glanced at it quickly, but he kept his hands on the wheel and made no attempt to take it.

'When did he give you that?'

'In Phuket. The hotel, after he'd met you. He came up to my room to fetch me, you remember, and we went out to Ban Yit in your car? While he was waiting for me to get ready he sat at the desk and wrote this note. "Give it to Aubrey," he said, "but only after you've been to the bank.

If he's not with you and he's fallen by the wayside, tear it up." Are you going to read it, or not?'

'D'you know what's in it?'

'Nope.'

'Then we'll hold ourselves in suspense until we get home and we'll read it over a little glass of lunch-time champagne!' His voice didn't change. 'What's in the bag?'

'Why don't we hold ourselves in suspense until we read what's in the little note.' She almost giggled; there was a lightness in her stomach to replace the heavy lump of fear that had been there for some time. She had a sense of achievement. She felt she'd almost reached the end of the road that had started when her father sat down in the Oriental Hotel and opened up a lifetime of secrets. Perhaps it was all over now. She had carried out her part of the arrangement; all she had to do was go to the States and wait for him and the new life he'd promised. He'd said it was a new life without fear or worry – and with the word worry the ice returned to her stomach. How in God's name was she going to carry several million dollars' worth of sapphires and money from Malaysia to the US, and via, of all places, London? Help, Aubrey!

'What does he say?' Theresa studied St Clair Smith's face as he read Logan's note, but there was nothing on display. She was surprised when he refolded the note and passed it across the table to her. She opened it and read:

Nice try, Aubrey!
  I almost bought the eccentric limey play but you over-played your hand. I'm sorry but the stuff your people sent you to have a look at is too expensive for you or London. But thanks for the help, specially as far as Theresa is concerned. Can I ask one more small favour? You would be more than within your rights to tell me to go to hell! T. will need help in getting this bag out. Can do? Either way, if everything goes to plan and you are reading this under the conditions I hope for, there is a packet awaiting you post restante in KL Main Post Office. In it you'll find details of TG activities in UK and the names of a few

330

financial institutions that should produce a rich rosy hue
to the faces of London's serious crime, fraud and anti-drug
units. Which is what you were looking for – wasn't it? This
is my way of repaying you for your generosity in helping
me out of what could quite easily have become a terminal
problem.
Regards – JL

'This looks to me as if you were sent to find my father. It
was all a put-up job – this whole business has been to get
to my father? You used me!'

'I think,' said St Clair Smith, calmly, 'that if you read that
letter again you'll find that it wasn't you or your father who
was used – it was me.' He suddenly lost his languid attitude.
His manner became abrupt and serious. 'But we've moved
on. Where've you put the bag?'

She hesitated.

'Be quick!'

She left the room, returned and placed the heavy bag on
the floor at St Clair Smith's feet. 'Money and sapphires,' she
said. 'No papers—'

He looked at her with raised eyebrows, then opened the
bag. She was right. He contained his disappointment. The
only paper in the bag consisted of high-denomination currency notes. 'Was there anything else?' he asked casually.

'Just this. Isn't it enough?'

'In his letter your father mentions something else.'

'This is all there was.' She was becoming very adept at
looking people in the eye and lying. 'I brought everything
there was in the box. Can you do what he asks? Can you
help me get this out?'

He'd already made his plans. 'It can go to London in the
British diplomatic bag. The person who'll take you on there
will arrange for its next destination. I presume the plan was
for it to end up in the States?'

She met his eyes for a moment, then nodded.

'OK,' he said. 'Take some of this money out and put it in
your own bag. This'll have to be sealed now, by you, and
then by the high commission people in Ampang Road.' He
clicked the locking device shut and pushed the bag to one

side. 'You can come with me to see that it's safely handed over.'

'Thank you, but I trust you, Aubrey.'

'That doesn't come into it.' He searched her face. 'A word of warning. Be careful about handing out your trust. You've chosen some strange people to run with, people who live in a strange world and take trust very lightly. Bear that in mind. Trust no one. That should be your philosophy from now until the curtain comes down. And just remember that from this moment you will be Miss Tan Soo Lee. You have her papers, now dress yourself in her psyche. Let's get you on the road, and don't look back—'

Theresa shivered involuntarily.

'Shall I see you again?'

'If it's written!'

Chapter 39

Kuala Lumpur, Friday, 1400 hours

Aubrey St Clair Smith and Theresa watched the high commissioner seal Logan's bag and authorise it for inclusion in the diplomatic bag leaving for London on Sunday night. This was a high commissioner who'd been spoken to; London's voice was a powerful one when the right tone was used. It had worked with this normally unapproachable mandarin and St Clair Smith nodded his thanks as the bag was placed in the security of the HC's safe.

When St Clair Smith returned from dropping Theresa off at Subang Airport he found Simon sitting comfortable and relaxed on the verandah with a long frosted glass of chilled Tiger beer in front of him. St Clair Smith came straight out with it – no preliminaries, no soft approach; Simon would have to take it or leave it. But Simon didn't need the explanation; he knew taking it or leaving it was for the other people; for him leaving it wasn't an option.

'It's just the one job down here for you, Simon,' said St Clair Smith. 'And then you move out of the frame. It's a job that'll take about four days, and it's a job that's fraught with a helluva lot of fucking strife. At the moment there are only four people in the world who know what you and I are about to discuss. You'll be the fifth. And, as far as I'm concerned, that puts you in chains for the rest of your life. D'you want me to continue?'

'In for a penny.'

'And if you refuse I'll have to kill you.'

'Don't be so fucking melodramatic, Aubrey. Tell me the story.'

'I want two men, who are in hiding, taken through about ten miles of serious jungle without sight or sound. That means sight or sound of any living creature—'

Simon refused to match St Clair Smith's seriousness. 'Aubrey, you've been talking to someone who knows of my youthful indiscretions! Is that the thing full of fucking strife – a stroll with a couple of guys through the forest?'

'If that's how you want to put it. You'll do it?'

'Of course. I don't want to have to put you to the trouble of killing me!'

St Clair Smith offered no reaction. 'One is James Logan, Theresa's father, and the other's a guy named Hagen. That's all you're going to need to know. When it's finished you erase both those names from your memory. You've never heard of 'em. Right?'

'I've got the picture. No facts, then, no background music. You want a couple of blokes taken from A to B and you don't want them seen. Where's A?'

'Cameron Highlands.'

'I know it well!'

'I know you do!'

'And B?'

'Up to you. I want them somewhere where they can be picked up. D'you want to look at a map?'

'Thanks.'

After a few minutes poring over an ordnance survey map, Simon looked up and said, 'I once ambushed a bandit courier who was part of a relay team carrying stuff from the big communist camp at Keroh on the Thai border. He was heading for Chenderiang, south of Kampar. I killed him near the Sungai Geroh – ah, let's have a look at that.' He pressed the crease out of the map and flattened it across the table with his hand. He stuck his finger on the road that went to the Cameron Highlands and then on to nowhere – except two hundred miles through the most impenetrable jungle in the world until it ran into the South China Sea. He lowered his head and traced his finger across the map. 'There, that's the river, the Sungai Geroh. We followed it with the body. There was quite a good track, about three miles of it. It's probably still there, still being used. It runs into a small Malay village.' He moved his finger again and ran it over the green area that represented secondary jungle on the map. 'Kampong Sungei Itek.' He looked up into St Clair Smith's eyes and shook his head slowly. 'You could get a Land Rover, even a car, to the village, but the minute you did so, night or day, you'd have every man, woman, child and animal coming to look at you.'

St Clair Smith continued staring down at the map. He made no comment. Simon waited a second or two then raised his finger from the small village marked black in a jigsaw of green and brown contours and lowered his head over it again. 'We could bypass it,' he said, as if to himself. 'Stay on the river's edge, cross this small range of hills, then get soaked again in the Sungai Kampar and hit the main Ipoh–Kampar road just south of Kampong Pulai.' He looked up again.

This time St Clair Smith said, 'Sound's OK. How long will it take?'

Simon stuck his thumb between the end of the Tana Rata road and the main Ipoh road and measured it against the scale at the top of the map. He wrinkled his nose. 'If that track's still in use, that's a plus. Are these two fellows fairly healthy?'

St Clair Smith didn't help him.

Simon paused and thought again. 'I'll take that as a no. Which is tough on them because it's very rough going at the start, all uphill, not too bad when we get down onto the flat, just a bit damp – swampy, and we can move only in daylight. Give or take a yard it's about twelve miles. That'll take two daylight sessions and one night laying up – say two and half days.'

'Fair enough. Let's hope they're up to it. How will you get there?'

Simon looked up from the map and met St Clair Smith's eyes. 'I'll play that one by ear if you don't mind.'

'Suit yourself. I'll leave everything up to you, then.' St Clair Smith studied his watch. 'Today's Saturday. Assume you leave Cameron Highlands first light Sunday, you said walk eight hours, sleep twelve and then Monday another eight—'

'Make it eight hours plus for the last stretch. Have somebody on the end of a two-way link near that stretch of road from twenty hundred hours – a couple of flasks of anything hot and wet, and some changes of clothes—'

'Leave all that up to me. You know where to find them. I'll warn them. If we talk on air your code-name'll be Porteus. Logan can be Item One, and Hagen Item Two.'

'And my contact?'

'Whitehead.'

'OK.'

'And, Simon—'

'Yup?'

'Don't turn your back on Hagen.'

'OK,' said Simon casually. 'If there's nothing else I'll be on my way.' He stood up and stretched. He looked relaxed and totally at ease with himself. He was going back into the jungle; he was about to do something for which he knew he had no peer in the country. He felt very good about it.

Chapter 40

Kuala Lumpur, Sunday, 1700 hours

The five o'clock news, the Mandarin version, finished with a fanfare, and then a pretty nineteen-year-old, the character and beauty of her face flattened by the heavy plaster-like make-up, took over and lost Francis Ong's interest. He heaved himself out of the low cane armchair, padded across the deep, rich, red Bukhara carpet in his bare feet and switched the television off. He picked up the phone.

'It won't be on the English news until six,' he told Aubrey St Clair Smith, 'but it appears that there is a bit of panic going on in the Cameron Highlands. Apparently, some rich American from Bangkok – you might know his name: James Logan – has gone missing from an early morning walk. His servant reported to the police when he didn't return for his breakfast; he, the servant, that is, said he thinks Mr Logan's been eaten by a tiger.'

'Fascinating,' replied St Clair Smith. 'Has the American embassy made any comment?'

'Not yet, but the police are moving up in strength to comb the area. Which, in my opinion, is a pity when I think of all those untrained boots clumping around before the real experts can get up and there have a proper look . . .'

'Why a tiger?'

'Some Chinese fellow in the Smokehouse put forward a theory to a *Straits Times* reporter, who just happened to be there for a weekend break, that he remembered a time when a visitor went missing and all they found after weeks

337

of searching was a bit of his shoe, and that had an animal's tooth marks in it. This Chinese chap reckoned it had happened on several occasions in the past. They say the Perak tiger is very partial to eating man – or woman!'

'Very coincidental, Ong, all these people being on hand during this trying time. Be interesting to see what happens next. Incidentally, why don't you join me for a drink in the Long Bar later on?'

'Harlequin in the Merlin would be better. I think there should be a good deal of knowledgeable speculation on these interesting events. Nice way to pass an evening.'

'I'll see you there.'

By the time Ong and St Clair Smith met in the Harlequin Bar, Logan's disappearance had lifted off with a bang. The American embassy had issued a statement on the disappearance of the millionaire, but insisted that, as yet, there was no cause for real alarm. They dismissed as fantasy reports of tiger tracks having been discovered in the vicinity where Mr Logan had last been seen, and that signs of a violent struggle and heavy bloodstains had been found by the police. A Malaysian Government source also dismissed it as rubbish. But the theory was a popular one and was rapidly gaining ground. Washington had been informed of Mr Logan's disappearance and were keeping a very tight watching brief on the progress of local Malaysian authorities in tracing him. St Clair Smith and Ong exchanged glances. It looked as though Jim Logan could very well be dead.

'My people have identified four of Liu Hongzhou's Touming actually in the area,' murmured Ong. 'One's carrying an official press pass, the others are on fairly legitimate business. They're not missing a trick; they've got their eyes on everything. Two of them are very, very smart cookies. If *they* accept death by tiger as well I shall be definitely worried about our friend Jimmy's health!'

'Anybody else about?'

'There are more Touming at Tapah and Gopeng, but they're watching people go up and down and asking questions – has anyone seen a tall American like this. They have photos of Logan, head and shoulders, not that they'd need 'em. Just the mention of his name in this atmosphere and anyone who's ever seen an American in his life'll come forward. It's all money. There's bound to be a reward. Vietnam's Cong An Bo have a presence. They're also dressed up as press.'

'Any Americans?'

'As you can imagine! But I've heard a whisper – there's a team of CIA people waiting on permission from Malaysian police to come and stick their oar in.'

'Will they get it?'

Ong smiled. 'Sure, when all else fails. It's good for PR when you've made a balls-up of everything to be able to say, Well, even the much-vaunted CIA did no better than our local boys. You must be happy.'

'Heard from your control in Washington yet?'

Ong continued smiling. 'Only an exploratory cough. But any hour now and the wires'll be burning. But it's so convincing at the moment the clouds above Langley must be pissing blood. He doesn't know whether the prize has pulled it off and cleared the air or whether he really has gone up the spout. I think the tiger thing's a classic, but I never heard of one eating a man right down to, and including, his shoes and socks. Still, if they'll buy it—!'

Chapter 41

James Logan sat in the darkened room and watched Simon as he stood unmoving, like a shadow, at the window, searching the black, unrelenting sky for the first glimmer of dawn.

Hagen, squatting with his back to the wall, made not the slightest movement; his breathing was regular and unhurried, there was no indication of a raised stress level. Hagen could have been asleep. But he was anything but that.

The half-moon that had turned the bungalow's surroundings to a ghostly silver had vanished half an hour earlier beyond the jagged line of trees, but still reflected a faint, lighter-than-pitch hue to the sky where it had dropped. The jungle hadn't yet woken up, but Simon waited, and listened, for the first signs.

Very shortly the night insects and the irritating, insomniac tok-tok bird would go to sleep and the gibbons, monkeys and other creatures would start yawning and stretching their mouth muscles to welcome a new but unchanging day. Somewhere down below the bungalow, where the jungle fringe ran into the end of the lawned garden, little mouse-deer, the *pelandok*, would begin rubbing the sleep from their bright, bulging eyes and start being afraid of the throaty cough of the tiger, and the wild boar would already be silently rootling for its breakfast. Simon looked over his shoulder and managed to pierce the darkness of the room.

'Jim,' he said softly. 'What time does your houseboy start moving about?'

'He'll light the fires about five,' whispered Logan. 'What's the time now?'

'Just gone four.' Simon made a last inspection of the non-existent skyline and said, 'Go to bed now and get ready to have a headache. We'll move out when we hear your voice. You know where to go when you leave the house. Do it openly, the way you normally do during the day. Just leave things as if you'll be back in half an hour.' He directed his voice at the man on the floor. 'Hagen, when you move down to the back of the bungalow don't touch the lawn, it'll leave marks until the sun comes up. You've got your face blacked?'

'Yeah.'

'OK, you go first. Don't break through the undergrowth, just slip into the fringe and then wait for me. Face the direction you've come and stick your hand against a tree – it'll show up in the dark. I'll make sure everything looks normal here. OK with you two?'

Logan and Hagen both grunted their assent.

Logan went to the door, opened it a crack and listened. The house was like a morgue. In the distance, somewhere in the back of the servants' quarters, he could hear someone hawking in their sleep; it was a prelude to waking up. In a few minutes the back light would go on and a whoof of flame would announce a dose of kerosene on the ashes of last night's fire. Then kettles and saucepans would start banging and clanging as tea and breakfast were prepared. Logan slipped out of the door and closed it behind him.

Hagen stood up and waited his turn. His eyes strained towards the outline of Simon's shadow by the window. He was glad to be on his way. He'd had enough of nature; he'd filled his guts to bursting point several years ago in that other jungle south of Saigon. And, although he might have forgotten the discomfort, he hadn't forgotten the smell. This brought it all back, both the stink of the jungle and its associates, the once-smelt-never-to-be-forgotten aroma of the mixture of cordite-impregnated flesh and blood. He reckoned this little stroll was going to be a cakewalk and

hadn't been put off by Aubrey St Clair Smith's briefing. But
he had come away with a marked impression that St Clair
Smith was an extremely fancy bastard, and his fat Chinese
buddy was no slouch either; they'd got this funny game well
tied up around here. He grinned in the dark. Old Reilly's
man, the Chink, the guy whose name Reilly didn't want to
mention because he was too exclusive to Reilly's bit of the
CIA, was even more exclusive to what was obviously a
British top spy. St Clair Smith and the Chinaman were
a team of some sort. Some goddamn team! Laurel and
Hardy of the Far East espionage circuit! Poor old Reilly!
But he wouldn't spoil his illusions. He dropped his lips over
the grin and considered Logan's disappearing act. When
he'd asked them for suggestions he hadn't expected to discover that Laurel and Hardy had already got it worked out.

'OK,' St Clair Smith had told him. 'You were marked by
the Touming Guanxi right from the start. They were on to
you, somehow, from the day your feet touched Bangkok
Airport. They might even have been with you when you left
Washington.'

'I'd have seen 'em.'

'But you didn't, did you? Of course you bloody didn't,
they're invisible. But they've had you in sight all along and
now you've become their number one. Theresa Logan's
gone. They've lost interest. They've got a body; they've put
a line through the name. They can't find Logan, but they
know where there's a man who's looking for him – you. So
go and let them see you again and take them to Logan.
There's no point in Logan disappearing if they're not there
to see it happen, OK?'

But it wasn't OK – not with him. 'OK, my ass! I'm not
going down as some fucking staked-out nanny-goat. If you
think I'm—'

St Clair Smith had studied him as he would a spoilt child.
'I thought we decided you had no choice in this matter,
Hagen.' He overrode Hagen's attempt at further argument
with an airy wave of the hand. 'Can I get on with it?' He
didn't wait for Hagen's permission. 'Right. You take the car
up to the Camerons; you book in under any name you fancy

in the Smokehouse or the Cameron Highlands Hotel and you've dragged a couple of Liu's Touming Guanxi boys along with you. Don't let them see Logan until Sunday when you start sniffing around his bungalow like a potential burglar; they'll be with you and they'll see Logan. When that happens they won't want you any more, so they'll kill you, if you let them, and concentrate on getting Logan back to Bangkok. You make a run for it first light Monday, by which time they'll have reported Logan's whereabouts and reinforcements will be on the way.'

'And me?'

'You're a big boy, you can look after yourself.'

'Like fuck I can! If I take part in this move I'm sticking. You forget, Logan's my problem, I'm looking after him. Think again, friends!'

'OK, if you want to do it the hard way—'

'Hard way or not, I want to do it the way I end up living happily ever after. I don't give a fuck how it happens, but that's how I want it. And I want Logan's sticky little hand held in mine when running time comes.' He stopped and considered it for a moment. His eyes never wavered from St Clair Smith's. 'What *is* the hard way?'

'You break out through the jungle – you and Logan.'

'I thought you said that was no deal.'

'We'll supply a guide.'

'Who I kill at the end of the trip because he'll know that the whole fucking thing is a snow job!' Hagen was serious. It showed on his face. Serious and wary. He meant exactly what he said.

St Clair Smith shrugged it to one side. Simon had taken care of uglier bastards than this one. He had no fears about who was going to walk out fresh and bright-eyed from a Malaysian jungle jaunt. 'Let's stick to facts.' He ignored Ong's eyes and the uneasy expression that flitted across his chubby features. 'We've got you running around in circles and Liu Hongzhou's people excited at the thought of seeing Logan again. You give Touming the slip, kill 'em if that's your fancy, and make your way, without being seen, into Logan's house. You'll have arranged this with him beforehand. Everything must be normal. The cook, or whatever he has in the bungalow, must not suspect that anything abnormal is happening. When he's been brought his early morning tea and biscuits Logan'll get up, complain about his terrible headache, and say he's going for a walk.'

'But it's still dark.'

'That's exactly the remark that Cookie will make as well. Logan will say whatever he has to say to his cook when he wants to go out for a walk in the early dawn and Cookie tells him it's still dark. He can tell him to mind his own fucking business if he likes, and anything else that comes to mind at that moment, providing it's not out of character. In the meantime, you're freezing to death outside waiting for the cook to go to bed so that you can crawl into the house and wait for Logan to do his act with Cookie. Then you slip out and go into the jungle at a pre-arranged spot. OK so far?'

'What about this guide?'

'He will appear like magic and whisper a code-word in your, or Logan's, ear and take over. You will follow exactly what he says; he is in charge from the word go and he'll lead you into, and out of, the jungle . . .'

'And what are the Chinese doing all this time?'

'I've just said, waiting for reinforcements to close in on Logan on Monday and do whatever they've been intending to do – presumably find out what all the fuss is about and whether he's going to damage them. As far as we know he's still a senior member of the Touming Guanxi, only his peers know what awful crime he's committed or is about to commit. That's none of our business. Our business is to get him out of here and somewhere where his, and your, principals can discuss matters with him. Clear?'

Hagen couldn't help admiring them. It had gone like clockwork. It had happened exactly as Laurel and Hardy had predicted. The only surprise to him was the ease with which he had thrown the Chinese watchers. Their knowledge of the jungle was nil; they were town boys, city dwellers who knew all about breaking arms and legs and sticking fingers down people's throats but absolutely fuck-all about the stuff that grew all around them. He'd strolled off the path into the jungle and within minutes he'd found himself on his own. He hadn't seen them again. Perhaps they were still floundering around in the cultivated jungle on the edge of the resort. And the simple-looking bastard, the guide, as St Clair Smith had described him, had arrived out of nowhere with a pack on his back and an M1 carbine under his arm and growled 'Porteus' in his ear.

Easy as pie! And here they were waiting for Cookie to bring Master his tea and bananas and biscuits and find out that Master had a headache and was going for a stroll in the early morning air to cure it! He stopped thinking about it and allowed himself to be joggled into action by his new pal Porteus.

'OK, move!'

Hagen left as silently as had Logan and carried out the first part of the plan. No problems. With his back resting against the trunk of a tree, he crouched in the dark with his hand on his chest and strained his eyes along the animal track he'd just traversed and waited for Simon to find him.

He'd barely scratched the itch out of his first mosquito bite when he felt a tap on his shoulder and nearly jumped out of his skin. He always reckoned he'd been good in the jungle. Perhaps he had been, by Vietnam standards. But this guy! Not a sound. It was as dark as Granddad's armpit and he'd come up behind him – behind him! He shuddered involuntarily and blamed it on the mist and the early morning chill that it brought.

They kept close together as Simon led him two hundred yards or so to the south, then he turned and touched his shoulder. He put his blackened face up close. His voice was less than a whisper. 'Wait here. Same procedure. I'm going to get Logan.'

This time Hagen did hear something. He wouldn't have staked his life that what he heard was the man called Porteus, but a few seconds later Logan, struggling with his breathing, was crouching beside him. Simon opened his pack and placed a neat bundle in Logan's hands. 'Bit of jungle green. Slip it on, wrap your own stuff up and hang on to it until I come back.'

'Where you going now?' Hagan could just make out

345

Simon's form and the shape of his head. Somewhere the sun was coming up, but not on Cameron Highlands. Not yet. It was just a suggestion of light, a fraction of a shade less than black.

'Two Chinese followed Jim down the track; they lost their nerve and squatted against a couple of trees to wait for him to come back. I'm going to have a look at them again to make sure they haven't done anything silly.'

There was no mistake this time; it was definitely getting lighter when Simon's outline appeared back on the track. 'OK.' He carefully packed Logan's clothes, checked thoroughly, with his face inches from the ground, that they had left no signs, and then with a flick of his hand led the other two off the track and began to move carefully, slowly, upward, away from where the sun was making its first tentative streaked pink-and-red marks on the fading night sky.

By the time it was light enough to see his hand, Logan felt the grip of age on his tired limbs. He kept his eyes glued to the fragment of white material hanging out of one of the pouches in Simon's backpack as he picked his way in his wake along the animal track, ever upward, always at a crouch, forever twisting and turning when something hooked onto his clothing: avoiding the searching barbed fingers that sprang out as Simon passed them and hooked onto his arms and pulled at his face. This had to be the worst jungle in the world. Eventually the will to pirouette his body out of the way refused to match the effort and he just barged on, head down, and after a while forgot to notice that the skin of his hands and arms was being torn to ribbons.

But his brain wouldn't leave him alone. Logan had lost the factor; he didn't feel lucky any more. He felt like that Italian – or was he Spanish? – in that old black-and-white film of the last ten yards of an early Olympic marathon. The poor bastard had given his all. There was the finishing tape a few yards away; he'd won! But then a couple of his pals, interfering bastards, decided to help him over the last couple of yards. The poor fucker was disqualified. Logan knew how he felt. This was the last yard of his marathon, but it wouldn't be disqualification; the end of this one would be a bullet in the back of the head. Forget the Italian, he'd been running for fun and it had only been the marathon. His run had been longer, the stakes higher and the tape suspended somewhere between life and death – his – and he couldn't even see the fucking tape yet. He was still running – he hadn't stopped, not since 1941.

Logan held his watch up close to his face, wiped the sweat from his eyes and estimated it was getting on for thirty-six hours since he'd begun hauling himself through the jungle. His age was telling on him; it had started telling on him an hour after they'd left Cameron Highlands. He glanced wearily over his shoulder and met Hagen's eyes, briefly. It was telling on him as well, but then Hagen had a few years in credit.

Simon brought them together in a huddle just east of the small Malay village. They crouched, soaked in sweat, their legs caked in mud. Hagen was dying for a cigarette but had neither the energy to dig one out of his pocket nor the inclination to ask the fresh-looking Simon if that would be OK. His impressions of this man were set in concrete – he knew exactly what the reply would be. He cocked his head towards him. Simon was whispering. 'One more little river, but it's got to be done in absolute silence. The people living there can hear a mouse fart a thousand yards away! Follow me and don't try to hurry. Once across the river we'll let it guide us to the edge of the road; it's easy going from there. Mainly chest-high *lalang*, but it won't make a noise. I'll find a path. Stick to it.'

'How much longer?' wheezed Logan.

'Not far.'

Logan peered up through the canopy of trees. The last time he'd had the energy, or the inclination, to look anywhere other than where his feet were going, he'd noticed the sky had turned navy blue. Now it was grey. Shortly, with a bit of moon, it would be almost black. It *was*, where he was sitting. He couldn't make out Simon's features but they were ingrained on his mind as those of someone he proposed hating for the rest of his life.

'Can't you be more specific than that?'

'I wouldn't worry about how long it takes,' murmured

347

Simon. His teeth, unusually, showed in some sort of smile – the smug fucker was actually enjoying himself, thought Hagen. 'Let's save it for a surprise!'

'And fuck you too!' hissed Logan. Hagen glanced quickly at him. He reckoned by the look on the old man's face killing this fucker was going to be a race between the two of them. But he knew who was going to get there first, and putting a couple of bullets into the smooth bastard's face was going to be one of the pleasures of the immediate future. It gave him added strength.

But surprise it was.

A few minutes later, and without warning, Simon stopped dead. He put his hand out behind him to stop Logan, head down and seeing nothing except the mud balls that were his feet going automatically one after the other in front of him, from crashing into his back.

'The road,' he whispered over his shoulder.

'I couldn't give a fuck any more!'

'Listen.'

And it was only when he held his breath to stop his heart thudding in his ears that Logan caught the sound. But it seemed miles away. The distant howl of a motor car engine. Civilisation. He let out his breath with a cough that brought a sharp hissed reprimand from Simon.

As they rose from the riverbank they'd been following and turned sharp right into the dense secondary jungle, Logan realised why the car's engine had sounded so far away. They were making their way through thick under-growth growing out of soft, wet, knee-deep mud. He felt as if he were bashing his way through barbed-edged kapok with his legs being pulled from under him at every step. He didn't realise Simon had found them an easy track through the otherwise impenetrable secondary jungle and up to the rise that overlooked the road.

It was now night and the headlights of thinly spread-out cars and lorries were insufficient to hinder their sliding and scrambling down the steep bank to the road. There they waited until Simon gave the word, then, one by one, they darted to the other side and clambered up the opposite bank.

Logan and Hagen lay flat on their backs and sucked air into their tortured lungs while Simon said, 'Don't move. I'll be back shortly.' It must have been ten minutes before he reappeared, then, checking that the two Americans were still alive, he moved slightly away and, still standing, opened a two-way radio. He switched on its power, pressed transmit, and said quietly, 'Porteus. Come in, Whitehead.

The set crackled briefly, then Aubrey St Clair Smith's voice, muted but clear, came from within Simon's cupped hands. 'Waiting for directions, Porteus.'

'383827—'

There was a pause, a crackling of paper, another pause, then, 'Got it—'

'There's a track wide enough for a vehicle. Reverse into it and put your lights out. I'll approach you.'

'See you in a minute.'

'Another little walk, chaps,' said Simon cheerfully when he joined the other two and crouched down with them. 'Not far – a couple of hundred yards, all downhill.'

'What direction?' rasped Hagen.

Simon jerked his head sideways. 'That way. It's a narrow path. There's a vehicle on its way.'

'Thanks,' said Logan. Hagen's hand came from under the back of his thigh and the worn military-pattern 9mm Browning he'd been given by St Clair Smith rested in his lap, pointing towards Simon. 'Looks like it's goodbye, then, pal,' he said, smoothly.

'I'm afraid it is, chaps. I've enjoyed the trip and I wish you every success in whatever your futures are. I'll come along with you, though, and hand you over to your next friend—'

'You're reading the wrong message, pilgrim. I said it's goodbye. I didn't mean good luck or cheerio, I meant goodbye.' Without moving it from his lap, Hagen lifted the muzzle of the Browning and shifted the safety with his thumb. 'The fewer the people who know . . . you know the sort of thing – you've been around . . . Don't take it personally. Think of it as one of those necessities of the game – one you lost.' Simon just looked at him. Perhaps a touch of contempt – it was hard to see in the shaded moonlight. He held his hand out. Hagen shook his head. 'They only do that in the movies.' Logan, his back resting against a thin sapling, looked on with dull eyes. He had neither the strength nor the inclination to join in the repartee, or to take sides – young men's business, fuck-all to do with him. But he watched nevertheless.

'Not this they don't—' Simon opened his hand. 'I think you'll need these if you're going to go around pointing that thing at people.' He tilted his hand and fourteen rounds of 9mm crunched softly into the leaves and soil at Hagen's feet. 'That includes the one that was in the breech. Shall we go and meet the car?' He crushed the bullets into the soft ground with his foot as he stood up, and Logan saw that the slim barrel of his M1 carbine had been pointing all the time at Hagen's midriff. It looked casual and unintentional. Logan wouldn't have bet money on it being unintentional, and he noticed that Simon kept it that way as he sent Hagen in front and directed him from behind, through the sparse undergrowth, to the narrow track.

They arrived almost at the same time as St Clair Smith, who had reversed into the cutting. The engine was still running but there were no lights on the big, dark-coloured Volvo. Simon held the door open for the two Americans to climb into the back. He didn't offer to shake hands. He went round to the front and leaned through the window. 'All present and correct.'

'Thank you, Simon,' said St Clair Smith in a low voice. 'You're not coming back with us?'

'Er – no, under the circumstances I think I'll go back the way we've just come. I'll hang around for a day or so and put my ear down to see if anybody noticed anything.'

'Jesus Christ! Am I hearing aright?' rasped Logan. With an effort he leaned forward. 'You're going back where we've just come from?'

Simon didn't reply. He continued, with his head close to St Clair Smith's, 'I'll let you know if I hear anything about these two. When I come down I'll go back up north and dig in again. Probably won't see you for some time—'

St Clair Smith lowered his voice to the merest whisper; he could hardly hear himself. 'Be warned, Simon. Both

Hagen and you'll go on a CIA project for check-out if this thing comes off. Logan'll go too in the end.'

'What about you?'

'Count on it. The CIA's got a special-treatment department for people they think might be carrying delicate and potentially damaging information. Just spend the next ten years or so with your face back to front!'

Simon held his hand up and then he was gone, back into the night without a sound. Hagen just looked straight ahead. He'd been done by an expert. He never even felt the bastard lift the Browning from him, let alone empty the breech and the magazine. And the fucker had stuck it back under his leg when he'd been sleeping. He should have broken the bastard's neck when he had the chance. He scowled to himself in the dark and blamed it on the fact that he was getting past his youth. And it had been a damned long walk.

Chapter 42

Aubrey St Clair Smith turned the dark grey Volvo off the Circular Road and into Ampang Road. He took the next right, then another right into the quiet, peaceful and leafy suburb known as, with good reason, Embassyville, and came slowly towards the Circular Road again, turning just before it reached the side entrance of the US embassy, KL.

They were waiting for them. It looked like a dead area. The main overhead light had been dimmed, the gate was open and the Marine guard, usually on full show during daylight hours, was hovering somewhere near the gate, fully armed and out of sight. There would be another across the road, and another on the far corner scanning the dark area behind the Volvo. The gate shut smoothly behind them.

Smith cut the lights and followed the shadowy figure that detached itself from the cover of the guardroom. He took the car at a crawl round to the rear of the embassy. Still dark. The shape he'd been following disappeared. There was no one else about. It was deserted. Beau Geste would have felt at home here.

St Clair Smith stopped the car, switched off the engine and waited. There had been little or no conversation between the two men in the back. Any talk between Logan and St Clair Smith had been desultory; no one was in the mood.

St Clair Smith stiffened as a new shadow appeared from the darkness of the main building and moved towards the car. A hand tapped on the window. The shadow had no face; nothing recognisable except a definite Southern accent.

'Get as close as you can to the wall, drop the two parcels and go back the way you came.' The shadow stuck its head into the window and addressed the blackness of the back seat. 'When the car stops hop out and stick close to the wall. I'll lead you home, OK?' It didn't wait for an acknowledgement. One minute it was hanging into the window, the next it had melted back into the brick wall of the embassy.

St Clair Smith did as he was told and the two Americans slipped out of his car and vanished. No thank yous; no gratitude; nothing. But St Clair Smith wasn't disappointed. He wasn't in the business for fawning gratitude; he'd done a job, done it well, and he'd achieved what he'd been told to do. London would have to be happy. If they weren't he didn't give a shit – that was what he told himself as he re-entered the Circular Road and made his way home. Tomorrow morning he'd visit the general post office and see what Logan had left for him. Then it would be down to Port Klang and, without a fanfare, he'd point *Claudia*'s bows towards the south and head for Singapore and then the South China Sea and the fleshpots at Pulau Tioman. It was time for a break; it was time to get out of everybody's way; it was time to go to ground for a couple of months while the disturbed undergrowth and vegetation of the jungle covered itself up and the peace and quiet of the Cameron Highlands were allowed to revert to their normal state.

But General Samuel Reilly played it for all it was worth. The American people, he pronounced to the world's media, demanded answers. American citizens didn't get eaten by Malaysian tigers, and if the guy was lost somewhere in the depths of the jungle, then no effort would be spared to find him. A unit of the Malaysian élite 2nd Police Field Force from Ipoh took to the jungle and helicopters arrived from the US base in southern Thailand and scoured the area from the air. Sam Reilly arrived personally to give added impetus to the efforts. Nothing was spared – but nothing was found either, and after ten days of intense activity the search was called off. As far as the world was concerned

James Logan had got lost in the jungle; he'd either been attacked and eaten by a tiger or he'd strayed from the known tourist tracks and fallen and broken his leg and died a slow and lonely death.

They could have it either way; but whatever way they chose, General Sam Reilly made his observations to the world loud and clear.

'James Logan, goddammit, is dead.'

Chapter 43

Kuala Lumpur, January 1975

Liu Zhoushiu sat in the low-slung bamboo armchair in the Touming safe house in Ulu Kelang, just on the north-eastern boundary of Kuala Lumpur. It was a very ordinary Chinese shop-owner's bungalow and matched the others that surrounded it. It was very safe.

He drank boiling-hot thin green tea from a small bowl and smoked a heavy black tobacco cigarette. The cigarette was doing his shrivelled lungs no good at all, and every so often the talk stopped while he went through an eye-bulging paroxysm of loose, wet coughing. He was there as head of the Touming Guanxi but, so far, had taken no part in the discussion.

They were all here, all Chinese, the godfathers and the executives of the most powerful criminal configuration in the world. And they were here for one purpose.

It was easier to gather here in Kuala Lumpur where any activity by the DEA, the CIA or any other American-controlled agency was strenuously suppressed by the fiercely independent Malaysian authorities. Any American in Malaysia, unaccounted for, would be listed by the highly secret special intelligence section, E3, and his every movement plotted and checked; his drinking companions, dining companions and sleeping companions would join his name on the list. This was a highly satisfactory state of affairs for the likes of the Touming Guanxi, and this was where the gathering could take place without fear of interruption. The whole of the immediate area of Ulu Kelang was under the control of these grey and serious men; they could sit and sleep and relax as if they were at home in Bangkok.

And now they sought a decision. But it was hard to come by. The elder Liu sat and drank his tea and smoked his life away and listened. Eventually, after everyone had had his say, all faces turned to the old man and the question was posed.

'Is James Logan dead?'

Liu Zhoushiu had already come to his own conclusion.

'James Logan is dead.'

'We have seen no body.'

'Then review the facts. Our people were present the day before Logan disappeared; our people have been there in ever-increasing numbers since he walked into the jungle. The Cong An Bo wanted him. They were likewise there and they are still there. Would they still be there if they had taken him back to Vietnam? The Americans want him very badly, not because he is one of them but because he has much that they need from him—'

One of the younger men tapped the table with his finger-tips. Liu stopped talking and turned his flat black eyes to the interrupter. The man didn't flinch but allowed his eyes to drop and his sharp features to assume an expression of respect.

'They also needed to protect him from the Viets. The fact mustn't be lost that we and the Americans still have mutual interests while this war goes on. I understood Logan had made provision in the event of his sudden death for details of this mutual interest to be made public.'

'You haven't said anything,' said Liu Zhoushiu, without taking his eyes off the man who had spoken, 'that answers the question of whether the man is dead or not.'

'With respect—' The younger man met the old leader's eyes. 'If the Americans didn't think Logan was dead they would still be there, combing the area. They want Logan alive, not dead. So, if they have given up after many days of searching, with the help of helicopters, American special agents brought in from Vietnam, CIA people, Malaysian soldiers and police – hundreds of them – they must have

356

given up hope of his still being alive. I stressed that they wanted him alive for the reason that our mutual interest with the CIA should remain within the minds of the people in this room and the principals in Washington – that was my argument.'

'You make an eloquent point, my friend,' conceded Liu Zhoushiu. 'I have said I believe Logan to be dead. Have you discussed the presence at Cameron Highlands of the other American?'

'We believe he was CIA-connected and was watching. Nothing more than that. Logan was seen in the Cameron Highlands after this American had left.'

'He was followed to his destination?'

'He was not our target. He was used only to keep us in contact with Logan. It was sufficient that he was not in the area when Logan entered the jungle.'

The old man lit another crumpled cigarette and coughed solidly for half a minute. When he'd recovered he said, 'Has anyone considered the coincidence of Theresa Logan's death such a short time before that of her father?'

Liu Hongzhou took up the question. 'Theresa was killed by accident. We know who did it. It was Peng Soon. He tried to take her from the American in Kuala Lumpur and was shot dead in the attempt by the American who was looking at Logan. His name was Hagen.' Hongzhou had his own version; it was more convincing than the real one and there was no need for the elders of this gathering to know that he'd had this American in a fish basket and had lost him. Touming Guanxi wasn't interested in the incompetence of one of its crown princes. He thus closed the subject of Theresa Logan. 'Her name need not be mentioned again. There is, however, a major problem remaining—'

'Logan's insurance?'

'Exactly. When this was discussed in Bangkok, Logan stated that should he die suspiciously the material he'd put away would be made public. Would this that has happened to him constitute suspicious death?'

'There is no body?'

'None has been found. No trace. He could have been

357

eaten; if he hasn't there will be only bones in a very short time. These will never be discovered.'

'We are satisfied that he is dead?'

'Are *you*, Father?'

'Yes.'

'Then so be it. But you haven't answered the question.'

The old man kept them waiting until he'd drawn smoke into his lungs and coughed away another few days of his life. 'We know he is dead; they know he is dead; but the law doesn't say he is dead until seven years have elapsed. There will be no disclosure of Logan's papers until then. Liu Hongzhou's agreement with the CIA is that our arrangement remains intact until the war ends for good in Vietnam. He estimates one year at the most. That is nothing to our disadvantage because only we and Logan knew the extent of our compromising these governments and our penetration into the intelligence services in this part of the world. Seven days is a long time in our terms – seven years is an eternity. In one year's time our establishment of a worldwide opium distribution centre in the United States will continue with or without the co-operation of the people who negotiated our freedom of action in return for intelligence information for their prosecution of the war. When that time arrives we shall have nothing to lose or gain. When Logan's disclosures are made it will be for them to explain their actions to the American people – it will not be our problem. In the meantime it is my verdict that James Logan is dead and no longer constitutes a threat to the Touming Guanxi.'

Chapter 44

Chicago, USA, January 1975

Jim Logan and Mark Hagen ducked beneath the wavering blades of the army helicopter and without straightening up trotted, heads down, into the back of the giant Hercules C-130 parked half in and half out of the huge hangar on the part of Thailand's Hat Yai airfield reserved for the USAF.

Dressed in GI fatigues, they looked like a couple of loaders. The fact that they didn't leave the aircraft went unnoticed, and it took off for Saigon with two passengers known to the captain of the aircraft only as Sergeants Wells and Day on relocation. Their presence didn't raise an eyebrow.

At Saigon they walked off with the rest of the crew, entered the operations room and walked straight through the shed, out the other side, and grabbed a couple of free bucket seats on a transport to Wake. Here they reckoned they'd done enough running and, reverting to being civilians, found a flight to Honolulu and then changed to a scheduled direct flight to Chicago.

Hagen booked the two rooms in the Park Hotel on Madison Street in the centre of Chicago; it seemed the right city in which to end a game of hide-and-kill, a game of gangmen, Tongmen and double doubles. He bought himself a cold beer from the miniature bar, took it with him and lay on the crisply made-up bed. He picked up the phone, dialled 9, waited to make sure he wasn't paying for someone else to listen in, then dialled 703 482 1100. It was nice to hear a female American voice.

'Two nine zero,' he told her.

'Graver,' came another voice after a few moments.

'Hagen, sir. I've brought Contractor home.'

'Where are you?'

'Chicago.'

'Chicago's not home, Hagen, Washington is. What're you doing in Chicago?'

'Contractor's decided this is where the game stops; his choice, he wanted Chicago, and I didn't want to put a gun to his head and run him all the way across to DC! I don't think he would have liked that.'

'OK, give me your phone number and I'll ring you back when I've made some arrangements—'

'He doesn't want that, sir. He says he'll make the arrangements. He's working on a little meeting, just you and him—'

'Hagen – is this man holding a gun to your head?'

'No, sir—'

Graver had been at the top too long to show his feelings to an employee. He carried on with the conversation as if he were talking to an equal rank – well, almost an equal rank; cool and calm, he assessed Hagen's words and their implication and then replied in the same manner. He could have been a doctor telling Hagen that the X-rays showed he'd got something unpleasant. He carried on with the diagnosis. 'Then I want that parcel brought to DC. No – better still, take him to Ashford and contact me from there. Keep him under wraps – he's not public property and he's not totally in the clear from the other players yet – we haven't had a definite from the other place yet, so keep a tight grip on things. OK?'

'I'll have to ring you back, sir—'

'Why?'

'Because, like I've just said, sir, he won't play. He's going to do this thing his own way and it's going to be on his terms. He's not frightened, quite the opposite, but he's very, very wary ... Just a minute, sir, let me finish!' Hagen inelegantly brushed aside the beginning of an interruption from his director. 'He reckons he's come home voluntarily;

if we play this thing the wrong way he's just as likely to fold his blanket and vanish again. I've got nothing to hold him with – and I can't sit here with my finger in his ear waiting for your people to arrive. It's taken a lot of hard work to get him this far. Why not go along with him? Listen to what he has to say—'

Graver's voice sounded very unhappy. 'I'll ask you again, Hagen, what's your phone number?'

'Sorry, sir.' Hagen put the receiver down and up-ended the bottle of cold beer into his mouth. It tasted as sweet as honey.

Logan didn't trust the hotel phone. No reason, they'd only just moved in; but this was a phobia, not a new one, one that had been brought out of its private limbo after the last three months of being back on the road. This was an old habit that was always going to crop up when the safety glands started sweating again. The phone he liked he found in a bar just across the road from the hotel. The safest phone in the world was the one at the railway station; if that was too far away, the next best was the first bar on the other side of the road, provided you could talk with your back to the wall. This one filled all the requirements.

Logan left his beer on the counter, looked up the code for Indiana and dialled Kendalville. Then he turned round and looked to see if anyone was interested. They weren't.

It was an elderly female voice that answered.

'Hilda—' he said into the mouthpiece. 'It's Jim. Don't ask too many questions, but have you received a parcel within the last couple of days?'

'One from Malaysia.'

'Anything else?'

'A couple of envelopes. Why don't you buy yourself a proper post office?'

'This one's worked fine for thirty-five years, no reason why it shouldn't continue. You complaining?'

'You talk too much, young Jimmy. You want me to do something with this packet?'

'Strip off the outer cover that's got your name and address on it and burn it. Then rewrap the inner packet and address it to James Goddard, c/o Rino's Hotel, Fourteenth Street, Pilsen, Chicago. Make it express delivery. OK?'

'You've got it, Jim. See you some time?'

'Sure.'

He returned to the bar, finished his beer, had another quick, if surreptitious, look around, and then left. He went back to the Park Hotel, and when Hagen came down looking for him he was relaxed in the front lounge with his head in a late edition of the *Herald Tribune* and a large double Scotch on ice clinking comfortably on the table beside him. He didn't move when Hagen approached.

'Have you thought about what you're going to do for Graver?' said Hagen as he flopped into the deep armchair beside him.

Logan put down his paper. 'Have you spoken to him?'

'No,' lied Hagen. 'I was waiting for you to give me something to tell him. You're the driver at the moment. Everyone's panting around with their tongues hanging out waiting for you to say or do something. That includes me. I'm pissed off with your company and Chicago I need like I need leprosy.'

'Have a Scotch,' responded Logan, 'and while you're doing it I'm going down the road here and when I come back I'll tell you what's going to happen.' He drained his glass and put it down with a chink of ice cubes that hadn't had time to melt.

'Forget the Scotch. I'll come with you—'

'Not down my street you won't, sonny.'

Hagen didn't take offence. 'OK, but don't forget I'm here to keep you upright. We might have put a few people in doubt about whether you are or whether you're not, but until someone signs a death certificate you're going to have to keep looking over your shoulder. While I'm here you don't have to do that. Take your choice.'

Logan stood up. 'I'll see you.'

'Sure. I'll come to the door. I need a bit of fresh American air. Don't worry!' He stuck up his hand with a sour grin. 'I'll go in the opposite direction.'

He stood on the sidewalk outside the hotel entrance and caught the eye of the taller of two Mexican kids sitting on the step of a boarded-up office entrance on the far side of the road. They had their backs against the blocked-off door and their legs splayed out, taking up half the room on the sidewalk. Most of the people stepped round them. Others, probably from the same bit of pampas, stopped and waited for them to move; it depended on size and numbers whether they did or not. When the youth spotted Hagen he got up and slouched obliquely across the road. He put on a burst of speed when he reached Hagen's side.

The deal had already been done. For the torn half of a hundred-dollar bill Hagen had, before meeting Logan in the lounge, bought the services of a tracker dog. All he needed was the sniff. Hagen gave it to him with a short jerk of his chin at Logan's back and watched the Mexican melt into the surroundings in Logan's wake. After a few seconds the other youth set off in support. Hagen went back into the hotel lounge and did as Logan had suggested.

He was still there when Logan returned two hours later.

Hagen gave him enough time to settle down, then got up casually and strolled about the hotel foyer and shopping arcade. After a while, when he was sure Logan had made himself comfortable, he strolled out into the gathering dusk.

His two Mexican pals were back in their position on the other side of the street, doing what they did best. He jerked his head as he left the hotel entrance and walked down the sidewalk in the direction Logan had taken. A few yards and he turned into one of the hundreds of bars that proliferated in the area and waited at the counter.

'Rum and nothing,' said the tall Mexican, and jerked his thumb at his friend. 'He'll have Coke with his.' His sidekick neither agreed nor disagreed but slouched in beside him, perched his bottom on a stool and laid his arms across the counter. He looked as if he were about to go to sleep. This must have been the hardest couple of hours' work he'd done since crawling on his belly across the border.

'I thought you tough guys normally drank tequila?' said Hagen.

'We normally only drink piss. That's all we can afford, but as you're buying—' The Mexican shrugged. This was

363

what it was like, it was the way of life. 'I'll have another one in a minute.'

Hagen paid for the drinks, picked up his Scotch and went over to a table in the corner. There was a quick scramble for who was going to sit with his back to the wall, but when that was settled and Hagen took the safe chair they closed ranks and, with their heads close, but not too close – chilli has a long memory and likes to announce itself at regular intervals – they got down to the second part of the business.

'It was worth more than a hundred—'

'It's worth fuck-all so far – and that's all you've got until you persuade me to part with the other half. Let's hear the story, Gonzales!'

'My name's not Gonzales!'

'It is now! Go on—'

'He was expecting a tail—'

'Which is why you got the job and I didn't.'

'He's good at losing people. He was suspicious.'

'OK – just cut out the crap. I can see you're the best little tracker in the county and you deserve a lot more than I'm paying, but if you don't soon stop telling me what a clever little fucker you are I'm going to call off the deal and go and waste my time some place else. *Comprende*, dickhead?'

The Mexican smiled. He had an excellent mouthful of large white teeth. Years ago he'd have made stand-in for Ricardo Montalban. 'He booked into a third-rate hotel in Pilsen – Fourteenth. Room Thirty-four, fourth floor, no phone, no bath, no shower – a cheap shit house—' He studied Hagen's face for effect but got nothing. He continued, 'Rino's Hotel.'

'What name did he register in as?'

The smiling Mexican held Hagen's eyes and turned his hand over and rubbed his thumb against the first two fingers. He said nothing.

Hagen took the other half of the bill from his top pocket, showed it to the Mexican, placed it on the table and put his hand over it.

'What name did he register in as?'

'Another fifty.'

'D'you want a smack in the mouth?'

The Mexican showed his lovely teeth again. 'Twenty.'

Hagen took out a ten and placed it under his hand with the half hundred-dollar bill.

'James Goddard. And for another ten I'll tell you something interesting that wasn't in the deal.'

Hagen did the business again.

'He told the guy at the reception that he was expecting an express packet and that the guy was to sign for it and hold it for him—'

'How did you hear all that going on?'

'We Mexicans are as thick as shit, gringo. Even if we're not Mexicans we're still as thick as shit provided we've got a bit of spic blood and no Yankee attitudes. The guy at the reception could have been my brother – he didn't like the Yankee who looked as though he could afford better than a scuzzy flophouse.'

Hagen lifted his hand and the money disappeared as if by magic. The Mexican could have made a living at it. 'Thanks.' Hagen got up and made to leave. 'What about my other drink?'

Hagen was about to tell him to piss off, and then changed his mind. He might need him again before the end of the story. 'Sure. You always in the same place?'

'I can be – for a price.'

'No thanks. I don't want a full-time employee, I'd end up having to pay social security for you. If you're there tomorrow, same place, I might be able to use you, otherwise—' Hagen smiled into his face. 'You got a contact?'

The Mexican scribbled on a piece of tissue he dragged out of a wad jammed into a much-handled glass tumbler. 'Ring this number, tell her where you want me.'

'She'll understand "Gonzales"?'

'She'll understand anything I tell her to understand.' He grinned broadly again. 'I like Gonzales – that will be my new name.'

'Sure it will,' said Hagen. 'What was that drink you wanted?'

Ricardo Montalban was so surprised he almost forgot what it was he was drinking.

Chapter 45

Hagen finished his eggs and bacon, wiped his lips with a paper napkin, screwed it up into a ball and swung round on his swivel seat at the bar of the diner. Logan had had nothing except three cigarettes and two large cups of black coffee.

'Jim,' said Hagen as he poured more coffee into his cup and lit a cigarette, 'it's crunch time. Some time today I've got to pass on the word that you're here safe and sound and want to talk a little business. Our friends in DC are not known for their infinite patience. They've probably already taken their nails down to the cuticles waiting for you to say something. So, what d'you say? I give the word?'

They were the only two people in the place. It was understandable. The eggs greasy and the bacon soft – it was one of those places deserving of one unlucky visit only. But it had privacy. The girl doing the eggs wasn't interested; it showed in her manner and the product. Hagen discounted her and spoke to Logan in a normal voice. She probably wouldn't have understood what he was talking about if he'd called her over and bellowed in her ear. But not so Logan. He thought for a moment, then in a very quiet voice said, 'OK. Tell 'em I'm ready to talk to Graver.' He stubbed his cigarette out aggressively. 'Just Graver, Hagen. I'm not interested in anyone else. I'm not holding a meeting or a conference – just Robert Graver and me. And that means not Hagen, either.'

'Got you, Jim.' Hagen leaned forward so that he could

366

look into Logan's face. 'But tell me one thing – why don't you make a run for it now? You're in the States, you're home and dry. I presume you've got your gambling chips all counted and neatly stacked and accessible?' Hagen waited. Nothing came, not even a change of expression. He tried again. 'Why sit around Chicago waiting, for whatever, when you could vanish into the great unknown?'

Logan looked him in the face as he lit another cigarette. He sucked on it hungrily. He didn't look very friendly. 'Good question, Hagen. But if I wanted to go running for the rest of my life I could have done it somewhere else. I'm fed up, son. I'm fed up with seeing smartasses like you every time I look over my shoulder. I don't want to be on anybody's list. I want to talk to Graver and then I want to crawl into the woodwork somewhere where no one's interested in Jim Logan.'

'You trust Graver to leave you alone once you've let him see your cards?'

'He's not a fool, Hagen. Once he's seen the disaster scenario, he'll be happy to let things stay under the blanket.'

'You're going to show him what you've got?'

'I might give him a page or two.'

'Isn't that a bit risky?'

'Not the way I see it.'

'You've got the stuff here?'

'Don't be so goddamn stupid! D'you think I'd tell you if I had?'

Hagen smiled, stubbed out his half-smoked cigarette and lit another one. 'It was worth a try.'

'Was it fuck!' But Logan wasn't smiling. He rolled off the stool, studied the chit under the plate and flicked it along the counter to Hagen. 'See you later.'

'Where're you going?'

'I said I'll see you later.'

Hagen remained where he was until Logan had left the eater, then went back to the hotel. He hauled the holdall from out of the cupboard, dragged out the bundle of dirty fatigues he'd worn on the trip out of Saigon and unfolded it. Aubrey St Clair Smith's Browning was wrapped in a pair of dirty underpants. He checked the magazine. He'd replaced the rounds Simon had casually ground into the dirt in Malaysia and, contented, he jammed the weapon into his trouser band.

No hurry. He caught a cruising taxi near the hotel and had it take him south to Pilsen. He paid off the cab on the corner of Wabash and 14th and strolled west until he spotted the dingy entrance with the dingy sign to the dingiest-lodging house in the street. Rino's. It was in between two cheap Mexican cafés and opposite were two more. Hagen felt like one of the Magnificent Seven; he could almost taste the air, and the atmosphere.

He crossed the road and went into one of the eating shops opposite and ordered a cup of coffee. It was good. He sat away from the window but facing it, and waited. It didn't take long. He was just about three-quarters of the way down the cup of coffee when James Logan came along the sidewalk from the opposite direction and walked straight into Rino's. He came out immediately and waited at the entrance, gazing unconcernedly in the direction he'd just come. Logan might be getting old, thought Hagen, but he still played the game. He must have thought he was back in the old days and looking for black caps, boots and swastikas. Logan waited another few moments and, satisfied, turned back into the hotel and disappeared from view.

Hagen gave him ten minutes. He didn't come out again. His package must have arrived. Hagen paid for his coffee and walked across the road to Rino's.

Reception looked up from his dirty magazine as Hagen strolled across the minute, and very dirty, foyer and towards the stairs. There was no lift. Hagen showed him his teeth, nodded, and pointed upward. He didn't stop to chat or gossip. The receptionist went back to his magazine. He wasn't interested; the guy seemed to know what he wanted and where he was going. None of his business.

Hagen walked briskly up the four flights of stairs and stopped in front of Room 34. He brought the Browning out from his waistband and tapped on the door.

'Whaddya want?' The door was paper thin. Logan hadn't even had to raise his voice.

Hagen put his lips near the door jamb and said, '*Señor!*'

Logan repeated his demand.

Hagen said '*Señor!*' again.

Logan gave in first. The door opened.

Hagen stroked the side of Logan's chin with the Browning, eased him back into the room and closed the door behind him with his foot. No words. Logan had a look of resignation; it was almost as if he'd been expecting this. Trouble – it was never going to be easy, even now.

'Turn round, Jim.'

Logan met Hagen's eyes. There was nothing in them; nothing he could work on. He tried a tentative 'Look, Hagen, I think we ought to talk a—'

'Just turn round, Jim.'

Logan shook his head. Whether in disappointment, sadness or just fear Hagen couldn't quite make out. It wasn't going to make any difference which of those it was. Logan's hands were still hanging at his side; Hagen, with an abrupt, unsignalled lunge, punched his left shoulder and, as Logan swung round with the blow, went up on to his toes and brought the Browning upward and, with an expert's eye, hit the unbalanced Logan hard just behind the ear with the full force of the weapon.

Logan went down like a stunned bullock. He remained on his knees for a second while Hagen measured him up for another one. Same place. Logan collapsed flat on his face, his knees drawn up, and lay there on the grubby, dusty, worn carpet as if he'd decided suddenly to take a little early morning siesta.

Hagen stepped over him and looked at the opened parcel on the bed. It was full of sheets of paper; some typewritten, some handwritten; some were documents – originals. Whatever it was there was a lot of it. He roughly rewrapped it, stuffed the Browning back into his trouser band, bent down and lifted Logan onto the bed. He rested his head on Logan's chest and listened to his breathing. It sounded all right, a little choked and laboured, but there was definitely something coming in and going out.

Hagen turned him over onto his face, whipped the belt from around his trousers and bound his hands. He stripped the one pillow of its covering and used that to tie his feet, then, making sure Logan wasn't going to suffocate, went out to the corridor, spotted what he was looking for and, leaving the door ajar, tiptoed down to the landing and picked up the pay-phone.

The woman barely understood English; she didn't speak it either. 'Can you tell Gonzales to ring me at—' He managed to decipher the number among the scrawls and wriggles around the board above the pay-phone. He didn't know whether she understood, he didn't even know whether she could write numbers, but he was encouraged that she managed a definite '*Conthaleth? Sí!*' before slamming the phone down in his ear.

Logan was still unconscious, and Hagen had just finished his second cigarette since putting down the phone when it rang. Nobody else seemed interested. There was no slamming of doors or the scurry of feet hurrying to get to it. He was the only person in the building, if indeed there were any more, who made any attempt to stop the high-pitched clamouring.

It was Gonzales. 'You got any doctor friends?' asked Hagen.

Gonzales was very quick on the uptake. He didn't need explanation, he didn't ask questions – unless it was 'how much?' – and he had connections everywhere. It was Mexico in Chicago – us against them. He made it sound a very normal request. 'Where shall I bring him?'

'Rino's. My friend wants a good long sleep; one of about a day and a half. He doesn't want to know anything about what's going on.'

'Cost you, gringo!'

'As soon as you can—' Hagen dropped the phone onto its hook while he consulted a small notebook. He lifted the receiver again and dialled a local, Chicago, number. When the metallic answerphone voice stopped talking he spelt out his code-number and listened to the keys being tapped. After a moment a real voice sounded in his ear.

'I need a safe house,' Hagen told it, 'thirty-six hours, say two days, not too far from O'Hare—'

'Take the north road from the airport then head for Schaumberg. About six miles you hit West Newington. Carry on through; second crossroad out go right then turn into Cutler's Farm. You'll be expected.'

'Got a car?'

'Where d'you want it?'

'This side of Newington?'

'You got it. Chevy station wagon, dark blue, maroon slash, Illinois plates.'

'Thanks.'

Gonzales's doctor friend was an unshaven, long-haired stretcher-pusher at one of the downtown hospitals. He didn't even look like a doctor.

'Does he know anything about medicine?' asked Hagen.

'Don't ask,' said Gonzales. 'He wants two hundred.'

'What for?'

Gonzales gave his friend the teeth. 'Tell him, Doctor.'

'You want this man asleep for day and a half.' He reached into his pocket and brought out a rolled-up plastic bag. He opened it and peered in. 'Omnopon,' he pronounced with difficulty, 'and scopolamine.' He emptied the contents onto the table and picked up a plastic syringe and a sealed packet of needles. 'I will give him first course, you will 'ave to carry on from there—' He narrowed his eyes at Hagen. 'Every four hours, before 'e wake up. That is what you pay two hundred for. Deal?'

'Go to work, Doctor,' said Hagen, and handed him four fifty-dollar bills. 'Can you find your own way home?'

Gonzales and his friend laughed into each other's faces. Hagen didn't see the funny side of it. 'I need a little bit more help, Gonzales – you free for a couple of hours?'

'Sure. You wanna negotiate before or after?'

'Is that all you ever think about – money?'

'Five hundred for the day.' Even Gonzales's doctor friend looked up from Logan's bare arm in surprise at Gonzales's audacity, but didn't linger; the 'om and scop' was still moving slowly into Logan's vein.

'Two hundred and fifty for the half-day that's left.'

'Plus one hundred for the car—'

'Fifty.'

'OK. And you fill her up.'

The youth pulled the needle out of Logan's arm and

wrapped the syringe up again with the empty phials and the unused needles. 'Don't forget, every four hours—' He didn't wait for Hagen's acknowledgement; he winked at Gonzales, showed him the flat of his hand and was gone.

'Where's your car?' asked Hagen.

'Over the road, outside Tomasito's.' Gonzales watched Hagen untie the unconscious Logan without curiosity. 'You want to carry him out?'

'Got a better idea?'

'You should have asked my friend. For another few dollars he would have provided a stretcher, but—' He looked out of the window. 'We'll pretend he's drunk, eh?'

'At eleven in the morning?'

'Around here, gringo? Any time! Nobody'll notice.'

Gonzales was right.

They carried and dragged Logan between them and made him comfortable on the back seat of Gonzales's battered Oldsmobile. Nobody gave them a second glance. Twenty-five minutes later, under Hagen's direction, Gonzales crawled into a picnic area just outside West Newington. There was one other vehicle already there – a Chevy station wagon, dark blue, maroon slash, Illinois plates, just like the man had said.

The driver, behind a dark smoked windshield, sat unmoving. All that could be seen of him was a sheepskin-covered elbow resting on the open window ledge being, every so often, massaged by a gentle cloud of cigarette smoke which came from within the cab.

Hagen uncurled himself from the springless passenger seat of Gonzales's Oldsmobile and, with his hands clearly visible at his side, walked slowly and openly towards the station wagon. The face, framed by the upturned sheepskin collar, was flat and unfriendly. The man only moved once, to transfer the cigarette from his hand to his mouth.

'You wanna take me to Cutler's Farm?' Hagen found no difficulty in being equally unfriendly. He didn't wait for a reply. The man wouldn't be there if he didn't. 'Come and give me a hand. I've got a fourteen-stone parcel with no legs.' He turned his back on the cowboy and returned to Gonzales.

'What d'you make the bill, Gonzales?' he said.

'We agreed three. You didn't give me gas, but as we're now friends I'll let you off that.'

'You're all heart, Gonzales. Here—' He rolled five one-hundred dollar bills into a tube and stuck them in Gonzales's jacket pocket. Gonzales didn't need to count them; he could feel what he'd got by instinct. He nodded seriously.

'I'm going to miss you, gringo.'

'Sure you are. So's your bank manager! *Vaya con Dios*, asshole!'

Chapter 46

The CIA's Chicago safe house was a replica of Ashford Farm in Maryland. Hagen had no difficulty making himself at home.

With the help of the taciturn minder, he carried Logan to the top-security wing at the back of the house. It had no windows; the vents were double-tiered and secure. Everything else had the appearance of a normal, comfortable room. A large wood-burning stove, standing in an open fireplace, was already blazing like a jet fighter on full boost – any minute now it looked as though the pressure building up inside would take them all off on a quick trip round the countryside. A large settee, deep, with a full back, made the ideal resting place for an unconscious man full of morphine-based omnopon and scopolamine. Which reminded Hagen – he glanced at his watch. Another couple of hours before Logan was due for his next dose. Time to kill. He inspected the cupboard in the corner and, as expected, found the usual quantity of high-quality booze. He poured himself a large Remy Martin, lit a cigarette, and sat beside the phone. Red for careful; green for secure – a direct line to Langley.

'Two nine zero—' he said into the green one.

'Graver.'

'Sir,' said Hagen, 'it's all arranged. Logan is waiting here. He is prepared to negotiate. He wants direct contact with

374

you and feels that this thing could well work out to every-one's advantage.'

Graver wasted no time. 'Has he got the stuff?'

'No—'

'What the—!'

'I've got it.'

'Everything?'

'I don't know. It needs checking by an expert.'

'Forget that. I'm coming down myself. I don't want to hear that our man has been exposed to any "experts". You follow me, Hagen?'

'Loud and clear, sir.' He cast his eyes over the unconscious man on the settee. 'Why don't I just terminate his contract and bring the stuff I've got to you?'

'Don't even think about it, Hagen! You wait there and sit in the man's lap until I arrive—' There was a pause. Hagen could almost hear buzzers being buzzed, bells being rung and airplane engines warming up. 'I'll be with you this evening. Tell Jenkins to meet the aircraft. He knows what to do. Don't let Logan, or his papers, out of your sight.'

'Goodbye, sir—' But Hagen was wasting his words. The phone was dead. Graver was probably already running for the aircraft.

Hagen decided to let Logan sleep it off. Forget the stuff Gonzales's friend had given him, the old man had had enough rough treatment for one day; that was the physical. The cerebral was on its way; they were going to give old Jim's brain a nasty battering.

He took the cocked Browning out of his belt and placed it on the table at his side. He made himself comfortable by the fire with the bottle of Cognac and a couple of packs of free Lucky Strike and opened up Jim Logan's life insurance policy. He was still engrossed in it two hours later when he glanced up and saw that Logan's eyes were open.

'Evening, Jim,' he said casually. 'Had a good sleep?'

Logan swallowed and nearly threw up his early morning coffees.

'You bastard!'

He ran the flavour round his fur-coated mouth and brought his memory into play. It didn't work. It was too long ago. 'OK, you motherfucker – what's that you've shoved into me?'

'The doctor said it was om and scop, whatever that may be. Mean anything to you?'

'What's going on?' Logan still wasn't with it. His brain wasn't doing its stuff. He felt he'd like to curl up and go back to sleep, but he was willing himself to stay awake. And his eyes were improving. He recognised the remains of the packet on the floor beside Hagen's chair. He blinked and forced some recognition out of his eyes. There were two piles – a lifetime's collection of insurance. He felt his hands. They weren't tied. His feet? He moved them about. Hagen was taking a risk – or was he?

Hagen read his mind. 'It's all right, Jim, I had thought to put you out for another five hours or so, but I was a bit worried about your ticker. The doctor said the stuff he poured into you was fairly strong. Didn't you use it on the Kraut in the good old days?' Hagen shrugged; he didn't think Logan would want to talk about the good old days – not just at the moment. 'Never mind. I've been on to Langley – Graver. He told me it would be a good thing if you got yourself shot trying to escape – once I'd told him I'd got all your stuff here. And, of course, being a loyal servant of the Company, I am always prepared to do as I'm told. See?' He picked up the Browning and held it up for Logan to inspect. 'Loaded, cocked and safety off. Take a chance if you feel like it.'

Logan studied the younger man for several minutes. 'What are you going to do?'

Hagen smiled mirthlessly. 'First of all pour you a large Scotch and then prepare you for your meeting with the lord and master. Graver's coming this evening. Wants an urgent talk with you. If Reilly's in town he'll bring him – and then we'll all be in the shit!'

'Why?'

'Reilly's one of your sort, Jim. A hard, calculating bastard with a lotta miles on his clock and enough scalps hanging from his belt to cover the wall in the Oval Office. Not good news is Reilly. Anyway—' He stood up, picked the Browning from the side table and walked over to the drinks cupboard.

He poured about a half a pint of Black Label into a glass, dropped a couple of ice cubes in it and, approaching Logan from behind, reached over his shoulder and placed the glass on the table beside him. He went back to his place by the fire and opened the door of the furnace with his foot. He leaned back out of range of the surge of heat and picked up one of the bundles of documents.

'This, Jim,' he said, looking at it and shaking his head, 'is pure dynamite. I can understand old Graver getting grey hair knowing this was sitting around somewhere waiting to be picked up by the world's media.' He stuck the rim of the brandy glass to his lip and up-ended it. 'I don't know what it's going to do to Graver but, Jesus Christ, Jim, it makes my ass twitch—' He studied Logan's eyes. 'If it's kosher, that is?'

Logan watched him but made no response.

'I'll take that as an affirmative.' Hagen glanced down again. 'You mean to tell me that, for all these years, I, among others, on behalf of the US Government, have been shuffling around helping the fucking Chinese Tongs make a nice time for themselves on drugs in the States? Big deal, Jim, but very, very naughty, even for us. You quite sure about all this?'

Logan broke his silence. His mouth still felt as though it belonged to someone else, but he stuck with it. 'It's all there,' he said. 'You don't need me to interpret it for you—' He stopped talking, gagged over a mouthful of Black Label and studied Hagen's face keenly. 'You interested in being made a partner in the firm?'

'What're you offering?'

'I've got a bit put away. Say a figure.'

'Money?'

'As much as you could handle.'

Hagen never really thought about it. 'Doesn't even cover the openers, Jim. Not with this stuff. If Graver has any idea what you've got here he'd stop everything else that's going, spend every penny in the kitty and turn every CIA employee who ever was onto the street looking for you and me. No thanks! But I tell you what I am going to do—' Before Logan could move, before the shock and horror could register in his eyes, Hagen leaned forward and, with both hands, shovelled Logan's life insurance policy into the furnace and closed the doors.

Logan sat mesmerised by the roaring flames coming from behind the fireproof glass door. The roar of the paper being turned into ash sounded like an elephant's howl of anguish. He just sat and stared, then slowly brought the glass of whisky back up to his lips. He looked fifteen years older. He looked exactly like that Italian marathon runner – he'd got to the winning tape and had had the prize dashed from his hand.

It took some time, another two or three large swallows of neat whisky, and then he managed to put a few words together. His voice had lost some of its strength. 'I had you figured for an asshole, Hagen, but I didn't think you would want to earn a look up Bob Graver's rectum over my coffin. Thanks, pal!'

Hagen watched him for a moment, then nodded. 'You're a man of perception, Jim. Couldn't you tell? I've always been a guy for ass-licking. Now you just sit there and let your blood pressure settle and say to yourself, "Well, at least he's left me a few bargaining chips"—' He touched the other pile of paper with the tip of his shoe. 'Maybe you can persuade Mr Graver that this is sufficient to earn you a few more years of life.'

Logan shook his head. 'The stuff you've just tossed on the fire is the only thing that has held Graver from telling you to put a bullet in my head. You've taken the one thing. This . . .' He pointed his chin at the pile of paper, 'is the best intelligence he, or anyone else that matters, is likely to receive in a lifetime. It'll send him to the White House if he wants it in a few years. That's the biggest intelligence coup in history, but there's nothing to say how it was bought; nothing once my head goes on the block.'

'Why don't we wait and see? Another drop of Scotch?'

Sam Reilly came through the door first. Graver was right behind him. They were both wrapped up for subzero but within seconds of entering the sweltering, overheated room their coats came off and they stood together studying Jim Logan, a look of curiosity on both their faces.

'Get me a large Jack Daniels, Hagen,' growled Reilly. 'Neat, nothing with it.'

'How about you, sir?' Hagen was hovering. He looked every inch Bertie Wooster's Jeeves. 'The same?'

'Scotch – a large one. Jesus, but it's bloody cold out there! OK—' He dispensed with the friendly observations and sat down and began wiping the mist from his glasses. He'd just carried them in from subzero to subtropical and they'd almost cracked with the excitement. He peered short-sightedly at Logan. 'You've been a fucking nuisance, Logan! I knew you were going to be a fucking nuisance when I met you in Malaya!' He lost interest in Logan for a second and turned to receive his drink from Jeeves.

'What've you got for us, then, Hagen?' Before Hagen could reply, he followed it up with, 'You haven't looked at that stuff, have you?' He stared myopically at the pack of documents by Hagen's chair. He wasn't the only one. Reilly's big head had been studying the sheets of paper on the floor ever since he'd sat down. That was his future. It was lying on the carpet for anyone to pick up. Secrets, secrets, secrets – Jesus Christ! But he controlled the urge to throw himself on them as if they were a live grenade and the room was full of his soldiers. He sipped his drink without tasting it and left it all to the man who was soon going to be the ex-Director of the CIA.

'No, sir,' replied Hagen evenly. He didn't appear to be overawed by the weight of brass in the room – polite and respectful, but definitely not overawed. 'I opened the parcel when it was delivered to Logan and what you see there on the floor is everything that was in it. Perhaps you'd like to look for yourself, sir?'

Hagen avoided meeting Logan's eyes. He glanced in his direction briefly and was pleased to see that Logan hadn't yet lost the art of keeping his thoughts and feelings off his face. He knelt down, gathered the sheets of documents together and dumped them on Graver's scrawny knees.

'If you don't mind, sir, I'll get myself another drink while you're checking them. Can I give Logan something?'

But they weren't interested in the civilities. Reilly had joined Graver on the arm of his chair and was staring down as Graver turned over the pages, first carefully, then faster, and then with a sort of controlled anxiety. Hagen left them to it.

'Another Scotch?' he asked Logan, and stared at him pointedly.

'Thanks. About the same size as the other one.'

Hagen didn't acknowledge. He turned away just as Graver's thick lenses rose from the paper on his knee and centred on a point just between Hagen's shoulder blades.

'There's something missing,' he said. There was disbelief in his voice.

Hagen turned. His face was a picture of innocence. 'Like I said, sir, that's what came in the packet. I, naturally, asked Logan if this was everything and he said that was not for me to know. It was to be the basis of the negotiation he would argue with you. This is why he stayed and didn't try to run for it. It was to discuss with you the provision of his security.'

'You seem to know an awful lot about this, Hagen,' interjected Reilly, gruffly. 'How close have you got to this man?'

'I've been breathing down his neck one way or another since you sent me to look for him, General, but he's never discussed his affairs with me. You asked me to kill him. I could have, quite easily, then Mr Graver rescinded that order and told me to keep him alive. I've done that. You told me to make him disappear. I did that. I've done everything you ordered me to do. In addition you asked me to find out whether he'd made any insurance. I found that out and persuaded him to hand this stuff over to you. He's been cracked across the head, threatened by me, tied up and drugged and brought here. What more did you expect me to do, sir? Have I read this? No, I haven't. Do I know whether there's any more? No, I—'

'OK! OK! Calm down and let's go through this rationally,' said Graver, taking up the reins of office again. 'You know the man better than any of us. Give me a few reasoned thoughts.'

'He arranged for his daughter to bring the stuff out of

Bangkok. She did that very successfully. She fooled an old British expat to sail her out of the country, but it went wrong after she collected the stuff.'

'Whaddya mean, went wrong?'

'Some Tong agents traced her to KL. They killed her.'

The two senior CIA men turned their heads simultaneously and looked at Logan. Hagen thought for a moment that one of them was going to say how sorry he was about it. But he'd miscalculated.

'She must have split the stuff into two packets,' said Graver, thoughtfully. 'Where did this one come from?'

'It didn't say, sir. It was a plain wrapper, no return address, just to him, special delivery, at a hotel in Chicago—'

'Where's the wrapper?' asked Graver, his thick lenses surveying the floor where the paper had been stacked.

'I threw it on the fire, sir.'

'Why would you do that?' asked Reilly suspiciously.

'No reason, sir. I just screwed it up, the fire doors were open, I flipped it in without thought.'

'Hmmm.' Reilly wasn't pleased. 'Where are we, Director?'

'Can I make a suggestion, sir?' said Hagen, politely.

'What?'

'Well, I've spent a lot of time with Logan, sir, and one or two things he's let drop make me think we're on a pretty good thing here—'

Reilly and Graver stared at him as if he were a raving lunatic. But they did nothing. They let him go on. They could have been in shock.

'That stuff' – Hagen jerked his chin at Graver's knees – 'I understand, gives us a total network of intelligence sources throughout the Far East. Logan said the Chinese Tong people in Bangkok were in a position to close the whole apparatus down; but now, with this in our hands, they could try, but the people they've placed for us would have to deal with you or go to the wall themselves. That pile of paper is worth a sackful of diamonds to us. I also understand from Logan that there's a lot of other stuff that came from his sources in Hanoi, via the KGB, dealing with the possibility of subversion here, in the States. This alone, I gather, would be political dynamite for the good guys if, some time in the foreseeable future, one or more of the names on those lists put himself forward for nomination to any office higher than shit-house cleaner to the White House guardroom. With stuff like that the CIA, in the future, could ensure that the wrong man, a man who'd been marked by the KGB as being a leading figure in the anti-war-in-Vietnam brigade, anyone who had been acknowledged by the KGB as a potential ally, would never, at least for the next generation or so, have an opportunity to try for the highest, or any other serious, government position . . .'

Graver and Reilly exchanged glances. They'd already come to a similar conclusion after a brief survey of Logan's papers. Reilly's eyes settled on Hagen's. 'Anything else about sucking eggs you'd like to tell your grannies?' he grunted. But his expression had relaxed. Hagen was making the right-sounding noises for him.

Hagen accepted his invitation. 'Well, sir – if there is anything else that may be detrimental to the CIA's position—'

'You sure you haven't seen something that you shouldn't have, Hagen?' It was Graver's turn again.

'No, sir, but as I was saying, if there was something else, surely Logan could be trusted to make damn sure that nothing came out to nullify all this. If there are any skeletons in the closet, and if Logan should know where that closet is, surely he should be allowed to hold on to that information – say for a specified term, like—' He looked Logan up and down like a horse dealer assessing the life left in a remount. '—Twenty years on the written promise that his will stipulates every document or paper in his possession, or that he has access to, be destroyed without examination.'

'You sound like a fucking sea lawyer to me, Hagen!' said Reilly. 'Have you finished?'

'There's only the alternative.'

'Your version? Tell us about it.'

'We could take Logan out and drop him over the cliff. And then sit around for ever wondering whether he'd dummied us with this lot—' Hagen stopped for a moment and studied his attentive audience, then gave a wry, humourless grin. 'Well, not for ever – only until the time limit he's set comes and goes and the *Washington Post* brings out a special edition of the back-up copy of how the CIA bought its information from the capitals of South-East Asia between 1957 and 1975 . . .'

'You know of a back-up copy?' snapped Reilly.

Hagen shook his head. 'I know less than you about that, sir – only what I've picked up from running in this man's shadow. What we've got here is all that I've seen, which is bad enough,' he conceded. 'But' – he nodded in Logan's direction – 'my experience and assessment of the man is that he wouldn't leave the job half done. Somewhere – somewhere very, very safe – there's gotta be a detailed account of the CIA's arrangements, negotiations and privileges handed to the Bangkok Chinese. Names'll be named, locations pinpointed, the whole depth of eighteen years' conspiracy – using the word guardedly, sir – not to put too fine a point on it.' Hagen was in danger of running away with himself. He brought himself up abruptly and shifted his gaze from the two senior CIA administrators to a po-faced Logan. 'But he's the only one who can answer that. And that's the problem, the way I see it—'

'OK, I've heard enough of that one, Hagen,' said Graver with heavy irony. 'Show me another scenario, one that gives me more confidence in the future based on what you've picked up from this man, running, as you say, in his shadow.' Graver's voice was thick with scepticism. He was head of the CIA, he wasn't a fool. Somehow Logan had screwed them and he'd got this smooth-talking asshole doing a PR job for him. But it was a salvage job he needed, and he wanted both Logan and Smartass to know that he knew. He caught Reilly's eye. He had a good idea what Reilly's inclination was – and it wasn't sitting here listening to a voice from the bottom of the ladder telling him how things should be done. But Reilly kept his mouth shut and his hands wrapped round his glass of Old 79 while Hagen offered them the benefit of his experience.

'The way I read it, sir, Logan just wants to come in and put his head down. He doesn't want to cause trouble to you, the Company, the country or himself. It makes sense to me. He's given you everything you need to keep this country firm and stable during the next few years when, as we all know, the bottom's going to drop out of Vietnam and all hell is going to break loose. Other than to preserve his life, there is no reason for him to bring out the stuff you were expecting. As far as the Chinese are concerned, and the Viets as well, Contractor is dead. They have no incentive to scrabble around among the ashes here. They'll all go home and leave us to it. Logan can disappear but he must have your word that his physical integrity will not be jeopardised. If you don't give him this word we'd need a thousand agents to keep track of him and make sure he remains intact whether he's got anything or not. If he has, he's been in the business far too long to leave it somewhere where we can pick it up. Wherever it is it's safe. You can relax, and so can he. I always thought there was a chance of doing something about him through his daughter. If we could have taken her we could have used her as a lever. But—' Hagen shrugged; he still hadn't met Logan's eyes. He wondered what he made of it all.

But he'd found a home for his theories in Graver's mind. Or so it seemed from the way the thick, impenetrable lenses locked onto his face and remained there while the brain behind them worked out the ramifications. But Hagen didn't squirm. He sat and gave Graver back as good as he got; nothing insolent, nothing for them to take exception to, and nothing to show the bottle bottoms what was going on behind his own flat eyes. It seemed to go on for ever. The silence; the muted roaring of the wood burner; the overpowering heat of the unrestricted wall-to-wall, ceiling-to-ceiling central heating; and above all the four men looking at each other like experienced poker players, but not a card among them. Graver broke it all up with the first call. Hagen kept his sigh of relief to himself. He'd won.

'Why don't you take Mr Logan outside and have a look at the roses while General Reilly and I have a little private conversation? Give us about ten minutes—' Always the gent; always polite, particularly when he lost a big hand. 'And then I'd like to have a private word with Mr Logan.'

Sure, why not? Hagen was already on his feet. He didn't smile. His face remained set and respectful. They were all calling each other Mister now – all of them, that is, except dogsbody Hagen. But it looked like Logan was off the hook. He could now go out in the world somewhere and wait for his grandchildren to be born. Take him out to see the roses! Sure – half past two in the fucking morning, minus six degrees and a howling blizzard hissing in from a black Lake Michigan and the nearest fucking rose is a thousand miles to the south. *But what does it matter?* Hagen nodded to Logan and led the way.

They huddled in the frozen conservatory with its windows opaque from ice, the ice shivering under the onslaught of the snow that was flung at it like handfuls of mud and made about the same noise. Logan, whose blood was still working at Bangkok levels, began shivering immediately and didn't stop until his corpuscles got used to it. Hagen shoved a lighted Lucky Strike between his blue lips. The smoke helped, but not so as you'd notice.

'That was an interesting performance, Hagen. Why?'

'Why what?'

'You know what I mean. You don't owe me anything. Why d'you go through all that fucking rigmarole?'

'You really want to know? OK. Until I read the stuff that got burnt I was quite happy for things to take their course. But you and I both know the damage it would have caused. Fuck it, man! Your revelations about the Touming Guanxi narcotic deals would blow the CIA apart. It would mean the end of the one organisation that can hold this country together when the big chopper falls. Can you imagine what would happen to America without a CIA? It'd fall apart in anarchy. I don't want that to happen. For good or bad we need the CIA. Why did I go through that rigmarole? That's why I did it.'

'You sure that's all?'

Hagen thought for a moment, then, for the first time in his adult life, showed that somewhere inside a rock-hard shell was a feeling. It was a brave admission. 'You saved my life back in Phuket. I couldn't think of any bastard who would even consider doing that, let alone risking his own to do it—'

'So you owe me one. It was no big deal.'

'It wasn't even that. The thing that got me was that when

you tried to buy your way out in that crummy shit house of a hotel you didn't attempt to cash that in. You could have said, "Look, you bastard, you owe me! I saved your fucking life." You were desperate. If I'd been in your position I wouldn't have given it two thoughts, no hesitation. Why didn't you?'

'Would it have made any difference?'

Hagen thought about it, then grinned. 'At the time? I doubt it!'

Epilogue

Paris, May 1997

Aubrey St Clair Smith committed what was for him an unforgivable lapse of manners. For a few seconds he took his eyes off the beautiful woman sitting opposite him in the Café Voltaire on Paris's elegant Quai d'Orsay and glanced briefly at the two men who came through the entrance. They were Americans, no doubt about it. There was something about Americans, particularly those in Paris, which betrayed instantly their nationality. One of them caught St Clair Smith's glance, brief as it was, and then followed his companion into the depths of the restaurant and out of St Clair Smith's sight. There had been no recognition in his eyes.

St Clair Smith's companion continued talking. She hadn't noticed a thing. She was a woman; she was spending more time inspecting and analysing the women at the other tables and paying them more attention than she was her elderly partner. She was one of those women who could look you in the eye, listen to every word you were saying but not see you nor hear what you were saying. It didn't worry St Clair Smith. He had *his* conventions; he lived by those and gave her his full attention. But with the entrance of the two Americans something ticked in the back of his mind and, unusually, he allowed his brain to pick up where his eyes had left off.

And then he remembered.

Hagen. Mark Hagen. Still fit and menacing, not an ounce of flab, his hair now tinged with a little iron grey. It suited him. But it didn't soften his features, quite the opposite; there were still no laughter lines around his mouth – something he was never going to acquire now – and his jawline looked as firm and unyielding as it ever had.

St Clair Smith had taken it all in in the one fleeting moment of eye contact – a twenty-year-older Mark Hagen had walked into the Café Voltaire in Paris and hadn't recognised him. St Clair Smith was, for a moment, annoyed. After all, a man of thirty something changes out of all recognition in twenty years; in the same period of time a man of fifty doesn't change at all – he just gets older. Perhaps Hagen had a reason. Perhaps he was still working. But it still rankled.

When he returned to his hotel, St Clair Smith poured himself a large Cognac and sat at the Directoire secretaire while he turned the leaves of a well-thumbed crocodile-skin address book. When he found what he was looking for he picked up the telephone and asked the operator to make the connection. He sat back in the heavily gilded, embroidered Louis XIVth chair, sipped his Cognac meditatively and waited for the phone to ring.

The melodious tinkle brought him back from a visit to the past.

'Lyndy,' he said without preliminaries. 'Can you trace an American for me? Gamesman of twenty years ago, could still be active.'

'I don't know why it is, Aubrey, that I always expect romance from a call from Paris and, instead, all I get is you – never mind! What's his name?'

'Hagen. Mark Hagen. Probably CIA. Can do?'

'I can but try. D'you want to tell me why?'

'Can I pass on that?'

'Sure. How urgent is this?'

'Shall I hang on?'

'I'll give you a call tomorrow. Did the lady say the Hotel Meurice?'

'Naturally.'

'What's your interest in this item, Aubrey?'

'None – now. Goodnight, darling.'

It had to be a long, convoluted exercise, with nothing given, nothing taken, nothing told – not without a struggle. 'Hagen? Hagen who?' *Try this. Try that. Try the other.* 'OK. Gimme a name—' *St Clair Smith.* 'Smith? Don't make me laugh!' *Aubrey St Clair Smith.* 'Now that really is hysterical! Where?' *Paris.* 'Paris, France? Gimme a number.' *Hotel Meurice.* 'No promise, Lyndy. See ya, honey!'

At four o'clock the next afternoon the receptionist saw Aubrey St Clair Smith enter the lift and kept the caller waiting until she estimated that St Clair Smith would be in his suite and sufficiently relaxed. It was a reception desk of the very highest quality.

'I set my stopwatch on you, Aubrey,' said Hagen. 'I didn't think it would take too long.' It was almost as though he had just stepped out of St Clair Smith's car at the US embassy, Kuala Lumpur, and then turned and poked his head back through the window. But it wasn't. It was twenty years later. 'D'you want to meet?'

'Fouquets – half past seven?'

No hesitation. The ritual disagreement. 'Make it the Scribe – same time.' Out in the open, nothing to hide.

The meeting wasn't spectacular. Hagen was already at the bar and halfway down a Chivas and ice. 'Same for you?' It took the place of a handshake. 'Long time, Aubrey. Everything settled down now?'

'It had. What are you doing here?'

Hagen studied St Clair Smith's pale blue eyes. Was there a trace of filming over them? Cataracts? Surely not, not Aubrey St Clair Smith, he wouldn't suffer anything as common and ordinary as eye cataracts. Hagen's expression remained neutral. He couldn't be that old. But he looked fit, well covered, good colour. There was nothing wrong with the appearance of Aubrey St Clair Smith.

'Bit of this, and a bit of that, Aubrey. You know what we old soldiers are like – always scavenging, always on the scrounge.'

'So you're still working?'

'Pass.' Hagen sidestepped with a crooked smile. 'You still chunting around Malaysia on that old tub of yours?' He paused for a moment without removing his eyes from St Clair Smith's. 'Talking about old tubs, I often wondered

389

what happened to that guy Krislov – you know the one? The guy with all the cancer scabs – remember?'

'I should think he'd have rotted away by now. Funny, I hadn't thought to ask.'

'You haven't been back to Ban Yit since '75?'

'Many times. But our paths didn't seem to cross. Why d'you ask?'

'No reason.'

Just to let Aubrey St Clair Smith know that Mark Hagen had a bloody good idea what had happened to the man with the cancer scabs and who else was involved. Like underwater explosions, news hovers for years below the surface. But it wasn't important, not after twenty years.

'What about Logan?'

'He went missing in the Cameron Highlands.'

St Clair Smith drained his glass and raised his finger to the bar. Two more glasses were placed before them.

'OK,' St Clair Smith said, 'so we've done our duty. We've pissed around like a couple of Bulldog Drummonds and shown each other that we haven't forgotten all we learnt from the comic books. Now let's talk like a couple of grown-ups. OK?'

Hagen took it in his stride. He looked at his watch. It didn't mean anything; he was trying to work out if there was anything left after twenty years to give away. St Clair Smith caught the gesture. 'How about dinner?'

'I promised my wife—'

'Your what!' Smith was genuinely surprised. Shocked, more like it. 'You're married?'

Hagen nodded, almost shyly. 'And two girls, twins, grown-up, seventeen.'

'It doesn't appear to have softened your demeanour.'

'Thanks. I try not to let my happiness show—' Hagen seemed to come to a decision. 'Come and have dinner with us.'

'I'm not sure—'

But Hagen was determined. 'And I'll tell you what happened to Jim Logan.'

St Clair Smith smiled his acceptance. 'Is he still alive?'

Hagen had to think about it, then conceded, 'Yeah. But

you don't want to know where he is. Changed name, shape, identity; you wouldn't recognise him if he was leaning against the other end of the bar. He's getting on a bit now, wrong end of seventy, but I'm sure he'll be pleased that you remembered him.' He locked his eyes onto St Clair Smith's. 'We close the book on him now, OK?'

'It's been closed since '75, Hagen. Did he get all his stuff back to the States?'

'Every last bit of it. Not only that, he got out clean. His Bangkok Chinese chums declared him dead when nothing was found in the Camerons. It was a good exercise; all down to you and that little fat Chinaman. I never did thank you. Is he still around?'

'Retired.'

'Funny. That's what he told me when I first met him. Give him my regards.'

'He won't remember you.'

'Thanks.'

'How about Logan's daughter? I heard she passed through London as arranged but then she dived into a deep hole. Clever girl. But I did see what she was carrying. If she got that through intact to Logan he wouldn't have had any troubles about living on his pension. Did she make the connection?'

After a moment's reflection, Hagen nodded his head. 'She made it all right. I ducked out when I landed Logan. He was hot and wanted to dig his own hole. They let him do that. Theresa found herself a guy and they had a great big thing going but the guy fucked up. After all that had happened between us I felt protective towards her. I liked her, she was a nice girl, so I had a private look at him. He was an asshole; a bum. These well-bred and well-educated girls never did know how to choose men. This guy, I did not like. Not a one-woman man, he reckoned the field was there to be played; he made her very unhappy.'

'Should I ask what happened to him?'

Hagen smiled and St Clair Smith saw, close up, that there were lines of some sort; they could even have been laughter lines. Perhaps marriage had put them there. That was all

Hagen did; he smiled and left Theresa and her ex-lover to St Clair Smith's imagination.

St Clair Smith didn't dwell on it too long. 'Tell me more about Jim Logan. What happened to him?'

Hagen took another big mouthful of Chivas from his glass. 'Sure. A good story. The fact that the Chinese had declared him dead made everything easy for the people from Washington who'd set him up. Langley wanted him out. They wanted him dead, and that's what he'd been working against. As you probably know, he gathered quite a portfolio together, enough to cause some serious rumbles in DC; but he got there and played the cards exactly right—'

'Were you with him during all this?'

'Me? I was just there to brush the dandruff off his shoulders and keep his glass topped up. He did it all himself. He negotiated a new bill of identity and a secured status with the two top Langley people in exchange for all the documentation plus his guaranteed silence. It worked. Everyone kept their part of the bargain and everyone lived happily ever after!'

'So you've no objection now to telling me what these documents were?'

'I think you'll find, Aubrey, that most of them are still classified. They were very heavyweight and did their job—'

'You mean they kept Logan alive?'

'More than that – they did their job. You remember Graver?'

'Knew of him. Never met him—'

'Sam Reilly?'

'Same.'

'OK. These two held the United States Constitution in their hands – thanks to some of the stuff Logan had given them. Owing to him they were in a position to dictate who could run for what; who could sit in judgement; who could dictate national policy; and even as far as a nomination for the highest office. As soon as someone's nose began to edge forward in any sort of political race or gubernatorial gravy train the two of them would pore over the Contractor documents and see whether that someone's nose was clean. Contractor gave them, among other things, something like

392

twenty-five thousand names of people involved in what they called anti-patriotic activities during the Vietnam War. Anybody whose name was on that list was fucked, politically, for the next twenty years.'

'A little bit tall, that, Hagen,' said St Clair Smith sceptically.

'OK, think about this one, then. Who came out of nowhere to snatch the Republican nomination for President in '80?'

St Clair Smith had to think about it. 'Reagan.'

'Exactly. The same Ronald Reagan who failed to get the nomination in '68 and '76 and suddenly, in 1980, out of nowhere, his two Republican contenders for the nomination pull out and the outsider romps home to oust the favourite, Jimmy Carter. For the next twelve years, him and George Bush. Think about it, Smithy – Graver heads off into politics in '76 and they call him the kingmaker; Reilly becomes head of the CIA and right-wing hawks are suddenly getting the influential jobs. Coincidence? This was about the time Contractor's papers were being analysed and lists being drawn up. Personally, I think Jimmy Logan did his country a great service.'

'What about drugs? Wasn't his name involved in massive penetration of Western markets on behalf of the Touming Guanxi?'

Hagen avoided the direct question. 'The Triangle narcotics situation in the States, or anywhere else, is now exactly as it would have been with or without anybody's help to get it established. A bit of co-operation here and there paid a huge dividend and, as I say, the end result's the same. There was no shit left sticking to the CIA once Logan had been bought off, and it's been that way ever since.'

'Glad to see your conscience is nice and clear, Hagen. How did you come out of all this?'

'Clean as a garden fairy. When they decided to let Logan go to sleep, Reilly gave me the long-term job of Logan watcher. He took me into the executive and laid my assignment down in black and white. It was a twenty-year contract. I'm still doing it – after a fashion.'

'Lucky you! What about Logan's daughter? You said everything except whether she lives happily ever after.'

'Sure.' Hagen brushed aside St Clair Smith's query and glanced at his watch again. He surveyed the busy bar area, nodded briefly to an acquaintance, and then said, abruptly, 'Let's finish this at home. Come and see whether my wife's capable of opening a bucket of Kentucky Fried Chicken.'

Hagen appeared to have done very well for himself. St Clair Smith stepped out of the taxi and gazed up at the top four storeys that constituted Hagen's flat in Boulevard Lannes and reckoned that somehow he must be in the near-millionaire bracket – unless he'd got something wet and sticky on the US Government housing procurement agency. It was even more opulent inside. An opulence of extreme good taste. St Clair Smith approved and stared at Hagen's broad back as he led him through the double doors into a sitting room, comfortable and relaxed, with the air of a much-used room. It looked homely and exclusive in the same glance. St Clair Smith began to worry about Hagen's choice of wife. A middle-aged lady, her grey hair swept back in a bun, appeared with a tray of drinks. Smith wondered if this was Mrs Hagen. She wasn't. She was a lady with a tray of drinks.

'Have a drink. I'll be back in a second.' Hagen picked up a newly poured glass of champagne and left the room. St Clair Smith helped himself, smiled at the lady and walked across the room to inspect a very pretty little modern Utrillo; it had to be Montmartre – he could almost touch the Place du Tertre and smell the garlic and the *saucisson*. And then he turned when he heard his name.

'Hello, Aubrey—'

She hadn't changed. The soft, rounded, girlish features had developed into those of a beautiful woman. Always elegant, her figure was, if anything, more sensual, more desirable, but, above all, the eyes, the beautiful, slightly almond-shaped eyes, were happy. Hagen must have been exactly what she'd needed.

'Hello, Theresa.'

394